REPARATIONS

STEPHEN KIMBER

REPARATIONS

HarperCollinsPublishersLtd

Reparations

This is a work of fiction. Any similarities between the events and characters depicted herein and actual events or persons, living or deceased, are purely coincidental.

Published by HarperCollins Publishers Ltd

First Edition

HarperCollins books may be purchased for educational, business, or sales promotional use through our Special Markets Department.

HarperCollins Publishers Ltd
2 Bloor Street East, 20th Floor
Toronto, Ontario, Canada
M4W 1A8

www.harpercollins.ca

Library and Archives Canada Cataloguing in Publication

Kimber, Stephen

Reparations / Stephen Kimber. — 1st ed.

ISBN-13: 978-0-00-200564-7
ISBN-10: 0-00-200564-6

I. Title.

PS8621.I543R46 2006 C813'.6 C2005-905574-X

HC 9 8 7 6 5 4 3 2 1

Printed and bound in the United States
Set in Monotype Baskerville

For Jeanie

REPARATIONS

1

July 1976

He shouldn't have been in this hellhole on a summer Sunday morning. He should have been home sleeping it off. So why was he standing here in his one, drizzle-dampened suit trying desperately not to let his brain process the smell of shit and salt that wafted up from the sewer outfall down the block? Those queasy-making odours were stirring up whatever remained in his stomach from Saturday's stew of beer, and rum, and grease. He almost wished he could just puke it all away. Almost.

The worst, he knew, was that he didn't need to be here. He could have handled all of this by phone a few well-slept hours from now. One call to the cops. Hit and run. Coloured kid dead. No name pending notification of next of kin. No suspects. Under investigation. Two paragraphs, three at most, for the "Briefs" section in Monday's *Tribune.*

No, the only reason Patrick Donovan was standing here in the wet and stink this morning was because Tom Harkin, the weekend City Editor, believed he was talking up the union. He wasn't. He wanted to tell Harkin about last night at the Victory, and how Saunders had tried to get him to sign a union card, and how he'd told him to go fuck himself. Patrick wasn't in the least interested in joining a union. Why should he? The old man had been good to him. Given him a five-hundred-dollar bonus when he got married, then an interest-free loan to cover the down payment on the house he and Emma bought after Moira came along.

Moira. Lovely little Moira. She was the reason he was in such sad shape this morning. No, check that. The real reason? Donovan had spent all day Saturday on the roiling waters off Peggys Cove, bobbing up and down in an old Cape Islander under a face-lobstering sun, chugging quart after quart of Schooner beer and not even pretending to care whether he caught a fish.

It was the something-th annual Imperial Oil Fishing Derby, a grand piss-up the company staged every summer to curry favour with local reporters. Teams of four reporters each from all the local media outlets got to spend their Saturday on the ocean, supposedly competing to see who could catch the most and biggest fish but mostly just drinking, shooting the shit, pissing—and occasionally puking—over the side.

At the end of the day there was an awards ceremony, and more drinks—hard stuff this time—back at the local Legion. Biggest Fish, Most Fish, Ugliest Fish, Biggest Fish That Got Away, Fewest Fish. Donovan's team tied with three others for the Fewest Fish caught. None. The PR guy emcee presented them each with a plastic fish—"so you'll know what they look like"—and a forty of Captain Morgan to share. Aye, aye, Captain.

He and the three other "*Tribune* Trojans," as they called their team, demolished the forty on the drive back to Halifax. Donovan couldn't remember driving but he was certain he had; his VW Bug had been in the driveway when he woke up this morning. He couldn't recall either whose idea it was to stop in at the Victory Lounge for a victory drink—or two—to end their day, but it must have seemed like a good idea at the time. By the time he finally got home—after one last side trip to Claudie's for a takeout order of two greasy plops of battered fish on a soggy bed of french fries—it was after midnight.

Emma was pissed. Understandably. She'd been home alone all day with a teething, crying baby and no car, and why the hell hadn't he called, anyway? Donovan stood dumbly by the door as Emma handed him the baby, declared she was now "officially off fucking duty" and disappeared down the hall to bed, not inviting him to follow. He had been exiled to the couch in the baby's room. Again.

Moira, of course, was wide awake. And baby-eager to play with her daddy. Donovan did his best, even got down on the floor with her, but he could barely keep his eyes open, let alone focused. He put Moira in her crib. She cried. He scooped her up, carried her to the bathroom, got some Ambusol from the medicine cabinet, rubbed it on her gums. Still, she kept crying. He went to the kitchen, warmed some milk for her bottle, rocked her in his arms, tried not to fall down, finally sat on the couch—better—and held her as she sucked on the bottle. Did Moira fall asleep first? Or did he? The next thing he knew Emma was standing in the doorway.

"Tom's on the phone." Her tone was still icy; there would be at least a week's worth of couch penance ahead. "Says he needs you to come in to work." She stepped into the room, scooped the still blissfully sleeping Moira out of his arms, turned on her heel and was gone.

"There's been an accident." Harkin's voice was almost as frosted as Emma's. "Down near the projects. Sounds like hit and run. Check it out. I'll see you when you get in." Donovan looked at his watch. It was 5:45 a.m.

Donovan hated Sunday shifts. Everyone had to do them, of course. One Sunday in four. No extra pay. During the week, Patrick Donovan was the *Tribune*'s legislative reporter. He lunched with Cabinet ministers at Chez Henri, drank with senior bureaucrats at the Victory Lounge and could get in to see the Premier himself if he needed a quote for a story. But one Sunday in every four he was back in the bullpen, chasing ambulances and scrambling to find something—anything—to fill up Monday morning's paper.

He'd been thinking he might spend the day cobbling together a spec piece. One of his sources had told him the Liberal brain trust wanted to replace O'Sullivan before the next election. Donovan doubted his source's insistence that Ward Justice was the man who would take the Premier's place. The Fisheries minister was a rising star, no doubt of that, but he was just twenty-seven and had won his first election only two years ago.

Still, Donovan could certainly believe someone in the Liberal backroom was plotting a coup. Electricity rates were going through the roof and, though that was really the Arabs' doing, O'Sullivan had won re-election by promising to keep rate increases in check. Plus, it seemed there was a new scandal every week. Cabinet ministers caught driving drunk. Millions in government money poured into a cruise ship venture that looked like a scam. It would make a good story, but not today.

It had taken him a while even to find the inappropriately named White Street, which was squeezed between Black and Grey streets. It was an alley really, little more than an unpaved gash between Barrington Street and the harbour. It was home to a dozen or more black squatter families, all squeezed into a few paint-peeling, plywood-shuttered buildings that might once have been privateers' warehouses but had long since been abandoned to displaced Africvillers. Africvillians? Who knew? Who cared? But judging by the mob milling about this morning, there were plenty of them.

So how come, he asked himself, you never saw any of those black faces downtown? It was, after all, just a few blocks from here. And why were there no black faces among the dozen or so uniformed cops congregated in front of the last building on the block? Maybe he could make a story out of that. Maybe pigs could fly.

"You a cop?" a kid asked him. He was about twelve with a coal-black face and a kinky Afro.

"Reporter," Donovan responded.

"I knew you wasn't from here." The kid smiled, satisfied with his powers of deduction. "You on TV?"

"Newspaper."

The kid looked less interested all of a sudden. "Where's the TV?"

"It's Sunday," Donovan explained. "They don't work on Sunday."

The boy took that in, rolled it around in his head, made up his mind. "I saw it happen," he said.

"Saw what happen?"

"The accident, what you think?"

"So what happened?" Donovan was only half paying attention. He could hear the cops laughing at some private joke. A hearse picked its way through the crowd along the potholed alley to where the officers were standing.

The boy eyed the hearse with renewed interest. "I heard this big noise," he said. "So I went to look. This car, big car, white, I think, kept backing up and smashing into this garbage can. Bang! See? There it is over there by the side of that building." He pointed. Donovan kept his eye on the hearse. "The guy kept spinning his wheels . . ." Donovan watched as one cop led a tearful young black woman over to a lumpy white sheet on the ground near the cluster of cops. He knelt down, pulled back a corner. The woman screamed. The kid at Donovan's side kept talking. "Anyway, he finally puts it into drive and guns it up the street past me. And that's when I looked back and I seen . . ." He paused, looking for encouragement from Donovan, got none and continued anyway. "I seen little Larry in his pyjamas, all bloody, on the ground right where the car was."

"When was this?" Donovan knew he should walk over and see if the woman would talk to him, but he hated doing those kind of interviews.

"Middle of the night. I don't know. Why?"

"Just asking. Did you see the driver?"

"Yeah. White guy. Old, older than you." The kid smiled, as if to say that was a joke. "He's been around here a lot. I seen him coming out of Rosa's place lots of times."

"Thanks," Donovan said absently. He hadn't taken out his notebook. The woman was being ushered into a police cruiser. It was now or ever. He moved away from the kid, hurried to the police car. The cop was closing the door.

"*Tribune*," he announced, as if that were sufficient explanation. "Is there anything you want to say, ma'am?"

The cop looked at him, incredulous. It was a stupid question; Donovan knew that. But he didn't know yet who she was or why she was crying. The mother? The accused? The accused's mother? A relative? She looked at him wordlessly. He could see the wet rivulets of tears on her cheeks.

"Why don't you go see the sergeant?" the cop said, as much to shoo him away as to assist him. "He's in charge."

The sergeant was, as sergeants are, determinedly unhelpful.

"Some kid called it in. Four forty-five," he told Donovan in his flat, official voice. Was it the kid he'd been talking to? Donovan wondered. "We found the dead boy in the street over there. Looks like he got run over." The sergeant laughed his black-humour laugh. "Yes, sir, that's what it looks like. Car tire went right over his chest. Flattened it like a pancake."

"You have a name?" Donovan had finally taken out his notebook. The kid had called the victim "Larry," but Donovan knew he needed an official source and a full name.

"Yeah, but I can't give it to you. You know better than that. Call the station in a couple of hours. They'll probably be able to release that information then."

Donovan sighed. "What about the woman?"

"Kid's mother," the policeman said. "She's a whore. Arrested her myself couple of times. What the hell's she doing letting her kid wander around outside in the middle of the night anyway? Stupid nigger bitch—and that's off the record. I catch that in the paper and you're a dead man."

Call the station . . . Off the record . . . What the hell was he doing down here anyway? Donovan wondered again. Damn Harkin. But he was stuck now. So he tried again. "Kid over there told me he saw a white guy in a big car run over the kid."

The cop's eyes hardened. "Don't start messin' with that shit, Mister Reporter. These coloured guys'll tell you anything just to stir stuff up. Ever since them Black Hands bastards came here, it's like they're all looking to start a race riot. Like in the States. So don't you go playing along just to sell some papers." He paused. "And that's off the fucking record too."

Donovan closed his notebook. He wanted to go back to sleep.

2

May 2002

Of course it was insane. Insanity, in truth, might be the young man's best defence. It would never work. And yet? Uhuru Melesse reconsidered the intense young man sitting stiffly, expectantly in the rickety, coming-unglued, straight-backed wooden chair across from him.

The young man, whose name was James Joseph Howe, was Biafran thin. His bulging, milky-white eyes strained to take flight from the tight, dark-chocolate cage of his face. His two-sizes-too-large black wool suit made him appear even more emaciated and, if possible, more out of sorts with himself and the world he'd suddenly found himself in.

That world, Uhuru Melesse's world, was a holding room in the bowels of the Provincial Court House where legal aid lawyers met their clients, usually for the first and only time. The small, windowless room reeked of stale sweat, the smoke of a thousand furtive cigarettes and the unmistakable odour of urine.

Uhuru Melesse wasn't a legal aid lawyer but he occasionally hung out at the courthouse on mornings when there were no wills to write or deeds to transfer. He would troll the corridors for clients who earned too much to qualify for legal aid but who needed someone to plead them guilty to whatever lesser offence the Crown prosecutor would reluctantly okay. But this time, for whatever reason, Melesse had been asked for, specifically.

Thanks to his familiarity with this particular room, Melesse knew better than to sit down on the room's only other piece of furniture, a wooden chair identifiable by the fact that some of the plastic webbing on the seat was missing. Though not apparent to the casual observer, the glue holding the legs fast to the seat had long since dried up. The sheriff's deputies amused themselves with it, banging the legs into place in order to catch new lawyers or their clients unawares. Melesse ignored the chair, perched one polished black shoe on the edge of a broken radiator and wondered at what he was considering.

The young man looked like one of those preternaturally beatific young men who occasionally showed up at Melesse's door wanting to know if he *knew* the Lord. But he was really a bookkeeper for the Halifax Regional Municipality. The City claimed he'd stolen $323,456.56 worth of taxpayers' dollars. Howe didn't deny taking the money. But he insisted it wasn't theft.

"Are you sure this is really the way you want to go?" Melesse asked.

"Absolutely. That's why I asked for you." Melesse looked puzzled. "I saw that film," the young man explained. "That Film Board film, about Black Pride. I knew you'd understand."

Melesse understood. The young man did not. That film was from another life. Melesse was no longer that person. He didn't even carry that man's name.

Still, Melesse could appreciate the young man's confusion. After all, hadn't he "shed" his slave name—he'd probably claimed that himself in some interview or other—and taken on one that better reflected his African roots? And hadn't he shaved off all the hair on his head, lending him the menacing persona of the aging but unbowed black radical? Melesse didn't want to confess, not to the young man and certainly not to himself, that he'd decided to change his name on a drunken whim one night five years ago. The whim had involved a blonde and a bottle of white wine. Shaving his head? One of the TV reporters—a white woman, of course—had made a big deal of it when she'd interviewed him last year for a story about Kwanza (which the headline referred to as "Black Christmas"). Truth? He was trying to hide the fact that his hairline was receding, and what was not receding was turning white.

"Even if we go the way you want to go," Melesse said finally, "there's no guarantee the judge will buy it. Chances are he won't."

"But it's true." Howe seemed almost childlike. "So we must."

"Okay, we can try. But let me ask you a question, Mr. Howe. It's not that I don't believe you, you understand, but I have to ask because the first thing the Crown is going to do is root around in your life looking for evidence. You're telling me they won't find anything. You're sure about that?"

"Absolutely. Not a penny went anywhere but where I told you." He reached into the breast pocket of his suit, pulled out a sheaf of papers, all neatly folded into a packet, and handed it to Melesse. "See?"

Melesse carefully unfolded the papers, read the names: Square Meal . . . Seaview Children's Trust . . . African–Nova Scotian Pensioners Association . . . Save Our Neighbourhood from Drugs Committee . . .

"You show this to the cops?"

"No. Just you." Howe's smile was full of expectation.

Uhuru Melesse didn't want to do this. It would mean more work than he wanted to take on. And he was no longer a fan of lost causes. Not to mention that Howe was probably lying. Melesse could not remember the last client who wasn't lying about something. Even—or especially—since he'd begun to specialize in real estate transactions.

There was a knock on the door.

"Okay," he said, looking toward the unseen door-knocker. "Be there in a sec." He turned back to the young man, more eagerly expectant now. "What the hell," he said. "Let's do it."

As the deputy led the young man out of the room to the elevator that would take them to Courtroom 1 for the arraignment, Uhuru Melesse hung behind, took a deep breath, seemingly lost in thought. But he wasn't thinking about what he was going to say in the courtroom; he was thinking about last night, about what had not happened. Again.

How do you plead? Guilty. *Three hundred dollars or thirty days. See the clerk on your way out. Next case* . . . Still not the case she was here for. So Moira Donovan resumed the less than artistic rendering of an unidentified, unidentifiable flower taking shape on the front cover of her steno pad. How many more peace bond breakers, break-and-entry makers, probation order violators, pot puffers, drunks and other assorted minor-league miscreants would she have to sit through before the judge finally got to the case she was here for?

She tried not to think about the much better story playing out at this very moment in Courtroom 5. By now, Abe Belinsky was probably on his fourth it-would-shock-the-conscience-of-the-community-Your-Honour diatribe. Belinsky was always good theatre and better copy. "Never in my thirty-six years of legal practice have I seen such a travesty of . . ." whatever.

Today the travesty would be that his client, a slumlord slug named Tony Karakis, was up for murder when all he was really trying to do was burn down his own apartment building for the insurance. How was he supposed to know his ex-wife and her new lover would be inside *in flagrante delicto*, crisped, as it were, in the act of congress?

Tony had conveniently—not to mention cheaply—provided his ex with an apartment in his tenement in lieu of spousal support. Abe would paint this as an act of incredible generosity to a woman he had earlier dissed as a "coked-up hooker" (without mentioning, of course, that Tony had been both her pimp and drug supplier, which was how they'd met in the first place). Not that Abe would ignore his client's seamier side, of course, just in case some esteemed members of the jury might have already read about Tony's exploits during one of his many previous court appearances for extortion, assault, living off the avails or even arson (this was not his first torch job).

"I won't pretend that my client is a model human being," Abe would allow, stating the obvious, leaning his arms against the jury rail, making eye contact, honey-coating each word. "Who among us is?" But Tony Karakis had never, as Abe was quick to point out, been convicted of anything. "And, members of the jury, you must keep in your minds the indisputable fact that my client is not on trial for being a person you might not invite home for dinner. Tony Karakis is on trial for murder." Pause. "And, my friends"—everyone was Abe's friend, especially when he was in mid-harangue—"Tony Karakis is no murderer . . ."

She could write that story without even being in the courtroom. Which is almost certainly how she would have to do it now. She'd have to ask Bonnie, Judge Adamson's clerk, to let her listen to the tape over the lunch break so she could get Abe's quotes exactly right. Another lost lunch hour. Not that she felt much like eating these days anyway. But still.

She looked at her watch. Ten forty-five. It had been two hours since Michelle had called. "Oh good, I caught you," she'd begun, as if Moira had been trying to escape. Michelle was Moira's City Editor at the *Daily Journal.* "Got a call from a friend at the cop shop last night," she'd explained confidentially. "Says they're going to be charging some City accountant with scamming a million bucks. Morton wants it big for page three, right next to a reprint of last month's story about property taxes going up. We'll send a shooter to get his mug on the in-and-out. All we need from you is a little colour from inside. Head down, tears in his eyes, doleful look back at the wife, you know, the usual." She paused for breath. "What was on your sked for today anyway?"

"Karakis. Closing arguments." Trying not let her frustration show.

"Morton wants this one," Michelle said, as if that trumped everything else. Maybe she really was sleeping with him. "Anyway, shouldn't take long. You can do Karakis after the arraignment."

Michelle, of course, didn't have a clue about the hoops Moira would have to jump through to do that. She had never covered courts, never covered anything except her rather largish ass, and that not completely. Which may have been why Morton . . . *Stop it.* Moira knew she wasn't being fair. Michelle might not be sleeping with Morton. Perhaps she was just stupid. No, that wasn't being fair either. The reality was that there just weren't enough reporters any more. Michelle was too new and inexperienced to know that, or what the lack of warm bodies meant for those left in the field.

When Moira started at the paper five years ago, there were two reporters covering courts full time, and they could always call the desk for help on a particularly busy day. Now, she was on her own; she had to handle the Provincial and Supreme Courts, criminal and civil cases, arraignments and sentencings—and woe to her if she missed a story one of the *three Tribune* court reporters had. The *Tribune* was the competition, the older, established broadsheet. The *Daily Journal* was the newcomer, the feisty tabloid that tried harder. It had been started back in the late seventies by a bunch of disgruntled *Tribune* editors, including her father. Even though they no longer owned the paper—they'd sold out to a businessman, who'd sold out to a chain, who'd sold out to a bigger chain—most were still working for the paper as editors, and they took it as a personal affront when the *Tribune* carried a story the *Journal* didn't have.

Moira did her best, but there were inevitably days like today when she was assigned to pursue some editor's hot tip. She'd already discovered from her friend in the prothonotary's office that the guy she was waiting to see arraigned this morning wasn't an accountant—just a lowly bookkeeper—and he wasn't being charged with making off with millions; it was a couple hundred grand at most. Still, she had to admit, it did sound like a good story.

Another *How-do-you-plead?* Not her boy. She looked up at the bench and saw good old Justice Justice. How she hated to have to write his name in a story; the paper's computerized spell-check system invariably choked on it as a double occurrence of the same word and helpfully tried to fix it by automatically eliminating one of them. That meant someone on the desk had to go in and manually override the system, provided, of course, a copy editor even noticed, which they seemed to do less and less. They were short-staffed too.

The judge looked almost as bored as she felt. How had he managed to draw this short straw? she wondered. The Supremes—that's what court reporters called the Supreme Court justices—weren't supposed to preside at routine arraignments. But there was a big

Provincial Court judges' annual convention at the Digby Pines this weekend, and most of them were already at the resort, golfing probably. Those who weren't in Digby—according to the clerk Moira had had coffee with that morning—were at home with a nasty flu. "God's bowling ball just rolled right over them," the clerk joked. Which was why Justice Justice had got the emergency call to handle this morning's arraignments.

Looking up at him on the bench, Moira found it difficult to imagine that Ward Justice had been handsome once. She'd seen proof in the tattered scrapbook of old newspaper clippings her father kept to remind himself—and her—of the journalist he'd once been. In those days, the judge had been a politician whose doings featured prominently in the news, or at least in the legislative stories her father wrote. Inevitably, the paper used the same studio-posed, black-and-white photo of Justice staring solemnly into the camera, his right hand beside his face, a lit cigarette held delicately in his fingers, smoke curling up and beyond the frame. When was the last time a politician had posed for a photographer with a cigarette in his hand? In her mind's eye, Moira lined up the head-and-shoulders shot of the young politician side by side with the image of the old judge in front of her. His then-trendy Afro (his "Art Garfunkel 'do," her father called it) was now close cropped and almost entirely white. And the young man's piercing eyes and swarthy, angular good looks had long since disappeared, buried under a layer of fat-puffed, wrinkled skin, freckled here and there with splotchy, penny-sized liver spots.

Moira brought her attention back to the flower she'd been sketching on the cover of her notepad. In her mind, the flower had magically morphed into a flying saucer because the ink from a few of the petals had fused together and made the flower look more like a spaceship. Maybe she should add a couple of stick spacemen to complete the—she felt a sudden wave of nausea bubble up. Thankfully, she hadn't stopped at Tim's this morning for a double-double and muffin. She hadn't felt like eating all week.

She put down her pen, stared up at the ceiling, waited for the feeling to pass. She was sure of it now. She would stop at SuperDrugs at lunch, pick up one of those test kits—Damn! She couldn't. She had to spend her lunch hour listening to the Abe reruns in the clerk's office. Which meant she'd have to get the kit tonight on her way home from work.

Moira wasn't sure what she thought about the idea of having a baby. She knew she wanted to have children. But now? With Todd? What would Todd say? First: *Great.* Second: *Now you can quit.* It wasn't that Todd didn't want her to work; he just considered newspaper reporting beneath her dignity—and his. Which, of course, drove her father to distraction.

Her father had never liked Todd, especially after he'd quit his law firm job (strike one: he was a lawyer) to become a real estate entrepreneur (strike two: he was a developer). Todd's current project was cobbling together a high-profile, high-rise luxury condo apartment project on the Dartmouth waterfront. His plan was to sell the units at inflated prices to the multinational oil companies that were drilling for gas off the coast. The companies, in turn, would lease them to their up-and-coming young managers at deflated prices in order to entice them to relocate to Halifax for a few years of outpost seasoning. Moira's father was dismissive. "You'd think Toddy owned the friggin' view."

Their father-daughter lunches had become more frequent—and her father's condemnation of her husband more virulent—since he'd left the paper himself with a buyout two years ago, one of a dozen senior employees eased out the door. Each new announcement that Todd had pre-sold yet another apartment seemed to make her father angrier. That Todd inevitably seemed to sell another one just after her father had been turned down for yet another job beneath his qualifications did not help matters.

She hadn't told her father she and Todd were trying to have a baby, or that Todd was pressuring her to quit her job at the paper. Strike three, game over. But the reality was she'd been thinking about quitting herself, maybe going to law school if she didn't get pregnant, writing a novel if she did. Why did her father care so much whether she stayed at a paper he'd already left?

Maybe she'd tell him over lunch next Wednesday, sugarcoat the quitting with the news about the baby. If indeed a baby was growing inside her. Something was certainly making her want to throw up.

"Case number 1-4-5-7-5-3." Finally. "*Regina v. James Joseph Howe.*" Howe stood ramrod straight, a six-foot-something rail of a young man, listening intently as the clerk read out the specifics of the allegations against him. Theft. Fraud. Breach of trust.

Had he been named after Joseph Howe, the famous nineteenth-century Nova Scotia politician? Moira wondered. She was surprised to see he was black; though the courts were clogged with black defendants, few were ever charged with such white-collar crimes. She'd just assumed he'd be white because she knew he was a bookkeeper for the City. Perhaps it was time for a reality check on her own stereotypes.

Speaking of stereotypes, she noticed that Uhuru Melesse was the young man's lawyer. Surely, Howe could have done better. Moira had interviewed Melesse once for a Sunday feature she did on the importance of having a will. He'd had nothing interesting to say, but she'd included him in the piece anyway so the paper could use his photo. Morton had been keen to get the faces of black professionals into the *Daily Journal* ever since a Media Watch report had criticized the paper publicly for "reinforcing negative racist stereotypes of African Nova Scotians." What Moira remembered most about Melesse was that he had never looked her in the eye; he'd stared straight at her breasts instead.

She'd never seen Melesse do an actual trial. She wasn't sure he had. When he did appear in a courtroom, it was usually just to enter a guilty plea on behalf of some poor schmuck who couldn't afford to fight the case against him.

"Is your client prepared to enter a plea, Mr. . . . Melesse?" Moira wondered if Justice Justice's pause was deliberate; a lot of lawyers she knew sniggered about Melesse's decision to change his name.

"We are, Your Honour."

"How do you plead?"

"My client wishes to plead not guilty but, with the court's indulgence, I would ask leave to raise a couple of issues I think may be critical for the court to consider as we proceed."

Justice Justice lowered his head slightly and stared out resignedly over his reading glasses at the lawyer before him. "Indulged."

"Thank you, Your Honour. As this court is well aware, the question of reparations for African Americans victimized by slavery is already a matter for civil litigation in the United States," Melesse began. He sounded almost wary about what he was getting ready to say. "I don't mean to suggest that the case before you this morning is about slavery per se," he added quickly. "It's not . . . but the reality is that the unequal treatment of black people in this country is a . . . fact, a . . . matter of . . . public record . . ." To Moira, Melesse sounded like a stutterer trying unsuccessfully to maintain control of his tongue. "While there is as yet no case law in this country, Your Honour . . . it has certainly become an area for academic research among . . . some of our brightest young . . . African-Canadian legal scholars." Melesse paused again, as if deciding to shift gears.

"My client is a proud descendant of the community of Africville. As Your Honour well knows . . ." Melesse attempted to make eye contact with the judge, who was staring at his papers. "During the 1960s, the residents of that poor but proud . . . African-Canadian community were expropriated, driven from their homes without consultation, or fair and just compensation. My client believes that because the City of Halifax, the Province of Nova Scotia and, indeed, the country of Canada have all failed to right this wrong over the past forty years, that it was his right, his duty as a citizen, to correct this unfairness, to provide *reparations* to the victims of this historic injustice."

Moira flipped open her notebook, suddenly interested, and began to play note-making catch-up.

"I'm not sure I follow, Counsel." Justice Justice no longer seemed bored either, but he wasn't eager to go where Melesse seemed bent on taking him. "I thought your client was charged with theft, fraud and breach of trust," the judge noted, looking down and adding, with what Moira took to be more than a hint of sarcasm, "At least that's what it says here."

"Begging your indulgence, Your Honour, I—"

"You're being indulged, Mr. Melesse. But don't take advantage. Save your argument for the proper forum. This proceeding is neither the place nor the time for you to play to the press."

Moira looked around. She hadn't noticed before, but the usually vacant spectator galleries behind her were now dotted with the painted faces of half a dozen recognizable, well-coiffed and groomed TV reporters. They rarely, if ever, darkened the corridors of the courthouse for less than a murder arraignment. Whoever had leaked word about Howe's arraignment to the *Daily Journal* had obviously been an equal-opportunity sieve.

"But, if it please the court—"

"It pleases the court that your client has pleaded not guilty," Justice cut him off. What was he so agitated about all of a sudden? Moira wondered. "So let's move on. Ms. Evans, do you have a recommendation with regard to bail?"

"But—"

"Sit down, Mr. Melesse, you'll get your chance."

Elinor Evans, the usually bustlingly efficient Crown attorney, seemed as nonplussed by the judge's sudden outburst as anyone. "Ah, yes, Your Honour . . ." She began riffling through her papers. "If you'll give me a moment—"

Justice was red in the face now. "You shouldn't need a moment, Ms. Evans. I didn't ask a complicated question."

"No, no sir, Your Honour, you didn't. I apologize." She gave up looking, decided to wing it. "Mr. Howe here is charged with a very serious offence, a crime that involves not only stealing money belonging to the taxpayers of the Halifax Regional Municipality but also with violating his sworn duty to his employer and to his fellow citizens. He is accused of taking . . ." She looked down at the papers on her desk, realized it was hopeless, "a great deal of money. The police have not been able to account for the whereabouts of all those missing funds and they believe Mr. Howe may still have access to at least some of them. As a result, the Crown believes Mr. Howe may be a flight risk. We would ask that he be denied bail or, failing that—"

"Mr. Melesse. Your turn."

Uhuru Melesse seemed to be struggling for words. "With respect, Your Honour, I don't believe I was given a fair opportunity to raise the issue of—"

"Hearing no objections to the Crown's recommendation, bail is denied. Mr. Howe is remanded into custody until his next court appearance. That's it for this morning, ladies and gentlemen." With that, the judge bolted from his seat and stormed out the back door of the courtroom so quickly his startled clerk didn't even have time for an "All rise . . ."

For a moment no one spoke, then the room filled with a sudden, dam-bursting cacophony of confusion. What had just happened, and why? Moira didn't know. Neither, judging by what the people around her were saying, did anyone else. Moira only knew that she now had a much more compelling story for tomorrow than Abe Belinsky and his predictable histrionics. Justice Justice was the story now. And, more to the point, since the judge wouldn't be granting interviews, the story would be what Uhuru Melesse had to say about the judge's behaviour. He was already making his way out of the courtroom into the camera lights, surrounded by a moving amoeba of journalists, thrusting their microphones and mini-disc recorders into his face, jostling each other, pushing for position, demanding he stop and talk to them. Moira hurried to catch up with them, felt another hot wave of nausea. Damn.

Truth to tell, Uhuru Melesse was grateful to Ward Justice for saving him, temporarily, from himself. He should have known better than to wade into such tricky legal waters so woefully ill prepared. What he knew about reparations for African slavery could be summed up in a single TV news clip he'd seen in which Johnnie Cochran announced he was filing a class action suit against a bunch of corporations, or maybe the American government, seeking millions, or perhaps billions, for centuries of slavery there. But what did that have to do with Canada or, more to the point, with Uhuru Melesse's sticky-fingered client?

Uhuru Melesse blamed his client. If the kid hadn't played the black card and, more importantly, the Raymond Carter Black Radical card, Melesse would almost certainly have tried to talk him into taking a plea. Perhaps he still should. *I can get you a deal. A year, two, tops, in Springhill. You'd be back on the streets in a few months. Come out with some money to spend if . . .*

Howe wouldn't have gone for it, of course. Melesse knew that. Perhaps that's why he hadn't suggested it. Or perhaps, more likely, he hadn't suggested it because he didn't want to disappoint the earnest young man who'd seen a film about another him from another time and decided he wanted that man for his lawyer. Maybe Uhuru Melesse still wanted to be that man.

At least Ward Justice had saved him from making a public display of his ignorance in court. And now most of the reporters seemed more interested in Justice's treatment of Melesse than in the substance of whatever it was he was trying to argue.

"How do you feel now, Mr. Melesse? Are you angry?" It was the TV reporter, the woman who'd tried to turn his shaved head into a political statement. She had nice tits. He tried not to look at them.

"I am more disappointed than angry," he began carefully, looking beyond her, directly into the whirring lenses of one of the half-dozen TV cameras behind her. "The judge's actions in court this morning simply confirm what we in the black community have known for a long time."

"Are you saying Judge Justice is racist?" Another TV reporter.

Careful now. He didn't need a rebuke from the Barristers' Society, or worse. "I'm not saying anything of the sort," Melesse replied evenly, smiling as ingenuously as he could while walking the skinny line between giving a good sound bite and getting cited for contempt. "I'll let others draw whatever conclusions they wish. I'm simply telling you that what we saw in the courtroom this morning—and you'll have to characterize that for yourself—comes as no surprise to the people of my community." *My community.*

"You talked about reparations." It was Donovan, a reporter for one of the newspapers. Melesse couldn't remember which paper, only that she'd interviewed him once and didn't seem to like him, which, as usual with white women, only served to make her more desirable. That and her tits. Better than the TV reporter's. "Are you planning to make reparations part of your defence?" she wanted to know. This time he didn't even try to look away; he spoke directly to her chest.

"I don't want to get into our legal strategy at this point, of course, but let me just make the point that black people in this country have endured hundreds of years of racism at the hands of white society, and we have a right—"

"But what's the connection between the fraud charges against your client and the idea of reparations?" She'd cut him off just as he was about to take rhetorical flight, frustrating the TV reporters, who'd sensed a six o'clock sound bite in the making. "I mean, he's charged with stealing money—how do you get from there to reparations?"

He looked up from her chest and into her eyes—they were green, Irish, he wanted to lose himself in them—and gave her his best call-me-later-and-I'll-tell-you-everything smile. "That's a very interesting question, Ms. Donovan, but, as I said, I don't want to get into the details of what I'll be arguing in court in front of these cameras." Smile. "All I can tell you for now is that my client is not a thief, that he is a principled, upstanding member of this community, and that, in the fullness of time, he will be vindicated."

The TV reporters had their clips now and were eager to leave, but Donovan, a dog with a bone, refused to be mollified. "But what's the legal basis for a defence based on reparations?" she demanded again. Melesse watched the TV reporter with the less-nice tits signal her camera operator with an economically raised eyebrow. As the two of them backed out of the scrum, so did the others. He and Donovan were on their own.

"Another very interesting question, Ms. Donovan . . . Moira," Melesse added, sliding into the familiar and as far away as possible from the fact that he didn't have a clue about the legal basis for a criminal defence based on reparations. "I don't have time to get into it right now, but why don't you call me at the office? We can get together, maybe have a drink, and I can explain it all then." Assuming he could figure it out by then.

Not that there would likely be a *then*. Moira Donovan shot him a withering look, as if she understood exactly what he meant by having a drink. And she did. But that made her interesting. As she turned on her heel and walked away, Uhuru Melesse admired her ass. He tried to hold the image in his head, tried not to remember last night. Perhaps he would call her.

Ward Justice stared into the nothingness of the white ceramic tile wall, rested his forehead against its coldness, felt the liquid draining out of his body. Almost all. Another sign. It was getting worse. This time he'd barely made it; had, in fact, felt the hot wetness ooze across the crotch of his grey wool pants even as he fumbled for the zip. Thank God for his judicial robes. So he'd squeezed harder, tensing every muscle in his midsection to try to staunch the flow. Finally, when he was able to let himself go, the pressure, which had seemed to fill to bursting in every pore and muscle and marrow of his being, dissipated like air being whooshed from a balloon. Relief.

Damn Carter, or Melesse, or whatever the hell he called himself these days. Ward Justice had not seen that one coming. A defence lawyer's familiar complaint about a lack of disclosure, perhaps, even accusations that some overzealous police officer had manhandled his client. He heard that often enough these days. But he'd never imagined that Melesse would try to turn a routine arraignment into a complex, convoluted and time-consuming argument about reparations. The young Carter might very well have played that game, but that was a long time ago. There'd have been Charter issues and jurisdictional questions. The Crown, quite rightly, would have wanted to insert its oar into the discussion by demanding to know what any of this esoteric legal talk had to do with the only germane question, which was whether the defendant had done what the police alleged he'd done. The lawyers could easily have gone on arguing those questions for hours, after which Ward Justice would have been expected to say something wise and judge-like.

As soon as he'd understood that Melesse wanted to raise an issue he could not dispense with easily or quickly, Ward felt the need to pee. No, that didn't quite capture it. He *had* to pee. Now. This instant. But Melesse kept talking, almost as if he knew the havoc he was wreaking. Ward's nerves jangled and his mind was frayed with the increasing urgency of his body's demands. He'd had no choice but to cut him off. And then the prosecutor, with her inept dithering . . .

As the torrent into the urinal in his chamber's private bathroom slowed to a trickle and then an occasional dribble, Ward Justice's mind unclenched too, and he was able to consider what had actually transpired in his courtroom with some equanimity. He knew it was silly to blame the lawyers for simply doing their jobs. Worse, he began to realize how others—the press, for starters—might choose to interpret his actions. And worst of all, Ward Justice understood finally that he was dying. Getting up to pee three and four times every night. No wonder he was so tired all the time. Yesterday, he'd almost fallen asleep on the bench during a defence summation. And the more he peed, the less he seemed able to completely empty his bladder, which meant he was not only dealing with the sudden, overpowering urge to urinate, but then, almost immediately, the need to urinate again. He could feel it now, the sense that, even after he had shaken the last drops of this pee, the next one was already pooling down there, waiting, ready to command his undivided attention again at the most inconvenient moment.

He knew what it meant; he watched television. But even that wasn't enough to convince him to make the appointment with his new doctor. Old Doc Wilson would have made a joke of it, a little male humour between friends, which is what they'd been for twenty years, and put him at his ease, even if the news turned out to be the absolute worst. But Doc Wilson had retired and his replacement—what was her name? another sign of aging, as if he needed any more portents—would be all business and tests and results. He didn't want results; he already knew what they would be. Besides, Dr. Thomas—ah yes, that was her name; maybe he wasn't quite as far gone as he thought—was a woman, and he was not about to drop his trousers in front of some woman, doctor or no, and present his backside for her to stick her fingers in.

Which is why he'd spent an entire evening a few weeks ago on the Internet. He'd first typed "prostate" and "symptoms" into Google and, "approximately" 0.16 seconds later, the computer spat up an index of 223,000 web sites, all of them seemingly shouting the same message: Ward Justice presented all the common symptoms of advanced prostate cancer. When he added "cause" to his search terms, he got 132,000 "hits," the gist of all of them appearing to be that, while no one knew for sure what actually caused a man's prostate to turn against him, Ward Justice was a walking risk factor: he lived in North America (check), ate too many dietary fats and too few cooked tomatoes (check) and had a close relative with prostate cancer (check—his eighty-five-year-old father had recently been diagnosed, among his many and various other ailments, with what he persisted in calling "prostrate" cancer). Although he was not African-American—another of the factors that could double your risk—that seemed small comfort in light of all the others.

He did find web sites touting "cures," miraculous and otherwise. "The prostate is a muscle," explained one article he read under the title, "Enhance Your Sex Life for a Healthier Prostate." "Like all muscles, the prostate must be used if it is to remain strong. It's no accident the highest incidence of prostate cancer occurs in celibate men." Far from offering the prospect of a cure for what ailed him, the article added one more risk factor.

The closest to comforting news among the thousands of pages filled with doom and gloom, surgery and pain, catheters and impotence, and, of course, decay and death, was the promise that his prostate might be saved by swallowing the oily essence of the berry of a dwarf palm tree. Doc Wilson would have laughed him out of the office if Ward had suggested such a "dumb-arsed New Age, natural, herbal bullshit cure-all." Ward would probably have laughed too. But he wasn't laughing now, and since Wilson was no longer practising medicine and since Ward had no intention of asking Dr. Thomas for her advice on any matter affecting his lower extremities, he had simply gone ahead last week and ordered a supply of sixty saw palmetto gel caplets over the Internet using an e-mail address he'd set up for those rare occasions when he wanted to surf porn sites that demanded you provide one to gain access. The address—250849@hotmail.com—wasn't a very clever choice; it was his real birth date. Besides, he'd had to use his real name and credit card to place the order. If anyone wanted to track him down, they could. But they could do that anyway.

He'd learned that uncomfortable truth while presiding over a child pornography case last year; the police had painstakingly tracked down a Halifax man who had taken nude photos of his sleeping, seven-year-old twin nephews while he babysat them. He'd sold the photos over the Net to faceless men who apparently got off on seeing photos of nude boys in the sexually charged act of sleeping. The cops pursued the man through cyberspace all the way from a Finnish-based chatroom, where he'd posted messages, back to his Internet service provider in Halifax. The service provider offered up the man's entire online history, even the fact that he'd once used the Internet to order flowers and send an electronic greeting card to his mother—"Your lucky, loving son"—to mark the occasion of her seventieth birthday.

Since Ward's personal interests didn't veer to nude sleeping boys, he doubted his own very occasional nocturnal wanderings through AllNudeAlways.com would attract the attention of the police. He worried more about *Frank* magazine. The local gossip sheet had already published details about a fellow judge's very messy divorce proceedings, in which his ex-wife had accused him of beating her with his belt because she had failed to maintain their household to his exacting standards of neat-and-tidy.

At least Ward didn't have to worry that Victoria would dish up the details of their married life in a public divorce proceeding. Victoria simply wasn't that sort of woman. Besides, they hadn't had what would be classified as a "married life" for the past twenty-five years, ten months and thirteen days. By his careful reckoning, it had been nine thousand, four hundred and thirty-eight days since the last time he and Victoria had made love. That was one week before the Premier's office issued its press release announcing that Fisheries minister Ward Justice was abandoning politics forever to become a justice of the Supreme Court of Nova Scotia.

Victoria Justice did not issue a press release to announce that she would never sleep with her husband again. But when she moved all his clothes into the guest room, he got the picture.

Which reminded him. Today was their thirtieth wedding anniversary. They would celebrate it as usual. Over dinner. At Valentino's, Victoria's favourite restaurant. Just the two of them. They would talk civilly about nothing of consequence, and then go home to their separate beds and lives. It was, all things considered, a good marriage. Which reminded him that he hadn't bought her a card yet. They always exchanged cards, never presents. It was not easy finding anniversary cards that did not refer to either sex or love.

He zipped up his fly. Perhaps if he stopped drinking coffee in the mornings. When would that saw palmetto arrive? he wondered.

"Saw you on TV tonight, man," the voice behind him shouted over the bar's Friday night din. "You were great."

Uhuru Melesse made the mistake of turning in the direction of the voice, which he hadn't recognized. Too late, he put the voice together with the face and the perpetual bed-head of dirty-blond hair. It was that annoying young reporter from *High Tide*, the one who called him "man" and inevitably wanted to talk to him about racism, or rap music, or racism in rap music, or any one of a dozen other topics Uhuru could care less about. What was his name? Calvin? Kevin? Whatever. Fat White Boy—that was his name now—was a short, fat, pimply-faced, just-past-being-a-boy young man who tonight was incongruously dressed in a checked sports jacket that just might have been popular in the seventies. Fat White Boy assumed a familiarity between them that did not exist.

"Got a question for ya," he continued, now that he had locked on Uhuru like a target. This was how it always began. And an hour later, Fat White Boy would still be asking questions. Desperate, Uhuru looked above his head and into the sea of bodies between him and escape. He should have known better than to come here tonight.

The Economy Shoe Shop was the downtown bar of choice for local politicians, lawyers, journalists, film types, secretaries-on-the-make—anyone in Halifax, in fact, who wanted to be seen being seen. Perhaps not surprisingly, the Shoe, named after an old neon sign for a real shoe store the bar's owner had picked up at an auction and installed over the entrance, was Uhuru's favourite bar. It was an ideal place for a black man to troll for white women looking for someone new and different and dangerous but not really dangerous. Unlike plenty of other places in town he could name, no one at the Shoe looked askance, or allowed themselves to appear other than blasé, at the sight of a black man in the company of a white woman.

The problem was that the Shoe was too popular. By eight o'clock on most Fridays—and tonight was no exception—the narrow, train-like aisle between the bar and the tables in the original section was jammed to more than fire-marshal-full with pre-weekend revellers.

Most of them appeared to have seen, or at least knew about, his appearance on the news tonight. As he'd worked his way through the crowd from the entrance to the far end of the bar—where Jason, the bartender who knew him too well, was already pouring his usual Jim-and-Ginger—people smiled, and winked, and high-fived, even offered up a solidarity fist in the air. Most of them, he was certain, didn't understand any better than he what the reparations issue, of which he'd spoken so eloquently, was really all about. Fat White Boy knew.

"I read *The Debt* so I think I understand the civil side, at least in the U.S.," he began earnestly.

The Debt? What the hell was *The Debt?* Why couldn't the kid just ask a question instead of making a speech?

"But that's all based on the history of slavery there. Now I know, I know, we certainly had slavery here, too. But I don't believe there was slavery in Africville. So is this just about the relocation, or is it from before that, you know, to when Africville was created?"

Uhuru did what he always did when someone asked him a question he couldn't answer. He smiled as if he knew something the questioner didn't. "You'll just have to wait and see," he said. And searched for an escape route. There was none. Just dozens of shouting-to-be-heard sweaty bodies jammed together. Uhuru hunched his shoulders and squeezed his arms against his sides as he tried to navigate the glass of bourbon to his lips without it being jostled by the undulating wave of humanity around him.

"And there's also the whole civil-criminal thing," Fat White Boy continued, not reading the get-lost message Uhuru hoped he had delivered with his eyes. "You know, like, I can see it as a civil case, I mean, that's what it is in the States, fifty thousand dollars for every African-American family to pay them back for two hundred and fifty years of slavery and discrimination, and you could probably make the same kind of case even here using, you know, the Charter and such. But as a defence for theft? How are you going to do that?"

"You'll just have to wait and see," Uhuru said again, his smile a little less fulsome. He began to try to edge out and around Fat White Boy.

"I was thinking I might try to sell a freelance piece to *Lawyers' Weekly*." Fat White Boy kept himself in front of Uhuru, shuffling sideways in step with him. "I think they'd be really interested. Can I give you a call, maybe stop by the office Monday? I'd like to talk to your client too, you know—" He stopped suddenly. "Shondelle! Shondelle! Over here," he shouted, waving his arms in the direction of a black woman. Shondelle looked over, then looked as if she'd thought better of her too-hasty glance, but had, like Uhuru before her, been trapped by Fat White Boy's riveting gaze.

Uhuru didn't know the woman but he knew her to see her. He knew too, without knowing her, that he wouldn't like her. Shondelle Adams was a prof at the law school, one of that new breed of professors whose chief qualifications, Uhuru imagined, were that she was a she, and that she was black. Uhuru knew it was wrong, especially for him, but he couldn't help himself; his first thought the first time he'd seen her interviewed on television was that she must be an affirmative-action hire. Perhaps it was because she was described as a specialist in "critical race theory." What the hell was that? Worse, she favoured colourful, tent-like African dresses with matching headdresses that made her seem, to Uhuru at least, like a walking cliché.

Of course, then, what was he? A middle-aged black lawyer with a faux-menacing shaved head and an unseemly thing for young white girls. Talk about clichéd. A cliché who, truth be told, was willing to wear a dashiki himself if the right photo opportunity presented itself.

"Hey, Shondelle, great to see you again," Fat White Boy greeted her like a long-lost sister. Did he know this woman any better than he knew Uhuru? "You two must know each other," he said, as if they were all part of some in-crowd. Why did white people always assume that just because two people were black they should know each other? Probably because, in Halifax at least, it was almost always true. But not this time. Uhuru smiled his best cocktail party smile.

"We haven't had the pleasure," he said, extending a free hand in her direction. "My name's Uhuru Melesse."

"I know who you are," she said, letting his hand hang empty in the air between them. "Shondelle Adams. Saw you on the news tonight. Interesting case you've got."

Interesting? Had she said the word dismissively? Was she dismissing him as well? Uhuru appraised her again. She was probably in her mid-thirties, though perhaps younger. Her skin was caramel brown. Smooth, soft, inviting. Her hair was hidden beneath a turban-like green-and-gold headdress. If, that is, she had any hair; perhaps she had shaved it bald like so many black feminists. Uhuru didn't like the way it made them look. He brought his hand back to his side, tried not to acknowledge the snub. Instead, he tried to imagine what lay beneath the billowing folds of the matching green-and-gold dress—Jamaican?—that gave away no secrets. She could be hiding 350 pounds beneath a dress like that. But he doubted it. Her face was all angles and high, hard cheekbones.

"Yeah," he replied. "Interesting." Be noncommittal. Let her talk first.

"Got any experience handling this kind of case?" It sounded less like a question than an accusation. Despite the fact that there were local black families named Adams, Uhuru knew this one must be from away. Local blacks, even ones who hadn't been alive in the seventies, knew Uhuru Melesse by reputation, even if he had done precious little to live up to it for more than twenty-five years.

"Experience? Oh, you know, a little. I'm not too worried."

"You should be," she fired back. "This isn't some commercial property case where the only important thing is whether you get paid. This is going to be a hard sell in the courtroom. It's too important to have somebody screw it up."

"What makes you think I'm going to screw it up?" he bristled. Bitch. He looked away, saw a blonde in a red party-time cocktail dress coming in through the door.

Shondelle followed his eyes, saw the blonde. She gave him a disgusted shrug. "Whatever," she said, and pushed her way back toward a crowd heading deeper into the bar. She looked back. "If you ever decide you need some help, you know where to find me."

This time, Uhuru didn't bother to excuse himself from Fat White Boy. He simply snaked around him, wordless, his eyes fixed on the blonde.

"I'll call you, man," Fat White Boy said. "Monday. Your office."

"Dessert, ma'am?" The waitress seemed to have materialized from nowhere, magically transforming their entrée plates into dessert menus. "And for you, Judge? Coffee? With a liqueur?"

This waitress was good, Ward thought, very good. He and Victoria had been dining at Valentino's since it opened thirty years ago, but usually only once or twice a year, on special occasions such as this. And yet the maître d' and servers inevitably addressed him by his title. Since judges were relatively anonymous, the fact that they always seemed to know what Ward did for a living impressed the former politician in him. So too did the fact that they remembered he preferred his dessert out of a bottle.

"Coffee would be great, thanks," he said, while Victoria gave Valentino's never-changing dessert menu a quick, just-in-case perusal. "Decaf. With a little Kahlua on the side." The decaf had been a recent addition to his post-prandial routine, another depressing sign that he had become one of those people he used to disparage. *Can't eat this. Can't drink that. Keeps me awake. Makes me sleepy. Gives me bad dreams. Gives me gas.* Now *he* was one of them.

"Ma'am?"

"Hmmm . . ." Victoria knew, had known all evening, what she would order for dessert. The anniversary special. "I've been saving myself for a little of your *za-bag-lee-own-ah*," she said sweetly, looking directly at the waitress and deliberately mispronouncing the name of the Italian dessert.

Ward smiled. There were times he could remember loving her. Did he still? The first time they'd come here—could it really have been to celebrate their first anniversary?—he'd mangled the pronunciation of zabaglione so badly he'd eventually had to resort to pointing dumbly at the menu to get the waitress to comprehend what he wanted. (Those were the days, he thought with a sudden wistfulness, when he could still order dessert *and* a liqueur.)

Victoria, of course, knew how to pronounce zabaglione. She'd learned to say it—and plenty of other words and phrases that sounded impossibly exotic to Ward—during her family's annual vacations in Europe. By contrast, Ward had lived the first fourteen years of his life in Eisners Head, a remote fishing village. No one in his family had ever had occasion to eat in a restaurant, let alone order zabaglione; Ward's parents believed food that didn't come at the end of a fishing line or out of a can wasn't real food. Even after his parents moved to Halifax in 1962, their idea of fine dining was Claudie's Fish and Chips, a neighbourhood greasy spoon owned by the brother-in-law of one of the trawlermen Ward's father had crewed with back home.

When Ward and Victoria first met, Victoria found Ward's lack of sophistication exotic. She'd barely managed to suppress her giggle until the waitress left that night. "You're such a Nova Scotian," she'd said affectionately, squeezing his hand. "You're *my* Nova Scotian. *Za-bag-li-own-ah, za-bag-li-own-ah* . . ." She'd repeated it like a mantra. "I'm going to call it that from now on too."

It was impossible for either of them to have known in the middle of that sweet memory-making moment so many years ago that, just two years later, everything about his career, his life, their life together, would shatter, altered forever in a single, still unacknowledged instant. "*Za-bag-li-own-ah*" was one of the few pleasant pre-apocalypse memories to survive.

"Excellent choice, Mrs. Justice," the waitress replied, affecting not to notice how badly Victoria had mutilated the word. "Some tea with that?"

Over the years, Ward was certain, Valentino's staff had learned to straight-facedly translate the many and various eccentric local pronunciations of its *Eye-talian* cuisine until nothing fazed them any more. When Valentino's opened its doors in 1972, there were only three or four restaurants in town worthy of the name, none more ethnic than meatballs-Italian-style or faux-French. Today, the city was full of chi-chi Thai, Greek, Vietnamese, Lebanese, even Ethiopian restaurants. Not that Ward ever ate in any of them, of course. He preferred to get Kathleen, his secretary, to buy him a bagel with cream cheese from the deli on her way back from lunch. Bagels! When Ward was first elected to the legislature, you still couldn't buy a bagel that hadn't been shipped in, frozen, from Montreal. Now you could buy them at Tim's. In flavours.

". . . that researcher from the Archives, that weaselly-looking fellow with the thick horn-rims and the bad breath?" Victoria was addressing him. What had he missed? How long had he been adrift in his tangential culinary ramble? He tried to focus. Researcher. Archives. Horn-rims. Bad breath. Oh, right. Oh no!

Ward couldn't help it if his father couldn't—or wouldn't—tell Victoria what she wanted to know. "I can't make the old man do anything he doesn't want to do," he'd explained when she'd tried to talk him into pressing his father for answers. "He's a stubborn old cuss."

"Just like you," she'd replied. Touché.

"Anyway, he called today," Victoria said now. "He thinks he might have found something about your family."

Tracing her own and Ward's family trees had been Victoria's most recent how-can-I-fill-up-my-days project. It wasn't the first. At one point, she was going to go into business as a high-end renovator, buying, fixing up and then selling dilapidated south-end mansions. At another, she was going to start her own high-fashion boutique for women of her age. And then there was the time she was going to go back to art school and open a ceramics gallery. And before that . . .

Ward had learned it was best not to take any of her schemes too seriously. Most never got beyond the talking stage. Their main purpose seemed to be to divert his wife's attention from the reality that she was middle-aged with two grown children, nothing to occupy her time and no marketable skills to offer the world.

Victoria was curiously both a woman of her times and also a woman out of time. Perhaps because she'd been the pampered daughter of a politician-businessman and his socialite wife, Victoria had grown up never imagining herself as more than an appendage—the daughter of a premier, the wife of a politician who would someday be premier and, then, the wife of a judge who could never be anything but a judge. But at the same time, she'd come of age in the sixties and had briefly fancied herself the rebellious, free-spirited flower child who smoked dope, tried acid and had sex with strangers in stranger places—which is the role she was living when she first met Ward.

When she got bored with living that fantasy, she married Ward on the rocks at Peggys Cove in a sunset ceremony she wrote herself and became the urban, pseudo-back-to-the-lander who baked her own bread, made her own yogurt and ground her own coffee. Then a mother, having their two children, Meghan and Sarah, one after the other, eighteen months apart. There might have been more, but then . . . what happened happened. So she got her tubes tied and assumed her next role as the overprotective earth mother who enrolled her fine and gifted daughters in all manner of self-improving music and dance lessons, soccer schools and summer camps. When the children got to be teenagers and stopped believing Mother Knew Best, she transformed herself into the new new Victoria, a perfect Martha-Stewart-dinner-party hostess who knew not only where to find—and how to use—fresh fennel and star anise but who could also set an elegant table for twelve every second Saturday evening. When had that phase ended? When she had the brief affair with the doctor-husband of her childhood best friend? She got more bored and then was diagnosed—by the doctor-husband—as clinically depressed. He prescribed Paxil; she gained weight, stopped taking Paxil, suffered withdrawal, joined a book club, drank too much, gave up alcohol, suffered hot flashes, married off one daughter and watched the other leave home for a job in Toronto.

Somewhere between the time she whacked up against menopause and Meghan announced last spring that she was going to marry Brad the architect, Victoria became obsessed with tracing their families' genealogies. The goal was supposed to be a personal, personalized wedding gift for Meghan and Brad, but this universe, like most, had not unfolded quite as Victoria intended.

The problem was not with Victoria's side of the family. There were two fawning biographies of her father, both written by self-publishing former aides. Victoria's grandfather had been a ship's chandler and prominent anti-Confederate member of the Nova Scotia Legislative Assembly; her great-grandfather was a wealthy sea captain. Her ancestors on both sides were United Empire Loyalists, but Victoria had also discovered—with the help of the horn-rimmed-glasses-wearing, weasel-faced archivist with halitosis—a branch of her mother's family that had remained in the Carolinas after the American Revolution. The "patriot" strain of Cullinghams produced both a state governor and a bank president, which Victoria duly noted in her genealogical charts. She did omit, of course, that the bank president went to prison for fraud.

Victoria was finding it much harder to trace Ward's family tree. It had no roots and only one branch—Ward. That wasn't quite true. There were church records in Eisners Head documenting his mother's side of the family for more than a hundred and fifty years, but nothing at all about his father's family.

The archivist had tried. He'd taken it first as a personal challenge, and a personal affront, that he could find no sign of Justice forbears before Desmond Justice's sudden, unexplained appearance in Eisners Head in 1932. He'd found Ward's parents' 1938 marriage certificate, but there were only blank spaces where Desmond's place of birth and the names of his parents were supposed to have been listed. The archivist had trolled through property and poll tax records in Eisners Head and other nearby communities, examined census documents, looked through family histories and come up empty.

"He's very excited," Victoria told Ward as the waitress set the snifter of liqueur in front of him.

"Coffee's coming right up," she said.

"He's such a strange little man," Victoria continued. "He's being very mysterious about whatever it is he's found. Says it could be nothing at all, but then, in the next breath, makes it sound like he's solved Rubik's cube."

She stopped talking while the waitress poured her husband's coffee. "Your dessert," she said, careful not to embarrass Victoria by pronouncing the name correctly, "will be along presently, ma'am."

"Anyway, we're going to meet at the archives Tuesday morning," she continued when the woman left. "You're welcome to join us if you like."

"Uh, I'd love to," he lied, "but we have our scheduling conference Tuesday morning."

"Here we are then, ma'am," the waitress said, placing a dish of zabaglione in front of Victoria. "You take milk with your tea, not cream, right?" Victoria nodded. "Coming right up."

They sat in silence then, Victoria picking at the edges of her zabaglione, Ward sipping his Kahlua. Occasionally, Victoria would look up, eye him intensely, appear about to say something, then look back down at her dessert, escaping into it. Finally, she found her courage, spoke, but without looking up.

"Ward, I think we need to talk—not now, not tonight. But soon." She looked at him finally. "I've been trying to figure out how to say this for weeks. And I know this is the wrong place and the wrong time. But I feel like I have to say it sometime. And there's never a right time." She took a breath, then another. "Ward, we need to talk about us. About what we're doing. About the future. The kids are gone. You'll be fifty-three, I'll be fifty-two. We've been married for thirty years, but it hasn't really been a marriage for most of that. We've done good things. We have two wonderful children. But they don't need us any more. And we both deserve to be happier than we are. We deserve the chance to find happiness, to find love—"

"More coffee, Judge?"

Ward shook his head, no. The waitress, who had seemed to materialize from nowhere to add tension to the moment, dissolved back into the shadows. Ward waited for Victoria to pick up her monologue, to drive this non-conversation down the road toward the cliff where he knew now it was headed.

"This is hard. It's very hard," Victoria tried again. She was looking into his eyes now. She put her hand on his. "But I think we have to be honest with ourselves. Face the truth. We haven't been happy together for a long time." Was this a royal 'we'? "We deserve better." She stopped again, let her words worm into his consciousness, allowing him to understand without her having to say anything more. But then she did. Say more. No misunderstanding her meaning now. "I want a divorce."

Ward wanted to reply, tell her he hadn't really been unhappy, but, even if he had, he understood he deserved his unhappiness. He wanted to tell her about his prostate, about how he was dying and she would be free soon enough. Why couldn't she just wait? That chance for happiness, for love, would be hers anyway. He wanted to tell her these things, but he couldn't. He *had* to pee.

"Drizzled! Smothered! Nestled! Coddled! Cuddled! Christ Almighty!" Patrick Donovan spat out each word like a swallow of sour milk. "Why don't they just call the goddamn food by its name instead of trying to make it sound like a whore at a fancy ball?"

Moira sighed. She'd invited her father to lunch at Richard's—"my treat"—so she could tell him her news. She'd finally found time to get to the drugstore for the pregnancy-test kit. No doubt about the results. And now that she'd had a few days to get used to the idea herself, she was ready to face her father. Richard's was the city's latest "in" restaurant, an airy, glass-walled dining room on the ground floor of Halifax's newest waterfront condo project. Richard's boasted not only hyperbolic descriptions of its otherwise undistinguished nouvelle cuisine but also—and more importantly—a spectacular, 180-degree snapshot of the waterfront, including a direct view of Todd's soon to be even newer and better condominium project rising up across the harbour in Dartmouth.

Todd knew his father-in-law disliked him, though he had no idea why. Which was the reason he'd mistakenly insisted Moira take her father to lunch at Richard's today. "My treat," he'd said grandly, and then called the restaurant's owner to tell him to forward the bill directly to his company. "I can write it off," he explained to Moira. His hope was that Moira's father would regard lunch at the city's most expensive restaurant—not to mention its view of Todd's fortune-making work in progress—as compelling evidence that Todd could provide, and very well, for both his only daughter and his soon-to-be grandchild.

What Todd couldn't seem to comprehend, but Moira knew full well, was that Todd's well-intended gestures would be a red cape to her father's raging bull, exacerbating Patrick's already barely veiled hostility toward him. Which is why Moira had told her father lunch was *her* treat. And why she'd made sure her father was seated with his back to the harbour and the view of the imposing skeleton of Harbourland Estates, Todd Eldridge, Esq., proprietor. "Daddy's not like you," she'd told Todd with uncharacteristic understatement the first she took him to meet her father.

Patrick Donovan fancied himself a socialist and claimed—wrongly, according to a former colleague Moira met at a party soon after she began working as a journalist herself—that he'd been fired by the *Tribune* for trying to start a union. "Is he still retailing that bullshit story?" The guy, whose name was Saunders, snorted derisively when Moira mentioned it in passing while introducing herself as Patrick Donovan's daughter. "He wasn't even a member of our little union-organizing cabal," the man told her, "but, for some reason, the bosses thought he was, so they fired him. And, ever since, he acts like he was some sort of fucking Eugene V. Debs." Suddenly realizing who he was talking to, he backtracked. "No offence. I mean, I like your father. He's a good guy most of the time—except when he's drinking, or when he claims he was the one behind the union drive. He wasn't even part of it."

The union-organizing/firing incident, which had occurred when Moira was barely a year old, had been one of the touchstones of her childhood. Her father referred to it often. *If I hadn't got fired for trying to organize that union, I'd still be married to your mother*, he would confide during almost every one of the two weekends a month they'd spent together during her childhood. Inevitably, of course, he would be drunk when he told her this, which perhaps also explained why he told her exactly the same story so often and in almost the same words. *I could have been the editor if I'd been like some of my so-called colleagues, if I hadn't stood up and been counted. But sometimes you just have to stand up and be counted.* Moira's mother told a different story. She blamed the collapse of their marriage on Patrick's drinking—"It started long before that union thing, and don't let him convince you otherwise"—and his frequent absences from home. "He was always working and, if he wasn't working, he was out drinking." Her one piece of advice to her daughter: "Never marry a journalist."

Moira had become one instead. What, she often wondered, would her mother have said about that? She had died of breast cancer nine years ago, while Moira was in her first year of university. Her slow and painful death was probably what lit the match to her father's last and longest full-blown bender, a two-week spiral into alcoholic oblivion that finally ended only when one of his fellow nightside editors at the *Daily Journal* bailed him out of the drunk tank. He'd been arrested for attacking a bartender who'd refused to serve him more drinks. By then, he hadn't shown up for work in more than a week. In the old days at the *Trib*, the editor would have fired him immediately; the enlightened management at the *Daily Journal* shuffled him off to Human Resources for employee assistance counselling instead. His counsellor made it clear his future depended on getting his drinking under control. So he did. He joined Alcoholics Anonymous and attended his weekly meetings faithfully until the day two years ago when the new publisher called him into his office to offer him his Hobson's choice: take a buyout or be laid off. He'd never been to an A.A. meeting since, but he hadn't started drinking again, either. "I wouldn't give those bastards the satisfaction," he told his daughter.

Today, Moira watched as her father took a long swallow of his San Pellegrino mineral water. "What's wrong with tap water?" he'd scowled at the waiter who had responded to Patrick's request for water with a list of bottled brands. Now he scanned Richard's noon-hour crowd of business types and lawyers with such a pained expression he could have been drinking sewage-polluted water from the harbour itself.

"They must be paying you pretty well if you can afford lunch at a place like this," he said finally. "Newspaper wages gone up since my day?"

Moira ignored his challenging barb. "Morton says to say hi," she said. "Said to tell you they still miss you on the night desk."

"*Hmmpf*," he replied, employing what Moira instantly recognized as her father's all-purpose expression of disgust. She'd forgotten. While Morton had not been the one to give him the boot two years earlier, Patrick had never forgiven the editor for standing by in silent acquiescence while the new publisher did the dirty deed on behalf of unseen owners half a country away. "Ah, yes, Massah Morton, the man with no balls."

This was getting worse. There was nothing for it but to plunge in. "Daddy," Moira said, "you're going to be a grandfather."

That stopped him. There was a long silence while Patrick did his best to make sense of this unexpected announcement. "Is this what you really want?" he asked finally.

"It is," she said, nodding her head in the affirmative and ignoring his unsubtle unhappiness at her news.

"Well, then . . ." he said in a flat-lined voice. "Congratulations, I guess." He raised his glass. He took a long swallow. Moira knew her father would have preferred to hear he was going to be the father of an editor than the grandfather of an infant.

"So I guess you're going to stay with that guy then." Her father rarely ever referred to Todd by name. Todd was too obsessed with making money, Patrick believed, too caught up in his work to be a good husband or father. The problem, though Patrick would not have put it in those terms, was that Todd was far too much like himself. How long before Moira found herself a single mother with a kid to drag her down, keeping her from ever—?

"Of course I am." Moira smiled, kept her tone light. She'd mastered the art of domestic peacekeeping during those teenage, post-divorce years when she'd been called upon to serve as the diplomatic envoy between her warring parents. "Daddy," she added, squeezing his hand in hers, "why can't you just be happy for me?"

"I'm sorry," he said after a moment. "I am, I really am. It's just . . . you're just so damned smart and talented. You're going to make a great editor one day and I don't want to see you get sidetracked by—well, you know . . ."

Time to release the second smart bomb to her father's heart. "I'm not even sure I'm going to stay at the paper," she said. "Todd wants me to come work for him, market his condos. And the fact is I am tired of being stuck covering courts. I've been on that beat for too long. Most days, I feel like I need a shower when I come home. Just to get rid of all the shit I pick up during the day."

"But you don't have to quit," Patrick replied. "I mean, you could go to Morton, get him to put you on the desk. That would be a good step up the ladder. Then maybe go for a section editor job and then—"

"But Daddy, I'm not sure any more it's what I want to do. Todd says—"

"What the hell does he know about newspapers?" he cut her off. "He's a . . . *dee-veloper*, for God's sakes. He builds buildings. You're a newspaper person. You're a different breed from him."

"*You're* a different breed," Moira corrected him. "I'm not so sure what I am. I like writing but I'm not passionate about journalism, not like you. Maybe marketing would be okay. Or maybe, you know, I could write a novel. Remember when I wrote that novel when I was a kid? You were so proud."

"But what do you need to write a novel for when there's so much more interesting real life you can write about? I mean, look at that story you covered last week about that black guy, the one who claims he stole all that money as reparations for Africville. You can't make that stuff up. You want to write a book? Reparations is a big deal in the States these days. I'll bet some publisher in Toronto or New York would pay a lot of money for a book about that. You could take a leave of absence, write the book and then, when you come back, you'd get promoted, maybe get your own column—"

"But Daddy, I'm pregnant!"

"That doesn't mean you have to roll over and die, does it? I mean, I could help you. I used to do court stuff. And I knew those guys. Justice, Melesse, both. Back in the day before anybody even knew who the hell he was, I had Justice by the short and curlies. If it hadn't been for publisher politics, I'd have nailed him." He saw Moira's look of impatience. "No, seriously. It's true. And Carter, he was my source. He had it in for Justice. There's lots of dirt I could dig up for you."

Moira tried to stay calm. It wasn't easy. "First of all, I'm not sure a publisher is going to be interested in a story from here, especially not one about a bookkeeper who steals money and then blames it all on racism. And second, I don't think you heard me. I'm pregnant.

I'm already falling asleep at the dinner table every night. I just don't have the energy to write a book right now."

Her father steamrollered over his daughter's protests about her pregnancy as if, by refusing to acknowledge its reality, he could make it disappear. "I think you're wrong about the publisher. Think about it. You've got Carter—I mean Melesse—as the kid's lawyer. His name may not mean much to you, but he was big into black power back in the seventies. A lot of book editors my age would remember him. And he's up against Justice. He was a big name when he was a politician. And those two, they have a history. Back in the seventies, Carter nailed Justice trying to buy votes from black families. Had him cold. Pictures even. I was going to write about it but the *Trib* wouldn't publish it." He stopped, as if remembering. "But that's another story. The point is, back then everyone thought Justice was going to be premier, maybe even prime minister. And you've got your storyline: thirty-how-many-years-later, they face each other in a courtroom. Black power versus racist judge."

"Whoa, Daddy. What do you mean, 'racist judge'?" This didn't sound like her father talking. "Why? Because he's white?"

"No, no. It was in your story. The way he treated Melesse in the courtroom—"

"But you know yourself judges do crazy things in court. That doesn't mean they're all racists."

Patrick Donovan smiled. "Ah, yes, my darling daughter. Which is why you need your father's help on this story. I just happen to know a few things about the good judge. Like the time when he was still a politician and he was guest speaker at the press gallery dinner. You know, one of those off-the-record, let-loose, nothing-gets-reported events we used to have before everybody got ethics. He gets up and he's as drunk as the rest of us, and then he starts telling this joke, this nigger joke—"

Moira blanched. "Daddy! Not so loud. People will hear."

"My point exactly," her father continued as if he'd been expecting just such an interjection. "What would people think if they knew the judge in the most important human rights case in Nova

Scotia history—isn't that what you quoted that Dalhousie law professor as saying?—if they knew that judge had a habit of telling nigger jokes in public?"

Patrick Donovan paused, took another drink of water, let his shimmering lure work its magic.

"What was the joke?" Moira asked finally.

"I don't remember now," her father confessed. "It was a lot of years ago. But I'll bet Danny Thompson would. He was president of the Press Gallery Association. He would have been the one to invite Justice to speak. I remember he was pissed off after. Thompson's still around. Took early retirement from Canadian Press. Lives on a farm up in the Valley. He wouldn't be hard to find."

"But would he talk? Didn't you say yourself that it was all off the record?"

"There's got to be a statute of limitations on that," her father replied. "Besides, Thompson wanted to write about it. He told me he even filed the story but his bureau chief wouldn't put it on the wire. So I don't see why he wouldn't be willing to tell you the story now."

"But even assuming this guy remembers, it would be just his word against Justice's," Moira said. "Morton would never go for that."

"Ah, but once again, your daddy to the rescue. I happen to have in my files in the apartment a list of all the members of the press gallery for those years." He grinned at her. "Among the names on that list is one Allen Morton, then the other legislature reporter for the *Tribune* and now the managing editor of the *Daily Journal* and therefore your boss."

"You're kidding—"

"Would I kid? But wait. It gets better. There was a CBC sound guy who did the audio for the dinner every year. Lambie. He was so into sound he recorded everything. And a pack rat, too. We used to joke he kept every piece of tape he ever recorded. He even had a special room in his basement—"

Moira had already taken her notebook and pen from her purse. "What did you say his name was again? And how can I get in touch with him?"

"See, I told you." Her father leaned back in his chair, smiled smugly, as if he'd mapped out this entire conversation and then followed its predetermined route to its inevitable conclusion. "You *are* a newspaper person. You'd never be happy as some marketing flunky for what's-his-name. And besides, there are way too many goddamn novels." He stopped then, continued to smile at her. "Moira, my love . . ." He stretched out each word to drive it home. "You—are—a—newspaper—person."

"Okay, okay," she said, allowing his gloat to go on a little too long before she answered. "I take your point. So how do I find this guy anyway?"

He reached into his sports jacket pocket, took out a clipping torn from a newspaper, slid it across the table to her. "I thought you'd never ask." He really had planned it all, she thought in amazement. "That story," he said, pointing to the clipping in her hand, "appeared in your Sunday paper last fall. Lambie was about to retire, sell his house and move to Florida, so he donated his entire personal audio library to the Public Archives." He looked at her. "And, before you ask, I already checked. The Archives lady says there are no restrictions on access. Lambie probably doesn't even remember what's on all those tapes."

"But why—?"

"I clipped it because I was going to try to get in touch with him before he left for Florida. But I never got around to it. And then he was gone. When I saw your story last week, I thought I could help my little girl get herself a big scoop. So I dug around and I found it in my junk drawer. Can't help it. Just like you can't help being a newspaper person. It's in the genes."

Moira looked down at the clipping in her hand and at the steno notebook on the table. She'd reached for it instinctively. Perhaps her father was right after all.

3

1964

Ward Justice *was* Elroy Face. He turned his head to the left, stared down Bobby Richardson. Elroy's vaunted pickoff move scared the Yankee slugger back to first base. Satisfied, Elroy swivelled his head toward third base, his eyes closed, his body still. To his left, ninety feet away, Roger Maris was crowding the plate, waiting for him to serve up a fat one he could pound out of the park.

It was the bottom of the ninth. The Pirates were leading by one run. There were two outs, Richardson on first. The count was three and two. The series was on the line. It was all up to Elroy now. If the Pirates won, the World Series title would stay in Pittsburgh. Where it belonged.

Inside his glove, Elroy splayed his index and middle finger around the circumference of the ball. Ward's hand was too small for the tennis ball; he could feel a burn in the crook of his fingers. But the fork ball was Elroy's signature, his go-to pitch, so Ward had to throw it.

Elroy brought his arms up over his shoulders, the ball hidden inside his glove, pumped his left leg in the air, leaned back on his right foot and fired the ball as hard as he could. As he opened his eyes, Ward heard a thunk as the tennis ball caught the sweet spot in the V of the concrete step leading up the hill to his father's workshop. It rebounded high into the air.

A fly ball into shallow centre, just beyond second base. Bill Mazeroski waved the other fielders away. This one was his. He leaped into the air, extended his arm higher than it could possibly reach. But he snared it, the ball slapping hard against the top inside webbing of his glove.

Ward fell backwards then, landing hard on his bum in a yellowed patch of tall grass just beyond the official backyard border his father had finally demarcated with his lawn mower last summer.

Mazeroski raised his left arm in triumph to show the screaming fans he'd caught the ball. It was over. The Pirates had won. They'd defeated the hated Yankees. They were World Series champions again!

And all because of Elroy and Bill—and fourteen-year-old Ward Justice, who was both of them. Not to mention Maris and Richardson and whoever else the play-by-play in his head required.

"Little early for baseball, isn't it?" Old Jimmy Parsons shouted across the field as he climbed out of the cab of his pickup truck. He was smiling at Ward in his goofy way. "Hockey's not even over yet."

"Spring training," Ward replied, and smiled back at him. "I think the meeting's already started," he added, nodding toward the house.

Jimmy was always late. Ward's father said it was on account of his drinking. Jimmy's wife—a *"Jee-hovah,"* according to Ward's mother—wouldn't allow alcohol in her house, so Jimmy had to keep his quart behind the driver's seat of his truck. Whenever he was anxious, which was most of the time these days, Jimmy would drive around town, drinking the rye straight from the bottle. *He must be really anxious this afternoon*, Ward thought as he took in the slackness of Jimmy's grin.

The strike had affected them all, including his father. But in a good way. Before the strike, his father rarely spoke to their neighbours. He wasn't unpleasant. He just preferred to keep to himself. "'Fore the strike," Jimmy had said, "nobody never heard your daddy say boo to nobody. Now, he's all the time tellin' them fellas in the gov'ment up in Halifax what we want. You're a lucky boy. You got a great man for a father. Remember that."

Ward would. It was his father, after all, who'd been responsible for starting the strike in the first place. Last February, when the *Sara*

Eisner had returned to port after an unsuccessful trip, Desmond Justice, Jimmy and Nigel Parsons and Martin Hennessey had drawn shore chores, so, while the rest of the crew got to spend the day with their families, they'd had to spend the morning unloading what little catch they'd brought back, the afternoon repairing tears in the trawl netting and the inky, early evening waiting for the truck from Eisners' General Merchandise to arrive so they could load and stow the provisions for the next trip. Only after all of that would they finally get to go home to their families, too.

This trip had been an awful broker—after nearly two weeks at sea, they'd hauled less than eighty thousand pounds of fish. On a good trip, they might bring in that much in a day. After his share of all the trip expenses had been taken off the top—food, bait, wages for the cook, wages for the engineer and, this time, seventy-five more dollars for what his pay stub described as "electronic gear"—Desmond Justice was handed a small envelope containing his net wages for the trip: one dollar and thirty-four cents. In cash.

"It's not wages," Dale Eisner corrected him when Desmond complained. "You're a co-adventurer, just like Dad and the company and me," he explained as if to a child. He had a smirk on his face. "That's what the court says. That's what the government says. And that's what I say. We share in the good times, and we share in the bad."

So how come, Desmond wanted to reply, *you live in a fucking mansion and I live in a prefab I had to put up myself?* The system was rotten, and everyone knew it. There may have been a time when fishermen really were co-adventurers, neighbours who'd go out for the day on somebody's Cape Islander, catch as many fish as they could, then steam back to port and split their earnings. But those days were gone. Now everyone worked for the company.

In this town, that meant J. F. B. Eisner & Company. Some people in town said the J.F.B. stood for "Jesus Fucking Bastard," but never to the old man's face. Dale—everyone called him Junior—was J.F.B.'s son. He was being groomed to take over from his old man.

The Eisner family had ruled the local fishing industry since long before Desmond Justice arrived in Eisners Head in 1932. Only it wasn't called Eisners Head then. It was Cabot Landing, named after the famous Italian explorer who may or may not have landed in the harbour during his ventures to the New World. If he did, Ward's father said, it was by mistake.

The community had been plunked down on a rocky, windswept promontory where what passed for trees refused to poke their heads more than a few feet into the salty sea air. The earth was so rocky no one even bothered to try to put a foundation under a house; most of the clapboard shacks squatted on posts or rested on great slabs of granite that had heaved up to the surface long before Cabot arrived.

Even today, the town seemed—to Ward at least—almost as isolated as it must have been in Cabot's day. It was twenty miles by dirt road to the nearest highway, and even that was an old secondary road, partly paved and partly not, depending on how the residents had voted in the last election. The residents of Eisners Head voted Liberal, usually the right choice in Nova Scotia. But the Tories had won the last election. Now they'd have to wait until the next provincial election to get the potholes filled.

Old Man Eisner was the chief Liberal in these parts. The chief everything, in fact. Back in the forties, he had successfully petitioned the Legislature to change the town's name, and the name of the harbour, and the name of the point of land on which the family fish plant sat, in order to recognize the Eisners' many and various contributions to the community. J. F. B. Eisner & Company's fish-processing plant and wharves now sat on the edge of the town of Eisners Head at a jut of land at the eastern end of Eisners Harbour known as Eisners Point.

No one had had to change the name of the building that housed the Eisners Head town hall. Back in the thirties, Eisner Contractors, another of the family enterprises Junior would soon inherit, had built the community's only three-storey building and named it after themselves. The Eisner Building on Main Street—thankfully, the family had left the street name alone—also housed the town's only general store, Eisners' General Merchandise, the post office and the liquor commission along with the offices of the *Eisners Head Gazette*, the local member of the Legislature and even the federal department where the fishermen had to go to file their unemployment insurance claims whenever they were out of work. Which, of course, they weren't eligible for now because they weren't technically unemployed; they were on strike. Or not. Depending on who you asked.

J.F.B. didn't own St. Paul's Anglican, the only church in town, but he didn't have to. The Eisners were generous contributors to the cause and had recently financed the acquisition of the new stained-glass windows Father Rhodeniser had been lusting after for so long. No one had to tell Father Rhodeniser where he stood on the strike. Over the past fourteen months, he'd made the strike—and the Godless communists who organized it—the subject of many a sermon. But his audience was diminishing. Many of the fishermen and their families, unhappy to be called Godless communists, or, worse, dupes of Godless communists, no longer attended services.

Was his father a Godless communist, Ward wondered? Perhaps, but it was only because Junior Eisner had pushed him too far. Desmond Justice had asked Junior Eisner to explain that seventy-five-dollar deduction for electronic gear. He wouldn't.

"If you don't like the way I run my business, *Mister* Justice"—the Mister dragged out and exaggerated to transform it into a mocking salutation—"well, why don't you just go out and start your own fish company?"

His father must have been seething, Ward thought, but still, he held his tongue, grimacing, swallowing the foul taste of his anger like a wad of snot caught in his throat. But then Junior, fresh out of the MBA program at Dalhousie University, ratcheted Desmond's anger one final notch. After they'd finished stowing the last of the provisions for the next trip, Eisner blithely announced that the *Sara Eisner* would be sailing again at first light. Desmond and the rest of the crew were to report back aboard at four in the morning.

Junior Eisner had never fished, never been to sea except on sunny Sundays in his daddy's sailboat. So he didn't have a clue what it was like to be a trawler fisherman. When you worked on a trawler, Desmond could have told him—he'd told Ward more often than he wanted to hear—you didn't catch fish, you chased them. Once you shot your trawl the first time, it became a race to fill the hold with fish before the first of the catch started to rot. If the fish were running, you could work eighteen, twenty-four, thirty-six hours without a break. Desmond himself had once worked sixty straight hours without sleep. You worked whatever the weather: rain, snow, sleet, a pounding gale. Lots of times, it was dangerous just being on deck. Over the years, Desmond had watched helplessly as three of his mates were washed overboard off icy or rain-slicked decks. They hadn't recovered their bodies.

Fishing, Ward's father said, was no choice for any man who had a choice. He had been pounding that mantra into his son's brain for four years. It had started when he was ten. It was his parents' anniversary, one of the rare ones his father had been home for, so his mother had organized a family picnic to celebrate. That afternoon, on their way to the provincial park just outside of town, Ward asked, for no good reason he could remember: "When can I go out fishing with you, Dad?"

His father was driving, his mother in the passenger seat, Ward between them. Desmond Justice shot a quick glance over Ward's head toward his wife. Then he slammed on the brakes and pulled the pickup off to the shoulder of the highway. His father turned on him. "You're *never* going fishing! You hear me?" he practically shouted in that scary God-voice he used only rarely, and only when Ward had done something incredibly bad. "You're going to go to school, and you're going to get an education, and you're going to get out of here. I'd rather cut you up for bait than see you grow up to be a fisherman."

His own hatred of what he did to make a living might explain why Junior Eisner's offhand order that night tipped his father over the edge. Desmond Justice had plans. He was going to go home, soak in a long, hot bath until all the salt and fish stink disappeared down the drain, and then make love to his wife. The next day he would sleep in, relax, probably do a few chores Ada had been saving up for him. Now, instead of that, he would have to squeeze what he could manage into less than eight hours.

"Tomorrow morning!" he shouted at Junior. "Jesus fucking Christ, we've been out for nearly two weeks. You're supposed to give us at least two days to do—"

"Who says? You? Listen, Mr. Justice. There's fish out there. The skipper of the *Mary Elizabeth*"—another company trawler—"just called in from the tail to say they hauled a hundred thousand of redfish in the last twenty-four hours. Their hold is full, but he says there's still plenty where they were hauling, so you guys are going to go out there and bring it back for us."

"But—"

"But nothing, Mr. Justice," Junior said, turning to walk away. "There's plenty more like you. If you don't want to fish, then stay home."

"Maybe I will," Desmond called after him. "Maybe all of us will. What do you say, boys?"

That got Junior's attention. He was halfway down the gangplank when he turned back toward Desmond and the others. He stared hard at the Parsons brothers and Hennessey, as if daring them and threatening them at the same time.

There was a long silence while Jimmy Parsons considered. There were rules against alcohol on board ship, and the skipper knew enough to keep an especially close watch on Jimmy. Jimmy had been looking forward to being home ever since they'd left port. Jimmy stared back at Eisner, meeting his dare.

"I'm with me mate," he said simply.

Nigel, who looked up to his older brother and followed his lead, nodded his head. "Me too," he said.

Martin Hennessey looked uneasy, but then he remembered his Uncle Eric. Last fall, his uncle had been swept overboard in a gale and drowned. Martin's own boat had been only a day out of port when it happened, but the company refused to allow him to hitch a ride back to port on the *Mary Elizabeth*, which was passing his ship on its way back. "Who'd do his job?" Junior had demanded after the skipper radioed in Martin's request.

"Count me in as well," Martin said quietly now. "Count me in."

And that was the start of it. That night, Desmond and the others called the rest of the crew to tell them what had happened. The next morning, no one but the *Sara Eisner*'s skipper and chief engineer reported for duty. When an angry Junior got on the phone to recruit replacements, he discovered that word of the "mutiny"—that's what he said it was—had spread. Not one fisherman in all of Eisners Head was willing to sail on the *Sara Eisner*. Or, it soon became clear, any other Eisner trawler either. That afternoon, Junior's father fired "every last no-good one of them," even though, as he himself had insisted for years, none of them were, in fact, employees of his company.

The next day the union reps from Halifax hurried to town with union cards and the promise that, if the fishermen signed them, they'd be eligible for strike pay. Most did.

The company tried to hire replacement workers from other ports along the coast, but it would have taken a brave man to walk past the fifty or so burly fishermen who blockaded the road from the plant to the wharf. No one was that brave.

In the beginning, most of the townspeople supported the strikers. But then the processing plant closed because there was no more fish to process. And since no one had any money to spend, the local merchants began to feel the pain, too. Now there was talk that old man Eisner might move his entire fishing operation fifty miles down the coast to Somerset, where the town council was offering to provide the company with land for a new plant free of charge. No wonder the plant workers, the merchants, all of the schoolteachers and most of the town employees—even some of the fishermen themselves—wanted the strike settled and didn't much care any more how it happened.

All of that, of course, eventually trickled down to the schoolyard. Ward learned the downside of having a father who was considered the person most responsible for the strike. Whatever criticisms the other children heard around the supper table at night they brought with them to school the next day. Manny Soloman, whose father managed the Steadman's department store, said Ward's father was a pinko and challenged him to a fight after school. Ward came home that day with a black eye. He refused to tell his parents what had precipitated the fight. "It just happened," he said.

The company, of course, was doing its best to single out Ward's father and the union agitators from away who were destroying the peace and prosperity of their town. Junior Eisner had let it be known he was willing to meet with a delegation of the fishermen to see if they could find a way to settle the dispute "like men," but only on condition that neither Ward's father nor the union be involved. After much argument, the fishermen agreed to Eisner's terms. Desmond Justice did not object. He told his wife he was fed up with being the focus of attention anyway.

So this afternoon, the fishermen, perhaps two dozen of them, had come back to Ward's house, still the unofficial strike headquarters, to find out what Eisner had told their representatives. Ward's mother had sent Ward outside to play soon after the first of the fishermen arrived. But the meeting had lasted longer than anyone expected. So, after he'd won as many World Series as he could stand, Ward slipped quietly back into the house through the side door. He was planning to go directly to his room and read but the shouting from the kitchen was loud and Ward was curious. He positioned himself at the top of the stairs, out of sight of the men, and listened.

It didn't take long to figure out what they were arguing about. Junior Eisner had made the fishermen a proposition. The company would take them back under the same terms and conditions as before the strike, provided they voted to get rid of their union and agreed the company would blackball Desmond Justice. If they didn't agree, Junior said, J. F. B. Eisner & Company would build its new wharf and processing plant in Somerset. The company would, of course, have to hire Somerset fishermen to crew their vessels. The choice was theirs, he told the fishermen, take it or leave it.

Henry Zinck, who'd been a mate aboard the *Mary Elizabeth* before the strike, had been one of the fishermen chosen to represent everyone else at the meeting with Eisner. And he'd come back from that meeting arguing in favour of accepting Eisner's offer. "What choice do we have now?" he demanded, his eyes sweeping the room. "We do it their way or they go away. Principles is fine but it don't put food on the table."

"Junior's just bluffing," countered Eddie Green. He was thirty-five and single. He still lived at home with his mother. "Eisners has been here for fucking ever. They're not going to just fucking up and leave and start over again somewheres else."

"Easy for you to say," shouted someone whose voice Ward couldn't identify. "Fuckin' momma's boy." There was a frantic scraping of chairs on linoleum then, and everyone seemed to be yelling at once.

"Enough," Henry Zinck bellowed finally, and calm slowly returned. "We've talked at this long enough. It's time to vote."

"No need." It was Ward's father. Ward hadn't heard him say a word until now. He imagined him sitting in his old wooden rocker in the corner by the woodstove enveloped in a haze of smoke from one of the Export As he always seemed to be holding in his hand. "There's no need to vote," Desmond said quietly. Suddenly, the room was as still as the church when Father Rhodeniser ordered his weekly moment of silent prayer. Ward could imagine the rest of the men leaning toward his father, waiting to hear what he had to say. "Henry's right," he said after a long pause. "Junior's not bluffing. He'll take the company and move it to Somerset. He's a stubborn one, just like his daddy, and he's going to win this thing one way or t'other."

The silence seemed to stretch on to forever as everyone drank in the import of Desmond Justice's words. Finally, Martin Hennessey broke the silence. He sounded to Ward as if he was about to cry again. "But what about you? I walked out with you and I want to go back with you." Ward heard murmurs of assent but he couldn't be sure whether it was the majority of the men.

"Don't you worry about me," his father responded. "There are some things you can change, and some you can't, and this is just one you can't. That's okay. I always said I was gonna quit fishing someday. I guess today's the day."

And so it was settled. The strike was over. The Eisners had won. Desmond Justice wasn't a fisherman any more. But what was he then? And what would Ward be now that he wasn't the son of a fisherman?

He knew what he wanted to be. He wanted to be Bill Mazeroski. But somehow he didn't think that was going to happen.

Raymond could already feel the sweat forming under his armpits. He wanted to loosen his tie—the tightness of his starched white shirt collar was scratching against his neck—and take off his wool suit jacket. But when he looked around he could see all the men were wearing suits too. They didn't appear uncomfortable. His father had insisted Raymond dress properly if he wanted to tag along to tonight's meeting at the church. And Raymond wanted to be there, wanted to see what all the fuss was about.

Raymond couldn't remember the church being so crowded, though it had been nearly a year since he'd last been inside. Last year, shortly after he turned thirteen, he'd announced to his father he was too old to be told what to do, and that he wasn't going to go to church any more. Ever. His father hadn't objected. Perhaps, Raymond realized later, it was the excuse he'd been looking for not to go himself.

That's not to say his father hadn't been inside the church at all. Seaview African United Baptist Church wasn't just Africville's only church, it was also its community meeting place. And there had been plenty of community meetings there lately. Most had to do with all the talk he'd been hearing about tearing down their houses and moving everyone somewhere else.

Tonight's meeting had been called so the residents could hear the latest report from an urban planning consultant the City had hired to advise it on what to do about Africville.

Raymond couldn't help but notice that most of the pews were filled with white visitors. Apparently, the other Africville residents had given up their usual pews to the whites. Not Raymond's father.

The women of the church auxiliary were standing, hovering near the back of the church, watching and waiting. They'd spent much of the day making the little quarter-sandwiches with the crusts cut off that Raymond loved, and baking the date squares Raymond loved even more. They were poised now, waiting for the meeting to end so they could serve them.

Sitting beside his father in their pew close to the front of the church, Raymond tried to identify the white people around him. He recognized the mayor. And their local member of the Legislature. Raymond remembered him—his name was O'Sullivan—from the provincial election campaign last summer when he'd led a cavalcade of horn-honking cars and trucks around Africville. The parade had finally come to a halt just outside the church. O'Sullivan got out of his car, a big white convertible, and shook hands with Deacon Johnstone, who'd assembled a small crowd of supporters to greet him. As the street outside the church filled up with other Africvillians like Raymond who'd been attracted by the commotion, O'Sullivan's workers took up positions beside the trucks and efficiently began handing out goodies. Balloons for the kids. Nylons for the ladies. Pints of rum for the men. There were even cardboard boxes filled with groceries. But only a chosen few seemed to get the boxes.

"How I get one of those?" Old Blackie asked. He was an elderly man whose last name was Black so everyone called him Old Blackie, even to his face. Old Blackie drank too much.

"It's easy, old fellow," answered a young white man in a cream-coloured summer suit. He seemed to be in charge of distributing the largesse. "We get your vote, you get your pint. Get five more people to vote for us and we'll give you groceries, too. How's that sound?"

Raymond's father was angry when he brought home one of the balloons. THE O'SULLIVAN WAY IS THE LIBERAL WAY, said the bold white lettering on the red balloon.

"I don't want that shit around my house," his father said. His father rarely ever swore, so Raymond knew he was serious. "I don't need any of them telling me which way to vote."

Raymond didn't know how his father had voted—"that's between me and the ballot box"—but he did know O'Sullivan had won. Which was why O'Sullivan was back here tonight, Raymond guessed, looking out for the interests of his constituents.

Raymond didn't recognize most of the other white men in the audience, but there sure were a lot of them. Raymond might not have even known he was in Seaview Church if not for the sight of the still-crooked painting of Jesus on the cross that hung beside the pulpit. Raymond used to stare at it during services, seeing if he could will it straight. He couldn't. Perhaps that was when he'd stopped believing; after all, he'd prayed to Jesus to straighten Himself out and He hadn't.

The Deacon finally made his way to the pulpit. Raymond's father looked at his watch. It was nearly 7:30, half an hour after the meeting was supposed to start. "Africville time," he muttered under his breath. His father didn't much like the Deacon. And the Deacon seemed to feel the same about him. That might have been another reason, Raymond thought, why his father wasn't angry at him for not going to church any more.

"Good evening, Mr. Mayor, Mr. M.L.A., aldermen, members of the Halifax Negro Betterment Association, distinguished guests and brothers and sisters of Seaview African Baptist Church," the Deacon began, in what Raymond's father would have dismissed as his "windbag way."

"For those of you who may not know me, I am Deacon George Johnstone, and I want to welcome you all here this evening, especially our esteemed visitors from the Province and the City and, of course, Mr. Wilfred Jamieson, our acclaimed guest speaker for this evening."

Raymond wasn't the only child there. Rosa Johnstone, the Deacon's daughter, was sitting in the pew ahead of them, squirming and fidgeting. The Deacon stopped speaking suddenly and froze her with a stare. Rosa was only eight, but she knew the look. She sat still and quiet. The Deacon had brought her along because Rosa's mother was working downtown. She was a cleaning lady—the Deacon referred to her as a "custodial specialist"—at the Dale Building. She began her job emptying wastebaskets and ashtrays, sweeping and washing floors after the building's white office workers had all left for the day.

Deacon Johnstone's own real job was as a porter on the CN railroad. His proudest moment came in 1939 when he was selected to be one of the porters on the special train that ferried the King and Queen of England across the country during their Royal Tour. "She was a gracious lady," he would say to anyone who would listen. A framed photo of the King and Queen hung in his living room.

Deacon Johnstone was also proud of his role as a deacon at Seaview. He'd wanted to be a preacher when he was growing up but he'd left the old Africville School after grade six to work in the railyard and never went back. That didn't stop him from talking and acting like a preacher whenever the opportunity arose. Seaview couldn't afford its own minister so it depended on other black ministers from around Halifax to conduct the services for them. When none of them could make it, the Deacon did it himself.

Mr. and Mrs. Johnstone's fourth child, their only daughter, Rosa, was born on December 7, 1955. It was exactly one week after a Negro seamstress named Rosa Parks had refused to give up her seat to a white man on a bus in Montgomery, Alabama, and was arrested. "My Rosa is going to be a credit to her race, too," Deacon Johnstone would say. He would not have said that tonight as she resumed fidgeting and fussing with the doll her father had allowed her to bring with her. Now he tried to ignore her.

"Mr. Jamieson brings with him a cornucopia of credentials," the Deacon said. Raymond's father snorted derisively, but Johnstone ignored him and proceeded to read from the man's lengthy resumé for five minutes. Raymond soon knew more than he cared to about Jamieson's education and professional accomplishments, even that he liked to garden in his "rare spare hours."

"Thank you very much for that most generous introduction,

Reverend," Jamieson began when he finally got his turn at the pulpit. "As many of you already know, City Council commissioned me last winter to investigate housing and social conditions in Africville and to make recommendations back to the members of Council by the first of September. I spent two days in Halifax in April consulting with City staff and meeting with community leaders. I met with Mr. Johnstone"—Johnstone smiled, pleased to be acknowledged as a community leader—"and he very graciously escorted me on a tour of this community. So thank you, sir," he added. The applause was tepid.

Jamieson became sombre. "I know I don't have to tell you what I discovered in my investigation. The conditions in Africville are deplorable, simply unacceptable in any community in Canada in the 1960s. Here you have close to seventy families, four hundred people, living in squalor on the very edge of a prosperous city." Jamieson seemed oblivious to the fact that he was addressing people who called what he called squalor "home." "They live in homes—shacks, really—with no indoor plumbing, no running water. Because the community is built on rock, most of the wells are shallow and, too often, right beside the cesspools from their and their neighbours' houses. The result is a health hazard of potentially catastrophic proportions." He paused to let that sink in. "I don't think it's unfair of me to point out that if the people of this community were of a . . . different racial background, this problem might have been solved a long time ago."

"Amen," Raymond's father said. Raymond was embarrassed. No one else had said a word. Deacon Johnstone looked at him disapprovingly.

"But that is water under the bridge," Jamieson continued. "We must deal with this problem as we find it. As you may have heard, my report, which is to be voted on by Council at its next meeting, calls for Africville to be demolished and all of the residents relocated to better and more modern housing in other parts of the city."

Old Blackie interrupted then. "Is it true you called Africville a 'shack town'?" It was obvious he'd been drinking.

"Well sir, look around you. What do you see? Tarpaper shacks with no foundations. People with no jobs. Bootleggers and worse. There are no paved roads. I've been to cities all over North America and Europe, and I can say to you that this is the worst situation I have ever seen. And you don't have to take my word for it. All the Toronto newspapers, even *Maclean's* magazine, have sent reporters down here to see for themselves. And they've all said the same thing. Africville is a national and international stain on the reputation of this fine community."

Old Blackie wasn't easily deterred. "George Dixon, the greatest boxer what ever lived, was born right here in Africville. And Duke Ellington's wife, the jazzman? Her people was from Africville, too—"

Deacon Johnstone stood up then. "That will be enough, Mr. Black. Please remember that Mr. Jamieson is our guest."

But Old Blackie had opened the floodgates, and no one was about to shut them now. "Why do you have to destroy our community and move us someplace else?" a man shouted from the back of the church. "Why not just give us city sewer and water and let us stay where we are?"

"Perhaps I can answer that, Mr. Chairman." It was the alderman, whose name was MacPhee. "It's just too expensive. City staff have looked very carefully at the numbers and they estimate it would take eight hundred thousand dollars to put in sewer and water lines to Africville. The city just can't afford that. Relocation is a better, less expensive alternative."

"Better for who?" It was Everett Dickson. He lived next door to Raymond and his father. "I read in the paper that you're only planning to spend forty to seventy thousand dollars in total to expropriate all the people here. That's less than six hundred dollars a family. Now, how we supposed to find a decent place to live on that? If we're going to be expropriated, we should at least get a house for a house."

There were cheers then. Up at the front, Jamieson was beginning to sweat. Raymond could see beads of perspiration on his forehead. It wasn't just the heat in the room, Raymond was certain. "Six hundred dollars?" he answered uncertainly. "No sir, not necessarily.

Some residents—ah, some homeowners, will do considerably better than that. As you know, many of the residents here have no proof they even have legal title to the land they occupy. Rather than just take that land, which it would be entitled to do, the City of Halifax is generously offering all of the squatters"—there were scattered boos at that—"compensation of five hundred dollars per family. That will mean more money in the pot for those residents who do have clear title. Subject to negotiation, of course. As for the question of a house for a house, I don't think that would be feasible. But Maynard Square is very nice, new . . . a wonderful housing project, and there are more public housing projects being built in the city even as we speak."

That's when Raymond's father stood up. The room became quiet, expectant. Raymond's father, Lawrence Carter, was one of the most respected men in Africville, more even than the Deacon. Born in Barbados, he still spoke with a lilting accent. He had arrived in Africville in the 1930s, to teach in the Africville school. He'd married a local woman, Desdemona Jones, and they had five children. Raymond was the youngest, an accident born ten years after his next oldest brother.

In 1951, when Raymond was just two years old, a fire that started in the chimney destroyed their house. Their next-door neighbour, Mr. Dickson, rescued Raymond—his father and brothers were at the school—but couldn't save Raymond's mother. The fire department eventually arrived, but there was no nearby source of water to connect their hoses to. Ray didn't remember his mother, but he knew by heart his father's bitter lament that if the City had provided Africville with water as the community had been demanding for years, there would have been fire hydrants and his mother would be alive today.

After the fire, the neighbours pitched in to rebuild the house, but smaller this time, just big enough for Raymond and his father. "I want the older ones to get away from this place," his father explained. "And I don't want them to have the option to move back." Raymond's brothers were long gone now, scattered all over

North America, with jobs and families and lives. They were Africville success stories, but they'd had to leave Africville to find that success. None of them had considered coming back. Not to Africville, not even to Halifax.

Five years after the fire, the provincial government shut down the Africville School in the name of integration and the students were all sent to Richmond, a white elementary school about a mile away in the city's north end. Raymond's father wasn't offered a job teaching there, which was all right because he'd almost immediately got into a shouting match with the principal, who wanted to shunt Raymond and the rest of the children from Africville into the "auxiliary class," which was the polite name for slow learners who became—if they weren't already—no learners. Raymond's father won the battle for Raymond, although some of the other boys and girls weren't so lucky. Raymond's father would delight in attending parent-teacher night and showing off his son's report card to the principal. "Number one in his whole class," he would marvel. "Some 'slow learner'!"

Since Lawrence Carter couldn't find another job teaching, he filled his days reading books he borrowed from the downtown library and his nights writing angry letters to the editor of the Halifax *Tribune.*

Everyone knew from his letters, as well as from his participation at earlier meetings, that Lawrence Carter opposed the relocation. That might have been why Deacon Johnstone only reluctantly recognized him, and only after scanning the pews hopefully in search of someone—anyone—else who might wish to speak.

"Thank you, Mr. Chairman," Ray's father said with exaggerated politeness. "I've been listening very carefully to what Mr. Jamieson has had to say tonight and I must say he has his answers down pat. But it seems to me he has missed a very important point. My question is this, Mr. Jamieson: Isn't this so-called relocation of yours just a fancy way of stealing our land so you can use it for industrial development?"

The Negroes in the crowd roared. "Amen." "You tell 'em, brother." "Tell it like it is." The whites sat on their hands.

Jamieson looked as if he wanted nothing more than to be on an airplane back to Toronto, to his comfortably appointed office, his loving family and adoring friends. "No sir, that is simply not true," he said finally, his words belying the anxiety his voice gave away. "This relocation is not about stealing land for industrial development, or more rail lines, or an expressway, or a new harbour bridge or any of the other wild suggestions I've heard. It is about urban renewal, about giving the people of Africville the opportunity to live in dignity in an integrated community with equal opportunity for all."

While his stirring words were still bouncing off the church walls, Lawrence Carter picked up a report from among the pile of papers he'd brought with him to the church tonight and began quickly leafing through its pages.

"Well, Mr. Jamieson," he said, "that's very interesting but not very comforting. I have in front of me a copy of the 1961 Halifax Development Plan prepared by City staff. Here's what it says, and let me read it to you: 'The City of Halifax will construct a limited-access expressway to pass through the Africville district after its residents have been relocated.'"

"But that's not my report," Jamieson protested. No one heard him. His voice had been drowned out by whoops and cheers. Raymond looked up at his father proudly.

The Deacon did his best to win back the audience but it was a losing battle. When he finally asked for a show of hands to see how many Africville residents favoured relocation, only a few raised them.

The meeting broke up with Mr. Jamieson thanking everyone for their input and promising nothing, and Deacon Johnstone calling on God to bless the City Fathers in their deliberations. As soon as it was over, Lawrence Carter left the church, avoiding the milling residents who wanted to thank him for saying what was on their minds.

Raymond stayed behind for the sandwiches and date squares, and to watch the adults mix and mingle. O'Sullivan, the MLA, gathered a gaggle of black men, including the Deacon, around him and began telling stories about the goings-on in the Legislature. Despite the tensions earlier, everyone was laughing now. Raymond wondered how they could do that after what had been said—and cheered—earlier. He would never understand adults.

As for himself, he'd almost raised his hand when the Deacon asked who was in favour of moving the community. He thought it would be exciting to move into a new home with new neighbours. If they ended up in Maynard Square, the public housing complex, that would be okay, too. It would be closer to his new school. He wouldn't have to get up so early, and he could stay after school for basketball practice. He was going into grade eight and his goal was to make the school's basketball team.

"I'd hoped for something more positive tonight."

Jamieson and the alderman, Mr. MacPhee, were standing next to Raymond now, drinking cups of coffee from the church china, and talking. They didn't pay any attention to him.

"No, really, I mean that. Don't worry," Raymond heard the alderman say. "It's already decided. The deal is done. We're going to—"

His words were drowned out by a thunderous roar. The whites looked startled; the Negroes paid no attention. It was the nine o'clock train hurtling through the heart of Africville on its way to Montreal.

Ward's first mistake was to be on the wrong playground. At exactly the wrong moment. But how was he supposed to know? It was his first day at his new school and he didn't know anyone. Besides, Richmond was at least ten times bigger than the school in Eisners Head. The school was so big, he would discover later, that it wasn't just divided into classrooms but into three distinct sections, each in the architectural style of its era and each housing a different group of students.

The main building, Old Richmond as it was known, was an imposing early-twentieth-century brick building constructed shortly after the infamous Halifax Explosion of 1917 levelled most of the city's north end. Old Richmond now housed the principal's office, the nurse's office, the library and classrooms for grades four, five and six. The newest addition was a modern, two-storey, glass-and-metal structure that had been grafted on the southern end of Old Richmond just a few years ago. It housed the gym, the teachers' staff room and classrooms for grades seven, eight and nine. Which is where Ward should have been. But he didn't know that. How could he?

His family had only moved to Halifax from Eisners Head the week before. His parents were renting a modest, two-bedroom bungalow a few blocks north of the school. It was the end of May, a strange time to be moving, but his father was eager to get away from Eisners Head. Ward's teacher had helpfully included a note with his school files, explaining Ward's situation and outlining his academic achievements. "I'm sure he'll do well in your school, too, as soon as he adjusts to his new surroundings," she wrote.

Ward wasn't so sure. He hadn't had time to meet any other kids or even check out the school building before he had to attend his first class. Approaching the school from the direction of his house, all Ward could see was the end of what he would soon learn was the new-old section of the school, a fifties-style, cream-coloured stucco building that housed primary, grades one, two and three, as well as the auxiliary class. Ward had never heard of an auxiliary class before. Back in Eisners Head, the slow learners didn't get their own space; in fact, there were three or four different grades full of all levels of learners in the same classroom.

When Ward saw a group of the slow learners—half a dozen boys his own age—huddling together in a far corner of the playground, he assumed he must be in the right place. The fact that all the other children on the playground were much younger didn't immediately register. As Ward approached, hoping to make a new friend, or at least an acquaintance, before the bell rang, the boys looked up from their huddle, guilty expressions on their faces. Ward could see one of the boys, a tall, gangly Negro boy, shoving a package of cigarettes into his pants pocket.

"Who you?" he demanded menacingly. He was as tall as Ward and very dark.

"Ward," he answered.

"Where ya from?"

"Eisners Head."

"Da fuck's dat?" The boy grinned at his friends and then back at Ward.

"Eastern shore," Ward said evenly. No point in antagonizing him. "It's a fishing village."

The boy sniffed the air in an exaggerated fashion. "So that the stink I smell." He was showing off for his friends now. "How much money you got, Fish Boy?"

Startled by this sudden turn in the conversation, Ward blurted out, "None." But that wasn't quite true. He had a quarter in his pocket. He was planning to use some of it to buy a bag of chips or a chocolate bar, at recess. He'd heard you could buy treats right in the school.

"You lyin'," the other boy said. "You think he's lyin'?" he asked the other boys. They nodded. That was their role in this little drama that almost seemed choreographed. "We think you lyin'." He turned back to Ward. "Show us your pockets."

Ward hesitated, scanned their faces for hope, found none. Could he outrun them? He could try. What choice did he have? He reached as if to put his hands in his pockets, then suddenly bolted. But to where? He couldn't go home. Not now. He had to stay on the schoolyard. The bell was going to ring any minute. Could he last that long? He made for the far end of the triangle-shaped playground as fast as he could, turned, ducked under the arm of his oncoming pursuer and roared past the others, who were trailing in the wake behind the two of them, hoping to see a fight. Ward could hear screams from the little kids in the schoolyard, whether from fear, or excitement, or both, he didn't know. He saw mothers who'd accompanied their primary school children shielding them from the commotion. Ward did his best to avoid knocking them over, but dodging around the children slowed him down. Finally, the other boy reached out and grabbed a fistful of Ward's shirt. The shirt ripped, but not enough for Ward to escape. He stumbled and fell hard on the asphalt, ripping a hole in the knee of his new khaki pants. He could feel the sting of scraped skin. He wanted to cry but he couldn't. The other boy was already on top of him. Ward squirmed to free his arms to fight back, but the other boy was too fast. He grabbed both of Ward's wrists and pinned them to the ground behind his head.

"Look in his pockets," the boy urged his companions, who'd encircled them. "Quick."

But the other boys didn't move. They weren't even looking at the two of them any more. Instead, they seemed transfixed by something behind Ward's head. Suddenly, Ward felt the weight of someone grabbing his tormentor and dragging him off.

"Leave him alone, Jeremiah," the new boy yelled, shoving him roughly to the asphalt. The new boy was black, too, Ward noticed, but smaller than the first.

Ward barely had time to digest this new development when a male teacher pushed his way through the crowd. "What's going on here?" he demanded.

"Ray hit me," the boy who was named Jeremiah said. Jeremiah looked as though he was crying, though Ward knew he was faking.

"Mr. Carter," the teacher said sharply, addressing the boy named Ray. "I expected much better of you. I guess my expectations were misplaced." Ray looked as though he wanted to speak, then thought better of it. "Picking on someone like young Mr. Black here. And you a senior student, too." He shook his head sadly. "You'd better go see Mr. Dunn. Let him sort you out."

Jeremiah was smirking as Ray turned and walked toward the school entrance.

"And who are you, young man?" the teacher asked finally, as if noticing Ward for the first time.

"Ward Justice, sir."

"Oh, yes, the new boy. They sent your files up the other day." He took in Ward's dishevelled condition. "Well, come along then," he said solicitously. "We'd better get you cleaned up."

The teacher—his name was Mr. Veniot—dropped Ward off at the nurse's station beside the principal's office. You had to go through the principal's reception room to get to the nurse's station, so Ward saw the boy named Ray already sitting on a chair in a corner waiting for his turn to see the principal. Ward tried to make eye contact with him, tried to express his gratitude, but Mr. Veniot urged him along.

The nurse's office was a small, spare room with just a cot in one corner, a desk in the other and an eye chart and a poster touting the benefits of the Salk vaccine on the walls. Ward remembered getting the vaccine at a special clinic when he was in grade two; he remembered because it was the only time he'd ever got medicine on a sugar cube. The teacher said it was to prevent him from getting polio like Nigel Parsons's boy, Trevor. Trevor was a cripple who couldn't walk without crutches. Ward didn't want to be a cripple, so he would have taken the medicine anyway. The sugar cube was just a bonus.

"So, what do we have here?" the nurse asked with a smile. She was a short woman, dressed in a white nurse's uniform, and she spoke with a clipped British accent but in an almost motherly tone of voice. She sat Ward on the cot and used a hot washcloth to clean the dirt and blood from his knee. "Now that doesn't look too bad, my lad, not too bad at all." She reached over to the desk and picked up a bottle Ward recognized as iodine. "This is going to sting a bit," she told him, "but just for a minute." Ward scrunched up his eyes in anticipation. Then he heard a sharp noise, almost like the report of a gunshot. There was a pause and then the noise again, and again. The nurse looked up, smiled at Ward. "I daresay somebody's getting a sting worse than you this morning." Was Ray getting the strap?

After putting a large bandage on his knee—"You should be shipshape in no time"—the nurse ushered him into the principal's office. There was no sign of Ray. "Here's the new lad, Mr. Dunn," she explained. "A little the worse for wear, but he's all right now."

Mr. Dunn, who was wearing a short-sleeved blue shirt and red-striped tie, was an imposing man, probably six feet tall, with a barrel chest, broad shoulders and biceps that were noticeable even under his shirt sleeves. Ward imagined he would wield a mean strap. Ward himself had never been strapped at his old school, but he knew other boys who had. Ward anxiously noted the black leather strap sitting on the principal's desk. But Mr. Dunn apparently had no intention of disciplining him. In fact, he was kind, even offering to show Ward around the school "so you'll know where everything is" before introducing him to his teacher and new classmates.

It turned out the teacher who'd intervened to break up the schoolyard fight was his grade eight homeroom teacher. The boy named Ray was in his class, too. It wasn't until recess that Ward finally had the chance to introduce himself and thank Ray for coming to his aid that morning.

"No problem," Ray said dismissively. "Jeremiah's not so bad. Just slow, that's all. He's okay by himself, but when he gets with those other guys he just likes to show off is all."

"Did you—?" Ward hesitated. "Did you get the strap?"

Ray grinned. "Yeah, but it's no big deal. Mr. Dunn, he looks mean but he doesn't hurt that much." Still, Ward noticed that Ray kept his hands in his pockets, even when Ray offered him a bite of his Oh Henry! bar. "Nah," Ray said, and shook his head. "You play ball? Me and Jason McInnes are going to get together a game after school. Wanna come? You can be on my team." He paused. "You any good?"

Ward was startled awake by the overwhelming, overpowering noise. Roaring. Coming closer. Another train? There were so many trains here. But no. This was something else.

Ward looked around, tried to adjust to the unfamiliar surroundings. There were no windows in the wooden shed, just a door made out of planks they'd hooked shut the night before. Dust motes danced in the morning light that streaked in through the spaces between the boards. What time was it? On the other side of the shed, he could see Ray sitting up in his sleeping bag too. Ward tried to read his face. Shocked? Surprised? Scared? All of that. So it definitely wasn't the train. Ray would have known the sound of a train.

Suddenly, the roaring gave way to an urgent, angry whine as whatever it was that was out there smacked hard up against something big and immovable. And then it moved. With a cracking, crashing, explosive whoosh of something collapsing in on itself. Ray and Ward looked at one another. Wide-eyed. And all Ward could think was: what would his father say?

His father wasn't supposed to know he was there. His mother knew; she'd lied to his father about it, told him Ward was sleeping over at Jason's house. Jason and Ward were friends, so it wouldn't seem illogical for Ward to be spending the weekend with him. Ward had already asked Jason to lie about the sleepover the next time he saw his father. The problem was simple: Ward's father didn't want his son hanging around with "coloureds."

It was his father's blind spot. Desmond Justice had a thing about Negroes and whites mixing together. "It's not right," he said. Ward's mother tried to excuse it, told Ward his father just didn't know many coloured people because there hadn't been any in Eisners Head, and the ones he'd met in Halifax he didn't like. Desmond was a janitor in a downtown office building where blacks, women mostly, were hired to do the routine cleaning of the offices each night. Ward's father claimed most of them were lazy and, worse, probably thieves too. "All the coloureds are."

Ward's mother, who didn't like confrontation if it could be avoided, encouraged Ward to let his father say his piece and then quietly go ahead and do whatever he wanted to do anyway. "There's no sense in trying to convince your father," she warned her son. "That's just the way he is."

Ward knew that now. He'd invited Ray home after school one afternoon last fall so they could watch baseball together on the Justices' new TV. His father hadn't said anything while Ray was at the house; in fact, he'd treated him with a kind of exaggerated politeness. But that night at supper, after Ray had gone home, he instructed his son: "Stick with your own kind. No good's gonna come, you mixing with the coloureds."

Was this what his father meant? Ward wondered now. He and Ray sitting in a shed in the Carters' backyard waiting, terrified, for whatever monster was lurking outside to kill them? Would his father be angry? Or sad? Or both?

Until the beast—that had to be what it was, Ward thought, an inhuman beast—had unleashed its mind-rattling roar, it had been the best sleepover Ward had ever had.

The strangest part of it all, the part he wished he could have talked about with his father, was that Africville reminded him of Eisners Head. He hadn't made the connection right away. He'd been too busy trying to keep up with Ray's whirlwind tour. Ray had met him at the corner of Duffus and Barrington Streets so they could walk the last half mile north to Africville together. Ray carried Ward's small suitcase; Ward slung his sleeping bag over his shoulder like he'd seen sailors carrying their duffel bags up by the navy base. Though Barrington was a main thoroughfare that ran all the way along the harbour from the very south end of the city through the downtown and north past the naval dockyard along the waterfront to Africville, the pavement stopped just as the street reached Africville. "That's how you know you're in Africville. Where the pavement ends, Africville begins," Ray said, and then pointed to a grassy patch of land sloping down to the water on their right. "That's Kildare's Field."

As small as it was, every section of Africville seemed to have its own name and purpose. "Used to be a bone meal plant here," Ray told him.

"What's that?" Ward asked.

Ray grinned sheepishly. "Don't know," he answered. "Just know that's what it was." These days, he said, people flocked to Kildare's to picnic and swim.

Just north of the field he pointed out Tibby's Pond, actually a shallow, saltwater inlet of the harbour that only turned into a pond at low tide. "When the tide's partway in and partway out," Ray told him, "you can walk across the edge of the pond out there like you were walking on water. Just like you're Jesus." There were half a dozen rowboats hauled up on shore at the edge of the pond. "We'll take one later, maybe go fishing," he said as he led the way to Up the Road, which was what the locals called the main part of Africville, a cluster of perhaps three dozen homes on either side of the dusty dirt road. Ray and his father lived in a small house at the far end of Up the Road. They dropped off Ward's suitcase and sleeping bag in the empty shed behind the house. "My father says we can stay out here tonight," Ray said happily.

Up the Road was just above Back the Field, a gully where some boys were playing pickup baseball. Seeing Jeremiah Black at the plate gave Ward a momentary fright, but then he remembered he was with Ray. Jeremiah knew better than to bother him when Ray was around.

They followed the railway tracks then, up past clusters of blueberry bushes—"Next month there'll be blueberries big as your balls"—and over Uncle Laffy's Hill to Round the Turn, another cluster of houses, where Ray's mother's family still lived. Ray introduced him to his grandmother, Ma Jones, who was tending the garden. "Now, mind you boys stay away from the Dump," she admonished as Ray gave her a kiss and told her they'd be back to see her later. "That Dump's a dangerous place for little boys," she said again as they left.

It literally was a dump, with huge mounds of trash—restaurant scraps, household leavings, car wrecks, car parts, construction debris, office papers, broken furniture, even bags filled with oozing hospital waste—dumped helter-skelter on top of one another to create a desolate landscape of smouldering garbage mountains. There were trucks everywhere, dump trucks, flatbeds, half-tons, delivery vans, all shapes and sizes of them, zipping in and around, heedless of the other vehicles or even the many pedestrians, mostly black but some white too, picking through the trash for treasures. The truckers would quickly disgorge their loads, then scurry back out through the gates and away from Africville as fast as the dusty, potholed road would allow.

Ray pointed to a big, blue five-ton truck at the top of one of the heaps. "Watch this," he said as the driver, the front of his truck pointing skyward at a forty-five degree angle, revved his engine. "There's no dump on his truck so he has to shunt everything off. Watch. This is amazing." The truck lurched, then picked up speed as it began hurtling backwards down the mountain. Suddenly, the driver slammed on his brake and the front of the cab reared up into the air like a wild horse, its cargo of trash flying out the back of the truck bed. For a moment, the truck remained suspended in place, its cab in the air, and then the weight of the engine brought the front end crashing back down to earth, spewing showers of dust and dirt into the air around it.

"Wow. That *was* amazing," Ward agreed. More amazing was that no one else seemed even to notice. There were dozens of people scattered all over the hillside, carefully picking through the garbage, looking for anything worth salvaging, focused only on the job at hand and ignoring the truck driver's inventive unloading method.

That changed as soon as someone spotted a big, orange Ben's Bread van driving in through the dump gate. There were shouts then, and most of the scavengers raced to the truck, descending like locusts on the driver, who seemed to know most of them by name. He laughed and joked with them as he walked around to the back of the van, opened the truck's doors and stepped back.

"My father won't let me," Ray explained as they stood on a hillside watching the scene below. "Says he won't take white bread handouts from white folks."

Ward smiled uneasily. He'd never heard Ray talk about white folks before.

"Come on," Ray said finally, "let's go fishing." But they didn't. At least not right away. Ray led the way to a small clump of trees beside the dirt road that hid them from view of the passing trucks. "Here," Ray said, handing Ward a handful of gravel. "Get ready." Just then, the big blue truck they'd watched unloading at the dump came round the corner and into view. "Now," Ray yelled, jumping out to the edge of the roadway just as the truck passed. He tossed his handful of gravel at the side of the truck. It pinged against the metal doors like a shower of hail. Ward didn't stop to consider what he was doing. He simply did as his friend had done. But his aim was not as practised, and some of the pieces of gravel he threw went right in through the open window of the cab.

The driver hit the brakes.

"Run!" Ray screamed. "Run!" And he turned on his heel and took off back into the woods. Ward followed as fast as he could. Behind him, he could hear the truck door open and then slam shut, the driver yelling after them: "Yeah, you'd better run, you little nigger bastards! I catch you, I'll tan your hides good."

Though the driver didn't seem to be following them, Ray kept running as fast as he could until they reached the shore. "Did you see that guy?" Ray asked between gulps of air. Ward had been too frightened to even look back. Ray laughed. "Was he pissed off or what?" He stopped then, waited until his breathing returned to normal. "But next time watch where you're aiming, okay? You're supposed to aim at the truck, not the driver." How was Ward supposed to know? "Did you hear what he called us? Nigger bastards." Ray raised his right arm above his head, brought it down gently on Ward's shoulder. "I dub thee Sir White Nigger Bastard."

Ward laughed. What would his father think of that?

When they got back to Tibby's Pond, there was a girl, a few years younger than them, playing by herself in the shallow water. Ray looked surprised. "What you doin' still here? I thought you moved."

"Did," the girl answered. "But I didn't like it, so Daddy asked Aunt Annie if I could stay with her till school."

Aunt Annie wasn't really the girl's aunt. She wasn't Ray's aunt either, even though that's what he called her, too. Her name was Annie Cole. She'd been a widow for at least as long as Ray had been alive. She ran the candy store in Up the Road and looked after the kids whenever their parents weren't around, often even when they were. Everyone, even the adults, called her Aunt Annie. She'd invited Ray, his father and "your school friend" to have supper at her place that night. "Nothing fancy," she'd said. "Just something to fill the hole."

"Rosa, this is my friend Ward," Ray announced. "He's sleeping over tonight. Ward, this is Rosa. Rosa used to live here but she moved."

Rosa smiled, Ward smiled back. The pleasantries over, Ray turned his attention to choosing a boat. "This one belongs to the Skinners." He pointed to a green, flat-bottomed, plywood vessel tethered to shore by a large rock and climbed in over its side. "But they won't mind if we take it out for a while. Get the rope, will ya?"

And that's when it hit Ward. The familiar, sharp, saltwater smell of the rope hanging from the dory's bow filled his nostrils. When Ward was a little boy and his father would take him out in their rowboat, Ward would sit in the bow as it bounced up and down in the waves, sucking on the end of the rope like a Popsicle, savouring its comforting, salty wetness. The smell made him wish he were back there now. Perhaps that was why, after Ray had dropped anchor at a spot about a hundred feet off the shore where he claimed the fishing would be best, Ward looked back toward the shoreline and was able to imagine, just for a moment, he really was back in Eisners Head.

If you looked in a certain direction and squinted into the afternoon sun just a bit, you couldn't see the rest of the city in the distance. All you could see was a jumble of small, multicoloured clapboard houses plopped, willy-nilly, among scrub trees and bushes, and connected to each other by foot-worn paths climbing up the hillside. Lines filled with laundry flapped in the breeze, only accentuating the greens and blues and browns of the houses. It was just like Eisners Head. His father, who hadn't seemed very happy since they'd moved to Halifax, would have felt at home here too. At home, except—

Ray jerked his arm suddenly. "Got one!" he shouted, pulling on the handline. Ward watched transfixed, his own line still hanging in the water, as Ray fought with whatever it was at the end of his fishing line. Ward's father would have been angry at Ray for not rewinding the line back on to its wooden core as he hauled in the fish. "Otherwise you just have a tangled mess at the end," his father had admonished Ward more than once.

"Oh shit," Ray said as the struggling, squirming, silver-bellied fish finally broke the surface. "An eel! I hate eels. They're so slimy." The eel flopped madly about on the floor of the dory. Ray seemed reluctant to touch it, so Ward grabbed it expertly by the neck with one hand and plucked the hook out of its mouth.

"Toss it?" he asked Ray.

"Toss it," Ray said, with a look of admiration for how easily his friend had handled the slippery eel.

By the time the fish had stopped biting and the flies had started in, they'd caught half a dozen cod and a few haddock, too. "We'll give them to Aunt Annie," Ray declared, adding, "Just as long as she doesn't make us eat them."

She didn't. Aunt Annie served plates filled with steaming servings of corned beef and cabbage, which also reminded Ward of Eisners Head. Before the strike, his mother had always served fish on Fridays, baked beans Saturdays and corned beef and cabbage—which she called Jiggs Dinner—on Sundays. During the strike, they ate mostly whatever his father could catch. After they'd moved to Halifax, his mother discovered the frozen TV dinners they sold at the Dominion Store. Salisbury steak with mashed potatoes was her latest favourite. Ward wouldn't have thought it possible after so many years of Sunday suppers, but he was glad to have a feed of corned beef and cabbage again.

"What are you hearing about the Deacon, Aunt Annie?" Ray's father asked, always curious about his rival. "He happy in his new place?"

"Oh, he's happy all right," she answered. "Braggin' to me about their fancy new bathroom. Says he can see the whole harbour right from his bathroom window. He's on the eighth floor of that high-rise. I told him living up that high's unnatural but he says it's the future. But he's the only one happy. Rosa"—Aunt Annie nodded at the little girl who was moving her corned beef and cabbage around on the plate, hoping no one would notice she wasn't eating any—"she called up cryin' and tellin' me, 'Aunt Annie, I want to come home.' Her daddy told me she misses all her friends." Annie shook her head.

Ray's father slowly chewed a bite of dinner, considered. "Guess it's too late now. Half the people gone and the other half just haggling over how much."

"Not me," said Aunt Annie. "They gonna have to carry me out of here." She looked accusingly at Ray's father. "Don't tell me you sayin' yes too?"

"Not me," Lawrence Carter replied. "I'm not going anywhere. They'll have to carry me out too."

Aunt Annie shook her head. "Well, I guess it'll just be me and you." She glanced over at Rosa. "You eat what's on your plate, girl. Or no treat for you."

As soon as dinner was over and the licorice was handed out—Rosa, Ward noticed, got her string of red licorice too, even though she never did finish her dinner—Ray excused them. "I'm gonna show Ward the train," he explained.

"I'm coming with you," Rosa declared. Ray looked unhappy but said nothing.

The train was as spectacular as Ray said it would be. They stood as close as they could to the tracks as the nine o'clock CNR train to Montreal roared through Africville without slowing down. The noise was deafening, the wind a hurricane as the cars hurtled past them. Ward could see the passengers in the lighted cars. Some waved as the train passed. Ward tried to wave back but he could barely raise his arm. Was it the force of the blast of warm air the train stirred up, or just fear from being so close to a fast-moving train?

After, Ray told Rosa that he and Ward were going to go to sleep now. "See you tomorrow," he said as he led the way back to his father's place. Rosa looked like she wanted to follow but thought better of it.

Inside the shed, Ward began to unroll his sleeping bag. "We're not really going to sleep now," Ray announced. "I was just saying that so Rosa wouldn't keep hanging around. Come on. We're gonna have some fun. Follow me."

Under the cover of enveloping darkness, they crawled to the Deacon's house next door and climbed in through an opening in a boarded-up window. The house had been emptied of all its furniture and was lit now only by the moonlight that leaked in through the cracks. "This was Rosa's room," Ray said as he moved like a cat from room to room while Ward followed tentatively in his wake. Ray wanted to stay and tell ghost stories, but Ward said he didn't want to. He didn't confess he was scared of the dark.

"I know what we can do," Ray said. "Let's sneak up by Aunt Lottie's. See who's there tonight." Lottie was one of Africville's best-known bootleggers. Her house on Barrington Street just beyond the end of the pavement was a favourite nighttime gathering place for Africville musicians, who'd stop by before and after their gigs downtown to do a little jamming and drink a little of what everyone called "niggershine," which was Lottie's special concoction. Ray and Ward took up a position in some bushes with an unobstructed view of the window of Lottie's place. They'd have to duck down behind the bushes whenever a taxi pulled into the driveway to pick up another bottle for delivery, but they could still hear the music—a saxophone, a piano, a bass—and the raucous laughter.

At one point, a police car stopped outside the door. Two white policemen got out and walked inside as if they owned the place. Ward expected the music to stop then and the policemen to begin arresting people, but the music continued as if nothing had happened. Through the window, Ward could see Lottie hand one of the policemen a glass. He toasted her and downed the contents in a gulp.

Ward wasn't sure how long they'd been watching; he only knew he was falling asleep.

"Can we go back?" he said finally. "I'm tired."

He didn't remember much about the walk back. Or anything else, in fact, until the morning, when the roaring monster woke him with a start from his peaceful sleep.

Ward remained frozen in place while Ray crawled tentatively over to the door and pressed his eye against a knothole in the wood.

"Shit!" he said, reaching for the hook and pulling open the door.

The sound they heard was not a monster, Ward realized when his eyes adjusted to the morning light. It was a truck—bigger even than the one they'd seen at the dump yesterday. This truck, which had the City of Halifax emblem on the driver's door, had a plow attached to the front that it was using to batter at the walls of the Deacon's empty house. The roof at the front of the house was sagging now, most of the wall that had held it up gone already. The remains of the wall—shattered posts, splintered clapboard siding, broken glass, smashed plaster—lay all around the truck, clouds of plaster dust rising into the air. The truck reversed then, repositioned itself in front of the far corner of the house—Rosa's bedroom? Ward tried to remember where it was—and rammed hard into it. Ward heard the crack of breaking wood and then the rumble as the roof collapsed totally, pieces bouncing off the hood of the truck and on to the ground.

"Shit," Ray said again. He'd just noticed Rosa standing near the truck, watching them demolish her family home. Ray and Ward could both see the tears in her eyes.

4

1967

"Well, merciful heavens, look who it isn't!" Before Ray could stop her, Aunt Annie had covered the distance across the gymnasium floor to where she'd seen Ward standing awkwardly with his parents and another man. Ray and his father had had no choice but to follow in her wake.

"Now let me look at you up close," Aunt Annie said to Ward. Ward's expression roller-coastered from surprise to pleasure to apprehension. "My, my, aren't you all growed up? And so smart. That was a wonderful speech, young man. Wonderful, wasn't it, Lawrence?"

"It was. Wonderful. Congratulations." Ray's father sounded decidedly unenthusiastic.

Aunt Annie didn't seem to notice. She hadn't had much opportunity to socialize since she'd moved into the apartment in Maynard Square, and she intended to make the most of it. "And you must be the proud parents." Aunt Annie turned to Ward's father and mother. "He's the spitting image o' both o' you. You must be very proud."

Ray looked at Ward's father. Shocked? Angry? Ray couldn't tell for sure, only that he didn't look happy.

"Yes, very proud," Ward's mother replied. "We're very proud." Her eyes anxiously darted between Aunt Annie and her husband. Ray eyed Ward. Ward stared at the floor.

"Been so long since I seen young Ward," Aunt Annie continued, oblivious. "He used to come 'round all the time back when I still lived out home. He and Raymond. Just like two peas in a pod. Always together. Always gettin' into mischief." She paused, as if caught up in some private thought. "Course that was a time ago. Been how long now, Lawrence? Two year since I sold? Wish I was still there but, well, what can you do? Not everyone like Lawrence here. I don't think he be leavin' except in a pine box." She laughed. "Right, Lawrence?"

Ray's father mumbled assent.

"Raymond?" Aunt Annie said. "You bring Ward round to see me, hear?" To Ward, "I don't have no store no more, honey, but if you was to come by, I think I could probably find a licorice treat or two . . . if you aren't too old for a little treat, that is."

Ward smiled, an embarrassed smile. "No, no, Aunt Annie. I'm not too old." He looked as if he regretted his familiarity. "And I'd love to come visit sometime." He kept his eyes on the floor.

"Sometime," Ray knew, meant never. It wasn't that he and Ward didn't get along any more. They just weren't friends. Nothing had happened between them. Nothing except life.

Sitting in the Queen Elizabeth High School auditorium that morning, listening to the principal drone on and on about how lucky they were to be graduating in 1967, Canada's Centennial year, with the future stretching out golden in front of them and *blah blah blah*, Ray couldn't help but feel a tinge of bitterness for his high school years. Bitterness mixed with a spicing of envy as the principal introduced "our valedictorian, our Head Boy, Ward Justice . . ."

They were a long way from Africville now. Though the entrance to the Q.E. auditorium was only a few feet from the school's north door, the entrance used by north-end students like Ward and Ray, the distance this morning seemed a million miles and a century or two from the sunny September morning in 1964 when he and Ward had arrived at the north door together to begin their first day of high school.

"Nervous?" Ray had asked.

"You?" Ward had answered the question with a question, as if he didn't want to be the first to admit apprehension.

"No . . . Sort of . . . Yeah, I guess." They'd laughed then.

"I'm scared shitless," Ward had said.

"Me too," Ray had replied. And they'd laughed again.

Although they'd sensed, even then, that their lives were about to change in ways neither could foresee, they'd assumed their friendship would remain constant. At least Ray had.

But the change had begun almost immediately. The vice-principal stood at the door with a sheaf of papers in one hand, calling out names in a booming voice, and assigning each name to a class and a room.

"Carter, Raymond. C-17. Mr. Dunphy's class. Basement level. Room 111."

Ray had no idea what the man was talking about, but he noticed the student whose name he'd called before Ray's was going in through the door. He decided he should follow suit.

"See you at lunch," he said to Ward.

They did meet for lunch and walked home together after school. But soon Ray had football practice. And Ward had met some new guys in his class . . .

It turned out that C-17 stood for the seventeenth of seventeen classes of grade tens, thirty students per class, more than five hundred in all. Just in grade ten! That was more than the total number of students in Richmond's entire primary to ninth-grade student body. Q.E.H.S. was the Protestant "and other" high school for all of Halifax, meaning it attracted students from as far north as what remained of Africville to as far south as the affluent south end. Ray had never met a Jew before high school; most of the south-enders, he guessed, had never met a black person before.

Not that the classes themselves were all that mixed. Close to half the students in C-17 were black. They accounted for all but a handful of the school's entire black population. C-17 was the class for the dumb newcomers—Mr. Dunphy was known, even to his face, as Dr. Dummy—as well as the even dumber ones repeating the grade for the second, sometimes third time.

Ray wasn't dumb; he just wasn't smart enough to know he was

being railroaded out of his future. His father would have known if he'd been paying attention. He'd fought similar battles for Ray's brothers, and for Ray too when he was younger. But Lawrence Carter had become so consumed by his own war with City officials he'd lost interest in almost anything that didn't have to do with Africville relocation.

Ray didn't put two and two together until the beginning of grade twelve, when he went to the guidance counsellor for help in picking a university. She told him he wasn't in the university prep stream; he was in the "general program." Which meant he was qualified only for vocational school or the lower rungs of the workforce.

"You didn't know you weren't in the university stream?" The guidance counsellor was incredulous.

"How was I supposed to know?" Ray demanded. She was making him angry.

"You just should have, that's all."

"What can I do now?"

She laughed. "Well, you could go back to grade ten and start over. Other than that . . ."

So Ray had sat in the auditorium that morning listening to all of the speeches about their collective future, hearing the scholarship announcements—this student to McGill, that one to Dalhousie—and planning his own escape. He had his train ticket already. He was leaving in two weeks. He wondered what it would be like sitting in the passenger car and passing the rubble of Africville, past the house where his father, the last holdout against progress, continued to live, past all the ghosts of his childhood. After a week in Montreal to see Expo '67, he'd continue on to Toronto, where he was going to live with his brother, go to trade school or get a job doing . . . something. He certainly wasn't going to stay in Halifax.

Ward was. Ward had a scholarship to Dalhousie University. Ray had already heard the principal announce it: "Our Head Boy, Ward Justice . . ."

Ward hadn't ended up in C-17 with Ray and the dummies. He'd

been placed in C-3, Mr. Golden's homeroom. C-3 was for students expected to go on to university. There were no black kids in C-3, but there were plenty of kids from the south end. Ward, in fact, was the only one of their Richmond class to make it to the exalted level of C-3. Except for Jason McInnes, of course. Jason, their other best friend from junior high, had done even better. He'd ended up in C-1 with the science and math whizzes. That much was fitting. Jason had been the top student in their class back at Richmond, Ward second. But what about Ray? He'd had the third highest average. How had he ended up in C-17?

Whatever the reason, Ray believed now it had marked the beginning of the end of his friendship with Ward. Ward began hanging out with the kids in his class. They introduced him to other south-enders. Someone invited him to join Hi-Y, a collection of social clubs modelled on fraternities, with Greek names and initiation rites. No blacks invited, at least none that Ray knew. And then they elected him as their class representative on Student Council. And one thing led to another. And finally he was Head Boy.

It wasn't just Ray and Ward who'd drifted apart, of course. Jason wasn't part of either of their crowds any more. He'd joined the math club, and Ray rarely saw him. Perhaps it was all just a natural evolution, like minds finding each other. Ray was not without his crowd. His friends were the jocks, the guys on the football and basketball teams. Ray was a runningback on the football team, a point guard in basketball. Sports became his claim to school fame, his cachet with girls, his own ticket into another world.

Becky Rutledge, who'd been his girlfriend for most of grades eleven and twelve, was a south-ender. Ray was convinced that it was their being opposites—she was rich, he was poor; she was white, he was black—that had attracted her to him in the first place. Was the same true for him? Probably. That and the fact their relationship came with a certain built-in intrigue and risk.

They'd met at an end-of-season team party. Becky was a cheerleader. Short. Cute. Curly blond hair. And bubbly. Ray still wasn't sure how they'd fallen into talking that night, but, very quickly, it was as if they were alone in the crowded, noisy rec room. By the end of the evening, they really were alone. Together.

That was one of the many things Ray still hadn't figured out. As soon as they'd become a couple, they no longer seemed to fit in with any of their old friends. It wasn't race. Or was it? No one mentioned that, of course, but no one seemed to know quite how to relate to them when they were together. Ray's black friends ignored Becky; Becky's friends would forget to tell her about upcoming parties. It was as if, by getting together, they'd crossed some invisible barrier that now kept them apart from everyone else.

Everyone except Alice. Alice was Becky's best friend. The go-between. That was because Becky wouldn't tell her parents about Ray, so he couldn't call her on the phone. And he couldn't pick her up at her house when they went out on a date. Instead, Becky would call Alice, who would call Ray: "Meet her at the field behind Gorsebrook at eight."

Afterwards, he could only walk her to within a block of her parents' house, and the best he could hope for was a goodnight peck on the cheek. "Someone will see." Luckily, Becky got her driver's licence near the end of grade eleven. After that, she could borrow her mother's car, a red Mustang—"she made Dad get it for her after she had her last nervous breakdown"—almost whenever she wanted it. They spent a lot of time in the car, much of it in the back seat. Sometimes, they steamed up the windows in a parking lot beside the harbour near Point Pleasant Park. But Becky wasn't keen on it; it was too close to her house, she told him, and her mother's car was too distinctive for anonymity.

One night, Becky drove them to a graveyard in Fairview, ostensibly to show him where her great-grandfather was buried. "He owned slaves or something, I think," she said, then added, as if it were funny, "Just joking." She'd brought a quart of vodka she'd stolen from her father's liquor cabinet. They drank it straight from the bottle. And then they made love. It was the first time for both of them. Becky cried, but when Ray got nervous and tried to pull out, she held him close against her. "Stay inside me. Please." Later, she joked that her great-grandfather must have been rolling over in his grave. "That's why the earth moved," she laughed. The graveyard quickly became their trysting ground, their secret spot. Her great-grandfather must have got pretty dizzy, Ray thought now. But after that first time, Becky made him wear a rubber, "just to be safe."

The secrets grew and the mysteries multiplied. Becky was worried that the principal or one of the teachers might tell her father about them. Her father was on the School Board and seemed to know all the teachers by their first names. So they stopped holding hands in the hallways between classes. And they stopped going to the Friday night dances at the Y because Becky's mother was on the board there. They spent more and more time alone together in the back seat. Until Becky broke it off. "I think we need to slow down for a while, maybe see other people," she announced one night just before she dropped him off at the end of the pavement on Barrington Street. Becky wasn't the only one who was worried about parental reactions. Ray's father had become increasingly vitriolic in his condemnation of white people, and Ray wasn't sure he could trust him to hold his tongue around Becky.

Becky said she wanted to break up—"for a little while, to see how we really feel"—because their relationship had become too intense. Ray wasn't convinced that was the real reason.

He'd been pressing her about the graduation dance. He wanted to make graduation their "coming out" event. He would pick her up at her house and meet her parents. They'd see he was okay, he assured her. Besides, they were both adults now, high school graduates, so they could do what they pleased, regardless of what their parents thought. Her "No" had been emphatic.

So Ray wasn't going to the prom tonight. Who cared? He was tired of high school anyway.

". . . the party is always looking for bright young men like yourself. Why don't you come along with Ward next week? We're going to pick a candidate for the election. Maybe I can get you a job on the campaign . . ."

Who? What? Ray had been so lost in his own thoughts he'd clearly missed an important part of this conversation. Who was this man? He remembered now. The man had been talking with Ward and his family when Aunt Annie first interrupted them. At some point, Mrs. Justice had introduced him. "This is Ward's friend, Mr. Eagleson," she'd said awkwardly as if she wasn't sure how to explain his presence. "Mr. Eagleson's a lawyer." As if perhaps that explained it.

Eagleson was smooth, polished, assured. He simply took over the conversation. "Yes, well I met Ward here at a conference we had last fall for young leaders and I was so impressed I just had to come and see him graduate."

"Ward's going to work for Mr. Eagleson this summer," Ward's mother said, still trying to make the connection to the older man's presence, as much for herself as the others.

"He is that, Mrs. Justice. And I'm delighted. Ward is a smart boy." He turned then to Raymond, whose own brain was still in the back seat with Becky. "You must be Ray. Ward's told me all about you." He had? "Maybe I can find a spot for you too. Everybody thinks the election will be late summer or early fall, and we're going to need all the help we can get to get rid of those Tories." He smiled indulgently at the adults. "Pardon my electioneering," he said. "Sometimes I can't help myself." Ray's father scowled. Eagleson turned back to Ray. "Here, let me give you my card. Just in case I can help in any way."

"I'm not staying," Ray said finally. "I'm moving to Toronto. Next week." That wasn't quite true; his ticket was for two weeks from now, so he could have attended the nominating meeting if he'd wanted to. But he didn't want to. There was something about Eagleson he didn't like. He was too smooth, too self-assured, too ingratiating.

"Well, no harm in trying, is there?" Eagleson said, as if he hadn't caught the undertone of hostility in Ray's voice. He handed Ray his card. "If you change your mind, the offer's open. Well," he said turning back to the others, "I must be getting back to work. Mr. and Mrs. Justice, thank you for letting me share this moment with you.

And it was very nice to meet you too," he said, addressing Ray's father and Aunt Annie. And then he was gone.

"Well," Ward's mother said to Aunt Annie, eager for it all to be over, "I think we should be going too. Desmond needs to get back to work. And I have to finish getting Ward's suit ready for the dance tonight. But it was very nice meeting you."

"You too," Aunt Annie said, turning back to Ward. "Now don't forget to come and see me. Make your friend here bring you," she said, poking Ray in the ribs. "I'll have the licorice waiting."

Jack Eagleson ushered Ward into his office. He closed the door. "Sit down," he said. His smile was almost conspiratorial. "I've got a special job for you this morning, Ward." There was a big leather suitcase on his desk. Eagleson sat down behind it, patted it with his hand. "All very hush-hush." He laughed his patented Jack-laugh. It was a booming, deep-in-the-bowels laugh that inevitably drew attention to itself, like a noisy, smelly fart in church. Ward had decided that Eagleson's laugh, which had at first struck him as self-conscious, even phony, probably wasn't. Still, it embarrassed Ward to be with him in public when he let loose. He was glad they were alone this morning.

Ward was nearly a month into his summer job as a messenger for Eagleson's law firm, McArtney, Eagleson, Cullingham & O'Sullivan, and so far, it was . . . well, boring. If he wasn't delivering briefs to the courthouse or picking up property documents from other law firms, he was playing the office gofer. Still, he shouldn't complain. The money was good, better than what his friends were making. With a scholarship to cover his tuition, he would end the summer with plenty of spending money for university.

He was even thinking of buying that 1961 VW Beetle Billy Henderson was selling. Billy, whose father had bought him a brand-new, baby-blue Chevy Camaro convertible for managing to graduate on his second try, was the reason Ward had this job in the first place.

That's not what Mr. Eagleson said, of course. Mr. Eagleson still claimed he'd "discovered" Ward at that leadership conference. But that wasn't quite the way Ward remembered it. The conference had been organized by the Second Century Canada Club, which, despite its lofty title, existed to recruit bright young high school students into the Nova Scotia Liberal Party. It was funded by the party but run by student Liberals from the local universities. They organized weekend "leadership conferences," to which they invited high school student leaders. Although there were panel discussions and even occasional speeches by senior Liberals like Jack Eagleson, the real purpose seemed to be to give underaged high school student leaders the chance to get drunk at party expense, thus making them more amenable to joining the party—if only for its parties.

It worked for Ward. Much to his father's disgust, he had joined the party six months ago. But Ward had been less interested in Liberal parties—or even Liberal politics—than in the fact that party membership might help him land a summer job.

Billy Henderson, who was more an acquaintance than a real friend but who seemed to have a way of attaching himself to whoever he thought was going places, had told Ward he'd have a better chance of getting hired if he joined. Billy's father was the president of a Halifax constituency association, and Billy promised Ward his father would put in a good word for him.

"It'll be great," Billy said. "We can work together."

But Billy—who wasn't, in fact, involved in any extracurricular activity other than going to the leadership conferences, and then only because his father insisted he be invited—got the only job at party headquarters, at least until an election was actually called.

"As soon as the Tories drop the writ," Billy's father reassured Ward, "there'll be jobs for everyone." To tide him over until then, Mr. Henderson said he'd speak to Jack Eagleson, a family friend who was a senior partner in the city's biggest law firm. "I'm sure Jack can find something for you."

Ward did remember Eagleson—sort of—from the Second Century conference he'd attended in the fall. Eagleson was physically striking, tall and lean, probably in his mid-forties. His fresh, unlined face, topped by a Beatles mop of prematurely white hair, gave him an air of eccentric, professorial *gravitas*. As did his choice of clothing: wrinkled corduroy sports jackets and colourful cravats. Ward was coming to realize that if you were to-the-manner-born, as Mr. Eagleson certainly was, you could get away with being unconventional. Everyone else had to dress and act according to their place in society. Or the place they aspired to.

Eagleson had made what Ward remembered as a boring after-dinner speech, something predictable about how everyone had a civic duty to get involved in the political process, and then shook hands with each of the three dozen or so students individually. What seemed remarkable about that at the time was that Eagleson knew all their names and even managed a quick, confidential chat with each of them as he moved through the group.

"Ah, Ward, nice to see you, delighted you could join us tonight," he'd said, pumping Ward's hand as though they were long-lost buddies. "I see where the Q.E. hockey team's having a good season." Then he leaned close and whispered in Ward's ear, "That fellow next to you on the right. I should know his name but I just can't think of it right now. Can you remind me?"

Ward was startled. "Ah, that's Billy Henderson, sir." How could he not know the name of his close friend's son?

Ward didn't actually speak to Eagleson again until he was invited to interview for the messenger's job. Once again Eagleson greeted him effusively, as if they'd shared a life's worth of intimate secrets. By then, however, Ward had become more skeptical. He remembered what had happened that night after he'd reminded Mr. Eagleson of his friend's son's name. "Ah, Billy," Eagleson had declared, grabbing Billy's hand and shaking it. "Wonderful to see you here tonight. Hope your dad's well." And then he'd leaned in, as he had done with Ward and the others, and whispered into Billy's ear. Eagleson's uncanny ability to know everyone's name wasn't so uncanny after all.

Despite that, Ward couldn't help but be impressed, even a little frightened, by all the unexpected things Eagleson did know about people, including himself. Knowledge seemed to be his way of demonstrating his power over others.

"Do you ever miss living in Eisners Head?" he'd asked him last week, for no reason Ward could figure.

"Yeah, I guess. Sometimes." Ward hadn't told him he was from Eisners Head.

"Who knows? Maybe someday you'll go back and get yourself elected as the MLA down there," Eagleson said, as if it were as simple as deciding to do it.

Eagleson knew other things, too. Sometimes, he'd slip them into a conversation. Like the time when Eagleson had asked him, again seemingly out of nowhere: "Your father ever get over that thing with Junior Eisner?"

"Yeah, I guess," Ward said. "It was a long time ago." What was he supposed to say? That his father harvested a bumper crop of resentment each and every morning? "That thing" didn't begin to cover it.

"Junior's not such a bad guy," Eagleson said. "Unless you try to start a union on him!" He laughed. Ward laughed too, though he wasn't sure why. Eagleson could be as disarming as he was charming.

Ward still couldn't figure out what Eagleson actually did at the law firm. Or, for that matter, what the firm did. With the exception of McArtney, who seemed always to be in court, the law was the least of the partners' concerns. Gerry Cullingham was officially listed on the letterhead as counsel to McArtney, Eagleson, Cullingham & O'Sullivan, but Ward had never met him.

The other two senior partners didn't appear to practise much law either. Seamus O'Sullivan was the leader of the Nova Scotia Liberal Party, which was currently the Official Opposition in the Legislature. He spent most of his time travelling the province, giving speeches and trying to convince people to vote Liberal again.

Back in the good old days, which Eagleson referred to as "B.S."—"Before Stanfield"—O'Sullivan's and Eagleson's fathers had been key figures in the last Liberal administration, which, probably not coincidentally, had been presided over by Premier Gerry Cullingham. But that was a long time ago. Robert Stanfield's Progressive Conservatives had been in power in Nova Scotia for eleven years and seemed destined to hold on for at least eleven more. Everyone, Eagleson confided to Ward, assumed that the new Liberal leader, Seamus O'Sullivan, would just be a caretaker until someone better came along.

"But then Stanfield took up ski jumping."

Eagleson talked like that a lot, assuming you would know what he meant. For once, Ward did. He remembered hearing on the radio once that Stanfield, a balding old man who spoke with what Ward imagined was a drawl, had initially dismissed speculation that he was thinking about running for the federal Tory leadership by saying he'd "rather take up ski jumping," but then had changed his mind, run and won. His replacement as leader of the provincial Conservatives was an even older and balder guy named Smith. "Smith's a Smith," Eagleson had said elliptically. "Beatable. But can Seamus? That's the sixty-four-thousand-dollar question. And if he can't, well, what then?"

Eagleson would often burst into this sort of disconnected monologue. Ward wasn't sure whether he was supposed to answer, so he said nothing, which seemed to work.

"You're the one, Ward, old son." Mr. Eagleson would often stop himself in mid-reverie, look at Ward and repeat those words like a mantra, usually ending with, "Some day," which he pronounced as if he were saying, "Amen."

Eagleson's role in the law firm seemed to revolve around politics. He spent hours on the telephone talking politics in a booming voice that carried all over the office, usually speaking in a verbal shorthand Ward couldn't decipher. Eagleson didn't seem to have any clients, at least not in the traditional sense. The only people who came to see him at his office—almost always late on a Friday morning—were various Liberal members of the Legislature. Ward knew that's who they were, mostly because Eagleson would introduce him. "I want you to meet the premier after next, Mr. Ward Justice," he'd say. "Pay attention, this young man may be your boss someday." The MLAs would smile indulgently but impatiently, too. It was as though they wanted to get in, do their business and get out.

Ward didn't know what their business was, just that it never took long. One by one, they'd go inside Eagleson's inner sanctum, spend fifteen minutes and then slip furtively back out past the receptionist, down the elevator and out the door.

One Friday morning, before they arrived, Ward was retrieving some papers for another lawyer from Mr. Eagleson's office. He couldn't help but notice a half dozen of the firm's business envelopes on Eagleson's desk, each bearing the handwritten name of an MLA, each apparently filled with something thick.

This morning, most of the surface of that same desk was covered by an oversized brown leather suitcase. "Want to see what's inside?" Eagleson was almost giddy as he flipped the gold latches on the suitcase. "*Et voilà, monsieur,*" he said with a wave of his hand across its contents. Ward had never seen so much money.

"Twenty-five thousand dollars," Eagleson announced grandly, "twenty-five big ones. Ever see that much cash money before, Ward?"

"No, sir."

"Impressed?"

"Yes, sir."

"Well, let's hope our friend is as impressed."

Eagleson said he needed Ward to carry the suitcase "and be my muscle if I need it." Ward wondered if he was joking. Eagleson was a big man, as tall as Ward but less gangly, and certainly capable of dealing with any sort of physical threat. "Not that I expect any trouble, but you never know," Eagleson said, adding with the same conspiratorial smile, "Besides, this will be a good opportunity for you to see how things really get done. No time like the present."

The suitcase was lighter than Ward had expected but it was big and awkward, and Ward struggled with it as he tried to keep up with Eagleson's long strides. They walked the four long blocks from McArtney, Eagleson's offices to the Dresden Arms Motor Hotel. The concierge recognized Eagleson as soon as he walked into the lobby. "Everything just as you requested, sir."

"Thanks, as always, Tony," Eagleson replied, smiling, handing him a two-dollar bill.

"Want someone to carry that bag for you?" Tony asked. "Looks heavy for the lad."

Ward might have taken offence at that but he was exhausted and would have been grateful to have someone take it off his hands.

"No thanks, Tony," Eagleson said. "We'll manage. Eh, Ward? Not too far now."

The room was on the third floor and there was an elevator, but Eagleson told Tony they'd prefer to walk. "Don't get enough exercise any more."

Ward followed behind.

The room offered standard-issue hotel furnishings: a double bed, a framed print of a seascape above the headboard, a long, low dresser on the wall opposite. The television, with built-in rabbit ears, sat on top of the dresser. Huddled in a corner by the window there was a small, round, dark wood laminate table with two chairs. Tony had already placed a forty-ounce bottle of Glenfiddich Single Malt Scotch Whisky, along with two tumblers and two champagne flutes, on the table. A bottle of Mumm's chilled in a silver ice bucket beside the table.

"For the celebration," Eagleson explained, then instructed Ward to put the suitcase on the bed. "And let's move this table a little closer so I can reach over and flip up the lid." He thought for a moment. "Don't undo the latches yet. No point in diminishing the drama."

What was going on? All Eagleson had told Ward was that the mayor, a former Liberal Cabinet minister, "wants me to do a little something for him that he doesn't want to be seen doing himself. Which is okay. I owe him a favour. Now he'll owe me one."

"What do you want me to do, Mr. Eagleson?"

"You just be here with me, Ward, but discreetly. I don't want to spook this guy." He laughed at that, as if at a private joke. "But I do want him to know I'm not alone. In case he gets any ideas."

Once the suitcase and the table were arranged to Eagleson's satisfaction, they sat in silence at the table. After about five minutes, there was a knock on the door. "Places, everyone," Eagleson said softly, pointing to a spot by the bed where Ward was to stand. Then he got up himself and opened the door.

"Come in, come in. So good of you to agree to meet me on short notice," he said, shaking his guest's hand and ushering him into the room.

Ward sucked in his breath in surprise.

"I think you know my assistant here," he said to the man, not bothering to introduce Ward by name. The man looked at Ward. His face was a mask. Did he recognize Ward? Ward certainly recognized the man. It was Ray's father, dressed in a dark-blue suit with a white shirt and tie. Except for the fact he was black—and that he carried what looked like a brown paper grocery store bag in his arms—he could have been a lawyer, too, Ward thought.

Seeing Ray's father, Ward suddenly felt guilty. He hadn't gone to visit Aunt Annie like he'd promised. And he hadn't seen Ray since graduation. Ward still didn't really understand what had happened to their friendship. Had Ward just naturally outgrown it after they'd started high school and made new friends? Perhaps. Probably. People changed, grew apart. It was no one's fault. But why then did he feel guilty every time he saw Ray? And why had Ray purposely ignored him whenever they happened to pass each other in the hall? Was he jealous? Resentful? Ward knew lots of the north-end kids he'd gone to Richmond with resented the south-enders. Even Ward had felt that way from time to time. Like the night Billy Henderson drove him home from a school dance. "You really live way up here, man?" he'd marvelled, gawking at the houses like a tourist on an exotic sightseeing expedition. Ward had directed him north on Barrington Street, past the imposing new public housing complex at Maynard Square.

"It's mostly niggers in there, right?" Billy asked, eyeing the row houses and apartment towers warily.

"Nah. Some. Maybe half, I guess," Ward answered. Ray had so

hated even hearing the word *nigger* that it was like fingernails on a blackboard to Ward, too. Ward wanted to stop Billy—tell him to say Negro, or maybe black, the word the civil rights types were using now—but he didn't.

"Fuck, man, this is the road to Africville, isn't it," Billy said suddenly. "Can we drive through?"

"Nah, I'm tired," Ward answered. "I just want to go home and go to bed. Besides, there's nothing to see there any more. It's almost all torn down."

"My dad says they're gonna call the new project on Gottingen Street 'Niggerville.' Niggerville Public Housing. Isn't that a laugh?"

Ward had laughed along with Billy, a short, sharp, go-along laugh. He wanted to tell Billy to shut the fuck up, but he didn't. It was easier to let it pass. Just as it was easier not to stop Ray in the hall at school, ask him what he was so pissed about. Maybe avoidance just ran in the family, Ward thought. Ever since graduation, his father had done his best to avoid confronting Ward about his relationship with Ray, even though he had to know now that Ward hadn't obeyed his instructions to "stay away from the coloureds."

Now Ward stole another glance at Ray's father. But he wasn't paying Ward any mind. His gaze was fixed on Mr. Eagleson.

"Have a seat, Mr. Carter," Eagleson said, indicating one of the chairs at the table. He sat down himself in the chair closest to the bed. "Can I get you a drink?"

"A little early, isn't it?" Carter answered, placing the paper bag on the floor beside him.

Eagleson laughed. "Never too early for a wee dram of Glenfiddich, my friend. Ever try it?"

Ray's father shook his head.

"You must, then," he said, taking the bottle and unscrewing the cap. "Single malt. Made from the best barley grown in the purest air on the banks of the River Fiddich, deep in the heart of the Scottish Highlands. I saw it with my own eyes last summer." He filled the two tumblers half full, slid one across the table to Lawrence Carter, picked up the other in his hand, sniffed the glass, smiled and offered a toast. "To perfection," he said, taking a long swallow. Ray's father took a sip, then replaced his glass on the table. His eyes never left Eagleson's face.

"You wanted to see me," Lawrence Carter said.

"I did, Mr. Carter, I did." Eagleson smiled. "I like a man who gets to the point." He paused then, took a shorter swallow of the whisky, held his glass up to the light and swirled the golden liquid around. "Perfection," he mused again, then put the glass back on the table. Ray's father, who had not taken a second sip, kept his focus on Eagleson.

"So . . . as you know very well, Mr. Carter," Eagleson began finally, "the City has been buying up properties in Africville as part of a major urban renewal initiative whose purpose is to relocate the residents to better quality housing, where they can get full access to City services. So far, this project has been very successful. Indeed—again, as you well know—all of your friends and neighbours have accepted the City's generous offers for their buildings and property, even in those cases—cases very much like your own—where the residents have no legal claim to the land on which those buildings sit. Now, the City would be within its rights to expropriate your house and take back the land on which it sits with no compensation whatsoever." He paused to allow that to sink in. Ward marvelled that Eagleson could be so clear and direct when he chose to be. "The City could do that, Mr. Carter, but it doesn't want to. That's why the Mayor has asked me to intercede, to talk to you man to man and find out how we can come to some arrangement that will benefit you and benefit the City, too."

He paused again, apparently waiting this time for a reply from Carter. But Ray's father just kept his gaze fixed disconcertingly on Eagleson.

"So . . ." Eagleson resumed at last, "I guess the question is simply this: What would it take to convince you to sell, Mr. Carter?"

"Not interested in selling, Mr. . . . ah, Eagleson. I like it fine where I am."

"But all your friends are already gone now, Mr. Carter. I'm sure it must get lonely out there all by yourself."

"Nothing wrong with being alone."

"No, of course not." Eagleson was doing his best to be patient. He wasn't used to dealing with someone who wasn't interested in dealing. "It's just that you're missing out on the City water and sewer services your former neighbours are getting now."

"Hard to miss something you never had," Carter replied. "Besides, the City could have given us all those services where we lived, they had a mind to."

Eagleson had been prepared for that. "But, as you know, Mr. Carter, it would have cost the City eight hundred thousand dollars to extend its services to Africville," he pointed out. "The City just couldn't afford that. As I'm sure you appreciate, eight hundred thousand dollars"—he said the words slowly, emphasizing the enormity of it all—"is a lot of money."

"It is," Raymond's father responded evenly. He leaned over and picked up the grocery bag, placed it casually on the table. "But not quite as much as the City has already spent trying to get rid of us." He pulled a file folder from the bag. "I been reading the City's financial statements for last year—I can show 'em to you if you want—and they show that the City has already paid more to move us than they claimed it would have cost to give us City services in the first place. Fifteen thousand dollars more. And that don't include how much you're going to have to pay to get rid of me. So who says the City can't afford it." It was not a question.

Eagleson did not try to answer directly. "You won't be very happy when you're living all by yourself in the only house left in the whole of Africville and you're surrounded by factories and noise."

Lawrence Carter grinned. It was a triumphant I-told-you-so grin. "I thought the City said this wasn't about industrial development, Mr. Eagleson. Thought they was just wantin' to help us coloured folk get a better life."

This wasn't going according to the script Eagleson had written in his head. He poured himself another whisky, slowly took another swallow. A long one, while he tried to think of a smooth segue to the suitcase. He couldn't.

"Look, Mr. Carter, I'm going to be perfectly straight with you. I'm trying to help you here but we've only got a very short time. The City has authorized me to make you a most generous offer for that small, rundown house you own and the half-acre of land you live on but don't own. But this offer won't last forever. Take it or leave it. Understood?"

"Oh, I understand all right."

Ward could feel the tension level in the room rising. The two men had dispensed with their cloaks of pretend politesse.

Without further preamble, Eagleson reached over and dragged the suitcase closer to him. He used his thumbs to pop the latches and pushed up the lid. Then he turned the suitcase around so Carter could see what was inside.

"There's twenty-five thousand dollars in here, Mr. Carter. That's a lot of money, more than the City has paid for any other single property in Africville, more, I dare say, than you ever made teaching at the Africville School. Am I right?"

Ray's father said nothing. His glance flickered briefly over the neatly stacked cash in the suitcase, then returned to Jack Eagleson's face.

"I can give you every last one of those twenty-five thousand dollars right now," Eagleson told him. "You can walk out the door with that suitcase in your hand and do whatever you goddamn well want with the money. It'll be yours."

Almost ceremoniously, Eagleson removed the whisky bottle, both their glasses and the two still-empty champagne flutes from the table, put them down on the floor beside him, then lifted the suitcase, still open, and placed it on to the table facing Carter.

"But this is a limited-time offer, Mr. Carter. It lasts only for as long as we're in this room. The moment you get up to leave, the moment you tell me, 'No, Mr. Eagleson, I'm not interested in having twenty-five thousand dollars in my pocket,' the offer is off the table, and the City will do whatever is necessary to achieve its objectives. Do you understand what I'm trying to tell you?"

"Do I understand?" Carter repeated the question as if considering. "I understand you think I'm just an ole nigger you can sweet-talk, or bamboozle, or intimidate into doing whatever it is you want. So yes, you could say I understand."

Eagleson closed the lid on the suitcase, put it back on the bed, tried again. "I'm sorry if you got the impression I was trying to intimidate you, Mr. Carter. That certainly wasn't my intention. I'm just looking for a solution that will work for everyone—"

"The solution that would work for me, Mr. Eagleson, is for the City to rebuild all them houses they tore down, let the people come home again, give us all the services they been denying us for so long and then just leave us alone. That's the solution that would work for me. Would that solution work for you?"

"Now let's just calm down and talk—"

"I think we talked all the talk we need to talk." Carter stood up then, picked up his grocery bag in his left hand and extended his right to Eagleson.

"Nice meeting you, Mr. Eagleson. I guess you can tell whoever sent you that we agreed to disagree. No hard feelings?"

Eagleson shook his hand without enthusiasm. "No hard feelings, Mr. Carter. But you do know you can't win, don't you? The City is going to win one way or the other, sooner or later. Why not just get the best deal you can and move on?"

"Because it's wrong, that's why. Somebody gotta stand up and say so."

"But what can you really do about it? You know and I know nobody cares much what happens to a bunch of coloured folk living in tarpaper shacks on the shore by the dump. People are just going to think you're ungrateful. Or crazy."

"Maybe. Maybe they will. We'll see. Eagleson? E-A-G-L-E-S-O-N? That how you spell your name?"

Eagleson looked puzzled.

"For the paper," Ray's father continued. "Young reporter called me this morning. Donovan. From the *Tribune.* Says he wants to interview me for a feature on what it's like to be the last person left living in Africville. I just want to make sure I spell your name right when I talk to him."

Eagleson was finally nonplussed. "This was a private conversation," he sputtered. To Ward, it almost seemed as if he was pleading. "Just between the two of us."

"And young Ward here," Carter replied, pointing at Ward. Ward couldn't hold his gaze, looked down at the floor. "And, as for this being a private conversation between the two of us—like friends, maybe?—I don't recall that, Mr. Eagleson. I think a lot of folks, even white folks, will be interested in this," he said, pointing to the suitcase, "interested in knowing how the City negotiates with poor people using suitcases filled with cash. You did say twenty-five thousand dollars, didn't you?"

Eagleson said nothing.

"Well," Carter said finally. "Nice meeting you, Mr. Eagleson. Good to see you again, Ward. I'll be sure and tell Raymond I ran into you. No need to see me out. I know where the door is."

And then he was gone.

For a long time, Eagleson didn't speak. Ward couldn't think of anything to say. The silence between them seemed to hang in the room forever. Eagleson finally picked up the whisky from the floor and took a long swig straight from the bottle. "That is . . . one . . . stubborn . . . nigger," he said, with what sounded to Ward like grudging admiration.

Then, after another long silence, "You think you and Ray will ever be friends again?"

Ward was startled. What did Mr. Eagleson know about his relationship with Ray? And how? Graduation? Perhaps, but there was something about the knowing way Eagleson asked the question, and something in the timing of it, too, that made Ward wonder if it wasn't some sort of test. But what was he testing? And what was the answer?

Eagleson picked up the two champagne glasses, filled them to the brim with the whisky and handed one to Ward. "Not much point in taking this back to the office. We'll just have to stay here until we kill the rest of it. We'll get good and drunk and you can tell me all about what you want to be when you grow up. Okay?"

He reached over and clinked Ward's glass. "To the Future Premier of Nova Scotia."

5

July 2002

Uhuru Melesse watched the Mayor squint into the shimmering late-morning sun. "On behalf of the City of Halifax and all its citizens," he began, standing behind an outdoor podium someone had placed incongruously in the middle of a grassy open field and addressing himself more to the TV cameramen crouched in front of him than to the dozen or so black faces ringing the podium behind them, "I am delighted to welcome you all here today to Seaview Park, to this beautiful National Historic Site, which was once the site of the proud community of Africville." The Mayor did not mention, of course, how the once proud *community* of Africville had become simply the *site* of the once proud community of Africville. "Today is a milestone," he continued, "the twentieth annual Africville Reunion Weekend."

The audience, which consisted mostly of the event's organizing committee, was clearly eager to get this over with and get back to the outdoor party and fair, which had already begun in the parking lot on the other side of the field. The Mayor, dressed casually for this photo-op in khaki pants and an official green City of Halifax golf shirt, seemed just as anxious to get his speech over with. He had a Saturday morning golf game and he was already late for his tee-off.

Uhuru Melesse was anxious, too. And hot. Standing at the edge of—but physically and psychically apart from—the audience of black men and women, he could feel the sweat pooling under his armpits, staining the front of his white shirt. He was wearing a suit, a dark-blue pinstriped banker's suit. That was a stupid mistake. He loosened his tie. What had he been thinking?

His excuse—he felt a need to explain, if only to himself—was that he'd forgotten just how casual this event was. The only other time he'd attended a Reunion Weekend was back in 1990 when he was still Raymond Carter, son of the recently departed Lawrence Carter, patron saint of Africville's dispossessed.

Reunion Weekend had begun in the early eighties when some of the grown-up children of displaced Africville residents met to plan an unpretentious get-together for themselves and their families. It was so successful it became an annual event, and was soon extended to a whole weekend instead of just a day. Reunion Weekend became *the* social event of black Nova Scotia's summer season.

Those who'd been ambitious enough—or whose parents had been smart enough—to take the money the City offered back in the sixties and head down the road to Toronto, or Boston, or New York, or anywhere industrious black people could find a better future for themselves and their children, came back to show off their good fortune. They drove up in their fancy Volvos and Mercedes, many hauling trailers or driving RVs bigger and certainly more luxurious than the shacks they'd left behind. With indoor plumbing! Uhuru was being unfair; he knew that. But he couldn't help himself. The more prosperous they became, it seemed, the more likely they were to return every year to rub shoulders with each other and, of course, to rub the noses of those who'd stayed behind in their successes.

The locals who came to the reunions were more mixed. There was the post-Africville generation of small businessmen and civil servants who could—and did—more than hold their middle-class own with those who'd found success elsewhere. There were also more than a few former residents whose lives had turned into one long disappointment after Africville, and who came to the reunions to wallow in shared nostalgia and pine for an idealized community that existed, if it ever did, only in their imaginations.

And then, of course, there were those who didn't show up at all. Some, like Ray Carter, were eager to leave their pasts in the past.

Others, like Ray's father, were dead. And still others—like J. J. Howe, to cite the most obvious example—were in jail. Or strung out on drugs.

The imprisoned and the addicted. Those were the ones Uhuru wanted to find out about today. For the case. Which was why he'd worn his suit, to make himself seem more official. Of course, none of the former residents had come here to talk about all the awful things that had happened to them or their children since the relocation. This was a family picnic, a chance to relax and celebrate the good times.

Another tepid smattering of applause. The Mayor had finished speaking. Damn. Uhuru had hoped he would at least mention the case of the *Africville Descendants' Association v. Halifax Regional Municipality*. Essentially, ADA—everyone called it Ada, as if the group were a person—had filed a civil suit seven years ago demanding the City give all Africville lands back to the former residents or their children and help them rebuild their community on its original site. With sewer and water services this time. Like most civil cases, it had quickly disappeared into lawyer limbo. But Uhuru had heard rumours there'd been a recent flurry of negotiations, and the two sides might be close to announcing an out-of-court settlement. Uhuru had tried to find out if that was true, but the Association's counsel, a young white lawyer named Davis, hadn't returned his phone calls.

Uhuru had hoped the Mayor might take advantage of today's friendly public occasion to announce that a deal had been reached. If the City said it was sorry, acknowledged it had screwed up when it expropriated properties and razed the community, Uhuru imagined—hoped against rational expectation—it might strengthen his own tenuous argument that J. J. Howe had simply been reclaiming what rightfully belonged to his community.

Uhuru wasn't convinced that laundry would wash.

The City had spent the last thirty-odd years defending what it had done. Even after it had no longer been politically palatable to claim that relocation was the best, or even a reasonable way to improve life for Africville's residents, City Fathers had continued to insist—probably on the advice of their lawyers—that their predecessors had made the best decision they could at the time. "You can't judge the actions of yesterday by the standards of today," as the current Mayor had put it almost pleadingly during a conference on Africville at one of the universities.

Uhuru wasn't sure he disagreed with that. He wouldn't want anyone judging him now on things he'd said or done—or not done—twenty-five years ago. Especially not . . . best not to think of her now. Was she here? He doubted it.

The Mayor was handshaking his way past the organizers, making haste in the direction of his car. Uhuru circled around the crowd and headed across the field toward the party. He wasn't about to ask the Mayor about the negotiations and he had no desire to shake his hand.

"Ray, Ray, wait up." It was Calvin Johnstone, the Deacon's oldest son and one of the leaders of the Descendants' Association. Uhuru hadn't seen Calvin since he was still Ray. Calvin's once sharp face had been swallowed by pudge, but Uhuru recognized him immediately, partly because his photo was often in the newspaper, promoting this or that black cause, and partly because of his prominent harelip, which had frightened Ray when he was a child.

"Good to see you, man," Calvin said, catching up to Uhuru. His breathing was laboured. How old was he, anyway? Uhuru had heard he'd retired last year after forty years teaching high school history out in the County somewhere. He tried to do the math: Uhuru was fifty-three, five years older than Calvin's sister Rosa, and Rosa was seventeen years younger than her oldest brother. So Calvin had to be sixty-five! He was grey-haired and balding, with a midsection that resembled an oversized spare tire. Like Eddie Murphy in *The Nutty Professor*. Calvin really did look his age. Uhuru didn't. At least, he didn't think he did.

"Been a long time," Uhuru said, warily shaking the hand Calvin extended. Calvin had never let on that he knew what had happened between Ray and Rosa. But he must have, Uhuru thought. How could he not?

"Sorry to hear about your father," Calvin said. Lawrence Carter had died twelve years ago.

"Sorry about yours, too." The Deacon had been gone at least half as many.

Neither, truth be told, cared all that much about the other's father. In life, their fathers had been rivals for the leadership of the Africville community. Though their sons were never directly involved in the rivalry and had, in fact, worked together at Black Pride, they carried the burden of their fathers' enmity, even now.

The competition between the two now equally dead men had been on relatively even terms until the provincial government had shut down the Africville School in the early fifties and Ray's father had lost his job. That had given Mr. Johnstone, the most powerful figure in the Africville church, the other key pillar of the local establishment, the advantage. And he'd happily lorded it over his rival. Until the relocation destroyed him. The Deacon failed to comprehend the obvious: that plowing under Africville and scattering its residents would leave him with no constituency to lead. And, worse, it would make him the easy scapegoat when things turned out, as they did, so badly. To make that even worse for the Deacon, his sudden, precipitous fall from community grace coincided with Ray's father's equally sudden beatification for having stood up so publicly against the cynical white power structure, a.k.a. Jack Eagleson *et al.*

After Ray's father died of a heart attack in the spring of 1990, organizers dedicated that summer's Reunion Weekend to the memory of "a true hero of Africville." That he'd lost in the end—the City had expropriated his house six months after he went public with his story of the suitcase, punishing him for having challenged its plans by ultimately giving him less than half of what had been in the suitcase—mattered less than the fact that he'd done the right thing. That he'd been vilified for his obstinacy at the time by many of Africville's community leaders, and not just by Deacon Johnstone, no longer mattered. Except to his son. Which is why Ray had felt obliged to attend the reunion that year. To see for himself how the community had come to terms with the reality of his father's protests and its response to them.

The Deacon himself had offered up a speech in praise of Ray's father. By then, of course, the Deacon had been busy rehabilitating and reinventing himself as one of the leaders—"along with my good friend Lawrence Carter"—of the anti-relocation faction.

The Deacon wasn't the only one who'd had a sudden, Saul-like conversion on the road to that reunion. Seamus O'Sullivan, the former premier, who'd been an enthusiastic booster of relocation when he was the MLA for the district, spoke about "the Lawrence Carter I was privileged to call my friend." His friend, Ray thought, who in turn had called him an "asshole." "Lawrence Carter was a man who cared deeply about his community and his province," O'Sullivan went on and on. But, like the Deacon, he managed not to mention anything at all about the suitcase full of cash O'Sullivan's law partner had used to try to buy Lawrence Carter off.

O'Sullivan, ever the politician even in retirement, came up to Ray after the "celebration service" to offer his condolences. "He was a fine man, your father, the finest," he said, holding out his hand. Ray shook it. It was clammy. "We still miss you around the firm," he added, as if he meant it, as if he'd forgotten that Ray had never been anything more than Jack's gofer and that the firm hadn't offered him a position after he graduated from law school.

The Deacon didn't shake Ray's hand that day, didn't even acknowledge his presence. But of course the Deacon hadn't spoken to him in sixteen years. And not just because of who his father was.

"I hear you've taken on young J.J.'s case," Calvin Johnstone came to the point quickly. "How's it going?"

"*W-e-l-l,*" Uhuru dragged out the word, trying to decide how much he should share. "We're still in the early stages."

"I read in the paper that you're planning to use reparations as a defence."

"Thinking about it. That's all. Just thinking." Uhuru wanted to see where Calvin was going with this before he offered more information.

"Well, I want you to know you can count on me and ADA," he said. "J. J.'s a fine young man, a volunteer in the breakfast program at our church, a counsellor in the drug program. Hard to believe how well he turned out. Especially with his parents."

Uhuru already knew all about J. J.'s parents. His father—also a J. J., but standing for Jeffrey Jack—was currently serving time for armed robbery. Two years ago, desperate for money to score some crack cocaine, he'd tried to rob a convenience store. The convenience store turned out to be in the same building as the North End Community Policing Office.

Unluckily for J. J. the Elder, two policemen had come into the store just before he did to buy snacks and shoot the breeze with its Korean owner. J. J. was either too high or too stupid to notice. Luckily for J. J., when he brandished his gun and began yelling at the owner that this was a robbery and he'd better hand over all his cash right away or he was a dead man, one of the cops casually grabbed the gun out of his hand and twisted his arms behind his back while the other cop just as casually handcuffed his wrists.

The cops knew J. J. was a crackhead but they also knew he was too strung out to be more than accidentally dangerous, and then mostly to himself. Unfortunately, the judge didn't understand that. He sentenced J. J. to seven years for pointing a firearm in the commission of a robbery.

J. J. the Younger's mother, Jaina, was a crack addict, too. Her addiction had only got worse since her husband and chief supplier had been packed off to jail. To support her habit, she'd become a street hooker, but she was too old and too emaciated to attract even the most desperate of ordinary johns, so she ended up trading blow jobs for crack with other addicts who were themselves too strung out to think about what they were doing.

J. J. the Younger had tried to get his mother into detox but Jaina wasn't interested, and the drug rehabilitation centre wasn't interested in someone who wasn't interested in getting help, so J. J. threw himself into helping others who might be more open to it.

He volunteered as a drug counsellor at his church. And, of course, generously donated City funds to a variety of drug education and prevention programs.

"J. J. turned out okay," Uhuru answered, and meant it. He'd come around, slowly and almost reluctantly to be sure, to the belief that J. J. was telling the truth about why he'd taken the money and what he'd done with it. But would the judge let him use that in his defence? Perhaps he should call J. J.'s parents as witnesses. That would, at the very least, gain his client some sympathy.

Uhuru remembered J. J.'s parents, but not well. He had known his client's grandparents better. Jeremiah Joseph Howe—J. J. the Eldest?—never held a steady job in his life, but his wife, Bea, kept the family going by working as a maid for a rich south-end family. Jaina, whose name meant "Jehovah has been gracious," was the daughter of one of Africville's most religious families. Her father, Caleb, was a janitor who had been fired by the School Board for proselytizing students in his white elementary school.

Both sets of grandparents were dead now, so they wouldn't be able to testify about the impact relocation had on their children, and on all the little J. J.s and Jainas yet to be born.

"If you're going to try to bring up the reparations angle," Calvin said, "you really should talk to our lawyer. We did some research on that ourselves."

"I tried. I called Davis, but he never returns my calls."

"Oh, we dropped him," Calvin answered. "I think his firm only took it on in the first place as penance for what that Eagleson character did to your father. Besides, we decided the optics were just wrong, having a white law firm speaking for a black community."

"So who's doing it now?" Uhuru made a quick mental checklist of the few black lawyers he knew in private practice and wondered why no one had contacted him.

"Oh, a real pistol, a woman who teaches at the law school. You probably know her. Shondelle Adams is her name."

Wonderful, Uhuru thought. The snotty bitch from that night at the Shoe Shop.

"She's something else, that one. And doing it all pro bono. Already got the City's lawyers racing around like a bunch of chickens with their heads cut off. The Mayor told me just this morning they're working on a new offer right now. Look, Ray, she's real interested in this reparations stuff. I'm sure she'd be willing to help with J. J.'s case."

"W-e-l-l," Uhuru stalled for time again. "maybe I'll give her a call."

"Oh, you don't have to do that," Calvin said brightly. "She's here. For the reunion. Invited her myself. I was going to introduce her around. It seems like she already knows half the old folks from out home. She's been interviewing them all for our case. I can introduce you if you want—"

"No, no, that's fine," Uhuru said quickly. "We met already. Maybe I'll run into her over the weekend."

"Whatever you say, Ray." He stopped. "Oh my. I am sorry. I keep forgetting you changed your name. What is it now? I've seen it in the papers but I know I'll mispronounce it if I try. How do you say it?"

"Uhuru. *Oo-who-ru.*"

"Ray's easier." He laughed. "Just kidding, Ray—I mean Uhuru. Some habits are hard to break . . . Well, must go see if I can track down the old ball-and-chain. We're expecting a few grandkids this afternoon. You got any kids?"

"No, not me," Uhuru answered quickly. Too quickly. He looked carefully at Calvin. Nothing. "Uh, Calvin . . . just wondering. What's your sister up to?"

"Rosa?" Calvin let out a sigh. "Sad, really. I don't know where she is or if she's even still alive. She took off, after, you know, after that thing with her son. And she never told a soul where she was going. Dad wouldn't even let us speak her name around him. My brother Gerry and I, we tried to track her down a bunch of different times over the years but it was like she'd just vanished. After Dad died, we tried again to find her to let her know, you know, but there wasn't anything to go on and we finally gave up." He paused, lost in some private thought. "Well, look Ray—sorry, Uhuru, it's great to see you again. I'm glad you finally made it to another reunion. And don't forget what I said about Shondelle. She'd be a real help on your case, I'm sure of it."

"Thanks, Calvin. Good to see you, too." Uhuru stood in the middle of the field for a moment, giving Calvin the chance to trundle off in the direction of the barbecue, before making his way to the Africville Memorial, a grey granite sundial with the names of Africville's families etched into the sides of its north-pointing dial. For some reason he couldn't explain, seeing his own family's names—Carter and Jones, his mother's maiden name—still gave him chills.

He tried to get his bearings. Where in Africville was he now? Although everyone expected the City to establish some sort of industrial park on the site, nothing ever came of those early schemes. Years after reducing the houses to rubble, somebody got the bright idea to turn the ugly wasteland into a civic green space. They called it Seaview Park, theoretically in honour of the Seaview African United Baptist Church but mostly because they didn't want to name it Africville Park. The City put out a few picnic tables, kept the grass mowed and otherwise ignored its existence until the Africville Descendants' Association began holding reunions there in the eighties.

These days, thanks in large part to the efforts of ADA, white liberal politicians were falling all over themselves just to get invited to the reunion. The night before, it had been Sheila Copps, the federal Heritage minister, breezing into town to anoint Seaview Park a National Historic Site and declare that she shared their pain—and hopes for a better future. "What we're doing today is the beginning of a process I hope will place the name Africville on the lips of every Canadian," she said. "If we can teach our children to avoid making the same mistakes, we can use this symbol as a way of changing Canada."

Uhuru had sat at home watching the speech on TV. "Way to go, Sheila, baby," he'd shouted at the screen. Sheila wasn't here this morning. *Must be the Mayor's turn in the black spotlight*, he thought.

Uhuru wandered back toward the parking lot, which had been transformed for the weekend into a country fairground. Dozens of youngsters careened down a huge, portable, plastic waterslide some adults had erected early in the morning. They screamed with joy and trepidation as their fathers or older brothers ambushed them with blasts of cold water from a garden hose just as they reached the bottom. Other teenage boys gathered around the dunk tank, taking turns drilling softballs as hard as they could at the tank's trigger mechanism and then cheering loudly whenever the platform dropped and another adult plummeted into the water. Directly across from the dunk tank, in a cavernous white canvas tent that would serve as the dance hall for the adults that night, a gaggle of teenage girls did their best Destiny's Child in a karaoke competition. Their mothers sat on blankets out on the grass behind the tent, loudly renewed old acquaintances and simultaneously supervised their husbands, most of whom were struggling manfully to light uncooperative charcoal briquettes for the hot dogs that would be lunch.

Uhuru rarely missed having had a family of his own, probably because he'd been born so long after his brothers and was raised like an only child. But this morning, watching children with their parents, husbands with their wives, he couldn't help but think again about . . . Uhuru missed her still. If only—

"Hey, mister!" a laughing teenage boy called to him from beside the dunk tank. "Want to take a turn?"

Uhuru was tempted. A quick plunge into icy water would be a refreshing escape from the stifling noontime heat. But his summer suit was still at the cleaners, so he'd need this one for work Monday morning.

"No. Can't," Uhuru said, indicating his suit. "Another time."

The kid shrugged. "Okay, Ms. Adams. I guess it's your turn then."

Unlike Uhuru, Shondelle Adams had come prepared. She was wearing a colourful sarong skirt over a blue, one-piece bathing suit. At the bottom of the ladder leading up to the dunk tank's drop-down chair, she loosened the skirt at the waist and let it fall away, then picked it up and handed it to the teenage boy to hold. He looked as if he could use a cold shower himself. Uhuru felt the way the boy looked. This was not the woman Uhuru remembered from the Shoe Shop, that woman of indeterminate size and shape whose features had been hidden under the folds of a shapeless tent dress. Now she was all curves and angles, which the bathing suit did nothing to hide and everything to accentuate. She wasn't wearing a turban today, either. Her Halle Berry hair was dyed a dark blond, giving her an almost regal look. A Caribbean queen, Uhuru thought.

"Step right up, gents," the middle-aged emcee shouted into the microphone as Shondelle Adams gingerly took her seat on the platform above the water tank. She smiled and waved to someone in the crowd. "So, gentlemen, do you have the balls try your luck at dunking the beautiful lady professor?" the emcee demanded. "You gotta have balls . . . Three balls for a dollar, ten for three dollars!" Everyone laughed. "Let's show this fine lady a little Africville hospitality." He recoiled theatrically then, as if he'd just thought of something. "Promise me you won't sue!" More laughter.

Uhuru raised his hand. "Give me a dollar's worth."

"Oh, my, my," the emcee said, looking at him in mock horror. "The lawyer versus the law professor." He winked. "Must be some scores to settle here. Hey, Mr. Boo-Who-Roo—did I get the pronunciation right?" He turned back to the crowd. "I knew him way back when he was just plain old Ray." Ray tried to place the face, couldn't. "Now you need a law degree just to pronounce his name. Anyway, Mr. Who-You-Are-Today, you sure you don't want ten balls? Just to give yourself a fighting chance? You're not as young as you used to be, you know."

"Three'll be more than enough," he shouted back, loosening his tie and taking off his jacket. He was getting in the mood now. "I'll dunk her in one, then do you for fun," he said in his best Muhammad Ali.

The crowd cheered. Shondelle laughed too.

But he didn't dunk her with one throw. The ball sailed over the target and into the netting behind.

"Been a long time since Little League," the emcee taunted. "Still not too late for the ten, Ray. We'll give you a cut rate. Just three-fifty for the other seven."

Uhuru ignored him. Concentrated on the target instead. He didn't want to miss this time. He stole a quick glance over at Shondelle Adams. She looked nervous. Good, he thought. He wound up and delivered a pitch that caught the target dead centre. The chair dropped away. Shondelle's shrill, giddy scream was swallowed by the splash and the cheers from the onlookers. Uhuru raised his fist in salute. It had been a long time since he'd done that.

Shondelle came sputtering to the surface. She was laughing and coughing at the same time. Uhuru watched her climb the ladder at the edge of the tank, the dripping wetness making the fabric cling even more deliciously to her curves. He felt a faint—and more than faintly pleasing—stirring. The teenage boy who'd been holding Shondelle's sarong almost reluctantly handed it back to her.

Uhuru waited for her to emerge from behind the tank. "Sorry." He smiled. "I couldn't help myself."

"Oh, that's okay. It felt good to cool off. I wish I could return the favour."

"Me too," he said. And almost meant it.

"I'm surprised," she said. "Are you really from Africville? I figured you for a come-from-away. Like me. Especially with a name like that."

"I was born and bred on this hallowed ground," he answered, though he still wasn't exactly sure just where on this hallowed ground he was standing. Ironic, he thought. Changing his name was supposed to bring him closer to his African roots. Instead, it had separated him from the only roots he had.

"So how's your case coming?" she asked.

"I should ask you the same thing. I'm hearing rumours you're close to a settlement with the City."

"Not that close. But I've got some research you might want to ask me about sometime."

"I might." Sometime? Was she just suggesting an exchange of information? Or something more? A date?

"Well, Lordy, Lordy, just look who it isn't. How come you been such a stranger all these years? Something I did?"

Aunt Annie! Uhuru instantly felt guilty. The last time he'd seen her was at his father's funeral. He'd promised to visit but never had. Now she was in a wheelchair being pushed by a young man. But her voice was still strong.

"Your lady friend here has been to see me plenty of times, haven't you, sweet thing?" Annie seemed more amused than annoyed.

Shondelle leaned over and gave her a peck on the cheek. "How you been, Aunt Annie?" *Aunt Annie?*

"I could complain, I suppose, but no one listens. 'Sides, if I'm not complaining, I'm probably dead."

"You're looking good," Uhuru said, mostly to be part of the conversation. But it was also true. She was.

"You remember my nephew, Charles," Aunt Annie said to him, nodding her head at the young man pushing her wheelchair. Uhuru didn't. Annie saw. "Oh Lord, how you supposed to know Charles? He be born in Toronto. Only come down home for reunions to wheel his old aunt around. And you"—she looked accusingly at Uhuru—"I ain't seen you at a reunion since your daddy died."

"I'm sorry, Aunt Annie." Annie was good at guilt. "I'll get over to see you. I will, promise."

But Aunt Annie had already moved on. "Speaking of your daddy reminds me . . ." She turned back to Shondelle. "Remember, Shondelle, honey, 'member when you came to ask me what it was like when the City came and took our land?" Shondelle nodded. "I said there was something I wasn't 'membering, but I couldn't think what it was. Well, now I did." She looked again at Ray. "I got your father's diary. When he went into the nursing home, he asked me to keep it for him." She looked at Ray, rebuke in her tone. "Said he didn't guess you'd be much interested." Would he have been? "So I kept it. Must be in the back of my closet at the home. I only just remembered when I seed Ray here. Ray, honey, you don't mind I give the book to Shondelle? She's working on a project."

"Uhu—Ray's working on a very similar project," Shondelle said quickly. "Maybe we could both look at it together." She looked at Uhuru.

"Sure."

"That's settled then," Annie cut in. "I'll dig it out wherever it got to. So why don't you two come over next week and I'll make you some tea and show you what I got?" She looked at Ray. "I don't keep licorice around these days . . ." Smiled. "But if I thought you was gonna come visit more . . ."

"How about I bring the licorice?" Uhuru replied, laughing. He paused long enough to change the subject. "Hey, Aunt Annie, you happen to know whatever happened to Rosa, the Deacon's daughter? Kind of thought she might be here this weekend."

Annie shook her head. "Nobody seen or heard of that girl in seems like forever. Wasn't even at her own daddy's funeral. You wasn't there either, but that's different. She's blood. Not that they got along. Ever since, you know, since the baby." She looked Ray in the eye then. "Sad it was, yes, very sad."

"Excuse me, excuse me everybody." A scratchy, disembodied voice booming out of the sound system silenced their conversation. "Okay, people, why don't you all join us here in the tent." Uhuru recognized Calvin Johnstone's voice. "Now that the Mayor and the TV cameras are gone, we're going to have our own Africville Descendants' Association welcoming ceremony. So come join me in the big white tent up by the dunk tank and the waterslide. We'll start in two minutes." As he took the microphone away from in front of his mouth, the shrill whistle of feedback and the crackle of microphone brushing clothing filled the air.

"So you see, Mrs. Justice, if you take this piece of the puzzle here and then combine it with this piece from over here, well, you could say it's all just a coincidence, it doesn't mean anything at all. But this"—David Astor's voice rose then, triumphant, as he scooped a sepia-tinted photograph from the tabletop and held it out at arm's length—"this changes things, makes all those other pieces seem less coincidental, if you see my point."

Victoria Justice saw his point.

The man stopped himself, suddenly aware that his own glorious moment of archivist's pride might not seem quite so glorious to the person on the other side of the table hearing the fruits of his deductive detective work for the first time. "Not that this is the definitive word, of course," he added, almost apologetically. "It could all still be coincidence. It might mean nothing. But then again . . ."

David Astor smiled. He couldn't help himself. He was giddy with the sweet satisfaction of discovery. After years of sifting through the detritus of lives lived—microfilmed birth, marriage, divorce and death records, property transactions, account books, letters, diaries, brittle newspaper clippings, even random notes and drawings—he had finally found something . . . surprising, startling, stunning, important. Ah, yes, important. This discovery would matter to more than just the great-great-great-nephew. His discovery involved a public figure. It would be news in Nova Scotia, especially now with the Judge involved in that big trial.

David Astor wasn't sure what he would have done if she hadn't showed up this time. She'd agreed to come see him twice before. Once, she'd called to cancel an hour before, but the second time he'd had to call her. She was terribly sorry, she'd forgotten. Forgotten! She was the one who'd come to him, looking. And he'd found what she was looking for.

What Victoria had been looking for was her husband's family history. When the archivist had failed to find any trace of Desmond Justice's ancestors, Victoria had even gone to visit her father-in-law in the senior citizens' home in Antigonish where he'd been living for the past ten years.

"Good morning, Da," she said, falling into the name Meghan used to call her grandfather before she could pronounce the word. He lay on his bed staring at the TV. The volume was high.

"Good morning, Da," she shouted this time. Why wouldn't he get a hearing aid? He looked at her now, did not smile. He didn't smile often, not since Ada died and his son and daughter-in-law forced him into this home with people he didn't know. But that was another battle line, one Victoria knew was no longer worth defending.

"How are you?" He shrugged. "I wanted to ask you some questions. I brought a tape recorder." She took the remote, turned off the TV, pulled a small black recorder the size of a cigarette package out of her purse, put it carefully on the night table, pressed the play and record buttons, then asked, "Is that okay?" He shrugged again. "Da, I'm trying to put together a special gift for Meghan"—he smiled for the first time; she noticed he hadn't put his teeth in yet that morning—"for when she gets married. A family tree. And I need your help."

Now he scowled, waved his hand dismissively at the tape recorder.

"I just need to know some things about your father, what his name was, where he came from, how you got to—"

"The coloured girl, the one that cleans the rooms, she stole my slippers," he said suddenly, cutting her off. "I want you to get them back for me."

Damn, she thought, *he's getting worse. Could it be Alzheimer's, or some other form of dementia?* More likely, Desmond Justice was simply being his usual curmudgeonly self. Over the last few years, her father-in-law had spiced up his contrariness with paranoia. Everyone was out to cheat him. The nurses, attendants, cleaning staff, even the doctor from town who came to visit him once a week, were stealing his belongings. Or his food. Or his photos of Ada. Sometimes Victoria was convinced the old man was simply acting out his anger that she and Ward had forced him to move out of his house and into this seniors' home in the first place. Whatever, it made her especially uncomfortable when he started talking, as he too often did, about the "coloureds" who'd done this or stolen that. What if someone overheard?

"I'll take a look for them before I go. Promise," she offered, hoping to win back his attention. She pointed to the tape recorder. "I tried looking up the Justices in the archives but there wasn't much there, so the archivist asked me to ask you about your father and mother, where they were living when you were born—"

"What's it matter? Doesn't matter."

"But I'm doing a family tree for Meghan and I want it to be complete with both sides of the family on it."

He shook his head. "I left, gone, good riddance, long ago. Why go back?"

"I'm not asking you to go back, Da, I just want to know where you were born. So the archivist can follow the family tree back. That's all. No big deal—"

"You're making the big deal. Your questions. Don't ask me questions."

This wasn't going the way she'd hoped. Desmond had become even more difficult ever since Ada died. Sometimes, it seemed, he couldn't have a conversation with his son or daughter-in-law without turning it into an argument. Perhaps that's why they visited so rarely.

"I'm tired," he announced suddenly. "Go find the coloured girl. Get my slippers back." He rolled away from her then, faced the wall, dismissed her.

That was a year ago. Victoria had tried to talk Ward into pressing his father for information but gave up when he resisted. At the rehearsal dinner before the wedding, she'd given Meghan and Brad a binder full of artfully arranged notes and pictures from the Cullingham family tree. "I'm still working on your father's side of the family," she said lightly. "It'll be your first anniversary present."

But she hadn't done anything about it since. She'd moved on, forgotten. Until the archivist called again.

David Astor glanced over now at the woman sitting on the other side of the table, a slight smile playing at the corners of her mouth. What was Mrs. Cullingham thinking? Of course, she wasn't Cullingham any more. It was a hazard of his trade, always at least a generation out of sync with current events. He tried to read her face. It was blandly unrevealing. Must be a product of her upbringing. Politician's daughter, judge's wife. They must need to practise that nothing-surprises-me look for cocktail parties and receptions. What *was* she thinking?

What Victoria Justice, née Cullingham, was thinking was that David Astor really did look like a weasel. Just as she'd described him to Ward. She thought this, not because it mattered, but because it gave her time to rearrange the expression on her face, to let him know none of this surprised her. It did. It made no sense. And yet, perhaps it made perfect sense. The hair, the features . . . If you looked at his face in a certain way, from a certain angle, you could . . . And then there was that woman. She had never understood that. They'd never talked about her again since that day she'd called. But Victoria had never stopped thinking about her. With revulsion. With anger. With curiosity. Even, perhaps occasionally, with envy. What was it about her that had drawn him to her? Perhaps this was what it was, something about *him*. Not that any of this should matter. It changed nothing. And yet it changed everything. What if she'd known this when they'd met? Would it have made a difference? It certainly would have changed her parents' perception, his good politics and prospects notwithstanding. And how good would those prospects really have been if . . . ?

She would have to reorder her thinking about so many things. The children! She had a moment of panic. Sarah might think it exotic; when she was a little girl she'd told her teacher she was Spanish because it made her seem more interesting. But Meghan, who wanted nothing more than to fit in, and with the right group, would be appalled.

All of these thoughts ricocheted through her mind, pinballing off one another, during the instant it took for her to rearrange her face. Victoria knew immediately what she had to do. She turned her attention back to David Astor, who was still babbling excitedly.

". . . very interesting but not as uncommon as you might think. I mean, there was Wentworth. We know all about him. And there have been others, less well known, granted, but the situation is the same, if you see my point. Anyway, I was thinking this might make a great article for the *Nova Scotia Historical Review*. I don't know if you're familiar with that publication, Mrs. Justice, but it's very prestigious. And I would write the article with the appropriate discretion . . ."

Suddenly, Victoria looked down at her watch, then, apparently startled by what she'd discovered, up at David Astor. "Oh dear, I had no idea it was so late. I shouldn't have, I realize now, but I didn't know your news would be so . . . interesting. So I scheduled another appointment for this morning and I'm already late." She looked at the photo still clutched in his hand. "Do you mind if I borrow this?" she asked. "I'd like to show it to my husband."

"No problem," David Astor replied, his voice betraying disappointment. "I made that copy for you anyway. The original's still in the files."

"We've known all along," Victoria lied, feeling the need to explain herself to this strange man, "but I don't believe my husband has ever seen a photo. I'm sure he'd be fascinated." It was all a lie. There was no appointment Victoria was late for. She'd known nothing of what the archivist had discovered and, she was certain, neither did Ward.

She saw the crestfallen look on David Astor's face as she stood up. "I'll give you a call next week, David, and we can talk some more about your idea of an article, which sounds very interesting to me. I'm sure Ward will think so, too."

That was a lie as well. Ward wouldn't think so because she wasn't going to *tell* Ward, or anyone else, what David Astor had discovered.

The classroom had the familiar smell—musty paper, pungent cleaning solvents, sweaty sneakers—Uhuru Melesse associated with his own school days. Late again. He tried not to draw attention to himself as he struggled to squeeze his oversized body into the undersized desk. It was hopeless. Some in the audience turned to see who was causing the fuss. A few smiled and nodded in acknowledgement before turning back to the woman at the front of the room.

"No, that's exactly right." Shondelle Adams resumed her explanation, doing her best to ignore Uhuru's late arrival. "The City hasn't offered one penny in direct compensation to any of the former residents. What they are offering is what they've been promising—but not doing—all along: rebuilding the church and setting up some sort of scholarship fund. But they can't, or won't, tell us how much they'll put in this fund, or who will be eligible, or who is going to decide who gets these scholarships. For our part, we have said there must be financial compensation for every surviving Africville resident, similar to that given the Japanese for their internment during World War II."

Uhuru's eyes swept the faces of the two dozen black men and women, all seated as uncomfortably as he in the horseshoe of student desks facing the front of the classroom. There were faces he recognized, Africville elders like Aunt Annie and Everett Dickson. Calvin Johnstone, the chair of tonight's meeting, was seated in a more comfortable chair behind the teacher's desk to the left of Shondelle. Though he didn't recognize anyone else, Uhuru would catch occasional glimpses of other elders in the faces and features of their now thirty-something children. This was the first generation to have grown up outside the comforting embrace of Africville, the ones Uhuru needed to talk to.

But not *these* people. These were the successes, the teachers and civil servants, entrepreneurs and social workers whose middle-class achievements—neat, vinyl-sided bungalows in Sackville, driveways filled with SUVs and Mom's Taxis, children studying computer science or commerce at college—could be bent and twisted to justify the City's decision to raze Africville and disperse its residents so they would have an opportunity to build better futures for themselves and their children.

Uhuru needed to talk to the others: the junkies and the jailed, the hustlers and the hookers, whose failures could be bent and twisted into an equally convincing justification for J. J. Howe's decision to play Robin Hood.

"You really are a cynic," Shondelle had said when he'd made just that point in her office at the university two weeks ago. They'd met at her suggestion to discuss what to do with his father's diary and, more generally, what she might do to help him with J. J.'s defence.

"Not a cynic, a realist," he'd replied. Her certainties made him want to play the contrarian. "You want to pin every bad thing that's ever happened to anyone from Africville on the relocation. But the fact is that a lot of *us*"—he emphasized the *us* to make it clear she was still a *them*—"turned out okay. Some people might look at me and say that I'm a success story . . ."

"Others might look at you and say you're a sellout." She said it with a smile. "Seriously, how can you provide J. J. with a proper defence if you're thinking that way?"

"Because I need to think like them if I'm going to win this case," Uhuru shot back. He was enjoying this. A good argument with a colleague. It was like being back in university—or it might have been if there'd been more black students studying law back when Uhuru was a student. In reality, this was a new experience. So, of course, was having a case worth arguing about.

Shondelle wanted to mount a defence of necessity. "J. J. had no choice," she rehearsed the argument aloud to Uhuru. "The City had more than thirty years to provide fair and reasonable compensation to the residents of Africville for the illegal and unconscionable seizure of their lands. It didn't. So J. J. Howe, a courageous young man who had experienced first-hand the impact of that failure in his own family and who saw its effect played out on the streets of his city every day, finally took matters into his own hands, not for himself but for his people, and began to redress the wrongs. He had no choice."

"Isn't that an argument for sentencing?" Uhuru countered. In fact, he wanted Shondelle to convince him otherwise. "I mean, there's no question he took the money. And there's no question the law says that's wrong. So how he used the money is irrelevant . . . except when it comes to sentencing."

"Unless we can turn it into a Morgentaler," she replied. "Everyone knew Henry Morgentaler was performing illegal abortions. But the courts couldn't get one single jury to convict him. Why? Because everyone also knew the law was wrong and that he was doing the just thing."

"Yes, but you're presupposing that we"—when had *I* become *we*, he wondered?—"will get to make this argument in front of a jury. What judge is going to allow us to claim justification?"

Shondelle had been waiting for that. "Certainly not Justice Justice," she said. "Which is why the first thing we need to do"—*we* again—"is file a motion demanding he step aside. After that first day in court, it's a slam-dunk."

Uhuru resisted; he wasn't sure why. Except perhaps that, unlike Shondelle, Uhuru couldn't buy the now conventional wisdom that Ward Justice was a racist. Since Ward Justice was one of the few white men to have experienced Africville close up, Uhuru believed, he might even be more sympathetic to their arguments . . . if indeed those were their arguments.

They agreed to disagree—for the moment. "We'll come back to this," she said.

What they decided was that Uhuru would read his father's diary looking for material, especially from the time of the expropriation, and share with Shondelle any entries that might prove useful for the civil suit. And that Uhuru would attend the next meeting of ADA to see if there were ways in which the association could support J. J.'s defence.

"Money would be nice," Uhuru said.

"Money's overrated."

"Easy for you to say, *Professor*."

She smiled. "So would you rather I took this burdensome case off your hands then?"

"No." He wasn't sure why he didn't want to do the sane thing and walk away, but he didn't. And he didn't want her to go away and leave him to handle the case alone, either. Perhaps it was because she prickled him in ways that annoyed him at the same time they invigorated him. It wasn't in a sexual way. Or was it? Could it be other than sexual if it was between a man and a woman?

"Now, I appreciate all you done for us, Mrs. Adams, we all do . . ." It was Everett Dickson. Uhuru tried to pull himself out of his reverie, concentrate on the conversation. "But the thing of it is I'm eighty-year an' three. My wife's gone. My boys is both dead. And I ain't got no grandkids. So money don't mean that much to me. What I want—all I want—is to go home to die."

There were nods and murmurs of support around the room. Uhuru had heard about this idea during the Reunion Weekend. Many former residents, especially the elderly, didn't want monetary compensation for their losses; they just wanted their land back, complete with new houses the City would build for them on the spots where their old ones had stood. Uhuru danced the idea around his head. The relocation had not turned out to be the romantic adventure he'd envisioned as a teenager. In his own life, in fact, it had marked the real end of his childhood and the beginning of his estrangement from his father and his community. But could he—would he even if he could?—turn back the clock to a time that was now as much imagined as real?

". . . so, Mr. Dickson"—how long had Shondelle been talking?—"I think, and the executive of ADA believes too, that arguing in favour of a house for a house, no matter how appealing that might be, would just be a recipe for an impasse that could drag this thing on for many more years and mean you and the others would never get redress of your legitimate grievances." She paused, looked around. "Does that answer your question, sir?"

"Indeed it does, Mrs. Adams," Everett Dickson said. "Unlike a lot of the lawyers we had here, you at least been honest with us."

There were "Amen"s and "You tell 'em, brother"s.

"Well, then, on that note, and if there are no other questions, I'd like to introduce another lawyer, another *honest* lawyer"—laughter—"who wants to ask for our help with a case he's working on. Most of you already know Mr. Melesse, and you know the case I'm referring too, so without further discussion, let me turn proceedings over to Uhuru Melesse."

The applause seemed heartfelt. And there were murmurs of assent as he laid out his plan—Shondelle's plan—to mount the Robin Hood defence. "We'll need to show two things," he explained, more confidently than he felt. "One, we must show that the City has failed over the course of the last thirty years to negotiate with us in good faith, and two, that our people suffered real harm as a result of the relocation."

Only Aunt Annie raised any objection. "I just hope you're not gonna call us down in public like the white folks, Raymond. They make it sound like all our kids got hooked on the drugs or ended up in trouble with the police and such."

"No, Aunt Annie, I have no intention of making our community look bad," Uhuru fudged. "I want to show what our community was like before and what happened after . . . the good and the bad."

Which was how the members of the Africville Descendants' Association came to agree to provide Uhuru Melesse with copies of all the affidavits Shondelle Adams had already collected, along with contact information for other former Africville residents she hadn't yet managed to reach. The motion, moved by Aunt Annie and seconded by Everett Dickson, was approved unanimously.

"Now you two," Aunt Annie looked sternly from Shondelle to Uhuru, "you be working together on this. 'Cause you know that two heads is better than one . . . and two black heads be better than a thousand white ones!" Everyone laughed. Uhuru and Shondelle exchanged glances. Uhuru couldn't tell what she was thinking, but he knew his own mind.

Ward Justice could sense the pseudo-solicitousness in the Chief Justice's earnest, I-care-about-you tone. David Fielding wanted Ward off the case, but he didn't want to have to order him off.

"It's not a problem," Fielding offered. "I can juggle the schedule and get you out of it. I'd be happy to do that. If you'd feel more comfortable, that is."

Ward smiled, didn't even nibble. He knew Fielding had read the stories in the papers. Who hadn't? He knew, too, from courthouse gossip, that the Chief Justice's secretary had ordered a transcript of the arraignment so that Fielding could study it, search for the reasons Ward should not preside at J. J. Howe's trial. Fielding, in fact, had admitted as much earlier in their conversation.

"When you just look at the words on the paper"—the Chief Justice often chose the second-person pronoun in order to distance himself from anything he was saying that might be construed as critical—"you get the sense that you may have been abrupt, perhaps even unfair, to both lawyers. But especially to Mr. Uhuru." Ward did not attempt to defend himself, or to correct the Chief Justice's use of "Uhuru" when he meant "Melesse." "And we"—now the inclusive *we*—"both know what the papers have done with that." Without, of course, ever saying out loud exactly what it was the papers had done with that.

Both local papers, as well as *The Globe and Mail* and CBC-TV's *The National*, had made the Howe arraignment their lead story. Given Melesse's declaration that he planned to raise the issue of reparations for the former residents of Africville in his client's defence, that was probably inevitable. But Ward's handling of the arraignment had added spice to the initial story and gave it legs.

The next day, the *Daily Journal* had another item quoting Calvin Johnstone, a spokesman for the Africville Descendants' Association: "Mr. Melesse may be too polite, or he may have to be careful for reasons of legal etiquette," Johnstone told *Daily Journal* reporter Moira Donovan, "but we are under no such constraints. So we can call it what it is. Racism, plain and simple. We have a racist judge in a racist legal system making racist decisions involving African Nova Scotians."

The *Tribune*, perhaps stung by its failure to follow up on the initial story, outdid itself the day after that by publishing two front-page articles, one quoting different black leaders saying much the same as Johnstone had, the other offering an interview with Dalhousie University law professor Shondelle Adams, who said the judge's outburst should be a reminder to everyone that Nova Scotia's judicial system had not changed much since the Marshall report. Donald Marshall, Jr., was a Native who'd spent eleven years in prison for a murder he didn't commit. A royal commission set up to look into the miscarriage of justice concluded that Nova Scotia had a "two-tier system of justice," with one law for the politically powerful and another for Natives, blacks and poor people. Part of the problem, the commission said, was that the process for appointing judges was corrupt and rife with political cronyism.

"Given that the judge in this case is a good-old-boy appointee from those bad old days, no one should be surprised by what happened in court," Professor Adams said.

The day after that, the *Tribune* weighed in with a thumb-sucking editorial that carefully steered clear of criticizing Ward personally—Victoria's cousin was the publisher—while obliquely noting that "Nova Scotians want justice not only to be done, but to be *seen* to be done as well."

All of which, of course, eventually made its way to the desk of the Supreme Court's Chief Justice and, even more eventually, to this awkward conversation in the Chief Justice's office.

"I'm not saying I pay attention to what the papers have to say," the Chief Justice continued, after yet another silence that had lasted too long. "I don't."

Ward knew he did. David Fielding was the first Supreme Court justice appointed under post-Marshall reforms to the judicial selection process, and he wore the fact that he'd never belonged to a political party as a badge of superiority. Since his elevation to the job of Chief Justice three years ago, he'd been praised for his stirring speeches touting the importance of judicial independence and the strides Nova Scotia had made in cleaning up its appointments process. He didn't need one of his own judges, even inadvertently, resurrecting the Marshall issue.

Ward may have been a "good-old-boy appointee," or whatever it was that professor had said, but he was proud of the judge he had become. At the time of his appointment, his legal experience admittedly had been—to be more charitable than precise—limited. But he'd worked hard, attended every conference, convention, seminar and professional workshop on offer, eventually graduating to seminar leader and even, at last year's provincial bar convention, keynote speaker on the subject of sentencing white-collar criminals.

The lawyer introducing him, a prominent criminal defence attorney, had called him "tough but fair—and I should know: he's sent some of my best-known clients to jail." Ward knew it was flattery, but he also believed it was true. He did try to be scrupulously fair, and, while he stayed within the federal sentencing guidelines, he made sure to reserve the harshest penalties for those he knew knew better—the lawyers who bilked clients, the stockbrokers who used inside information to fatten their bank accounts at the expense of others, the politicians who abused their public trust.

There was an irony in that, of course, one that was not lost on Ward. But it would take a lifetime of shrink appointments to sort it all out. And Ward didn't believe in shrinks. Sometimes, he wished he did. Whenever he thought about the unlikely twists his career had taken, which he was doing more and more often lately—his prostate worry playing with his mind?—it would come flooding back, seemingly out of nowhere, to whack him. Guilt. It would wash over him at the most inopportune times. For reasons only he understood. Like that moment during the arraignment when he'd looked down at J. J. Howe, all skin and bones and big, open eyes looking back at him, so confident, so serene, so young. Ward tried to do the math. What if . . . ? And at that moment Ward truly believed that he should not be up on high, sitting in almighty judgment on others. He should be down there, the one being sentenced, made to pay for his sin. Which was far greater than anything J. J. Howe might have done.

"But I know you've been under a lot of pressure lately," David Fielding said.

What did the Chief know? Ward wondered. That Victoria wanted a divorce? That the saw palmetto hadn't worked, that he was now peeing four times a night and that, as a result, he was more tired than he'd ever been and had developed a chest cold he couldn't shake? And, oh yes, that he couldn't stop thinking about how he'd become a judge and how much he needed to do penance before he died? Ward was sure Fielding didn't know that.

The divorce? Perhaps. Victoria and Fielding's wife were in the same book club. But he didn't think Victoria would have confided in anyone yet. She was much too private and proud for that, and besides, nothing had been settled. Had it? They'd not spoken of it, or anything else of substance, for that matter, since that night in the restaurant.

Ward looked at Fielding. The Chief Justice didn't know. He couldn't. "Pressure?" Ward said. "Not really. Nothing out of the ordinary."

"No, of course not," Fielding answered, disappointed; Ward seemed determined not to make this easy for him. "But this is a pressure-cooker job. People just don't know what it's like. The caseload. The demands. The decisions. So it's understandable, you know. We all get fed up from time to time—"

"Exactly," Ward cut him off. Fielding had given him the opening he needed. "You're absolutely right. I did have a bad day that day. But it happens, right? I'm fine now. I'll be fine."

The Chief Justice exhaled slowly. He had trapped himself. "All right then," he said slowly, looking for another way, and finding none. "You'll handle the trial. But if you change your mind, or run into any concerns, or, you know . . ."

"Yes, yes, I won't hesitate to call you," Ward said, rising from his chair to go. "But I'm sure it will be fine."

"Right then," Fielding replied uncertainly. "That's settled." He paused, not knowing how to end this conversation. "Hope everything else is okay?"

"Fine, thanks. Everything's fine." Ward was perfunctory. He needed to pee. And then he needed to call the doctor. He couldn't put it off any longer.

Moira Donovan looked again at her watch. It was ten past one. Didn't these guys know that other people have deadlines to meet, jobs to do? Fucking civil servants. She'd be late for work.

In fifteen minutes, Dr. Earl Cathcart was scheduled to take the stand at the Law Courts Building across town to try to explain the inexplicable: why a prominent, well-respected family doctor, who'd practised medicine for forty years without one single patient complaint, had gone home after work each evening for at least fifteen of those years and had his sexual way with one or the other of his twin daughters. The abuse had begun before the girls reached puberty and lasted until they left home. They were in their thirties now.

Moira had cried so uncontrollably listening to the women testify that she'd had to leave the courtroom twice. That had never happened before. Neither had she ever before experienced the blinding rage that had boiled up in her yesterday morning as she watched Cathcart blandly watching one of his daughters describe, in graphic, horrific detail, exactly what she said he'd done to her. Moira would have happily gone over to the prisoner's box, cut off his dick and shoved it up his ass . . .

Whoa! She couldn't believe she'd even *thought* such thoughts. It had to be the hormones. She'd stopped throwing up in the mornings, but now she felt as if she were living her life like an insect under a magnifying glass in the sun; everything was intensified, larger than life. Painfully so. Her anger, her sadness, her fears. She'd wake up in the middle of the night convinced the baby inside her was dead. She'd understand—*know* even—that this wasn't so. The rational part of her could label this panic as irrational, understand it as one more unpleasant side effect of her pregnancy. But that didn't make her any less frightened, or any less sad, less angry.

As a court reporter, Moira had, in fact, heard everything the daughters claimed happened to them—and worse, much worse. And she'd seen more than a few accused, even innocent men, reacting inappropriately while listening to themselves being described in monstrous ways by their accusers.

And the Cathcart case was certainly no slam-dunk. The lawyers were still arguing over whether the defence should be allowed to introduce similar fact evidence that the daughters had previously accused their parish priest of sexually molesting them. The scuttlebutt around the courtroom was that Cathcart's lawyer might even call the girls' mother to testify on her husband's behalf, perhaps later that afternoon.

Moira needed to get back. Now. She looked again at her watch. One-twenty. She couldn't wait any longer. She started to get up—

"Found him!" The woman's voice was shrill, triumphant. It intimidated Moira back into her chair. "Hiding in the stacks," she offered as she led a sheepish-looking man in a rumpled suit and unfashionably oversized horn-rimmed glasses to the table where Moira was seated. "Whenever David goes missing, that's usually the first place we go to look. But he was supposed to be in his office today doing his monthly reports. Weren't you, David?"

David, who looked as if he was used to being talked to—and about—in such patronizing ways, gave no sign the woman's tone irked him. It irked Moira.

"Anyway," the woman said, turning back to Moira without waiting for David's response, "David's the man to see. He knows everything there is to know about our audio collections. Don't you, David?"

David grunted, whether in acquiescence or irritation Moira couldn't tell.

"I'll leave you two to it, then," the woman said. "And don't forget those reports, David. I need them by the end of the day."

David grunted again. But when he looked up at Moira, he smiled. This woman had come to the Archives to look for something and he was, as always, eager to help. He looked like a ferret, Moira thought. Bits of green—lettuce from lunch?—flecked his top teeth.

"Shelly says you're interested in the Lambie collection?" he began.

"Uh, yes. But just one item, really." Moira wasn't sure why she was even bothering. She didn't have time for this and, besides, what difference did it make if Ward Justice made some racist joke a hundred years ago?

"Oh, that's too bad." The archivist looked deflated. "Just one item, eh? Well, here's the problem then, Miss . . . ?"

"Donovan. But please, Moira is fine."

"Miss . . . Moira, then. Well, Moira, here's the problem. Mr. Lambie was a wonderful collector and, of course, it was generous of him—most generous—to give his tapes to the Archives. I only wish others cared as much about our history. But that's the problem, you see. Some people don't care in the way Mr. Lambie cared. And some of those people who don't care, unfortunately, are the politicians downtown. They've been cutting our budget, and cutting our budget, and then cutting our budget again. As if history didn't count for anything." He paused to let that sink in. "That means we're years behind in cataloguing donations. It's got so bad the director has said we can't accept any more until we clear up the backlog. But we can't clear up the backlog because we don't have the people or the time. We—" He stopped suddenly, aware he was off topic. Moira, who'd gotten caught up in his emotional outburst, had already made a mental note to tell the Sunday Editor about Astor. It might make a good human interest piece.

"I'm sorry, Miss . . . Moira. I get carried away sometimes. But it is an important issue. Maybe you'll write to your MLA about—there I go, off track again. Bad habit. Anyway, the tragedy of the Lambie collection is that Mr. Lambie never catalogued his tapes. And there are thousands of them. One of the summer students counted ten thousand before he had to go back to school. But we haven't had the funds to hire anyone to count the rest, let alone listen."

So that's it then, Moira thought. *Well, at least I tried.*

"But perhaps . . ." David saw disappointment in her face, disappointment which might actually have been relief. "I have listened to a few of the tapes," he continued helpfully. "Perhaps if I knew what you were looking for . . ."

What was she looking for? "Ah, it would be a tape from the mid-seventies. Nineteen seventy-four, or perhaps -five, maybe even seventy-six." She paused then, unsure what to say next.

"Was it of some specific event?"

"Yes. A press gallery dinner."

"Oh, dear, there was nothing like that on the tapes I listened to . . ."

"Oh, that's okay."

"Why were you interested in those dinners anyway?"

"Well," Moira improvised quickly, "my father was a reporter back then and, well, you know, his birthday's coming up and I was just trying to find him something different as a present. I know he enjoyed that time of his life."

David smiled. "What a lovely idea, Miss, er, Moira. I wish I could help."

"Oh, no, that's—"

"Would a tape from any of the years you mentioned work, or—?"

"No, not really. There was an after-dinner speaker he keeps talking about. A man named Ward Justice. He was a Cabinet minister back then. Now he's a—"

"Oh, the Judge." David Astor beamed. "It just so happens," he said, leaning toward her and speaking in a conspiratorial whisper, "I've been working on a project myself involving the Judge."

As he leaned forward, Moira recoiled instinctively. His hot breath smelled of onion, garlic and undigested food. "That's very interesting, uh, David, and I'd love to hear more, but I'm late for work." She stood up and backed away from him, glancing furtively at her watch. One thirty-five. She really was late. And had nothing to show for her wasted lunch hour.

"Why don't you leave me your card?" David said. "That way, if I happen to find what you're looking for, I could give you a call."

She fumbled in her purse for a card, handed it to him. "Oh, a reporter," David said, smiling again. Moira turned away. "I guess I should have been more careful about what I said."

Moira didn't reply. Coming here had been a dumb idea. The only thing she'd really learned was that she wasn't completely past the nausea stage yet.

The doctor sat opposite Ward Justice in a white plastic chair in the middle of her small, windowless examining room, speed-reading the contents of the slim file the nurse had left for her. The file represented

Ward Justice's entire adult medical history: a pesky flu here, a wart removed there, an allergic reaction to penicillin, a few annoying sinus infections that had led to an operation to straighten a deviated septum and, six years ago, Dr. Wilson's final cryptic notation that Ward had developed adult onset asthma. Ironically, Ward had been diagnosed soon after he'd given up smoking and taken up running (after which he gave up running, but never resumed the smoking). The final page of his file, which the doctor was examining now, contained the results of a complete physical—his first and last—which indicated that, in early 1976 at least, Ward Justice was a healthy human specimen.

Ward sat across from Dr. Thomas now, willing himself not to think about what she would tell him. As the doctor read, his eyes darted around the room. The examining room was a sterile study in black and white that reminded Ward of a *Psychology Today* poster popular when he was in university. He tried to remember the details. There was a black man—or was it a black boy? He would be how old now? Stop it. Maybe a girl . . . dressed all in white and sitting in a white room full of white furnishings.

This room was like that room. The walls were plain white, with the exception of a single, black-on-white vision chart tacked up, with black pushpins, on the wall to the right of where Ward was sitting. In one corner, there was a white-enamelled scale with a black weight-balance mechanism and a folding swing arm the doctor used to determine her patients' heights. To his left stood a white laminate cupboard with melamine countertop, on which sat a white cardboard box filled with packages of disposable plastic gloves. Ward's eyes skipped past those. Along the opposite wall, just behind the doctor, he could see the metallic white examining table with its black leather mattress cover, partially covered by a white disposable paper sheet. In a few minutes he would be bent across that table, his pants and underpants at his ankles . . .

Dr. Thomas herself was also a study in black and white. And bronze. And red. She was wearing a white lab coat over black slacks and a plain black sweater. Her hair was black and sleek and pulled back in a bun. Even her ankle boots were black. All of which only served to accentuate the soft, brown-sugar hue of her hands and face. And the incongruously bold red of her lipstick.

She wasn't beautiful so much as striking. Ward was struck by what he saw as her beauty. There was a time when he might have noticed only her faults—the wisps of black facial hair that made her appear to have sideburns, the slick oiliness of the skin around her nose, the slight plumpness around her middle—but those days were long past. He regretted now that, when he was still a young man and somewhat attractive himself, he had been so selective about what constituted beauty. These days, he could see splendour in almost any female form—old, young, plump, skinny, black, white, bronze—but this admiration was no longer reciprocated. He could understand why. He had become fat and grey and wrinkled, an old man at fifty-three. Women also seemed more discerning now. Was that the ultimate fruit of women's liberation? For women to be able to judge men as men had always judged women?

Ward had begun to think about such questions in the two months since Victoria had told him she wanted a divorce. He couldn't imagine how he would ever meet another woman. Kathleen, his secretary—did he even know her last name?—was happily married (was that possible?) with two young children. She kept a framed Sears Family Portrait Studio photo of her smiling husband—Tim was his name; she mentioned that often enough—and the boys on top of her desk so they would face her while she worked. She would not have been a good candidate to replace Victoria even if Ward were interested. Which he wasn't. He had enough trouble thinking of things to say to her at work; he couldn't imagine a conversation over dinner or, especially, in bed. Not that she would be interested.

After Kathleen, there was . . . well, there was no one.

Dr. Thomas? He'd only met her once before today, during a perfunctory visit a year ago to renew his prescriptions for asthma medications. He remembered being surprised at the time to discover she was Indian. When he'd initially received Doc Wilson's letter announcing his retirement and welcoming his successor, "Dr. Elizabeth Thomas, a native of Uganda," Ward had assumed she would have the blue-black skin of an Idi Amin. And was strangely disappointed to discover she did not.

All the new doctors seemed to be immigrants from Asia or India; a black doctor from Africa might at least have spiced up that mix, even become a role model for local black children. Ward had begun to fret about the lack of positive black figures. Perhaps his perspective was just skewed by his job; the only black faces he saw were the ones parading before him charged with this or that crime, usually selling drugs or peddling girls for the purposes of prostitution. None seemed remorseful, or even concerned they'd been caught. They'd swagger into court in their oversized painter pants, their chests festooned with gold chains, smirking to friends in the gallery while the Crown and defence presented their let's-get-this-over-with plea agreements and joint sentencing recommendations that, most often, didn't involve more than few months' real jail time, if any at all. No wonder the drug dealers and pimps returned to their neighbourhoods as heroes, role models for the next generation.

Ward could have done his part to change that, of course, could have wiped the smiles off their faces and shaken the lawyers out of their going-through-the-motions stupor. But he didn't. It was simpler—and safer—to go along with whatever the defence and Crown had worked out in advance, so long as it didn't stray too far from the established sentencing guidelines. But was his reluctance as simple as that? The guilt again? Or was that giving himself too much credit for conscience? Maybe Ward was just content to go along to get along.

Is that also what had happened to Ray Carter? Ray could have been that role model. He was not only a black lawyer, he was from the local community. From Africville, for God's sake. And smart, smarter than Ward. Of course he'd been a shit-disturber back in the day. Back in the day when Ward was a politician. But then Ray had abandoned that role, as suddenly and completely as Ward had given up politics. He'd gone to law school, and the next thing Ward knew, Ray was going through the motions like all the rest. Ward wanted to ask him what had happened, but he was afraid of what he might hear. In court, Ray never gave the slightest hint they'd been friends. Neither, of course, did Ward.

He wondered what Ray—Ward's mind still tripped awkwardly over Uhuru Melesse—thought about what had happened in court the day of the arraignment. He'd been half expecting a defence motion to ask him to recuse himself from presiding at the trial. But it hadn't come. At least not yet. He wasn't sure why. Neither was Ward certain why he'd insisted to the Chief Justice that he wanted to hear the case.

Perhaps J. J. Howe would become the new role model for local black children. They could do worse, Ward thought. He had tried not to read the stories about the case in the newspapers, or listen to the gossip in the courthouse. His job was to interpret the law, not be swayed by the circumstances of a particular human situation. But this particular human situation was particularly compelling. Ward knew that from the few brief snatches of the TV reports he'd caught before quickly switching channels. And then there was last weekend's *Globe and Mail* front page: a large photo of the young man, staring hard at the camera as he was being led away by sheriff's deputies. "Is this the face of the new Robin Hood?" the caption read, promoting a feature in the paper's Focus section on "the issue of reparations and the criminal case that has become the talk of Canada's legal community." Would Ray really try to argue that the kid was justified in taking the money? It was risky. If Ward ruled against that defence—which he couldn't imagine not doing—Ray's client would have as much as admitted his guilt. Better to plead guilty and then use his client's circumstances to argue for a reduced sentence. Maybe, in the end, that's what Ray had in mind. Stir things up, and then . . . Perhaps that's why Ray hadn't tried to get him removed from the case. Perhaps he figured Ward owed him one. Perhaps—

"So." Dr. Thomas closed the file folder and looked up at Ward. "What brings you here today, Mr. Justice?"

"Well . . ." He coughed. He did that more often now, whenever he was nervous. "Nothing serious. It's just that, I guess, I'm getting a little older and, well, you know, you read the stories, see the ads, and you start to worry, think maybe you should get yourself checked out."

"Is there anything in particular you're concerned about?"

"No—well, yes, I suppose there is. I've been noticing that I sometimes have to go to the bathroom more often these days."

"To pee?"

"Yes."

She made a note on the file. "Just at night?"

"Yes . . . Well, no. Sometimes in the day, too."

"How often at night?"

"Three, maybe four times."

"After you finish, does it feel like you've completely voided your bladder?"

And so it went. Matter-of-fact. Question, answer, question, answer. It became easier not to think of her as a stranger, or even a woman.

"Any erectile difficulties?"

"No." Too quick. Would he even know if he had erectile difficulties? He didn't want to get into that. She knew enough already.

"Any other problems? Tiredness? Trouble sleeping?"

"No . . . Well, you know, sometimes when I get up to go to the bathroom, I'll have trouble falling back to sleep and I'll be tired the next day, but that's about it." It wasn't really *about it.* In the past few months, he'd begun feeling exhausted and was falling asleep with alarming regularity while reading case files in his office; he'd even, occasionally, drifted off in the courtroom in the middle of important testimony. He put it down to overwork; the court dockets were overcrowded and backlogged and he, like the rest of the judges, was struggling to keep up. But he was certain that had nothing to do with the state of his health . . . or his prostate.

"I noticed you have quite a persistent cough." Did he? He hadn't noticed. "Do you smoke?"

"Gave it up ten years ago, longer probably."

"Good for you. How long have you had that cough?"

"Uh, I didn't really even notice until you mentioned it. Just nervous, I guess. Sometimes I cough when I'm nervous."

She smiled at him. "There's no need to be nervous of me, Mr. Justice. I won't bite, I promise. Is it a productive cough?"

Productive? "Sometimes." Should he tell her about the green gobs he'd been coughing up in the morning. "A little sputum now and then."

"What colour?"

"Greenish, I guess. I try not to examine it too carefully." He tried to smile, but she was already looking back down at her notes.

"It's been a long time since you've had any sort of thorough checkup, Mr. Justice, so I think I'm going to send you for some tests. An EKG, blood tests, routine stuff, you know, check your thyroid and cholesterol, things like that, mostly just to give us a baseline for the future. One of the tests will be to determine your PSA levels. It's one of the two tests we use to check on the state of your prostate. The other test is the one I'm guessing you're probably nervous about."

She smiled. He smiled.

"It's not nearly as bad as you imagine, Mr. Justice. A little discomfort, that's all. And then it'll be done. Perhaps we should do that now and get it over with so you'll be nice and relaxed when we check your heart rate and blood pressure. That sound reasonable?"

"Yes." No.

6

1970

"Mr. Former Premier, meet Mr. Future Premier." Jack Eagleson laughed.

After three years, Ward had not only got used to Jack's Jack-laugh but also to hearing Jack introduce him as Nova Scotia's future premier. Ward had finally come to understand this was just Jack's way of making conversation, and that Ward was far from the first—and certainly would not be the last—bright young man Jack would single out in this way. It was almost as if Jack Eagleson was hedging his bets; if one of his protegés ever became premier, he could proclaim his prescience.

"Gerry Cullingham," the man said, extending his hand. He was tall, slim, grey-haired, with an unnaturally ruddy complexion that could have been the result of too many hours at the golf course or too much wine at that afternoon's garden party, maybe both. As he stood by the iron gate leading into the huge backyard, shaking Ward's hand, he stage-whispered in his ear: "You'd best watch yourself with this bugger. He's the reason I'm now Mr. Former Premier."

"Touché," Jack answered. "But you should tell our young man here that I'm also the reason you were ever the premier in the first place."

"Touché to you, too."

Ward tried to piece together what he remembered of The Recent Political History of Nova Scotia, as told by Jack Eagleson.

Gerry Cullingham was the wayward son of James Cullingham, founding partner of McArtney, Eagleson, Cullingham & O'Sullivan. After graduating from law school with a well-earned reputation as a ladies' man and an equally well-earned C average, Gerry was brought into the firm by the old man, who asked Jack to be Gerry's mentor. "If anyone can save him, you'd be the man," the senior Cullingham had told Eagleson. Or at least that's what Jack had told Ward.

Jack quickly understood that, while Gerry had no understanding or appreciation of the finer points of law, he was a first-rate public speaker who could be taught to follow Jack's script. In 1952, Gerry, with Jack pulling the strings, won the Liberal nomination in Halifax South. Jack then ran his first—and only—successful election campaign. Cullingham was never "the shiniest apple in the barrel," as Jack put it, but he was, with Jack and his father twisting arms and calling in favours, named a junior Cabinet minister anyway.

In 1955, after legendary Liberal premier Andrew Hamilton died suddenly of a heart attack, Cullingham became everyone's surprise second choice to succeed him. Jack Eagleson had stage-managed that, too, fomenting a nasty feud between the two front-runners: William Davies, the veteran provincial Highways minister, a Haligonian and a Roman Catholic (not necessarily in that order), and Donald Farrell, a former federal MP who happened to be a Protestant from Cape Breton. "It was easy," Jack bragged to Ward. "I told Davies's people that if Farrell became premier, he was going to sic the Mounties on the church bingos and put the priests behind bars. And I convinced Farrell's people Davies was going to renege on Hamilton's promise to build the causeway to Cape Breton from the mainland. By the convention, they hated each other so much Gerry was the only one both sides could stomach."

Cullingham's own brief moment in the sun lasted less than a year. "When the fat lady sings, you just gotta dance," was how Jack cryptically explained the party's defeat in the next general election. In Jack's version of events, he bore no personal responsibility for the Conservative landslide that ended nearly two unbroken decades of Liberal rule and cost Gerry Cullingham his seat in the Legislature.

Ward didn't contradict his mentor, but he knew now that there were other, less flattering interpretations of Cullingham's defeat. In "The Politics of Nova Scotia: 1867 to Now," a senior history seminar he'd taken last year, the professor, once a Liberal Cabinet minister himself, had blamed Jack. "As campaign manager, Mr. Eagleson tried to control the whole campaign from provincial headquarters in Halifax," he told the class. "That upset the good folks in the local constituencies, who figured they knew a thing or two about running election campaigns. Most of them decided to sit out the election. With predictable results."

Not that Gerry Cullingham ever complained about his fate. He'd managed to be premier long enough to make it the centrepiece of his resumé for the rest of his life, and for his father to die a happy man. The day after his son was sworn in as premier, James Cullingham had a massive heart attack. Since his wife had died a few years earlier, Gerry, his only child, inherited everything: the mansion on Young Avenue where Jack and Ward had come for this afternoon's garden party, the country estate near Chester, a thirty-six-foot, hand-crafted wooden schooner, memberships in the Royal Nova Scotia Yacht Squadron, the Chester Yacht Club, the Ashburn Golf and Country Club, the Chester Golf Club and, of course, the Halifax Club. He also inherited his father's carefully managed portfolio of stocks and bonds, which his father had insisted—wisely—continue to be controlled by his executor, Jack Eagleson.

Perhaps because of that, Gerry Cullingham seemed to take his electoral defeat as a kind of liberation and had happily spent the years since drinking, sailing, travelling and, of course, hosting occasional fundraising functions like this one, basking in his role as Mr. Former Premier.

Ward had never been to an event like this before. He couldn't help but marvel at the Cullinghams' huge, treed backyard, now crawling with dozens of loud, laughing downtown lawyers and business types, many of whom he recognized from having seen their photos in the *Tribune.* Tanned ladies in colourful summer frocks and all manner of straw hats accompanied the men. Ward accompanied

Jack. Uniformed black waiters circulated among the guests, bearing trays of wine and canapés. In one corner of the yard near the garden, there was a portable bar where the men lined up for cocktails.

Gerry and his wife, Irena, had organized the first annual Cullingham Gala in 1957, after his electoral defeat. Ever since, it had served as a kind of consolation prize for Liberal socialites who'd been unceremoniously dropped from the guest list of the annual Lieutenant-Governor's Garden Party after the new Tory administration got control of the invites.

The Liberals had now frittered away fourteen years trying to regain control of the garden party guest list and, coincidentally—at least for some in the party establishment—the government.

Many Liberals, like Ward's political science professor, blamed Jack Eagleson not only for the party's initial defeat in 1956 but also for its continued inability to oust the now entrenched Tories. But while they might grumble about him over their Scotch and sodas at the Halifax Club, none was brave, or foolish, enough to challenge Jack for the party presidency or, more important, his self-appointed role as its Provincial Campaign Co-ordinator.

That's because Jack Eagleson had sole control of the Winners' Club, the secret trust fund his father had created. Jeffrey Eagleson, a lawyer, chartered accountant and secretary-treasurer of the provincial Liberal Association, had quietly set up the fund after Andrew Hamilton's Liberals first came to power in the early thirties. During the next twenty years, Jeffrey Eagleson had funnelled all manner of political bribes, payoffs and kickbacks into the ever-expanding fund.

No one knew how much he collected but everyone knew it was a lot. Liquor companies that wanted to do business in the province, for example, had to pay five cents per bottle to the Winners' Club for the privilege of having their brands listed by the provincial liquor commission, which was the only way they could legally peddle their booze. That alone must have added up to millions of dollars' worth of kickbacks. But there were other sources, too. Anyone who wanted to win a highway paving contract, or rent office space to a government department, or sell staples to some secretary in some rural government outpost knew that their bid would not even be considered if they hadn't first paid a courtesy call on Jeffrey Eagleson, cheque book in hand.

Cash was acceptable if the donors—usually Upper Canadian business executives unaccustomed to the local ways—were nervous about paper trails. Not that there wasn't one. Jeffrey Eagleson kept meticulous records of every donation, partly to protect himself from potential allegations he'd siphoned off any of the money for his own use and partly because it gave him power. Though he never threatened anyone explicitly, Jeffrey Eagleson liked to talk about his obsession with keeping records of everything he did. Everyone got the message.

Eagleson was just as careful to detail every expenditure he ever made from the fund, including not only those for running election campaigns but also the occasional, instantly-forgiven-but-not-quite-forgotten loan to a Cabinet minister to cover a gambling debt, or a mistress's abortion, or an annual Caribbean vacation with the missus, or the mistress. Jeffrey Eagleson was just as careful to document the weekly cash payments he made to each Liberal MLA when the House was in session, and even itemized the expenses for the semi-annual Members' Appreciation Nights, when Eagleson would book the entire top floor of the Nova Scotian Hotel and hire a dozen of Monique's best girls to provide the politicians with all manner of sexual services all night long.

Because the trust fund had been created and then filled with what some uncharitable authorities might regard as illegal political kickbacks, the Winners' Club was never officially on the books as a Liberal Party asset. Which gave Jeffrey Eagleson, its sole trustee, even more power and influence. Which may explain why his son Jack, who'd run only one previous local campaign—Gerry Cullingham's—was chosen to quarterback the party's disastrous provincial election campaign in 1956. And which would also certainly explain why Jack, who succeeded his father as Winners' sole trustee after Jeffrey Eagleson died in 1964, was still masterminding strategy for the party's campaigns today, despite having never emerged victorious from a single one.

But now, with another election in the wind, Jack Eagleson's unbroken string of four straight electoral defeats seemed set to be broken. It wasn't that the party's current leader, Seamus O'Sullivan, was that much better or brighter than his predecessors, or that Jack himself had improved as a political tactician. It was that the Tories, as all governments eventually do, were imploding.

The sainted Stanfield had left—after promising he wouldn't. His successor, by unfair comparison, was a mere mortal. In the election three years ago, the Liberals had picked up five more seats, but not enough to take power.

But then the scandals, the kind that plague every government too long in office, came home to roost in newspaper headlines. Nova Scotia voters, Jack explained optimistically to Ward, were tired enough of the Tory gang to give the Liberal gang—whose own sins they'd by now finally forgotten if not forgiven—another turn at the trough.

"You just have to be there when the love affair ends," as Jack had put it one night a few months ago. He and Ward were examining the results of the latest secret public opinion poll Jack had commissioned. It showed the Liberals ahead of the Tories in support among decided voters for the first time.

Officially, Ward worked as an office assistant at McArtney, Eagleson—part time during university terms and full time in the summers. Unofficially, he did whatever Jack Eagleson told him to do, which mostly involved picking up Winners' Club donations from local companies that wanted to position themselves for contracts after the next election (in case the Liberals really did win) and delivering Winners' Club cash to worthy recipients. And listening to Jack talk, of course. That was part of Ward's job, too.

Though he was theoretically employed by the law firm and had a desk near the entrance to Jack's office, Ward's weekly paycheque came out of the Winners' Club account, which is how he came to discover it existed. It took him longer to understand its real purpose. "More grease for the political machinery," Jack would say with his room-filling laugh whenever Ward brought him an envelope from a local business favour-seeker. "More mother's milk for the democratic process," he would say when he handed Ward an envelope to deliver to some local constituency president.

Truth be told, the job bored Ward. But it came with a boat of a Chevy Caprice that Ward could use as his own whenever he wasn't acting as Jack's messenger boy or chauffeur. And there was the promise of more interesting assignments to come. Jack told him he would run O'Sullivan's constituency office during the upcoming election campaign.

The problem was that everyone was expecting the Premier to call the election in the fall, which was when Ward was supposed to start law school. "Don't worry, the Dean and I are old friends," Jack reassured him. "He'll understand." Ward wasn't so sure. He'd heard first-year law was demanding. "You'll do just fine," Jack insisted. "Trust me. If Gerry Cullingham can get through law school, anyone can."

Before today, Gerry Cullingham had been nothing more than the name on the door of a never-used corner office next to Jack's and the butt of countless Jack Eagleson jokes, asides, disparaging references and snide remarks, most of which revolved around Cullingham's stupidity. Gerry Cullingham, Ward had been surprised to discover this afternoon, didn't seem stupid. Merely congenial. And perhaps a little drunk.

"Jack tells me you're off to law school," Cullingham said. "Good on you, son. Who knows? Maybe you'll end up actually *practising* law. We could use a lawyer in the firm!" He laughed at his own joke. Ward laughed, too.

"Oh, our Ward's way too smart to end up practising law," Jack said, adding as he looked meaningfully at Cullingham: "He's just like you." They both laughed. Ward did too, but mostly out of politeness. Given Jack's often expressed views on Cullingham's intelligence, he wasn't sure if he shouldn't read more into the remark. With Jack, you never knew.

"Well," Cullingham said, looking beyond them, preparing his exit strategy, "let's see if we can't get you boys a drink." He raised his right arm into the air, caught the attention of the light-skinned coloured man who appeared to be in charge of the other waiters, brought his arm back down to his mouth, mimicked drinking out of an air glass and then pointed in the direction of Jack and Ward. The head waiter acknowledged his request with his own response-nod and, with a subtle turn of his head and a lifted eyebrow, signalled to a waiter bearing a silver tray filled with glasses of white wine above his shoulder, who then navigated his way through the crowd across the lawn toward them.

Satisfied his guests had been taken care of, Cullingham began to edge away from them. "Now gentlemen, if you'll exc—ah, if it isn't the Princess herself come to join us." There was affection, Ward thought, but perhaps a hint of rebuke, too, in his tone. Ward turned to follow Cullingham's eyes.

"Jack, you know my daughter Victoria."

"My goodness, she's grown since the last time I last saw her," Jack said, looking at the young woman but still talking to her father. "But that was a long time ago. She's blossomed into quite a beautiful young woman."

She was beautiful, Ward agreed, trying not to stare. During his travels with Jack, he rarely ever encountered women, and almost never young women, at least not young women who had not been paid for from Winners' Club funds.

Ward reconsidered. This girl was not beautiful in the look-at-me way some of those bought-and-paid-for women were. In fact, quite the opposite. She was beautiful because she seemed so casually indifferent to her good looks. Even if that casual indifference was, as he suspected, deliberate. Like her dirty-blond, pigtailed hair, at once unfussy and calculated. She wore no makeup, but she didn't need any. When she smiled, as she did now, dimples traced parentheses around full, rosy, kissable lips. Those lips framed orthodontia-straightened white teeth that seemed somehow even whiter against her freckled summer skin. Ward guessed she spent her summer days on the tennis courts or by the pool. Today, she was wearing a short, strapless, floral-patterned dress, and Ward couldn't help but notice the pale outline her bathing suit top had left on her shoulders and the tops of her breasts just above the elasticized top of her sundress. He felt a prick-stirring in his pants, and quickly looked down from her chest, which only made matters worse. Her legs were tanned and shapely and her feet were bare. He gulped down his drink.

"Beautiful, yes," Gerry Cullingham replied with a shake of his head, "but headstrong, too." He appraised his daughter. "I'm surprised you decided to grace us with your presence this afternoon, dear." Then he smiled. "But delighted, of course, delighted."

She looked at Ward, rolled her eyes confidentially as if to say: *Parents, what can you do?*

"Victoria, this is, ah . . ." her father began, forgetting his name already. Perhaps that was why he was Mr. Former Premier.

"Ward," Jack rescued him. "Ward Justice. Miss Vicky Cullingham, the beautiful daughter of the Former Premier of Nova Scotia, meet Mr. Ward Justice, the Future Premier of Nova Scotia."

Vicky looked less than impressed. As Ward and Victoria nodded at each other in acknowledgement, Jack turned back to her father. "I see Seamus has arrived. Why don't the three of us get together and figure out some dates when you two can campaign together?" He turned to Ward, winked. "I'm sure you two can amuse yourselves for a while."

Ward blushed. Vicky didn't seem to notice. Or at least pretended not to.

"So you're Jack's latest 'Future Premier,'" she said when they'd left. "Don't take it too seriously."

"I don't."

"Had the tour?"

What? "No, I guess not . . ."

"Well, we'd better fix that then. Follow me, Future Premier . . . what was your name again?"

He said it, but he wasn't sure she heard. She was already walking toward the house. He followed, trying not to stare at her ass. He failed. She walked with the kind of loose-limbed grace that invited staring. Stopping a passing waiter, she took Ward's now-empty glass, put it on the tray and selected two more. She handed them both to Ward. "Two for you . . . and two for me," she said, taking another two from the tray and continuing on toward the house.

"This is an early Andrew Cobb," she called over her shoulder.

"A what?"

"Ah, I can see you're not from here."

Ward bristled. She reminded him of those south-end girls from high school who had a way of employing their sophistication to make him feel dumb. "I *am* from here. Just not *here* here," he said, more defensively than he'd intended.

She affected not to notice. "Andrew Cobb was the famous architect who designed this place for my grandfather. My father is very proud of that, so he always makes it a point of dropping his name whenever he can. Guess I picked that up from him. Anyway, it was built in the early twenties just after Cobb got back from Paris. Ever been to Paris, Mr. Future Premier?"

"No."

"Don't bother. It's smelly and disgusting."

Meaning, Ward thought to himself, *I've been there and you haven't.* He wished she weren't so attractive. He wished he weren't so attracted.

"Granddad liked to entertain, so the rooms downstairs are all oversized—it's a very open concept," she called over her shoulder as she led him past the deck and into a kitchen that looked as though it could have served a good-sized restaurant. Waiters bustled in and out refilling their trays with wine or with the canapés that a uniformed chef was busy preparing at one corner counter.

She pushed through the swinging kitchen door and into a huge ballroom that took up one entire side of the house. Ward tried to picture his parents' bungalow; the whole of it could have fit into that one room, with space to spare.

"The Queen's Ballroom," Vicky announced with a mock flourish. "Granddad named it that after the Queen and the Prince came here for a reception during their Royal Tour in '53. I don't remember. I was only two." She was younger than Ward by two years. He liked that. "That's why we have that godawful portrait of her on the wall."

Ward looked at it. It reminded him of the picture of the Queen in her robes and tiara that decorated the front of every school classroom he'd ever been in, except this one was bigger and was clearly an oil painting instead of just a photograph. The room matched the painting: austere, forbidding. Dark mahogany wainscotting and trim surrounded the echoey hall, which was empty except for a piano in one corner. The walls above the wainscotting were a dingy cream colour. The high white ceiling was bordered with delicate gold mouldings and festooned with ornate chandeliers. Even the large bay windows at either end couldn't lighten the mood; they were mostly covered by thick, red velvet curtains that kept the sun at bay.

"I hate this room," she said suddenly. "Let's go."

She led him into a large centre hall with a wide curving staircase. She opened a door opposite the ballroom. A musty smell escaped. "Granddad's library," she said, not entering. "Daddy never uses it." Ward caught a glimpse of a far wall covered floor to ceiling with books. Vicky pulled the door shut. "I get bored quickly," she said. "Down the hall is the dining room and off that, the den. TV, stereo, the usual. Bunch of bedrooms on the second and third floors. We'll skip those." Ward was vaguely disappointed. He wanted to see her bedroom. "But I will show you my favourite place in the whole house. Come on, Mr. Future Premier." She ran up two flights of stairs. Ward followed, trying not to spill his wine on the thick carpet. They went down a long hallway to a bright, airy sunroom with floor-to-ceiling windows that looked out on the milling crowds below. "Over here." She led him to a corner of the room, where he noticed a wrought-iron circular staircase that had been painted white to blend in with the walls. "Follow me," she instructed as she began her ascent. And he did. But far enough behind her so he was able to drink in the picture of those long brown legs that disappeared into a tantalizing glimpse of white panties. He froze the sight in his mind for future reference as she pushed open a trap door in the ceiling. Light streamed in, temporarily blinding him for the sins of his mind.

"So," she said when he emerged onto the rooftop balcony, "the pièce de résistance. Like it?"

"Wow!" he said. And meant it. The wooden balcony, which measured about twelve-by-twelve with benches built into the railing on all sides, offered a magnificent, above-the-treetops view in every direction: the harbour to the east, Point Pleasant Park to the south and the broad, tree-lined residential streets of the south end to the north and west.

"What a great widow's walk," he said.

"What?" Now it was her turn not to know something. Ward liked that.

"A widow's walk. That's what they'd call it back where I come from. They built them on the roofs of sea captains' houses, supposedly so the captain's wife could go up there and watch for her husband's ship to return from sea." Ward tried to sound nonchalant in his wisdom, but the truth was that the only widow's walk in Eisners Head was on top of J. F. B. Eisner's mansion. Needless to say, Ward had never seen the view from there.

"So why do they call it a widow's walk?"

"Because so many of the ships sank." Ward wasn't certain this was the correct etymology but he said it with an easy confidence designed to impress. He hoped she might imagine him as the son of a swashbuckling sea captain who'd been swept overboard in a gale, rather than the son of a lowly deckhand who'd been blacklisted from the fishing industry for leading an illegal strike.

"So if you're from here, but not from *here* here, where are you from then?"

"Eisners Head."

She looked puzzled.

"Little fishing village. In the middle of the middle of nowhere. Grew up there." The wine was beginning to work its magic on him.

"Were you a fisherman?" Suddenly, she looked interested.

"Fisherman's son." It had been a long time since he'd volunteered that fact. The pride he'd once felt in his father, the fisherman who'd stood up to a bullying fish company owner, had soured into embarrassment for an embittered old man who cleaned washrooms for a living, and lived to see his son make something of himself.

Desmond Justice had become impossible to satisfy. Though he'd never been to university, or even high school, his father expected Ward to bring home nothing but top marks. A "B" wasn't good enough. "You want to end up like me?" he'd shout. "You gotta work, you gotta be somebody, somebody better than your old man." But Desmond seemed equally dismissive of his son's successes. In his freshman year, Ward had been invited to pledge at Phi Delt, a top fraternity, where Jack Eagleson had been a brother. "Rich boy shit," his father had said. Ward had twice been elected an Arts representative on the Student Council and was planning, with Jack's encouragement, to run for president after his first year at law school. "Sandbox stuff," his father had said, with a wave of his hand. When Ward told his father he'd been accepted into law school, he'd expected him to at least be proud. "Lawyers," his father had replied, spitting out the word likc a swallow of battery acid. "What do you want to be one of those bastards for anyway?" There was no pleasing his father.

Which was another reason Ward was looking forward to moving into his own apartment in September. That and the fact he'd finally have a place he could take girls. Maybe even this one.

"So how'd you end up in Halifax?"

It must have been the wine for her, too. Whatever it was, Vicky Cullingham seemed genuinely interested in Ward's story, and the more he told her about his father, and Junior Eisner, and the strike, and the blacklisting, the more he felt forgotten filial pride bubbling back up from the depths of the black ocean of his subconscious.

"So that's my story," he said, when he felt he'd finally exhausted her tolerance for his tale of woe. "What about yours?"

She laughed. "*B-o-r-i-n-g!*" But it wasn't. Perhaps because her life story was so foreign to anything he'd experienced or could imagine, he listened with the same rapt attention she'd offered him.

She'd spent most of her childhood shuttling from boarding school to boarding school because her mother—a forbidding woman who'd met her father in Paris after the war—decided, after a term or two, that each new school wasn't up to her own exacting educational standards. There was also the reality, Vicky confided, that she also wasn't meeting their too-lax educational standards.

She'd got accepted at Dalhousie University two years ago because her father was on the board of governors. But that wasn't enough to keep her there. She'd flunked every single course her first year, largely because she hadn't attended one class since October. She'd spent the next year—last year—in happy exile in Europe. "I smoked a ton of dope," she boasted, "screwed a Greek poet ten years older than me and painted all sorts of pictures of nothing in particular." A Greek poet? Still around? "And now I'm back. I'm going to NSCAD in September."

"Nascad?"

"Nova Scotia College of Art and Design. Used to be called just the Art College, you remember, the place where Anna Leonowens taught? Anna and the King of Siam? The movie? Yul Brynner?" He didn't have a clue. The wine had him now. She could see that. "Oh, never mind. Anyway, it's all changed. They've got a new president and he's bringing in all his conceptual artist buddies from New York. Everybody's stoned all the time. It's going to be fun." She'd lost him totally now.

She reached over, grabbed hold of his tie and pulled him toward her. She kissed him full on the mouth. Just like that. "Why don't you take off that stupid tie?" she said as she released him. "You're making me hot." He thought he understood. "No, dummy," she said when she saw the look on his face. "Not that kind of hot. Warm hot. Temperature hot. Uncomfortable, stuffy hot. You need to relax." Ward took off his tie. "Better," she said. "Wanna smoke a joint?"

"Sure." Did he? He'd smoked up. At parties, mostly. But it made him nervous every time. What would getting caught mean to his political ambitions? He now *had* political ambitions. Ward wanted to be premier some day. Or at least he thought he did. Being arrested for smoking marijuana would not look good on a campaign poster. He wasn't quite sure why it would be worse than getting caught collecting kickbacks for Jack, or attending, as he'd done twice now, a Members' Appreciation Night, but he knew it was. And that it was probably even worse to light up on a rooftop balcony overlooking a garden party full of the city's most prominent Liberals. But breaking the mood of this moment would have been worst of all.

He watched as she pulled the elasticized top of her sundress away from her skin, reached in and fished out a fat joint and a book of matches. "Storage," she said as she lit the joint and took a long, deep suck on it. "Bras are good for storage."

For reasons that made no sense—he hadn't yet taken a drag—Ward found this incredibly amusing. He began to giggle. When she handed him the joint and he tried to inhale, he ended up coughing and sputtering, which triggered a laughing fit in her. Pretty soon, they were both doubled over, not sure what was so funny, but trying their best not to attract attention from the revellers below.

After they'd finished the joint, they sat down on the benches on opposite sides of the balcony, quiet, lost in their own thoughts. Ward's thoughts were simple. And complicated. Why had she decided to sit on the other bench rather than beside him? Should he go over and sit beside her, show her he was interested, or would that break the spell, end the sweet illusion in his head?

"What're you thinking?" he said finally, breaking the silence.

"Nothing," she said. "You?"

"Nothing." He was lying. He suspected she was too. Was she hoping he would make a move? Or worrying how she would let him down if he did? Perhaps she was remembering what it had been like to fuck her Greek poet. He hoped not. He needed to do something, needed to go and sit beside her, ask her to a movie, or dinner, a drive in the country. He couldn't. He needed to. He should. He—

"Coming up." It was her father's voice calling from the sunroom below—the warning call of a father who didn't want to discover his daughter doing something he wouldn't approve of, even though he knew she probably was. Ward tried to wave away any telltale smells. Vicky shook her head as if to say it didn't matter.

"Thought I might find you two up here," he said as he popped his head through the opening in the roof. He didn't come up all the way. He turned to Ward. "Ever since she was a little girl, we always knew where to look for Victoria when she disappeared, usually in the middle of a party, even when it was her own. Right, Princess?"

"Right, Daddy."

"The only thing that's changed," he added, theatrically sniffing the air, "is what she does up here." He caught Ward's surprised look. "Oh, don't worry, young man, your secret is safe with me." He turned back to Victoria. "Just don't let your mother catch you. Anyway," he addressed Ward again, "your friend, Mr. Eagleson, is getting anxious to leave and he's looking for his driver. I'll let him know you're on your way," he said as he turned around and made his way back down the circular staircase.

Ward stood up. So did Victoria.

Later, when he tried to recreate the moment in his head, he couldn't decide if he'd reached for her first, or if she had opened her arms to him. Not that it mattered. What mattered was that they'd kissed and held each other like neither wanted the moment to end.

"Why don't you come back later," she said finally. "Come back and I'll show you my etchings." She stood on her tiptoes and kissed him on the lips.

Patrick Donovan stood in front of a third-floor window in the press room at City Hall, looking down on a sea of chanting, singing humanity surging below him along Barrington. To the north, the parade of people—black, white, men, women, young, old—stretched into the distance until it disappeared into the enveloping October night. To the south, he could see the front line of marchers make the hard right turn into the Grand Parade about five hundred feet beyond his vantage point. He tried to determine the number of demonstrators arrayed in loose rows across the street in front of him but the rows kept shifting and he lost count.

He hurried into the Council Chambers and, standing on his tiptoes, peered out over the heads of a cluster of nervous-looking aldermen who'd gathered to watch the spectacle outside. He could see a crush of protestors in the parade square, and more pouring in, not only from the main group of marchers on Barrington Street but also in ones and twos and groups of a half-dozen or more streaming into the square from Citadel Hill and the side streets above City Hall. He tried again to count them, but there was no order to their array, and no one seemed to stay still long enough.

Figuring out the size of the crowd was one of the reasons he was there. He couldn't fail. He turned to Mo, the veteran *Tribune* photographer who seemed to know more about reporting than many real reporters. Mo was standing on a chair using his wide-angle lens to try to get a shot that included both the backs of the heads of the gathered aldermen and the demonstrators gathering outside.

"How many?" Patrick asked.

"Four thousand," Mo answered, without taking his eye from the viewfinder.

"How you figure that?" He seemed so sure of himself, Patrick thought.

"Easy," he answered. "I asked the cops. Cops get the last word. Besides, if everybody uses the same number, nobody can be wrong."

Patrick Donovan still had a lot to learn about reporting.

Getting names right, for starters. He could still feel the panic from three hours earlier when Tom Harkin, the assistant City Editor, had bellowed his name across the newsroom. He was sure he was about to be fired. The day before, he'd written a story mixing up the name of a man arrested during a fair-housing rally with the name of the landlord whose apartment building was being picketed. The landlord was not amused; he had called to give Patrick shit and warned him he'd be calling his bosses, too, to tell them what a chump they had writing for them. "I hope they fire your stupid ass."

But Harkin hadn't called him over to fire his stupid ass. "You're going to help Morton cover the demo," he'd announced. Morton was the paper's City Hall reporter. There was talk the demonstration would be the biggest gathering in downtown Halifax since the VE-Day riots back in '45.

Last week, word had leaked out that the aldermen had secretly agreed to appoint an outsider, a former policeman turned security consultant from Columbus, Georgia, as Chief of Police. That upset Halifax cops, who'd been supporting one of their own for the position. And it angered the local trade unionists, who'd discovered the new top cop had a history of hiring strikebreakers to help his corporate clients rid themselves of pesky unions. It also pissed off black community leaders, who hadn't been able to find out much about the man's civil rights record but knew enough to know they didn't want some white Georgia cracker as their police chief. Not after what the City had already done in Africville. They had put aside their mutual animosities—blacks usually blamed union closed-shop policies for keeping them out of the local workforce; unionists believed blacks wanted to take their jobs; and cops distrusted, and were in turn distrusted by, both the blacks and the unionists for every reason you could think of. The rally would be a show of force just before Council met to ratify its choice of a new chief.

"Morton's gonna have to cover the meeting after, so you do whatever he needs you to do," Harkin instructed Patrick. "You get the crowd numbers for him. Talk to Black Pride and the rest and then feed him some quotes he can use. Maybe even get a little *vox pop* stuff. That would be good. And if there's any trouble, I want you right in the middle of it with your notebook. Got it?"

"Got it." Patrick Donovan was relieved and excited and pissed off all at the same time. He was supposed to finish his shift at seven, so he'd made plans to meet Emma. She'd said she'd wait for him outside the LBR. Thanks to the province's archaic liquor laws, men weren't allowed into places like the LBR, properly known as the Ladies' Beverage Room, unless accompanied by a lady; ladies, of course, weren't permitted in taverns at all.

Patrick looked at his watch. It was past six already. Emma would have left work and, since she had no phone in her apartment, he couldn't call to cancel. She wouldn't be amused.

They'd met nearly a month ago when he'd been assigned to cover the Lions Club monthly luncheon; Emma was the secretary to the club's president, a car dealer who made her hand out copies of the guest speaker's talk to the reporters covering it. But Patrick was the only reporter unlucky enough to have been assigned to cover this particular nothing speech by some local doctor just back from Africa. For reasons Patrick couldn't fathom, he and Emma had hit it off. He'd asked her out. But then he'd had to cancel twice because the desk had decided at the last minute to make him work extra shifts. Luckily, he'd been able to call her at work and reschedule both times. She hadn't been pleased. After tonight, he wasn't sure she'd even speak to him.

Oh, well, he had a story. And not just any story. This could turn out to be the story of the year, especially if, as callers to the radio open-line shows were predicting, the demonstration turned violent. Part of him hoped it would. What would the cops do then? He was just Morton's legman, of course. Morton would write the story, get the byline. But he was part of it. Not bad for a rookie reporter.

The *Tribune* had hired him that spring, ostensibly as a summer vacation replacement. But when the summer ended and no one told him to leave, he stayed. He didn't drop out of Saint Mary's University so much as he just didn't show up when classes began. Not that it mattered much. He joked—though not to his parents—that he was majoring in the campus newspaper, which, unfortunately, wasn't a credit course.

Harkin made him spend the first month doing obits, most of which didn't get into the paper the way he wrote them. He'd progressed since then to rewriting press releases, covering service club meetings and, in the past month, a few small stories like yesterday's demonstration at the apartment building. He'd only got that assignment—Black Pride had organized the rally to protest what it claimed was the landlord's refusal to rent to a Negro couple—because none of the more experienced reporters thought it worth a story. And then he'd screwed up. Had the landlord called the desk to complain about mixing up the names—maybe Harkin was just waiting until after the demonstration to fire him—or had yelling at him over the phone been enough to sate the man's anger? Patrick hoped so. He hoped, too, that somebody from Black Pride would agree to talk to him after the speeches tonight. They weren't happy with the *Trib* either.

The provincial government had made a big deal of announcing the establishment of Black Pride last spring. No one said so publicly, of course, but it was the government's pre-emptive, pre-election response to what had happened at that "Halifax 2000" conference a few months before, not to mention a way to defuse the fuss black community leaders had stirred up after the Africville relocation. And then there were all those race riots in American cities. The government didn't want their local Negroes getting any dangerous ideas.

Officially, Black Pride was touted as an independent grassroots organization, but it got all its funding from the province, and the province chose its directors. The problem for the government was that its tame board quickly lost control. The board made the mistake of hiring local coloured social workers, some of them almost certainly communists. They'd begun organizing protests and making public statements.

Earlier this summer, Black Pride had even staged a small protest outside the *Tribune*'s offices, handing out leaflets accusing the paper of having no black reporters in its newsroom. The *Tribune* didn't cover the protest, but the CBC (which didn't have any black reporters either) did. The story even included an interview with a protestor who claimed the paper was "a racist organization."

The *Trib* had retaliated this week with an ostensibly unrelated editorial criticizing Black Pride for being involved in organizing tonight's rally. "It ill behooves an organization that suckles at the public teat, as the so-called 'Black Pride' does, to undermine the legitimacy of elected municipal officials and their institutions by using such bullying, extra-parliamentary tactics," the paper harrumphed. "We call on the Premier and the Provincial Government, who loosed this scourge in our midst in order to appease Upper Canadian agitators and other do-gooders, to rein in the radicals and troublemakers who pretend to speak for our Negroes."

Patrick Donovan wasn't sure anyone from Black Pride would talk with him after that. Worse, the only person he knew at Black Pride was Ray Carter, the field worker who'd organized the rally against the landlord yesterday. But he was also the one who'd called the *Trib* racist on TV. Even if he did convince Carter to talk with him, he wasn't sure the paper would publish it.

Patrick took one last look out the window. The speakers were gathering near the podium. He'd better find Morton and see if there was anything else he should be doing.

═══

They shouldn't have been having this conversation. Not right in front of the loudspeakers, where they had to yell to make themselves heard. On the stage behind them, an old white folk singer was noisily exhorting the crowd to join with him in one more chorus of "Solidarity Forever." Ray knew it would be way too easy for some snooping reporter to overhear them. So he put his hand lightly on the other man's shoulder, hoping to steer him to a quieter spot behind the portable stage. The man slapped his hand away as if it was contaminated, or perhaps, Ray thought, as if it was black.

"Don't you fucken' touch me again or I'll take your fucken' head off and shove it up your fucken' arsehole!" The white man was so close to his face Ray could see the hard drinker's map lines of broken blood vessels crosshatching the man's nose and cheeks, could smell the rum on his breath, could feel the man's warm spittle landing on his own cold cheeks. "Unnerstand?"

Ray understood. He'd tried to tell Calvin this was a mistake. They should have staged their *own* rally. So what if it would have been smaller? So what if the newspaper wouldn't cover it? They wouldn't get it right anyway. Nothing Black Pride did or said was going to make the City change its mind, so why not think strategically, use the demonstration to heighten the contradictions, to force black people themselves to see the system for what it was? He'd learned that much in Toronto.

But Calvin and the other board members were still playing Martin Luther King, waiting for the white man to come miraculously to his senses and give black people what was rightly theirs. The white man already had his senses, thank you very much. He had the power; why should he give that up just because a bunch of niggers asked him to? No one gave you power in a capitalist, racist society. You had to take it. Maybe, Ray thought, he should go back to Toronto. It wasn't any better there, but it was bigger, and there were more people who thought like him. Here, he felt alone.

He'd imagined it would be different, that Halifax had really changed. Last winter, in fact, when he'd come back for a visit with his father, the city had seemed alive with possibility. Some white liberal do-gooders had organized an event called "Halifax 2000: Facing the Future." They'd convinced the provincial and city governments to underwrite it, even though Ray was certain the government hadn't understood it was popping the cork on so much bottled rage. It was supposed to bring citizens together, but it had turned into a week-long confrontation—between black and white, young and old, good and evil, the powerful and the powerless.

The organizers had put together a high-powered panel of a dozen experts, including an economist from Harvard, a labour leader from Toronto, an architect from California, even a black preacher-politician from Atlanta. They were to spend a week in the city, meeting and talking with locals from every social class, and then, at the end, come up with a single report, the sum of their collective wisdom, telling Halifax how it could magically transform its current backward, backwater self into a modern, cosmopolitan city thirty years from now.

During the days, the experts wandered the city, tailed by a phalanx of reporters from the local media and the Toronto papers. The experts would descend en masse on key companies and civic institutions, questioning their managers and leaders in front of the TV cameras about what they did and didn't do. About everything. And anything. The preacher, whose name was Bartholomew Andrew Jackson III and who spoke in a voice-of-doom preacher voice, asked the manager of the old Capital Fisheries plant near Maynard Square how come he hadn't seen a single black face on the company's processing line.

The man shrugged. "We don't have no coloured folks working here."

"None!" the preacher thundered. "And why not?"

The manager looked stunned. This was not what he'd expected. "Ah, I guess it's because none of them ever applied," he said lamely, hoping the preacher would yield the floor. He didn't.

"So are you saying then that if a qualified black man applied tomorrow, you'd hire him?"

The manager knew he was being led into a trap. "Well, yes, but—"

"You heard the man." Jackson cut him off, turning back to the reporters who were furiously writing down every word. "Now I want you all to report what this man said, and then tomorrow, I want my black Nova Scotia brothers lining up outside the gates here asking for the jobs that are rightfully theirs, the jobs this man just promised them."

The manager looked as though he was about to upchuck his breakfast.

At night, the experts held televised town hall meetings in a hotel ballroom to talk about what they'd seen that day and hear anyone from the community who wanted to speak. The owner of the local private TV station, who was also one of the event's organizers, had eagerly agreed in advance to broadcast the sessions live. By the end of the first hour of the first broadcast on Monday night, Ray thought, he must have been regretting his enthusiasm.

A long-haired Dalhousie student, who said he represented Socialist Solidarity, stood up at the microphone to denounce "your fucking racist honky police pig force" for beating up on a group of anti-war protestors.

Watching the TV in his father's living room that night, Ray almost choked on his cigarette. He'd never heard anyone say "fucking" on television before. And "racist honky police pig force"? Who was this white guy? American? Couldn't be a local. Probably a dodger. The universities were full of them. Even in Halifax.

"Thank you, young man." The camera was back on the men on the stage now. The black preacher was speaking. The camera zoomed in on him. "You know, I've been in your city for three days and you're the first angry young man I've heard. There is a lot to be angry about in this place. Especially for my people. But I hardly see any black faces in this audience here tonight. Where are they? I was told there were black people in this city. But I haven't seen them. Where are my black brothers and sisters? Why aren't they here like this young man expressing their anger and their outrage?"

Ray was there. Tuesday morning, he joined a small group of a half-dozen blacks and whites, including the angry young man from the first town hall meeting, who'd attached themselves like barnacles to the panel of experts, trailing them from meeting to meeting.

No matter which group the panel met with, Jackson kept asking the same question. Where are the black people—the businessmen, merchants, legionnaires, naval officers, board members, university students, teachers, doctors, lawyers, reporters, editors, politicians? By the middle of the week, his prey knew to expect it, but not how to answer.

Some organizations, like the School Board, put a few of their very few black employees on display, but they quickly discovered that was even more dangerous. During the meeting with the School Board, Reverend Jackson asked one of the black employees sitting in the spectators' gallery, to which the chairman had pointed so proudly in his opening remarks, exactly what he did for the Board.

"Janitor, sir," he replied.

"A janitor?" Jackson appraised him. "You always wear a suit to work?"

"No sir. Principal said I should, sir. Said they want to show me off."

There was a titter among the reporters. Embarrassment on the face of the Board chairman.

"I see," Jackson replied. "Wanted to show you off? Tell me, Mr. . . . ?"

"Dickson. Everett Dickson, sir."

Old Everett Dickson! Ray hadn't recognized him at first, perhaps because he hadn't expected to see anyone he knew inside these executive offices and dressed like an executive. But Everett Dickson wasn't just someone he knew. He was the man who'd literally hauled him out of the fire the day his mother died.

"Well, Mr. Everett Dickson," Jackson continued, in a tone Ray heard as both friendly and condescending. For the Reverend, Everett seemed not so much a person as an exhibit in his prosecution of the School Board. "Let me ask you a question, since these folks all seem so proud of you. Let me ask you this. How long y'all been working for the School Board?"

"Fifteen years, sir."

"Fifteen years. That's a long time. How much do they pay you?"

"One dollar and twenty-six an hour, sir," Everett answered, bragging.

"One dollar and twenty-six cents an hour," Jackson repeated, rolling the number around in his head as if trying to recall something. He looked to his fellow panellists. "Any of you gentlemen remember hearing a number like that?" No one spoke. "Ah, yes, now I remember—it was when we met with the Premier. Isn't that right, gentlemen?" The gentlemen looked nervous, embarrassed, as if they weren't sure where the Reverend was going this time but knew it wouldn't be good. It was clear, Ray thought, that the Reverend Bartholomew Andrew Jackson III was on his own among these gentlemen, too. "One dollar and twenty-*five* cents an hour. The Premier told us that's the minimum wage in this province. So, Mr. Everett Dickson, you say you've been a loyal employee of this here School Board for fifteen long years and you get one cent more an hour than the minimum wage." His voice rose at the end of the sentence. Then he paused, the silence now all the more electric. His eyes swept the oak boardroom table where his fellow experts and the School Board members sat, and then beyond them into the audience in the spectators' gallery—to the half-dozen Exhibit A black men in their Sunday suits, then beyond them to the reporters and the hangers on, all the way to the back of the room where Reverend Jackson knew the TV news cameras were now trained on him. He waited, made sure the cameramen had time to get him in focus.

"Shame!!" he cried. "Shame on this School Board! Shame on this city! Shame! Shame! Shame!"

"Right on, man." It was the long-haired young white guy from the first night's town hall. "Power to the people," he shouted, standing and turning awkwardly away from the Reverend to face the cameras. Ray and the others cheered and shouted encouragement—"Right on!" "Tell 'em, brother!"—as the cameras pulled back to include them too.

Everett Dickson, Ray couldn't help but notice, was silent. He didn't cheer. Neither did any of his fellow Exhibit As. Everett looked as though he was wondering what he'd said wrong.

It took Ray two nights to convince his father to come to a town hall meeting, two more to get him to stand up and tell his story of the suitcase.

Though the local reporters had heard it all before, the out-of-towners crowded around Lawrence Carter after he spoke, begging for details. Ray's brother David told him later the story was on the front page of both *The Globe and Mail* and *The Toronto Star*. "Fucking newspapers," his brother said. "When it was happening, they were all for it. Clean up the slums, they said. And now they're all crocodile tears. Fuck the vultures."

David Carter didn't like newspapers. He also didn't want to see or read anything that reminded him he came from Halifax. He hadn't been back since his father had sent him to Toronto to live with his uncle. He'd been thirteen then; he was thirty-one now, and just as angry as he'd been the day his father told him his mother had died because there were no fire hydrants in Africville.

When Ray moved to Toronto after high school, David, ten years his senior, took him in, showed him the city, helped him find a job at New Word Order, a radical bookstore near Rochdale College. The bookstore was where Ray got his own political education, gobbling through the store's entire collection of books on Negro history and black power between waiting on customers and stocking shelves.

Soon after Ray arrived in Toronto, David took him to his first

Black Hands meeting. The organization had begun in Washington in the late fifties when a group of Howard University students set up a breakfast program for kids in the city's ghetto. The idea quickly spread to other American cities and, eventually, to Toronto and Montreal. By the mid-sixties, however, the breakfast program was just the public relations face of a controversial political agenda. Black Hands now described itself as the vanguard of the New Africa Movement; its goal was to take over Mississippi and Alabama and transform them into one self-governing, blacks-only state. Ray was never sure how much he subscribed to that objective, but the specifics never seemed as important as the symbolic notion that blacks should control their own destinies. He could certainly agree with that.

Within a year, Ray had been elected the vice-chairman of Black Hands (Toronto), which didn't mean much since there were only a dozen members. But it did mean he got to attend central committee meetings in Washington, where American Black Hands members talked about how to jump-start the revolution.

It was just talk, of course, but that hadn't stopped the FBI from recruiting informers. One of them, a social worker from Atlanta named Franklin, whom Ray had met a couple of times in Washington, ended up dead. Black Hands (Atlanta) issued a communiqué blaming the local cops for "assassinating" him. But the rumour Ray heard was that the local branch had discovered his treachery and that the chairman, Tyrone Vincent, had executed him, then pinned the killing on police to stir up anger in the black community.

Strangely, Ray's decision to return home to Halifax last spring had begun with an offhand question from Tyrone. "You know anything about some place called Halifax?" he'd asked while they were getting coffee during a break at a central committee meeting.

"Yeah . . . What about it?" With the exception of his brother, no one Ray had met in Black Hands—including Black Hands (Toronto), whose members were all either draft dodgers or refugees from one of the Caribbean countries—seemed to have the slightest idea where Halifax was, let alone that black people lived there.

"One of our guys was there for a conference," Tyrone explained. "Says it's ripe for recruiting." It turned out that, unknown to Ray, Reverend Bartholomew Andrew Jackson III was a member of Black Hands. After his week in Halifax, he'd returned to Atlanta telling anyone who'd listen that the city was fertile ground. "It's where the South was ten years ago," he said. "They need us up there." Since no one in Atlanta was interested in taking up the Reverend's challenge, Tyrone figured he'd pass the idea on to Ray, "since you live in the cold already."

When Black Pride began advertising for field workers, Ray decided to apply. But, except for Black Hands, which he wasn't sure it would be wise to advertise to the Black Pride hiring committee, Ray had no qualifications whatsoever. Not even a university degree. "No sweat, man," one of his bookstore customers, a Rochdale student, told him. "Got twenty-five bucks?"

Rochdale had recently declared itself a "free university." There were no formal curricula, no classes, no exams, not even any degrees. Since Rochdale's governing council believed degrees were bourgeois affectations, it decided to sell them as a way of undermining the elitism of formal education and, not coincidentally, raising money. You could buy a Rochdale B.A. for twenty-five dollars, an M.A. for fifty and a Ph.D. for a hundred. To get the B.A., you had to answer a skill-testing question of your choosing. Ray's question: "What was the name of the black community Halifax City Council destroyed in the sixties?" He only hoped no one in Halifax had heard of Rochdale.

Ray did get the job, but not, as he later learned, because he'd faked his credentials. Calvin Johnstone, the Deacon's son, who was the head of the hiring committee, knew Ray hadn't gone to university. He even knew about Black Hands. "Wouldn'a mattered if you claimed you'd been one of them moon-walkers," he chuckled later. "We'd a hired you anyway. I told the committee, I said, 'We gotta have at least one guy from out home.' And nobody else from Africville applied."

The province had chosen Calvin to be the first chairman of Black

Pride's board of directors, partly because he was the son of a politically well-connected moderate black religious leader who taught high school history, lived with his wife and two children in a small bungalow in a new suburb outside the city, was active in his local church and chaired his neighbourhood improvement committee—and partly because he seemed so unthreatening. And, up to a point, he was. He preferred to go along and get along. But Calvin also knew the best way to get what he really wanted was to appear to be the lesser of the evils. In order to be that, he needed . . . well, a greater evil. Ray Carter filled the bill.

Ray's protest about the *Tribune*'s lack of black reporters, for example, had generated a torrent of phone calls from other businessmen practically begging to meet with Calvin to talk about how they could find more qualified Negroes to work in their shops and offices. And, thanks to Ray's highly publicized rally against the landlord who wouldn't rent to a black family, Calvin would meet next week with the Municipal Rental Property Owners' Association to talk about a voluntary code of ethics for landlords.

So Calvin had been more than willing to let Ray stir things up. Up to a point. He wasn't so sure about Ray's latest scheme. Ray wanted Black Pride to sponsor a visit from the Black Hands' new secretary of state, Tyrone Vincent, so he could talk about the organization's plan for a blacks-only state in the United States. "You do like to stir up the shit, don't you?" Calvin laughed when Ray had broached the idea a week ago. "Let's just get this rally out of the way first."

Ray had been Black Pride's representative on the organizing committee for tonight's rally. He thought everything had been settled, but now Spittle Man, one of the union reps, was telling him plans had changed. "We're runnin' late," he'd told Ray, so instead of two speakers—Calvin and his father—Black Pride could now have only one, and he could only speak for five minutes.

None of the speakers for the unions—there were four of them, plus the president of the Trades Council, who was acting as emcee—had been dropped from the speakers' list or had a time limit put on them. And there should have been time, Ray knew; none of the provincial politicians they'd invited had shown up. Nova Scotia was in the middle of what everyone said was going to be a very close provincial election and none of the candidates wanted to have to take a stand on such a controversial issue.

But Ray's protests had been in vain. Standing now, toe to toe, eye to eye with the union rep, Ray wanted nothing more than to take one good roundhouse swing at his fat, ugly, drunken white face. But he couldn't. Not here. Not now.

"Fuck it, and fuck you," Ray muttered finally, then turned on his heel and walked away. He would have to find Calvin now, tell him.

"Ray . . ." It was a woman's voice. Calling. From behind him. "Ray." He turned back toward the sound. It was Rosa, the Deacon's daughter, Calvin's little sister. Ray hadn't seen her since he'd left for Toronto three years ago. She'd been twelve then, an awkward, pudgy, preadolescent girl. She wasn't twelve any more! Now, she'd grown into her woman's body; the curves were all where they should be. Ray's eyes swallowed her full breasts, which were pushing out against the tight fabric of her white sweater.

"Daddy wants to know if he can speak first," she said when she caught up to him. "His breathing's bad and he's getting cold."

Ray ripped his eyes from her chest and focused on her face. It wasn't so hard. Her smooth skin was the colour of dark chocolate, which only made her eyes seem brighter, her perfect teeth whiter. But it was no easier to concentrate on what she was saying. What? Her father. Speak. First. Shit. Should he tell her? He didn't want to, but he didn't want her to go, either. Keep talking.

"There's a problem," he said. He didn't need to tell her about Spittle Man. "Things are running late so they're trying to cut down on the number of speakers." Ray knew Calvin, as chairman of Black Pride, had to talk. "So I don't think there's going to be time for your father tonight. I'm sorry."

She laughed. "He's not going to be happy when I tell him that."

"Do you want me to come with you? I can tell him if you want." Ray just didn't want her to leave.

"No, no, that's okay. You're busy. I'll tell him." She turned to go.

"Rosa?" She turned back. Now what? "It's nice to see you again. What are you doing, anyway?"

"School mostly. Grade ten. I hate it, but Daddy says I have to finish high school. Besides, there's only me at home now. Mama died last year."

"Shit, I didn't know. I'm sorry."

"Thanks. It's getting easier."

Now what? Keep talking. "Are you in academic?" She looked puzzled. "You know, the stream that lets you go to university if you want."

She shrugged her shoulders. "I'm not interested in that."

"That's what you say now." He was sounding like the voice of experience, an adult talking to a child, an older brother. He didn't want to sound like either. "But you might change your mind, so you shouldn't let them stream you out."

"Sure, okay." He could see she was losing interest. "I better go tell Daddy."

"Right, right." She was staring at him now too. Expectant? Expecting what? Was Rosa feeling what he was feeling? "Uh, look, Rosa, maybe we could get together some time, have a coffee or something, talk about old times, Africville, you know, maybe I can help to, ah, make sure you don't get stuck in the general stream." Why couldn't he just shut up about that?

"That would be nice," she said. *Nice?* "Why don't you give me a call? Like I said, I'm still at home. In the Square. Daddy's number's in the phone book. So call me." *Yes!* "I better go."

He watched as she walked away. Damn. She looked fine from behind, too.

"Repeating our top stories to this hour," the announcer intoned gravely, his radio voice pushing up from somewhere deep in his large intestine. "In Ottawa, thousands of soldiers are standing guard outside federal buildings. Meanwhile, in Quebec, police are stepping up their search for the men who kidnapped British diplomat James Cross and Quebec Labour minister Pierre Laporte. Contemporary News next at five to the hour . . . or *whenever* news breaks." The news reader paused, waited while the musical lead-in to Neil Diamond's "Solitary Man" established itself, then smoothly shifted emotional gears and added brightly: "And now back to Brian's Breakfast Club, on CHAX, 920 Radio . . ."

Ward Justice reached over and snapped off the radio on the credenza behind Gerry Cullingham's desk. He was thankful, relieved and apprehensive, all at once. He was thankful—though he would have been ashamed to admit it—that the FLQ had hijacked the headlines. Eight days ago, just as the Nova Scotia election campaign was moving into its final full week, a group calling itself the Liberation Cell of the FLQ had kidnapped the British consul in Montreal and threatened to kill him if authorities didn't meet their demands—release of political prisoners, broadcast of the group's revolutionary manifesto, five hundred thousand dollars in gold and an aircraft to take them to Cuba or Algeria. A few days later, another cell upped the ante, snatching the Quebec Cabinet minister. Then, last night—the night before voting day—the federal government had ordered the army into Ottawa. There were rumours Trudeau might declare martial law today.

No wonder most of the reporters from the Toronto papers and the TV networks who'd come to Nova Scotia to cover the last few weeks of the election campaign had already decamped for Montreal or Ottawa. Those who remained knew better than to believe that anything they wrote about Nova Scotia politics now would make it onto the front page or the evening newscasts.

Which was just fine with Ward.

He'd also been relieved earlier that morning when he'd picked up a copy of the *Tribune* and seen that its election day set-up story, while still on the front page, had been shuffled to a less prominent bottom corner of the page in order to make room for more dramatic news unfolding elsewhere. The innocuous headline over the story—"Nova Scotians Vote Today"—made it clear this was not the exposé Ward had feared. Was that Jack's doing?

But Ward was also apprehensive. Had Jack really managed to kill the story? Or just wound it, holding it at bay until the votes were counted? Ward was sure that was all Jack cared about. Ward was the one whose face was in the photos, whose name featured in the affidavits. Would this mark the end of his law career before it had even begun?

What would Victoria think? She was probably still sleeping. In his bed. In his apartment. Naked. He wished he were there. But would she still be there if his name ended up splashed across the front page? He could see the headline already: "O'Sullivan Worker In Vote-Buying Scandal."

Ever since a Tory campaign manager had indiscreetly confided to a Toronto reporter during the last election that the practice of exchanging votes for rum, cash and other commodities was alive and flourishing in rural Nova Scotia, vote buying—along with Africville—had become Nova Scotia's national media shame. Toronto reporters, who saw the issue as an easy avenue to a front-page story about the backwater politics of eastern Canada, had eagerly trooped through Jack's office throughout this campaign in search of quotable quotes, hoping he might be as indiscreet as his Tory rival. He wasn't.

The Tories, chastened by their campaign manager's gaffe in 1967, were responding to questions this time by alternately claiming piously that vote buying was a myth perpetuated by mischievous outsiders, and pledging apologetically that they would never, ever do it again. Jack responded by not responding. Or at least not directly, or helpfully. When the reporters would ask their inevitable question, Jack would appear to ponder for a pregnant extra beat, then declare enigmatically, "Ah, yes. *La politique du ventre*." Then, after a suitable silence: "But enough about *la politique du ventre*." And he'd wait, silent and sage, for the next question.

The reporters, puzzled but not wanting to appear stupid—at least that's what Ward assumed—dutifully wrote the phrase in their notebooks, probably thinking they'd look it up later, if they had time and if they hadn't misspelled it, and hurried on to their next question.

They rarely followed up, but even if they did, they would have learned from Jack only that the phrase had been coined by the French—literally translated, "the politics of the abdomen"—to describe the bureaucratic infighting and petty corruption that often followed independence in post-colonial Africa. Making a direct link between Jack's obscure reference to the political adjustments of newly liberated African nations and buying votes in backwoods Nova Scotia inevitably turned out to be far too tangled for the reporters to easily unravel, so they left it out of their stories entirely.

Which was, as Jack explained it to Ward, the whole idea.

That's not to say that Jack didn't really believe that his interpretation of *la politique du ventre* applied to Nova Scotia politics, and not just in rural areas either. But when he was speaking to Ward instead of a reporter, Jack preferred the looser, more colourful English translation—"belly politics"—which, even to Ward, made some sense.

"See, it's like this," Jack would explain. "The farther down the political food chain you go, the more important belly politics becomes. If a man is down and out, you appeal to his belly, get him to give you his vote for something for his belly. A few bucks, a pint of rum." He stopped then, laughed his room-filling laugh. "Works when you go up the chain, too. The difference is it costs more—a government contract instead of a few bucks, a political appointment instead of a bottle." Then he laughed some more. "Dealing with a voter is like dealing with a whore. It's never a question of will she or won't she; it's just a question of how much it's going to cost you. Let that be your lesson in *realpolitik* politics for the day, Mr. Future Premier."

Ward's role in this election campaign had not turned out to be the one Jack had initially promised him. Instead of managing Seamus O'Sullivan's local campaign, Jack had put Ward in charge of belly politics in his riding.

"This is the most important job in the whole campaign," Jack insisted when he saw Ward's disappointment. "Halifax North is not only the bottom of the bottom of the food chain, but this is going to be a very close race. If we don't get the belly politics right, we won't win. And that's why I need you as my man on the spot."

Belly politics, it turned out, covered a much wider swath of electoral skulduggery than merely buying a few votes.

One of Ward's most important jobs, for example, was assisting the dearly departed to cast ballots for O'Sullivan. He'd complied a list of the names of every resident of O'Sullivan's constituency who'd died since the last election, then assembled a half-dozen ringers—men and women, young and old, Liberals all—whose assignment was to go from poll to poll on election day posing as the very alive Mr. So-and-So of Roome Street or Mrs. Such-and-Such of Union Street, and demanding a ballot. Since a ringer could not produce proper identification ("My house was broken into and all my ID was stolen . . ." they would explain. Or, "I lost my wallet yesterday . . ."), each ringer was accompanied by a bona fide voter, a dependable Liberal campaign worker who would swear they were whoever they were claiming to be at the time.

The challenge, Jack told Ward, was that since the Tories were almost certainly using the same tactic, Ward had to make sure his ringers registered to vote before theirs did. It would be embarrassing to demand your ballot only to find a Tory ringer had already cast it. The ringer got five dollars for every vote he cast; the handler got a flat twenty dollars for the day for vouching for his identity and keeping score of how many ballots the ringer cast.

Ward looked at his watch. Eight-fifteen. With luck, the first six dead people had already voted for Seamus O'Sullivan. What if one of the ringers got caught? Jack said nobody ever got caught. But that was before Ward himself got nailed. Photographed, identified.

Which reminded him. He needed to call Ernie Scali, who was in charge of getting out the vote at Northland, to warn him. Northland, the riding's largest senior citizens' complex, with more than five hundred eligible voters, was a key belly politics battleground. The Liberal weapon of choice there was chocolate, heart-shaped boxes of Moirs Pot of Gold chocolates, to be more specific.

On Saturday, Ward had dropped a supply of them at Ernie's

apartment. Handing out the Valentine's assortment instead of a regular, boring box of chocolates had been Ernie's idea. Ernie was a retired math teacher and lifelong Liberal who lived in the building and volunteered to coordinate the party's campaign with seniors. "The old gals love their chocolates, and they especially love the ones that come in those heart-shaped boxes. We gave them out in 1967 and won both our polls," he told Ward proudly, "86 percent of the vote!"

"We probably would have got 85 percent of the votes there anyway," Jack said later. "But the old folks are so used to getting a treat, they won't vote until we give them one."

Ernie's most difficult task was to get the seniors to the two polling stations in the high-rise's main lobby. Many had trouble walking, others were bed-ridden. Ernie assembled a team of younger residents to go up and down the halls with wheelchairs, knocking on every door and offering to ferry the occupant down to the polling booth and back to their rooms. "And we'll have a nice treat for you for after," they were instructed to say.

The volunteers used to be permitted to accompany the seniors right into the voting booth to help them cast their ballots—and make sure they cast them the right way—but the Returning Officer had announced he was clamping down this election. No one except the voter was allowed inside the voting booth today. The problem was that many of the seniors were senile or forgetful, and might not remember who they were supposed to vote for. "So we're improvising," Ernie had confided to Ward. "If my students could write the answers to my tests on their hands, we can do the same." Ernie had handed out felt-tipped markers to his volunteers and instructed them to write "O'SULLIVAN" on the forearm of any senior they thought might need "reminding." "There's more than one way to win a vote," he said.

But what if . . . ? Oh, God. What if some photographer got a photo of that? Or, perhaps worse, walked into Ward's office at this very moment and saw all these empty cartons on the floor, each with its own incriminating listing of contents on the side. Instead of working out of O'Sullivan's official headquarters on Gottingen Street, Jack had set him up away from the rest of the campaign in Gerry Cullingham's unused office at the law firm. "Gerry'll never even know you were here." The big, sparsely furnished room served as Ward's office and—most important—his storage locker.

During the last two weeks, Ward had gathered most of his belly politics arsenal here: five hundred pint bottles of rum, five hundred boxes of Pot of Gold, one thousand pairs of nylons of various brands, sizes and shades and two hundred crisp, fresh-from-the-bank-vault five-dollar bills. With the exception of the cash, which Ward kept in a locked briefcase he carried with him everywhere, the supplies were all stored in plain view in the office.

Most of it was gone now, distributed to where he hoped it would do the most good. To Ernie at Northland. To the homes of various party faithful throughout the constituency who'd agreed to accompany their neighbours to the polling station and then bring them back to their own kitchens, which had been turned into portable bars and treat-distribution centres for election day.

And, of course, to the Deacon, who was handling the handouts today in Maynard Square. The Deacon! Why had he been so stupid? Ward wondered. Why hadn't he let the Deacon handle everything instead of—?

The Deacon wasn't really a minister, Ward knew. Jack called him the Deacon because he'd been involved with the church in Africville. The Deacon was a long-time Liberal supporter who served as the party's general in the black community. Whenever there was an issue involving the black community, Jack would instruct Ward, "Ask the Deacon."

The problem was that the Deacon and Ward disliked each other immediately. When Ward had called him last week to arrange to drop off his election day supplies, the Deacon had imperiously informed Ward of exactly what he wanted. "I'll need two hundred pints of rum, dark, Captain Morgan," he'd begun, as if calling in a grocery order. "Three hundred of those Pot of Gold chocolate boxes, the ones with the extra maraschino cherries. Five hundred pairs of stockings, all sizes, light-coloured ones work best here. Fifty turkeys, fresh-killed, for that special list I talked to Jack about. And five hundred dollars in fives, 'cause nobody's using twos any more. And make sure they're new ones. My people like the feel of the new ones."

When Ward pointed out to Jack later that the Deacon was asking for more treats than there were black voters in all of Maynard Square, Jack just laughed. "The Deacon delivers, so if he wants a little something extra for his troubles, that's okay with me. Give him what he wants."

"And what's this about turkeys?"

"Oh that," Jack answered. "The Deacon's got a special list he wants us to buy turkeys for. Because election day is the day after Thanksgiving. He wants to make a big show of handing out the turkeys just before Thanksgiving, he says, so other folks'll come looking for one too. When they do, he says he'll tell them they're too late for this election—all the turkeys are spoken for—but if they work for him between now and the next election, they'll be eligible for one too. And then he'll offer them one of the old standbys, a pint or cash, for their vote this time. The Deacon calls it his bait and switch."

Ward was dubious. "What's to guarantee that if we give someone a turkey on Saturday they're going to vote for us on Tuesday?" Ward believed, though he didn't say so to Jack, that the turkey giveaway had nothing to do with winning votes for Seamus O'Sullivan and everything to do with helping the Deacon bolster his image with his friends and neighbours.

"You, my young friend, have no faith in the honesty of the dishonest," Jack told him. "If the Deacon says they'll vote for us, they will."

For reasons that now made absolutely no sense, even to him, Ward decided to accompany the Deacon when he delivered the turkeys—partly to make sure O'Sullivan got the credit, and partly, perhaps, just perhaps, to bring the old bastard down a peg or two.

Which was how he'd got caught. His own damn fault.

On Saturday, Ward, driving Jack's Caprice, had led a cavalcade of a half-dozen horn-honking pickup trucks through Maynard Square's narrow laneways. Each vehicle was festooned with red balloons and O'SULLIVAN FOR PREMIER posters and jammed full of energetic, placard-waving young campaign workers Ward had recruited. The idea was to lure the residents to the main parking lot, where he and the Deacon could hand out the turkeys.

The Deacon wasn't amused. "Folks ain't gonna like that," he said. Ward ignored him, although he let the Deacon use the bullhorn to announce that Mr. and Mrs. So-and-So were about to receive a Thanksgiving turkey, "compliments of Seamus O'Sullivan, your Liberal candidate in Halifax North and the *next Premier of Nova Scotia!!*" On cue, the drivers all began honking their horns.

Ward thought it went well. In fact, he was back in his apartment that night celebrating with Victoria in his new double bed when Jack called and told him to get his ass back to the office immediately.

"Why is your friend Carter trying to fuck us over?" Jack demanded without preamble when Ward arrived.

What? "He's not my friend. I haven't seen him in years." *What a stupid answer.* "How's he fucking us over?"

It turned out the turkey giveaway had not gone as well as Ward believed. Someone from Black Pride was in an apartment above the parking lot snapping pictures the whole time. There were apparently photos of the Deacon with the bullhorn and some of Ward handing out turkeys from the trunk of Jack's car. After the Liberals had left, Black Pride workers had fanned out, interviewing residents and collecting affidavits from some who admitted they'd been given turkeys as a bribe to vote for O'Sullivan. And now Ray Carter was trying to peddle the story to the *Tribune.* One of the reporters at the paper, the one who was covering O'Sullivan's campaign, had called Jack to tip him off.

Once Jack had satisfied himself that Ward had had no contact with Ray since high school, his tone changed. "Okay," he declared, "we have some cards to play too. This fucking story will never see the light of day."

And it hadn't. Not yet anyway. Ward looked at his watch again.

Seven minutes to ten. Almost time for another newscast. He turned the radio back on.

For most of the past forty-eight hours, Patrick Donovan had wanted more than anything to be home in his bed asleep. But now that Harkin was telling him he should go and do exactly that, he resisted.

"But—"

"Look, kid," Harkin said, not unkindly, "you did what you could. It didn't work. It's not your fault. It's not our fault. It's not our paper. It's not our call."

"But—"

"Go home, kid. Get some sleep. Things'll look better when you wake up."

Patrick doubted that. He'd lucked into the biggest scoop of the election campaign, maybe the biggest story of the year, and the *Trib* wouldn't print it.

Late Saturday afternoon, Ray Carter, the Black Pride guy he'd quoted in a bunch of stories now, had phoned him at home, asked if he was interested in "a big story." When they met for coffee at Black Pride's offices a few hours later, Carter laid it all out. Affidavits, photos, everything. "Signed, sealed and delivered," he said with a smile.

But not published. When Patrick brought the materials back to the newsroom, Harkin was skeptical. "How do we know these people even exist?" he said, pointing to the sworn statements from eight Maynard Square residents, who each claimed a Liberal campaign worker named Ward Justice had given them a Thanksgiving turkey to vote for Seamus O'Sullivan. "Have you talked to any of them?"

"No, but—"

Harkin was incredulous. "You want us to put our asses on the line and you haven't even talked to them?"

"I will. I just got this stuff a few minutes ago and—"

"And these photos. Look at them. Grainy. Taken from miles away. You say this guy in the suit is that Liberal campaign worker talking to a coloured woman. What's that prove? Is she one of the affidavits? You say he's giving her a turkey, but all I see is a grocery bag. How can you tell what's really happening? Black Pride could have set the whole thing up just to make O'Sullivan—and us—look bad. Don't forget they don't like us very much."

"What about the picture of the guy by the car?" Patrick persisted. In the photo, the same man stood beside the open trunk of a car, handing what looked like a liquor bottle to a black man. Other men stood in a line behind him. Beyond them, you could clearly make out the outlines of the project's townhouses. The photograph had been taken in Maynard Square.

"Okay, so you can see his face in that one, and, yes, it could be the same guy in the other pictures . . ." Harkin took his loupe out of his desk drawer, placed it on the photo over the trunk of the car. "What were you saying about the licence plate?"

"Carter told me somebody in Motor Vehicles ran the plate for them and came up with the fact that it's registered to . . ." Patrick flipped through his notebook looking for the name. ". . . Jack Eagleson," he said triumphantly. "The party's provincial campaign manager." He hadn't known who the campaign manager was until Carter had told him a few hours ago. He hoped he was right.

"That could be worth a story, no question," Harkin mused. He seemed to be warming to the idea. "A very big story. But we'd have to confirm it. *You'd* have to confirm it. That and everything else. Interview everyone who gave a statement. Talk to their neighbours. What do they know? Did they see anything? Eyeball this Justice guy. Who is he? What does he do for the campaign? Is he really the same guy as in the pictures? And what's he have to say for himself?"

"I can do that." Patrick wasn't sure how, but he wasn't going to let this story slip away from him.

"And you don't have much time either, kid." Harkin looked at his watch, more for effect than for information. "The polls open in forty-eight hours and this is a holiday weekend."

"I can do it," Patrick repeated, more confident this time.

And he had. Patrick had done everything Harkin asked. He'd re-interviewed everyone who'd given a statement. They'd all confirmed what they'd claimed in the affidavits. Some had even shown him the turkeys and told him about the arrangements they'd made to be picked up and driven to the polling station by a Liberal volunteer on election day. One thing missing from the affidavits Black Pride had gathered was any reference to the role of a black man named George Johnstone; he was, they told Patrick, the man who'd initially made all the arrangements. Patrick included that in his story, too. And he got the paper's police reporter to call in a favour and confirm that the car was indeed registered to Eagleson. He found out Justice was a law student working on the O'Sullivan campaign out of Eagleson's law offices. He even tracked down the wholesaler who'd sold Justice fifty fresh turkeys—paid for in cash—and found out he'd picked them up from the depot on Saturday morning. When Patrick reached Justice at Eagleson's law office Sunday evening to ask for a comment, Justice hung up on him.

He called Eagleson, too. Eagleson listened quietly while Patrick laid out the story.

"I was wondering, sir, if you have any comment you want to make?"

"Only that you should be very careful what you print, young man," Eagleson replied evenly, more calmly than Patrick had expected. Then, after a pause, "You went to Saint Mary's, didn't you?"

"Ah . . . yes."

"You must know Father Hanrahan, then."

"He was my History professor."

"Great man. The best. Give him my regards when you see him."

"But—"

Eagleson cut him off. "I've been told that you're a clever young man with a very bright future," he said slowly. Who would have told him that? Patrick wondered. And how did Eagleson know who he was when Patrick had never even heard of Eagleson before yesterday? "I wouldn't want to see your career go off the rails before it's begun." Eagleson sounded solicitous. "So my advice to you, young man, is not to let yourself be used by some radical group with an axe to grind. That's my comment. But it's off the record. I don't want to see it in the paper. Understood?"

Patrick understood it was a great quote. In his first draft of the story, he put in the entire exchange, even including Eagleson's warning not to use it. Harkin took his red pen and carefully stroked out the entire paragraph. "This isn't about you," he grumbled. Instead he wrote in the margin: "Reached by the *Tribune*, Mr. Eagleson said he had no comment."

He also cut out the reference to Justice hanging up on him. "How do you know he hung up on you? Maybe there was a problem with the connection." He replaced it with a simple, "Mr. Justice could not be reached for comment."

Harkin finished editing the piece early Monday evening, the night before the vote, while Patrick sat in the straight-backed wooden chair besidc his desk, feeling like an errant schoolboy in the principal's office. Finally Harkin put down his pen, shoved his glasses on top of his head and slumped in his chair.

"Not bad, kid, not bad. I'd say it's ready for the lawyers now."

And that was the last anyone had told him anything, until just after nine this morning when Harkin told him to go home.

Harkin had called Mr. MacDonald, the Managing Editor, at home to tell him about the story. Within the hour, MacDonald had breezed into the newsroom, motioning for Harkin to follow him. Soon, his big, glass-windowed office at one end of the newsroom began to fill with men in suits.

MacDonald and Harkin were joined by two men Patrick didn't recognize. Their conversation was animated, much of it directed toward Harkin, who seemed alternately angry and resigned. By midnight, the publisher himself had arrived. Within a few minutes, he was talking to someone else on the telephone.

While the publisher talked, Harkin came out into the newsroom to dispatch a copy boy to the all-night restaurant a few blocks from the newsroom to get hamburgers and Cokes for the men in MacDonald's office.

"What's going on in there?" Patrick asked apprehensively.

"Horse-trading," Harkin replied. "Stuff you don't need to know, stuff you don't want to know." And went back inside.

Over the course of the night, while Patrick remained rooted to his chair, the newsroom emptied out as the last of the night editors went home, and then, a few hours later, just before dawn, it began to fill up again as the first dayside editors arrived to put together the afternoon edition.

Sometime around five in the morning, yet another man, this one dressed more casually in a sports jacket and wearing no tie, arrived. Patrick didn't recognize him either. Soon after, he and the publisher left and took the elevator up to the publisher's office. Patrick knew that because the brass half-moon floor indicator above the elevator jerked its way haltingly up to the fifth floor. An hour later, the two men returned. The publisher, looking pleased with himself, was holding a piece of paper in one hand. As they walked through the empty newsroom, seemingly oblivious to his presence, Patrick couldn't make out what they were saying, but he couldn't help but notice the other man's booming laugh, which filled the newsroom.

A few minutes later, the publisher, the Managing Editor and the men Patrick didn't recognize emerged from the office. No one looked at him; in fact, they seemed to deliberately avoid looking in his direction. Harkin accompanied them to the elevator, where everyone solemnly shook hands and talked quietly until it arrived.

After the others had left, Harkin slowly, almost reluctantly, returned to his desk and gestured for Patrick to join him.

"The good news," he began, trying his best to smile, "is that we still have our jobs." He let that sink in. "The bad news is that we're not running your story."

"Why not?"

"Well, for starters, the lawyers think we'd get sued—"

"But we've got affidavits, pictures, everything!"

"I know, I know, but they—"

"What do they need? I'll go back and—"

"The story's not running, kid. Not today. Not tomorrow. Not ever." Harkin sounded tired, defeated.

"What! Why not? You said—"

"I said it wasn't a bad story, and it wasn't. But there's more going on than you know."

Patrick was fighting the tears now. *I must be really tired*, he thought.

Harkin looked at him thoughtfully for what seemed like hours, then, apparently deciding to risk it, said, "Okay, I'm going to tell you what's going on, but you have to promise you won't breathe a word of it to anybody. Anybody! Got me?"

"Yeah, sure, but—"

"Not buts. Nobody. Understand?" He waited while Patrick nodded that he did. "You know that parliamentary committee, the one looking into newspaper ownership?"

"Uh-huh."

"Well, the publisher's heard from his buddies in Ottawa that the committee's final report is going to piss all over us for being a lousy newspaper, so he's getting his ducks in a row so he can piss right back at them."

Patrick was confused. What did this have to do with—?

"He figures the Liberals are gonna win today and O'Sullivan's going to be premier," Harkin explained. "Why do you think the paper endorsed him?" Patrick was dimly aware of Saturday's signed editorial in which the publisher had announced that, for the first time ever, the *Trib* was supporting the Liberal Party. Patrick had been too busy with other matters to bother reading it.

"He wants O'Sullivan to intercede with the Prime Minister, get him to put pressure on the committee to rewrite its report before it's released. So the last thing he wants right now is for his own paper to starting gumming up the works with the new government."

"You mean he—?"

"Exactly. But don't worry. He's not pissed off at us. In fact, he's delighted with us. We gave him the ammunition he needed. Tonight was all about making a deal. That's why Eagleson was here."

"He was?"

"You didn't know that was him?" Harkin laughed. "You *are* young. Eagleson was the last guy to come in, the one not wearing a tie. Those two other guys were lawyers, ours and theirs. But Eagleson was the only one who could make a deal. That's what he and the publisher were doing when they went upstairs. They were agreeing on the wording of the letter O'Sullivan's going to send to the Prime Minister and what he's going to say when the PM phones him later tonight to congratulate him on his election victory."

"But what about—?"

"About nothing, kid. It's over. Finished. The good news is we live to fight another day."

Somehow, at that moment, that didn't seem like good news to Patrick.

On his way back to his apartment, he stopped in at the Black Pride offices. He hadn't planned to tell Carter what had really happened, simply that the lawyers had decided the story could be libellous, but then he couldn't help himself and the whole mess spilled out.

He was surprised Carter was so unsurprised. "Don't worry," he said. "I knew they'd find a way not to print it."

Patrick made Carter promise not say a word to anyone—"I'm not even supposed to know"—and then continued the walk to his apartment. On the way, he passed his local polling station, thought briefly about going in to vote—it would be the first election in which he was old enough—but decided against it. Who would he vote for anyway? He went home and went to sleep instead.

"One more round, then we eat. Okay?" Ward must have looked dubious; he was hurtling past tipsy on the way to drunk. "Hey, don't worry, Ward, this one's on Canada. Your friend Pierre's buying this round." He raised his still half-full glass. "To Pierre . . . I mean, what the hell, eh? It's almost Christmas, you've finished your exams, your team won—"

"Okay." *What the hell,* Ward thought. *Why not? It* was *almost Christmas.*

"Waiter . . . Another draft here. And can we see some menus?"

"Team, what team?" It was John, a beat behind the conversation. Or was he Tom? Were those even their real names? They both wore dark-blue suits with red ties. They both looked like they'd be more comfortable without the ties. One was bald, one wasn't. That was the difference. Ward decided Baldy would be Tom, and Not Baldy would be John. Just to keep them straight.

"Liberals," Baldy Tom answered his buddy. "Our boy here helped get O'Sullivan elected down here this fall, didn't you, Ward?" He looked at Ward, winked. "My friend doesn't get out of Ottawa much."

Oh God, this was going to be about the election, about the affidavits and photos. But why would these guys care about that?

"Politics." Not Bald John emitted a bubbly beer belch of dismissal. "I thought you meant somethin' interesting. Like hockey." He turned to Ward. "You like hockey, Ward?"

"Yeah . . ." Ward needed to slow this down, figure out what was really going on. One of them—Ward thought the one who said his name was Tom, whichever one that was—had called him at home this morning. Victoria had answered. He'd asked her not to; he was worried his parents might call. He hadn't told them about Victoria.

"Some guy," she said, putting her hand over the mouthpiece. "Deep voice." She was sitting cross-legged on the bed, dressed only in one of his old sweatshirts. She still hadn't moved her clothes into the apartment. He'd asked her to. He reached out, took the phone.

"Yes?" he said. He needed to brush his teeth, blow his nose, expel last night's smoke from his lungs. After his Criminal Law exam yesterday, he'd bought a bottle of Mateus to celebrate. He thought he'd done well enough, but he knew the profs liked to be hard-assed with Christmas marks to send the first-years a message. Victoria knew he was worried. Which was why she'd scored a couple of joints from one of her friends at the Art College. They'd got drunk and stoned and made love, and since it was only ten o'clock, they'd gone over to the law school bar, and drank and danced until they were the last ones there. When was that? The bar was supposed to close at one, but it never did. "We're on west coast time," one of the bartenders told him. "We close when it's one o'clock in Vancouver." Which would have made it five in the morning Halifax time. He looked at the clock on the night table. Nine forty-five! No wonder he was—

"... maybe for lunch. We were thinking the Downtowner. The boys here claim they have the best tavern steaks in town."

What was he talking about? Who was he? Ward had drifted in and out, and could bring back only snatches of what the man had said. Tom something or other? Security? "Sorry," he said finally. "Can you run that by me again? I'm not quite awake ..."

"Hard night last night." The man hadn't asked it as a question. "Sorry, let me rewind. My name's Tom Aniston and I'm with the RCMP in Ottawa. My partner John and I are in town on other business and someone suggested you might be able to help us. So I decided to give you a call, Ward, see if you were free for lunch."

"Ah ..." He looked at the roach in the ashtray. Was this ... ?

"Don't worry," Tom said, as if anticipating. "You're not in any trouble. We just think you might know some things that could help us."

"Ah ..." What kind of information? Ward wanted to ask. But he couldn't. Victoria had submarined under the covers. She was kissing his chest now, using her teeth to tease his nipples. Her hand was on his penis.

"I'd rather not get into the details on the phone," Tom continued, answering the question Ward hadn't asked. "Why don't you just let us buy you lunch and we can lay it out for you?"

"Ah ... sure," he said, the "sure" a sucking in of breath as Victoria's mouth wrapped around his penis.

He and Victoria made love, showered, made love again. He didn't even leave the apartment until after eleven-thirty. He'd already decided to spend the afternoon looking for a Christmas gift for her. Something personal. A ring maybe. Not an engagement ring; she'd think that was stupid. But something personal. And expensive ...

He took a sip of the draft the waiter had put on the table. Was this his fourth beer? Fifth?

"Now you take the Leafs ..." Ward tried to snap himself back into the conversation. Not Bald John was still talking hockey. "I mean, the Leafs won the Cup—what was it? Four years ago? Centennial Year. Now look. Out of the playoffs two out of the last three years. Expansion. That's the problem. Fourteen fucking teams! The fucking California fucking Golden fucking Seals for fuck's sake! I mean, there's not enough hockey players for fourteen NHL teams. The—"

"But that's not Toronto's problem," Bald Tom cut in. "Toronto's problem is incompetent management. They let Imlach go to Buffalo, and he takes half the Leafs with him. He even got Eddie Shack back from L.A. or California or wherever he was . . ."

"I still say expansion is ruining hockey." Ward suspected they'd performed this routine before. "I mean some *defenceman* winning a scoring title. What kind of shit is that?"

"Bobby Orr? Bobby Orr's not some defenceman." Bald Tom again. "Did you see that goal he scored against St. Louis in the finals last year? Flying through the air and he still scores—I'm sorry." He stopped suddenly, looked at Ward. "We get carried away sometimes. What it is to work with someone for so long. We're like some old married couple."

"Except you're not nearly as good looking as my wife," Not Bald John added. They both laughed. Ward was sure this was part of their shtick. Which had now served its purpose.

"Anyway," Bald Tom said, "we didn't ask you to lunch to hear us bitch. How's school?"

"Fine." If this wasn't about vote buying, what was it about?

"Tom's thinking of going back to law school himself," Not Bald John said. "If any place would have him . . . You like the new apartment?"

Wha—how did they know about the apartment? "Good."

"Your girlfriend's a looker," Not Bald John added. "She move in yet?"

Were they just showing off their knowledge of the intimate details of his life, or trying to intimidate him with them? Did they know about the gift he was planning to buy Victoria, or that she'd invited herself to Christmas dinner at his parents' place? "I can't be your secret forever, you know," she'd said. He didn't know why not.

He visited his parents less often since he'd got his apartment. The apartment, in the south-end university ghetto, was close to law school and close to the law firm, close even to Victoria's parents, but as far as possible from his parents' north-end bungalow. Even though he had Jack's car for his own use, and even though he'd spent a good deal of time in the old neighbourhood during the election campaign, he'd only visited twice, both times at his mother's insistence, for perfunctory Sunday dinners. "You have to have a home-cooked meal every once in a while," she'd said.

Ward didn't tell her he'd developed a taste for something other than overcooked roast beef, mashed potatoes and canned peas. When he wanted roast beef now, he ordered it medium rare at Chez Henri, where it arrived with Yorkshire pudding and an assortment of fresh vegetables. Not to mention a carafe of red wine. Followed by an after-dinner Kahlua and a cigarette. His mother didn't serve alcohol or allow smoking in the house; whenever his father wanted a nip of rum or a quick smoke, he slipped away to his workshop in the basement.

What would Victoria really think of his parents? He couldn't decide whether she was genuinely interested in getting to know them or whether, like him, they were members of an alien species she found exotic in an anthropological way: the working poor.

She never tired of being amused by the things he didn't know—about music, travel, theatre, art. She insisted on bringing him along to openings at the college gallery. Once, it was an exhibition by one of her favourite professors. The centrepiece was a slide show in which a series of words, with their definitions, were projected on a white wall for ten seconds at a time, one after the other after the other. The work was titled *Four-Letter Words*, and it purported to be a complete listing of all of the four-letter words in the dictionary. From "Abba: *noun* Father: a title anciently used with the names of patriarchs" to "zeal: *noun* Ardour for a cause or, less often, a person."

"But what's the point?" Ward wanted to know.

"The point is the point," she'd answered.

And then there was the night they'd gone up on the roof of the Art College building to watch a visiting artist from New York, whose performance art consisted of walking around naked with his entire body painted green. It was titled *Envy*. Ward didn't envy him. It was a cold fall evening and the man's cock had shrivelled up into his balls until it had almost disappeared completely.

"I don't get it," Ward had said.

"What's so hard to get?" she'd answered. Ward sometimes thought Victoria probably didn't understand it either but knew enough—from her upbringing?—not to let her ignorance show. He loved her for it. He loved her because she was nothing like him.

"We're talking about living together," he said finally, answering Not Bald John's question. "Maybe after Christmas." How long had that silence gone on? He'd almost drained another beer. Four? Five? He couldn't remember. It dawned on him that Bald Tom and Not Bald John hadn't been matching him round for round. They each had almost half a glass left. Of how many? Two? Three?

"Waiter?" It was Bald Tom. "We're ready to order. How about one of your rib steaks, medium rare?"

"Medium rare?" The waiter laughed. "You can have it undercooked or overdone. Your choice."

"Undercooked, I guess. What's it come with?"

"Well, you can have fries or fries. Your choice."

"Well, since you put it that way, I guess I'll have fries."

"Good choice. And you, sir?"

They all ordered the same. "And another beer here for my friend, Ward, when you get a chance."

Ward knew he should protest but he didn't. Maybe he wouldn't go shopping after all.

"Well, Ward," Bald Tom began again when the waiter had gone. His tone had changed. "You're probably wondering why we wanted to talk with you. I told you when I called this morning that John and I work with S and I, Security and Intelligence, in Ottawa. I don't know how much you know about us; we're members of the RCMP, but a special section off on our own. Our job is to collect information on people who might want to do harm to Canada—from inside or outside the country—and make sure they don't get that chance. Finding Cross?" he said proudly. "That was us."

He had Ward's attention now. Last week, Ward had watched it all on the old TV with the broken rabbit ears Victoria had stolen for him from her parents' house. He'd been studying for his Christmas exams when Victoria called to tell him the authorities had found British diplomat James Cross; it was on TV. Ward could still recall watching the news a few days after the provincial election when police had found the body of Pierre Laporte, the Cabinet minister who'd been kidnapped by another FLQ cell. He'd been strangled and stuffed into a car trunk. James Cross was still very much alive.

Ward had to insert a coat hanger into the hole where the rabbit ears had been and then twist it this way and that to get a snowy picture. He'd watched for hours, even though there really was nothing to see. Mostly just a static wide shot of what had been the grounds of Expo 67 in Montreal. The announcers talked endlessly about the almost nothing they knew about what was really going on. "We're expecting a bus carrying Mr. Cross and his kidnappers to arrive here any moment," they repeated every five minutes. "That car you can just make out in the distance"—Ward couldn't see beyond a few ghostly outlines of buildings—"is the Cuban ambassador's limousine." The only thing the journalists seemed to know was that the police had found the FLQ's hideout and made a deal with the kidnappers; the police agreed to provide them with safe passage to Cuba and, in return, the kidnappers agreed to hand Cross over to the Cuban ambassador, who would hold him until the kidnappers' plane touched down in Havana.

"Really?" Ward said. He wasn't sure he believed Bald Tom.

"Really," Bald Tom answered, then amended his reply. "I mean, not 'us,' specifically, but 'us,' as in S and I." Ward was disappointed. "John and I work mostly on the English side. Campus radicals, communists, labour activists."

"I can see you're puzzled," Not Bald John cut in, "like, 'What does any of this have to do with me?'"

Ward nodded, felt the beer dizzy him.

"What do you know about an organization called Black Hands?"

Black Hands? "Nothing," Ward said. "Never heard of it."

"Black Pride?"

Ah, so this *was* about the photos! "Just that it's an organization, you know, the government set up. A self-help group for black people. Is that right?"

"What can you tell us about a guy named Raymond Carter?"

Ray? Ray Carter? "Ah . . . I knew him. When I was a kid. I haven't seen him in . . . I don't know? Years, at least . . ."

"We know that," Bald John said. If they knew so much, Ward wanted to shout, why did they ask him so goddamn many questions? "And we know you don't have anything to do with the stuff he's involved with these days."

Which was?

"We're just trying to put together a file," Not Bald Tom added. "Background stuff. We thought you could help us fill in some of the blanks from his childhood. When you *did* know him."

"Has he done something wrong?" Ward asked, not expecting an answer.

"He's just someone we're interested in knowing more about," Bald John answered. "He's been involved with some people who are involved with some people we're interested in. That's all. So you met him when?"

What the hell? Ward thought. They didn't seem to care about the vote buying. What harm could it do?

"I met him my first day of school . . ."

"Ssshhh," Rosa giggled, guiding Ray through the darkened living room, around the Christmas tree, by the fake mantelpiece her father had transformed into a photographic shrine to the memory of Rosa's mother, past a wall festooned with framed certificates attesting to Deacon George Johnstone's many and various good works and then down a long, echoing—he should have taken off his boots—parquet hallway, where she finally ushered him into her bedroom. As Ray allowed himself to exhale, Rosa gently closed the door behind him and flipped on the overhead light.

It was a little girl's room, soft pink walls, frilly white curtains, a collection of stuffed bears neatly arranged at the head of the bed. He shouldn't have been there.

That had been made very clear to him three weeks ago, at the Queen Elizabeth High School Christmas dance, when Ray had run into his old teacher. At first, Mr. Dunphy had seemed delighted to see him. "Seems like I see you on the news most every night," he'd said, pumping his hand like a long-lost friend. Ray guessed that not too many students in Dr. Dummy's class ever ended up on TV, unless it was in film footage showing them being led into or out of a courtroom, probably in handcuffs.

"What brings you back to your alma mater tonight, Mr. Carter?" he asked, cheerfully enough. But when Ray nodded in Rosa's direction—she was pouring them glasses of punch from the bowl in the corner—Mr. Dunphy did what seemed to Ray like a double take.

"Oh," Mr. Dunphy said, arching his right eyebrow in a look that mixed surprise and disapproval. "I see." And Ray could see that he did. Or was Ray just imagining censure in his tone. Because of his own insecurity.

After that night at the demonstration nearly two months ago, Ray had flipped it back and forth in his mind—he would/he wouldn't; he should/he shouldn't—before he'd finally called, asked Rosa if she wanted, maybe, to have a coffee with him, if she had time, of course, and only if she wanted to.

She'd laughed at his awkwardness. He liked her laugh. "Sure," she'd answered, then laughed again. "Just as long as you don't talk about that academic-streaming stuff."

He didn't, and they hadn't. They'd talked about growing up in Africville, happy childhood memories, Aunt Annie's treats, their fathers' rivalry.

Their first "dates" had all taken place in the same tucked-away booth at the far end of Calhoun's, the very same booth where he'd met—no, don't think about him.

Truth? He couldn't stop thinking about *her*. Between their first coffee and their second a week later, Ray had become so distracted he'd missed an important meeting Calvin had called so Ray could explain to some angry Black Pride board members why he'd agreed to limit the number of black speakers at the City Hall rally. "Oh, don't worry about it," Calvin had said the next day, reporting to Ray on what had happened at the meeting. He'd been more gracious than Ray had any right to expect. "You didn't need to be there. They just needed to get it off their chests was all."

Ray wondered if Calvin would have been so understanding if Ray had confessed he'd forgotten the meeting because he was too busy fantasizing about Calvin's baby sister?

Ray knew it wasn't right. He was twenty-one, Rosa only fifteen. "I'll be sixteen in a month," she'd said defensively when he'd finally raised the issue of their age difference, while simultaneously confessing he was in love with her.

She already knew that, of course. She was in love with him too, she said. "But we can't tell anybody," she added. "Not yet." It was their age difference, of course, and more. Her father mostly. Deacon Johnstone's dislike of Lawrence Carter had become a blanket bitterness about his entire family, especially Ray.

"He thought it was deliberate," Rosa had confided during their first coffee. "He figured you wouldn't let him speak that night because no one had bothered to invite your dad."

Ray had tried to explain about Spittle Man, but she'd cut him off with a smile. "Don't worry about it. I'm not my father."

Still, it was her father who loomed like a dark cloud over the sunny skies of their first days. Ray would wait for Rosa after school and walk her home along circuitous side streets, but only to within a few blocks of Maynard Square, where they'd exchange a furtive kiss before she continued on to her apartment and Ray went back to work. At night, Rosa would tell her father she had to go to the drugstore—"I say I need some 'girl stuff' and he doesn't ask any more questions"—and they would meet at Fort Needham, a grassy park overlooking Maynard Square, where they would lie on the ground and neck for as long as they could withstand the cold and for as long as they dared.

"I only wish . . ." she would say.

"Me too."

But there was no place for them to go to be alone together. Ray couldn't afford a car. And he was still living with his father, sleeping in a sleeping bag on the floor in the living room amid the stacks of boxes his father kept packed for his return to Africville. In his first six months back in Halifax, Ray had been working so hard at Black Pride that he only ever came back to his father's apartment late at night, and only to sleep. It seemed pointless to waste his salary on rent. Now, suddenly, he needed a place of his own. He'd found one last week—a bachelor apartment on Brunswick Street—but he couldn't move in until the beginning of January.

Rosa hadn't wanted to wait.

"Don't worry," she'd said when they'd rendezvoused earlier that night at the entrance to Fort Needham Park. It was December now, and far too cold to lie on the frozen ground. "Daddy's a heavy sleeper. He won't know we're there."

Which was how they'd ended up in Rosa's little-girl pink bedroom, Ray staring at the stuffed animals and wondering what in hell he was doing there anyway. He reached behind him to turn the light off.

"No," she said, drawing him closer. "I want to see your face."

The next thing he knew, he was squinting awake to sunlight streaming in through the bedroom window. But it wasn't the sunlight that woke him. It was the sound of arguing from down the hall.

"Your mother, God rest her soul . . . Her only daughter! And under her own roof? What would she think? What would she say?"

"She would say, 'Do you love him?' That's what she would say."

"Don't you go blaspheming your mother's memory like that. Don't you dare! Not after what you've done. And with . . . that one!"

"What one? Just because you and his father hate each other doesn't mean we have to be that stupid—"

"Don't you call me stupid, young lady! I'm still your father and you'll do as I say, so long as you live under my roof."

"Well maybe it's time I moved out from under your roof then!"

Ray rolled over, away from the light, pulled the covers up over his head. Maybe he was dreaming. He had to be dreaming.

7

Fall 2002

"Please hang up and try your call again . . . This is a recording . . . Please hang up and try your call again." Uhuru Melesse sat hunched over his desk, the telephone's handset still pressed against his ear. How long had he been listening to the insistent thrum of the dial tone before that disembodied voice finally cut in? What was he thinking? He should have said, *Yes, thank you.* Or, *I wish I could, but I'm just too busy right now, call me again next month* . . . Not: "I'm out of the property business." Spoken with finality, even a kind of spiteful distaste.

And to one of his best clients, a real estate developer whose buying and selling Uhuru had been handling for at least ten years. He wanted Uhuru to handle the legal work for a new apartment complex he was buying. It would have meant a substantial fee at a time when there were far more bills than cheques in his inbox. Still, he'd said no. What was he thinking?

He replaced the handset in its cradle, turned his attention back to the folder in front of him:

Interview with James Joseph Howe
Det. Fred Hopkins
02/05/06
13:15–15:45
Interrogation Room 3

As confessions go, it was full and complete and, based on the policeman's numerous cautions and warnings—spoken, written, signed and witnessed—about as defence bulletproofed as the Crown could have hoped. During his interrogation, J. J. had not only happily, eagerly confessed to taking the money, he'd also explained—without being asked—exactly how he did it, all of which forensic auditors had since confirmed, thanks in no small measure to the road map to his crime J. J. had voluntarily provided them.

What J. J. had not turned over to the police—though they quickly got a court order to seize them, too—were his bank records, which showed all the inflows and outflows. *Those* he'd turned over to his lawyer.

Which only served to confirm that J. J. had no hidden ill-gotten gains to pay for his defence. Worse, J. J.'s modest salary as a bookkeeper for the City was not modest enough to qualify him for legal aid. Worst, J. J. had used most of his salary to top up his contributions to various African–Nova Scotian charities, programs and good works, meaning he had no valuable assets at all to contribute.

He lived in a rented room on Agricola Street smaller than his cell at the Correctional Centre. With the exception of a used radio and a cheap microwave, the furniture all belonged to the landlord. With the exception of the suit he wore to his arraignment, the clothes in his closet were so worn and threadbare they would not have passed inspection by the buyers at Value Village.

Uhuru had discovered all of this the day after J. J.'s arraignment. "I need you to get something out of my room," J. J. had whispered to Uhuru just before the sheriff's deputies led him away. Uhuru imagined J. J. was about to tell him where to find a secret stash of cash. He'd hoped so, partly, of course, because that would mean J. J. could afford his fees, and partly because the idea that J. J. might really be as selfless as he seemed scared the hell out of Uhuru. His hope was in vain.

"I have some library books that are due back tomorrow," J. J. confided, handing Uhuru a key. "Could you take them back for me?"

The library books, it turned out, were the only items in the room offering even a hint about its occupant: *Soul on Ice* by Eldridge Cleaver, *Ready for Revolution: The Life and Struggles of Stokely Carmichael (Kwame Ture)*, by Stokely Carmichael and Ekwueme Thelwell, *Revolutionary Suicide* and *To Die for the People* by Huey Newton, and *The Autobiography of Malcolm X*.

Uhuru had returned them, then checked them out using his own card. Reading them—some for a second time—had taken Uhuru back to the New Word Order bookstore in Toronto, to his own political awakenings. Had J. J. felt the same connection, the same surging power coursing through his veins when he read the words of all those righteously angry black men for the first time?

Whatever happened to that Raymond Carter, anyway?

Uhuru looked around at his own sparsely furnished office. If he'd sold out, it had been for too little. The furniture was a mishmash: mismatched desk, dark wood veneer; and chairs, one oak rolling, one metal folding, one plastic stackable. Along the wall between his office and the reception area there were cardboard bankers boxes instead of filing cabinets stacked floor to ceiling. On the opposite wall behind his desk there was a haphazard bookshelf made of cinder blocks and unfinished planks, filled with unread legal tomes Uhuru kept for decorative purposes. The office itself, on the fourth floor of an unrenovated old building downtown, was in desperate need of a paint job, or at least a good cleaning. But the landlord—whose application to tear down the structure and replace it with condos was slowly working its way through the labyrinthian approval processes of the City's Development Department—wasn't about to waste his money on such frivolities.

Not that that mattered to Uhuru. He had alienated most of his best clients in order to devote all his time to the lost cause of J. J. Howe, who, of course, was still languishing in jail and unable to drop in for tea, so Uhuru had no need to impress visitors. Or visitors to impress.

That wasn't quite true. Shondelle Adams had become such a regular the last few months that he'd given her his secretary's desk in the front office. There was no secretary; there never had been, though Uhuru did keep a vase with plastic flowers on the otherwise empty desktop to make the room look more lived in. A woman used to come in every two weeks to invoice clients and update his accounts, but he'd replaced her last year with a computer program he was sure he could master. He hadn't. Luckily, there wasn't much billing to do.

Shondelle had become more than just a visitor in Uhuru's office. Because she was there and because neither of them had anyone to go home to, they began having dinner together. At first just once in a while, then more often, now every weekday evening. Uhuru couldn't remember who had initially suggested dinner. In the beginning, the plan was to discuss some aspect of the case they were working on—even though, in the end, they often didn't even get around to talking about that. After a while, they stopped needing a reason. That didn't mean there was anything more to it than convenience. Was there?

Shondelle, of course, had an office at the law school, but she claimed she couldn't get any work done there because students were always interrupting her. She'd even moved her files for ADA's civil suit to Uhuru's office, "in case we need to look at them."

We had become the operative word. Shondelle had become his unofficial partner in defending J. J. Howe. They had never discussed collaborating; it had just happened. Uhuru wasn't sure what he thought of that.

On the one hand, she was annoyingly self-confident. On the other, she was smart, smarter than he was. She could weave together disparate legal threads and transform them into the whole cloth of what seemed, to Uhuru at least, to be compelling arguments explaining why J. J. was justified in doing what he'd done.

Recently, for example, she'd begun studying cases involving battered wife syndrome, searching in the language of those decisions for some elastic to stretch the legal justification from the right of an abused woman to shoot her abuser in the back in his sleep to the right of a black man abused by a racist legal process to take the law into his own hands.

That was the first hurdle: convincing a judge to let them present a defence based on what amounted to justification. And not just *any* judge; they had to convince Ward Justice. Uhuru had been surprised that Justice still wanted to preside over the trial after the controversy at the arraignment. But, for reasons he couldn't quite articulate, he resisted Shondelle's suggestion that they file a motion asking him to recuse himself. Perhaps it was because he couldn't square the Ward Justice of that day in the courtroom with the Ward Justice he'd played with as a kid. Or perhaps it was more calculating; having come under fire for his actions in the courtroom, maybe Justice might actually be inclined to respond favourably to such an unusual defence to demonstrate he *wasn't* a racist.

Even if Justice did allow them to argue justification, of course, they would still have to figure out how to pick a suitably compassionate jury. Would it be possible to get a majority of blacks? Would that even be helpful? Would blacks be more sympathetic, or less patient with an argument that assumed they were helpless victims of a racist society? Whether the jury was black or white, could he convince it to pull what amounted to a Henry Morgentaler and acquit J.J. in spite of the fact he'd admitted doing what the Crown accused him of doing, which the law clearly said was a crime?

A knock on the door interrupted his reverie. It was a perfunctory knock; Shondelle Adams didn't wait for him to respond.

"I think I found something very interesting," she announced breathlessly. She was holding his father's diary.

Uhuru had been afraid to read it, afraid of what he might learn about what his father thought of the choices he'd made. Still, he'd given his okay when Shondelle asked a few months ago to read it, "to see if there's anything we can use." She hadn't said anything more about it, except one evening at dinner last week when she'd said, without preamble, "I find it hard to think of you as Raymond. Did your father always call you Raymond?"

"Only when he was angry," he replied.

"He doesn't seem to be angry in the diary," Shondelle said. "The opposite, in fact. It's 'Raymond did this,' and 'Raymond did that,' especially after your mother died and it was just the two of you. He was very proud of you."

And now here she was back in his office, holding the diary in her hands. "You never told me you were friends with Ward Justice!"

"That was a long time ago. Doesn't have anything to do with now . . ."

"Don't be so sure, Raymond." She'd begun to call him that. Usually when she was trying to make a point. He liked the sound of it in his ears, though he never told her so. "Did you know that Ward Justice was there the day Jack Eagleson tried to bribe your father with that cash?"

"What!"

"It's in the diary. Your father wrote it all down—the meeting in the hotel room, the bottle of Scotch, the cash in the briefcase, and then this . . ." She opened the diary, began to read: "'I wasn't surprised by anything except for the presence of Raymond's young friend, Ward, who accompanied Mr. Eagleson. From the look on his face, I could tell he was as surprised to see me as I was him. When I was leaving, I told him I'd tell Raymond I saw him, but I won't. I don't want to embarrass him. Unless Mr. Eagleson tries to claim he didn't offer me a suitcase full of cash. If he does, then I guess I'll have to tell the reporter there was a young man present too. What will the boy do then? Tell the truth? Or back up Mr. Eagleson? I hope I don't have to find out.'"

Shondelle looked up. "This is it!" she said excitedly.

"What is?"

"The bullet in the chamber, that's what. All we have to do is pull the trigger to turn it into a smoking gun. I mean, we're not just talking about some judge's racist attitudes to black people any more. We're talking about his part in a plot to deprive the people of Africville of their land. He'll have to step aside—"

"No."

"No?"

"No."

"What do you mean, 'No'? We can get this guy off the case and maybe get somebody more sympathetic—"

"No."

"Why not?"

"Because." He couldn't tell her the real reason, not without telling her other things he wasn't ready to confess. Not yet. "Just because," he said. He paused, then added, "You ready to eat?"

"Because! Because? That's your answer? That's all you're going to say?"

"It's complicated," he said. "Stuff I don't want to get into now. So you'll just have to trust me." He tried his best reassuring smile. "Besides, it isn't going to disappear. Think of it as insurance. There if we need it later . . . How about Ethiopian? I read in *High Tide* there's a new Ethiopian restaurant on Quinpool Road. I've never had Ethiopian food before, have you?"

She shook her head, more in resignation than response.

She could have been more grateful, David Astor thought as he watched the pregnant young woman in the audio booth beside him. She was listening through her oversized headphones, jotting the occasional note in her steno pad. He glanced at the counter on the Ampex tape deck. Less than a minute to go before—how would she react? Once he knew that, he would decide whether to tell her the rest.

He'd been disappointed when he called earlier in the week to tell her he'd found the audio tape she was looking for. It was almost as if she resented him for having discovered the very tape she said she wanted. Women. He would never understand them. Like that Mrs. Justice, who'd seemed so pleased when he showed her the picture. *Oh yes, David, I'll give you a call next week . . .* She never had.

He wasn't sure why he bothered. It had taken him hours, unpaid nights and weekends, to finally decipher this Lambie fellow's indexing system. Some of the audio tapes were filed by the name of the speaker, some by the event, some according to no logic David Astor could determine. He'd almost given up then, but something—his own obsessiveness, probably—kept him rummaging through tapes until, finally, three weeks after he'd begun, he'd stumbled across the motherlode: the audio tapes of speeches from annual press gallery dinners.

The first tape featured a droll, self-deprecating speech by Premier Robert Stanfield. David guessed, since Stanfield referred to Prime Minister Pearson and not to any national Tory leadership controversy, it must have been recorded sometime in the mid-sixties. The next speech, by someone whose name he didn't recognize, made reference to the new Canadian flag—1965?—so he decided to take a chance and skip ahead nine reels. Since Justice was elected in 1974 and resigned in 1976, his press gallery speech, if there was one, would have had to be from one of those years.

It wasn't the 1974 dinner. That one featured a very drunk Seamus O'Sullivan announcing the date of the next election—six months in the future—and then taunting the reporters that everything said at the dinner was off the record. Despite himself, David had stopped listening then and looked it up in the *Canadian Parliamentary Guide.* O'Sullivan had indeed given away the actual date of the election that night; was it really possible that not one single reporter had broken the ban on publishing what the Premier said?

The 1975 dinner apparently didn't have a politician as guest speaker; the audio featured a very bad rock band performing covers of Beatles songs. The group, David discovered when he skipped past the music, was called Press Runs and it featured five members of the press gallery.

The next year, the emcee began by announcing "the good news first. Press Runs has run its course. So tonight, we're gonna do what we usually do. Listen to some political palaver from some electoral cadaver." Whoops, shouts, cheers. "No, no, not Seamus O'Sullivan. We still haven't forgiven him for his cunning linguist's routine with the election date two years ago!" More cheers, laughter. Why did drunks always think they were funny? David wondered. "Instead, tonight, we have a *very big shoo* for you," he said, in his best Ed Sullivan voice, which was not that good. "On our stage, we present for your listening enjoyment the man who will *be* Seamus O'Sullivan . . . just as soon as his good friend, Jack Eagleson—is Jack here tonight? There he is. Down there in the corner. Just back from the backroom, Jack? Or was that the bathroom? Just as soon as his friend Jack Eagleson can organize the coup that will keep Jack himself in power for another four years . . . Ladies—who let them in tonight, anyway?—and harsh men—I said *harsh* men, not hard men, Allen, not yet, anyway—I give you our guest speaker, the Honourable Ward Heeler . . . er, Ward Injustice . . ."

He'd found it! The speech.

"Moira? It's David . . . David Astor." Who? She rummaged through her mental Rolodex. A defence lawyer?

"From the Archives?" Why did he sound like he was asking her a question? "You were looking for some audio tape?" Oh, right. The tape. The Archives. "Well, I found it!" His tone was triumphant. Found what? Was it pregnancy, or had she always been so forgetful, so scattered? Audio tape? Oh yes. The "nigger joke" story.

That was months ago. She'd long since given up chasing that. She'd tried to find Danny Thompson, the Canadian Press reporter her father thought had taken early retirement and bought a farm. The problem was he'd "bought the farm" a year later. A heart attack. He was beyond confirming her father's story.

Moira could have asked Allen Morton, but she feared Morton might be too keen on the story. She wasn't, in part because she found the idea of dredging up a twenty-five-year-old joke for a reporting point vaguely distasteful, and, in much larger part, because she had resolved to do no more work than absolutely necessary for the rest of her pregnancy.

She was past the morning sickness and overwhelming exhaustion of the first trimester. But now she'd become fixated on preparing for the baby's arrival. She filled up every waking hour—and a few sleeping ones, too—sifting through the results of consumer safety tests on baby car seats; selecting stimulating but not too stimulating, soothing but not too soothing wallpaper for the baby's room; choosing a crib rated number one by *Consumer's Own*; ordering the one-hundred-and-fifty-coil spring mattress recommended in *Baby's Best*, then cancelling and returning it after discovering that chiropractors in a new study had decided foam mattresses were healthier for baby's delicate backs; ordering one of those and then worrying whether she'd made the wrong decision; auditioning animal mobiles to hang from the ceiling above the crib . . .

Todd was no help. He said she was being stupid.

"Are you saying you think I'm stupid?"

"No. Just that getting all balled up about something as trivial as which animal figure you want hanging over the crib seems . . . well, stupid."

"So you *are* saying I'm stupid."

Todd hadn't said much after that. Most nights, he managed to find things to do at his office until Moira was asleep. She wondered if he was having an affair. Not that he had time for an affair. His business was collapsing. One of the big oil companies—Moira couldn't remember which one—had announced late in the summer that it was scaling back its offshore exploration program. It was no longer interested in buying condos in Todd's development.

"I thought you had a contract with them," Moira said, incredulous.

"I do," Todd snapped back. "Of course I do. But not everything is as simple as it is in your newspaper."

Another unsubtle dig at her job. At least he wasn't suggesting she quit any more. Who knew? She might soon be the sole breadwinner in the family.

"But now they say they won't honour the contracts," Todd continued. "And they've got an army of lawyers preparing to tie us up in court forever."

Most of Todd's financing had been contingent on the condos being pre-sold. Now that it looked as if the companies might find a way to wriggle out of their contracts, Todd's investors were threatening to pull the plug. They were already holding back on an interim payment he was supposed to have received three months ago, which meant he couldn't pay his contractors and suppliers, which meant they were threatening to slap liens on the property, which meant he could soon be pushed into bankruptcy. Moira hated the idea of bringing their baby up in an apartment, hated Todd because it might happen.

She still hadn't told her father what was going on. He'd inquired, though. "What's all this talk about the oil companies mean for our Toddy?" he'd asked a little too quickly, too smugly, at their last lunch.

"Nothing," she'd said. "He's got signed contracts." And she'd quickly changed the subject. At least her father would be pleased to know she was now planning to take just three months' maternity leave after the baby was born. But Moira couldn't tell him that yet because she'd also have to tell him about Todd's business problems. And listen to him gloat.

She hadn't told Morton, either, probably because she didn't want to admit to herself she'd have to come back to work so quickly. And she wasn't sure how he'd react to her request to get off the court beat when she returned. She couldn't handle the courts any more. She'd been thinking a lot about child murders, child abductions, child sexual assaults and all the other bad things that can happen to children. In fact, last night she'd been woken up by a nightmare that she was covering the trial of the man who'd abducted her child. She couldn't see his face but she thought it was Todd—*Stop it,* she told herself. She couldn't think about that. What was the question? When did she want to come in and listen to the audio tape? She didn't.

"Ah, I'm really busy this week, Mr. . . . Astor."

"Oh." He sounded hurt. Why did that upset her? Hormones?

"What about next Monday, then? Say, around lunchtime?" Damn. Why did she do this to herself?

"That would be wonderful."

David Astor was excited again. "And, Miss . . . Moira, you won't be disappointed, I promise. There's some very interesting material on the tape . . ."

Oh my God! Moira grabbed for her notepad, began to scribble furiously. David Astor wasn't kidding. She'd heard the voice on the tape often enough to be certain it belonged to Ward Justice. He didn't sound drunk, certainly not as drunk as the man who'd introduced him.

"One more, just one more," Ward Justice was shouting now as the furor in the room threatened to drown him out. "What word starts with 'N' and ends with 'R' that you never want to call a black person?" There were scattered cheers but more jeers.

"Siddown! Siddown!" Was that her father's voice? She would need to rewind the tape, listen to it again. How had it all started anyway? Justice had been talking about . . . what? About how he supported his leader, and how proud he was to be a member of the Liberal team, and—then something happened. What?

"Have the waiters all left?" he asked for no reason she could fathom. There was a pause, and then his question began to make sense when he asked, "Do you know when a black man turns into a nigger?" There was an embarrassed silence—even back then, Moira noted with some surprise—at the mention of the "N-word."

"As soon as he leaves the room!"

The laughter was awkward. No one seemed sure how to react.

He kept talking. "What does NAACP stand for? . . . Niggers Are Always Causing Problems . . . What do you call a nigger in a courtroom in a three-piece suit? . . . The defendant . . ." The delivery was staccato now. There should have been a cymbal crash to coincide with each new punchline. "What do you call a nigger with a Harvard education? . . . Nigger . . ." That's when the boos really began.

"One more, one more . . ." Ward Justice pushed on with his bad stand-up comic routine. "What word starts with 'N' and ends with 'R' that you never want to call a black person? . . . Neighbour!" he shouted after a suitable pause.

The audience was in a complete uproar now. She could hear a

scuffle, someone bumping against the microphone and then silence.

"Thank you, Mr. Minister, thank you very much . . ." Another voice she didn't recognize. "Enlightening as always. But the hour is late and I'm sure our friends in the press"—he had to be a politician, but which one?—"need their beauty rest so they can be ready for another day of scandal-mongering in the morning. For those of you who are beyond beauty rest—Danny, that means you—your friends in the Liberal Party are pleased to offer you complimentary liqueurs and cigars in the lobby."

With that, there was a shuffling of chairs and a cacophony of shouting. Then, suddenly, the recording stopped.

Moira Donovan slumped back in the chair. It was much worse than she'd expected. Worse? Or better? She looked over at David Astor. He was grinning.

"Interesting?" he asked.

"Very," she answered.

"If you think that's interesting," he replied, the grin now a smirk, "I think you'll find what I have to tell you even more so."

Strangely, knowing he was dying had given him a new purchase on life.

"So," Ward began pre-emptively as the doctor walked into the examining room clutching Ward's red medical file folder against her chest and staring at the floor, apparently deep in thought about how to tell her patient the worst. "It is prostate cancer, then. How bad?" Ward had been reading up on the stages of the disease. He was sure it must be at least Stage Three by now: "the cancer has broken through the covering of the prostate and may have grown into the neck of the bladder or the seminal vesicle"—or worse (better?), Stage Four: "spread to another part of the body."

Dr. Thomas looked at him, startled, then smiled. She put the file on the white countertop, turned and closed the door.

"No, Mr. Justice, your prostate is fine. In fact, you have the prostate of a much younger man. Which is good, very good."

"But why—?"

"Frequent urination can be a sign of many things, Mr. Justice, or of nothing. I didn't detect any abnormalities when I examined you, and the blood tests indicate your PSA results are well within the normal range. So, while your PSA score is not a 100 percent guarantee, the reality is that none of the tests we have at our disposal suggest prostate cancer."

"But—"

"But that's not to say we shouldn't be vigilant. You should schedule an annual prostate exam so we'll know quickly if there are any changes in the size and shape of your prostate, or in your levels of prostatic specific antigens."

"I really don't have prostate cancer?"

"No, you don't, Mr. Justice, but . . ."

Ward Justice had been so sure of his own diagnosis that he was still having difficulty rearranging his thinking to accommodate this new reality, this new . . . disappointment.

How could he be disappointed? Was it that he naively saw his own death, or at least impending death, as an easy, perhaps even romantic way to pull positive attention toward himself? *Look at me, look at me, I'm dying.* Or could it be that his life had been such a failure that jumping out of it now in the middle of middle age seemed preferable to staying the course? Or could it be that knowing he was dying liberated him, gave him a free pass to do that which he'd wanted to do for so long but had been afraid to pursue? Could he live now with not dying?

". . . some anomalies in some of the results that I think we need to explore further." Dr. Thomas was still talking. She opened his file, withdrew a number of forms that were already filled out. "I'd like to send you for some more tests, Mr. Justice, just so we can—"

"What did you find?" He could feel the panic bubbling up. Why was he panicking? Wasn't he, just a moment ago, eager to welcome death? And now he was afraid of what he wished for?

"It may be nothing," she answered, her tone soothing. "It probably is nothing. But"—she looked at him, smiled reassuringly—"one of the benefits of socialized medicine is that we can send you for tests to be sure."

"What tests?"

"A second chest X-ray to begin. The radiologist detected a slight abnormality in your left lung. So he thinks we should get another X-ray, using a higher resolution this time, perhaps with an injection to increase the contrast so we get a better look." She paused. "And I'd like to set up a consult with Dr. Bennett—he's a pulmonologist—and with Dr. Hussein. She's a very well-regarded oncologist."

Oncologist? "That's cancer, right?"

"Mr. Justice, there's a saying we were taught when I was in medical school. The saying is this: 'If you hear hoofbeats, think first of horses, not zebras.' There are many things that could cause the anomalies we noted. Most of them are benign. Because we don't have any recent baseline chest X-rays to measure these results against, it could very well be that this is simply a pre-existing tumour that's been around so long it's not a major concern. But since we don't have that historical data, we need to err on the side of caution, to rule out any of the more serious possibilities."

She paused, waiting for Ward to ask another question.

Oncologist? Abnormality in his left lung? Lung cancer?

"But I don't smoke. I haven't for years. I stopped. Ten years ago. At least. How—?"

"Giving up smoking is good, Mr. Justice, but it isn't a guarantee. There are no guarantees. But we're getting ahead of ourselves."

"What else? How else can you get lung cancer?"

"There are all sorts of ways people can get lung cancer. Smoking is the best known, of course, and we focus on it because it's the most preventable. But there's also second-hand smoke. And exposure to asbestos. And family history. There are also factors we still don't understand. African-American men, for example, get lung cancer at a rate that's one-and-a-half times greater than white men, but we don't know why. So there's . . ."

Smoking? It had to be from smoking. Damn that Manny Soloman. Ward had been just eleven, and he and Manny had been hanging out one summer night in the parking lot behind the Steadman's in Eisners Head. Ward could still vividly recall how Manny had hauled the half-crushed package out of his ass pants pocket, opened it, removed a cigarette, tapped the non-filtered end against the pack like Ward had seen movie stars do, then tucked it into the left-hand corner of his mouth so it hung just so. Then he lit a match, cupping the flame between his palms and raising it to the cigarette, nonchalant, as if he'd done it all a thousand times before. Ward was impressed, more so when Manny blew smoke out of his mouth and nose at the same time without coughing.

"Here, have a puff," he offered, extending the hand with the cigarette toward Ward.

"No," Ward answered, as if he'd been threatened.

"Yuh scared?"

"No."

"Well, do it then." Manny put the cigarette up to Ward's lips. Ward turned away. "'S'not like it's going to kill you. Just one puff."

Ward turned back then, tentatively opening his mouth in a small "O" to accommodate the cigarette. He breathed in. The hot smoke burned the back of his throat, tickled the passages of his nose. He coughed, sputtered. Manny laughed. Ward felt dizzy, light-headed.

He took the cigarette from Manny's hand, took another puff, and then another. He didn't cough.

"Hey, don't smoke the whole thing," Manny said finally.

And that was the beginning. By the time he was in his twenties, Ward was smoking a pack a day, sometimes two. He'd tried to quit when Victoria did, when she was first pregnant. And then again a year later. And a year after that. He'd lost count of the number of times he'd quit before he finally gave them up for good. But it wasn't ten years ago, as he'd told Dr. Thomas. It was six. And now he had lung cancer.

Should he tell Victoria? When he believed he had prostate cancer, Ward had decided he wouldn't tell her. Was he trying to be a martyr? Or did he want to punish her for wanting a divorce? *Think how sorry she'll be after she finds out . . .* But now that the doctor had told him he had lung cancer—she hadn't said it exactly, but Ward knew—his first instinct was to call Victoria and tell her the news, let her take care of him. Tell her. Don't tell her. Happy to die. Not happy to die. Why couldn't he keep his emotions straight?

". . . usually long waiting lists to see specialists these days. But Dr. Bennett's office says he can see you late Thursday afternoon. And we're waiting on Dr. Hussein. Her nurse says she'll fit you into the first cancellation she has." Dr. Thomas gave him her best reassuring smile.

He was not reassured.

8

1974

Ward should have been downstairs partying with the others. So why was he up here on the roof, alone, leaning against the railing on the seaward side of Junior's widow's walk, blowing smoke rings into the still, salt-damp night air and staring out into the inky blackness, trying and failing to make out the outline of his family's house in the distance, trying and failing to be happy?

The election was over. He'd won. No surprise there. The incumbent, a dentist named Dauphinee from Holden in the Tory end of Cabot County, who'd sat on the back-est Tory backbench for three undistinguished terms during the Stanfield era, had become even more marginal after Seamus O'Sullivan's Liberals formed the government four years ago. With the fishery in a mess and everyone in Cabot County in need of government assistance, voters understood they needed to be with the winning side this time.

Dauphinee had not helped his own cause, either. A few years ago, he'd taken up with a much younger woman in Halifax. That wasn't the problem—he certainly wasn't the only MLA on either side of the House with a wife at home and a mistress in the city. The problem was that Leila, the mother of his three grown children, was raising holy hell and not caring who knew. The Liberals were happy to heap manure on her garden of gossip, even adding spicy, if untrue, details, such as the fact that the mistress had borne Dauphinee a son and was now threatening to sue him for support.

The Liberals didn't have to make everything up, of course. The tale of Dauphinee's serial car crash wasn't a tall one at all. One night last fall Dauphinee had got falling-down drunk at the Holden Legion, poured himself into his car and proceeded to pinball into four different parked vehicles during the half-mile drive to his house, stopping at none of the accident scenes. Not that there was any doubt the next morning who'd done the damage. Dauphinee's recently acquired Ford Mustang—more evidence the dentist was going through a late mid-life crisis—sat in his driveway, looking like the loser in a demolition derby.

Holden's police chief, a friend of Dauphinee's who was also treasurer of the local Progressive Conservative Association, investigated but refused to press charges. His inquiries, he said, determined that Dauphinee had had only one drink that night. (He never questioned the bartender at the Legion, who told a different story.) The problem, the chief insisted, was an unfortunate combination of that single shot of alcohol with a painkiller the good dentist had prescribed himself (for reasons unknown), resulting in his accidental impairment, which had led to the multiple accidents. "You can't arrest somebody for taking medicine," the chief said. That Dauphinee agreed to pay the owners of the cars he'd hit for all necessary (and some unnecessary) bodywork kept him out of the courts and his name out of the papers. But that didn't keep people from talking.

During the all-candidates debate in Eisners Head two weeks ago, Old Jimmy Parsons, who knew a thing or two about drinking and driving himself, stood up to ask Dauphinee why he hadn't done anything to help the fishermen in Eisners Head. After Dauphinee huffed and puffed up his modest accomplishment in getting the government to extend the lobster season by three days, Jimmy thanked him, then added, as the crowd tittered, "You have a safe drive home now, Dr. Dauphinee."

Ward couldn't help but notice Junior sitting in the front row, a satisfied smirk on his face, as if he'd orchestrated the whole thing. Which he might have. Strange. The man who had blacklisted his father and sent the Justice family into exile in Halifax more than a decade before was now Ward's chief financial backer and main behind-the-scenes supporter in his election campaign.

Ward's candidacy had been Jack's idea. Of course. Jack and Junior were friends, though Ward didn't know much about the history of their relationship. Had they simply grown up together in the Liberal Party, both sons of prominent party power brokers, or was Jack, as many speculated, the brains behind Junior's wildly ambitious corporate expansion plans?

Whatever the basis for their friendship, Jack was now on the board of Eisner Fisheries International (Junior had dropped the J.F.B. from the company name within days of the old man's death and added the International after he struck some joint-venture deal with a fishing company in Argentina). Jack was also in charge of the company's legal and financial affairs. His duties consisted primarily of buying up struggling Nova Scotia fish companies using as little of Eisner International's cash as possible. Preferably none.

The east coast fishing industry was in a sorry mess and had been for most of the decade. There were fewer and fewer fish. And more and more foreigners catching them, using ever larger, ever more sophisticated factory freezer trawlers equipped with all the latest fish-finding, fish-vacuuming gear.

Nova Scotia fish companies, most small-town pop-and-son operations, were caught in a double whammy: there were no longer enough fish to catch, and the fact that they were catching so few made it impossible for them to convince bankers to lend them money to upgrade their fleets to compete with the foreigners.

Some of the owners, well-educated second- or third-generation types, not unlike Junior himself, were happy to walk away from their fathers' debts and into new lives in the city. Unlike them, however, Junior saw a future—though a very different future—in fishing. He was only too happy to help them out by taking over their parents' antiquated processing facilities, cold storage plants and aging wooden trawlers. He paid fire-sale prices. If the company owed the provincial government's Fisheries Loan Board for money it had borrowed in more optimistic times, Junior would offer to take the company off their hands in exchange for taking over their loan payments. Then Jack would use his connections to negotiate a deal with the Liberal-appointed Loan Board not only to forgive the company's outstanding debt but then also provide Eisner with new grants and no-interest loans to upgrade the plants and build new, modern, steel-hulled trawlers.

Following that neat template, Eisner Fisheries International had quickly transformed itself from a modest catching and processing operation in Eisners Head into the largest privately owned and vertically integrated fish company in Atlantic Canada. It had a fleet of three dozen, mostly antiquated trawlers and eleven small plants dotted from one end of the province to the other.

Junior and Jack had what Jack called "the five-year plan." It had begun recently with a lobbying effort in Ottawa, trying to convince their political friends there to forget the plodding, bureaucratic United Nations Law of the Sea Conference and unilaterally declare Canada the lord and master of all it surveyed for two hundred miles off its coasts in every direction. The government could then kick all the foreigners out so Canadian companies could replace the foreign factory freezer fleets with homegrown ones. Like Eisner Fisheries.

Which is where, Ward guessed now, he was supposed to come in. Ward was a lawyer (though he'd never practised a day since he graduated) and the son of a local trawlerman (though his father had never fished a day since Junior blacklisted him). That made Ward Justice the ideal person to represent the interests of Cabot County and the fishing industry of Nova Scotia—which is to say Eisner Fisheries—in Halifax. And in Ottawa, too.

The Liberals were still in power in Ottawa, but Nova Scotia voters had sent very few MPs from the province to sit on the government side. Since the party's prospects in the next election seemed almost as dim, Jack and Junior decided a strong provincial Fisheries minister could lobby his federal counterpart on their behalf. Ward was the next best thing to having a Fisheries minister of their own in Ottawa.

Even before they'd asked Ward to run and let him in on at least part of their plan, Jack and Junior had cleared his path of all potential rocks, brambles and other unpleasant obstacles.

First, they'd convinced the incumbent Fisheries minister, Etienne Thibeault, a folksy fisherman from the Acadian shore, to retire from politics. Before surprising everyone by winning a seat in the Legislature in 1970, Thibeault had been a longline fisherman of the sort who'd leave his home port each morning before dawn, bait the hooks on his lines, toss them over the side, haul away, fill up his Cape Islander with whatever fish were running that day and return home to sell whatever he'd caught to the local buyer at the wharf.

Etienne Thibeault had won his seat in 1970 by tapping into the frustrations of independent inshore fishermen just like him. They believed the real reason there were so few fish to catch was not just because the foreign fishing fleets were taking them all but because the entire offshore industry, foreign and Canadian, was using destructive trawling technology. They argued that the offshore fleets' huge, bottom-scraping trawls scooped up everything in their way, including spawning, endangered and undersized fish and the plant life that nourished them. They wanted the government to ban trawling entirely.

Thibeault agreed. Which made him an unlikely candidate to lobby Ottawa on behalf of Eisner's planned deep-sea factory freezer trawler fleet.

Thibeault had to go. So Jack offered Thibeault a new position as Eisner's vice-president, Inshore Division, at slightly more than twice his Cabinet minister's salary. What Jack didn't tell Thibeault was that the company planned to scuttle the aging inshore fleet as soon it got the okay from Ottawa to lease its own factory freezer trawlers. Just as it planned to close all the seasonal fish plants that depended on those outdated vessels to supply them with fish.

After Thibeault's surprise announcement that he wouldn't run for re-election, Jack and Junior secured Seamus O'Sullivan's pledge that if the Liberals won, as seemed likely, and if Ward could win the Cabot County constituency, as seemed just as likely, O'Sullivan would name Ward his new Fisheries minister.

All that was left was to orchestrate Ward's nomination, stoke the gossip fires already burning around Dauphinee and paint in broad strokes a picture of Ward as the bright young fisherman's son from Eisners Head who'd gone off to the big city, made good, and was now coming back home to do even better for his people. A few details had been conveniently airbrushed out of that feel-good portrait, including, most notably, the circumstances under which Ward's family had left town. The strike was now an unpleasant memory best left unplumbed.

The only person, in fact, who seemed reluctant to let it go was Desmond Justice. There'd been a flicker of fatherly pride when Ward told him he planned to run for the Legislature in Eisners Head, but it had been snuffed the moment Ward said he'd be staying at the Eisners' old house during the campaign.

"What the hell you wanna do that for?"

"Because Junior offered." Ward had expected this. He just hadn't figured out how to respond, so he responded in the worst possible way. "Junior's supporting me," he said. "He was the one who asked me to come back and run."

His father said nothing.

"Besides, it's convenient," Ward tried again. "I mean, there isn't a hotel in the whole friggin' county . . . and I'm going to be there for six weeks or more campaigning . . . so I'll need a place to stay." More silence. "Anyway, Junior doesn't live there any more." Why did Ward feel the need to make it sound as though Junior's not being there was somehow a good thing? He had no beef with the man; that was all between his father and Junior. And it was in the past.

Ward, in fact, quite liked Junior. Jack had first brought them together for lunch at the Halifax Club six months ago. He'd introduced them, of course, in his Jack way: "I just thought that the Future Premier of Nova Scotia and the Future King of the World of Fish should get to know one another," he'd said, and his delighted-with-himself laugh filled the club.

One of Junior's first questions that day was about Ward's father. "How is your dad, anyway?" he asked after they'd ordered drinks.

"Good."

"As I'm sure you know, he and I had some problems," Junior continued. "I've always regretted that. Your father's a good man, even if we didn't see things the same way. But that's all water over the side now, and it shouldn't get in the way of our being friends."

Ward should have told his father what Junior had actually said about him instead of saying Junior didn't live in Eisners Head any more.

Junior's, of course, was far from the only family to have abandoned Eisners Head. About half the houses in town, including the one where Ward had grown up, were empty. Ward never knew who his father sold their property to when they left town, but whoever it was had apparently decided he couldn't afford to stay either, and since, by then, no one was buying houses in Eisners Head, he'd just walked away.

Junior had held on to the family homestead. Old Jimmy Parsons, who had lived in the Eisners' guest cottage down by the wharf ever since his wife threw him out, took care of the place when Junior wasn't there, which was most of the year. Three years ago, Junior had bought a house in the south end of Halifax and moved his family there in order to be nearer Eisner's new head office in the old Capital Fisheries Plant. Just before he died, Junior's father had bought Capital for far more cash than it was worth. That was, in fact, one of the causes of his falling out with Junior and the reason, probably, that Junior dropped his father's initials from the name of the company as soon as he took it over.

Junior and his family spent July in Eisners Head, mostly because the kids, who were nine and eleven, still liked it there. In August, they decamped to the new place Junior had had built in Chester so he could enjoy its annual Race Week festivities and, not coincidentally, hobnob with the province's elite. Junior had written off the purchase of the Chester place as a business expense.

After Ward agreed to run, Junior suggested he and his family spend July in Chester while Junior's family was in Eisners Head.

"The cottage will be a good place for you to rest up," Junior said. It was, but it was no cottage.

The Fish House, as envious locals called it, was a sprawling mansion with a basement-to-roof glass wall that enclosed the entire front of the house facing their sheltered cove. Watching Junior's racing schooner bobbing at its mooring made looking out the window seem like admiring a living oil painting. "Take 'er out for a sail," Junior had urged him, but Ward didn't. He didn't know how. Victoria did, but she was too busy mothering and smothering Meghan to have time for sailing. Or, later, for campaigning. Or even coming down to Eisners Head tonight to celebrate his election victory with him.

"I'm pregnant," she'd screamed into the phone that morning. "Fucking pregnant. In case you hadn't noticed. But how would you notice? You haven't been home in five weeks."

Ward had given up trying to understand. Victoria was the daughter of a politician, so she had to have known the demands of the political life. Yet she'd encouraged him to run, even after he'd been the one to fret about leaving her at home with an eighteen-month-old and another on the way. "We'll be fine," she'd said. "Don't worry about us." That was then.

She'd even posed for the requisite family photo for Ward's campaign flyer. You couldn't tell from the photo that Victoria was pregnant again. And you wouldn't know from the brochure that she'd been four months pregnant when they married "in a sunset ceremony on the rocks at Peggys Cove." That bit had been Jack's idea. "Connects you to the sea," he said. "People like that. Too bad you didn't decide to do it in Eisners Head, though."

Peggys Cove had been Victoria's idea. She liked the stark beauty, she said. Her father had got special permission to have the wedding there. Victoria wrote the ceremony in which they pledged to "be there" for each other. And picked the music, "A Groovy Kind of Love." The soloist—a friend of Victoria's from her school days in Switzerland who was, apparently, a minor rock star celebrity in her native Belgium—sang it in heavily accented English while Ward and

Victoria and their attendants (Jack was Ward's best man) disappeared inside the lighthouse to sign the official papers.

Was that the beginning of the end? Ward asked himself, taking one last drag of his cigarette before flicking the glowing butt off the roof and down through the darkness to the wet grass below. From a wedding on the rocks to a marriage on the rocks?

Victoria's mood could careen from bubbling optimism to boiling anger in the course of a short phone conversation. This morning, she'd seemed to be in an upbeat mood, telling him excitedly about a house she'd seen for sale just a few blocks from her parents' place. "It's perfect for us. Four bedrooms, a big fenced backyard for the kids. It needs work, of course. The kitchen looks like it's out of the fifties and there's no bathroom on the first floor, but it's just up the street from the Grammar School. The kids wouldn't even have to cross a street . . ."

Ward had tried to be encouraging. He hadn't even raised the can-we-afford-it caveat he usually fell back on whenever Victoria started talking about houses. It wasn't that he didn't know they needed a bigger place, especially with a second child on the way, and he agreed an apartment was no place to raise children. But the very idea of debt scared him. And a mortgage? His parents would be dead before they paid off their little bungalow. He had to keep reminding himself he wasn't his parents. He had an education, a law degree, the promise of a Cabinet position. And he had friends.

Even though Ward had never asked, Junior had offered to help him get a mortgage. "You're going to be a Cabinet minister," he'd said. "You'll need a house where you can entertain." He hadn't explained what he meant by helping out, but Ward knew Junior had good contacts in the upper ranks of the banks. Maybe he could get him a favourable interest rate.

"How big is the living room?" Ward had asked Victoria, trying not to ask the how-much question. "We'll need a big living room for parties after—" He was getting ahead of himself. "—*if* I win tonight."

"Oh, you'll win all right," she said. "You're a winner."

"Which is why I called this morning," he said by way of segue. "It'd be great if you could come down for the party tonight. Junior's hired this Irish group to play. Everyone says they're great for dancing. I'll even dance, if you want! Old Jimmy said he'd drive down and get you this after—"

That's when she'd exploded. And hung up. He was alone again tonight.

The truth was that no one in Ward's family had been there to support him during his entire campaign. He'd tried to talk his father into campaigning with him—"You could see all your old friends again"—but he'd flatly refused.

"And where would I stay?" Not, it was clear, at Junior's house.

People did ask after him, though. "How's your dad?" they'd say. No one mentioned the strike. "We still miss your mother at the church," one old woman said to him when he knocked on her door. "She made the best date squares."

Even his mother had turned down his request to come to Eisners Head. "I've been having problems *down there*," she said delicately, pointing toward her nether regions. "You don't want to know. But I shouldn't be straying too far from home." Ward wasn't sure she was telling him the whole truth; she knew he wouldn't press her for details on whatever was wrong "down there," so it could be left to hang, ominously, in the air. Most likely, she just didn't want to get caught in the crossfire between father and son, and so chose to absent herself instead. He couldn't blame her.

Ward's eyes had adjusted to the darkness now and he could finally make out the outlines of the clapboard bungalow where he'd grown up. It was probably only a few hundred yards away but the life distance was an Atlantic Ocean. And yet he'd made it. He lit another cigarette, cupping his hands around the lighter to fend off the wind, which had picked up in the past few minutes.

So why did he feel like shit? Perhaps he was tired; it had been a long campaign. But he didn't feel tired. Just depressed. Maybe it was his conversation with Victoria that morning. She had an uncanny way of making her mood his. As if his mood only existed through hers. That was it, he thought to himself. It was not so much their conversation that had depressed him as the realization that he could be so easily bent and shaped, even twisted, by other people's moods, or beliefs, or desires, and make them his own.

Did he even want to be a politician? He'd never thought about that or—more to the point—allowed himself to consider any other possibility. *Was* there any other possibility? Jack had never left him alone long enough to explore any other path. No, he was not being fair. Why was he always so eager to blame his inadequacies on others? On Jack. On Victoria. On Junior.

Ward hadn't been prepared for Junior. "A surprise," was all Jack had said when Ward asked who they were meeting for lunch that day at the Halifax Club. His first thought when Jack led him to Junior's table had been to turn around and walk out. He hadn't. He didn't want to be disrespectful to Jack. Or cause a scene. At least that was how he rationalized it after. So he sat down, shook Junior's hand, nodded as Junior explained away those "problems" he'd had with Ward's father. Part of Ward wanted to confront the man who'd ruined his father's life; instead he smiled and made polite conversation and then went along with Jack's suggestion that Junior become the chief fundraiser for his—or was that Jack's?—election campaign in Cabot County.

Ward knew, without anyone saying so, that there would be a price to pay for Junior's support. He understood how Nova Scotia politics worked; he'd got his education at the feet of the master. He'd gone along with all that too, of course. Perhaps, at first, he'd been too awestruck by the newness of it all to know how to react. But gradually, he'd decided, without ever actually deciding, that this was just the way the system worked, that there was nothing he could do about it, that everyone did it, and now . . . well, he was part of it too. No wonder his father didn't like him, or at least didn't like what he'd become. For all his many faults, and Ward could list them too, his father understood who he was and what he believed. His father had backbone, character. Unlike his son.

Suddenly, from behind him, Ward heard the door to the widow's walk open and the sounds from the party below—fiddles and the noise of revellers shouting to be heard over them—spill out onto the deck. He turned around. It was Jack, followed by Junior. Junior was carrying a forty-ouncer of rum in one hand, three glasses in the other.

"You're missing a good party, Mr. Future Premier," Jack said as Junior set the glasses up on the balcony railing and began to fill them with straight rum.

"Just having a smoke and enjoying the air."

"You missed your phone call," Jack said. "We looked everywhere but we couldn't find you. It was your new boss, Premier Seamus O'Sullivan himself, calling to congratulate the new MLA for Cabot County."

Junior handed a glass to Ward and one to Jack, then raised his own. "To our new MLA—"

"Not just MLA," Jack cut in. "Our esteemed Premier asked me to ask you not to make any plans for next Tuesday."

Ward looked puzzled.

"Next Tuesday. Swearing-in day. New Cabinet. He said you have to keep it under your hat until he makes it official, but you're going to be his Fisheries minister. The youngest Cabinet minister in Nova Scotia history. I'll have to check to see who the youngest premier was. So, Mr. Minister, Mr. Future Premier, congratulations." He paused, raised his glass. "To the Premier-to-be." Jack clinked his glass against Ward's and took a swallow of the straight dark rum. Ward and Junior followed.

So this is what it feels like to win, Ward thought. He took another mouthful, bigger this time, and swished the harsh liquor around inside his mouth, felt it anesthetize his tongue and teeth. If only it could do the same, and as quickly, to his brain. Ward raised his glass in the general direction of Jack and Junior. "And to the men who made him what he is today," he said.

The two men offered up their glasses in response to his toast, but Ward had already emptied his. He looked at them, looked away, and threw the glass as hard as he could into the night.

"Good morning, Mr. Carter." Cecil Montague smiled, nodded and continued on his way down the long corridor that connected the professors' offices with the law school's main classrooms.

"Sir," Ray acknowledged, then thought: What did Montague mean by that? Was it simply a tossed-off greeting from professor to student as they passed in the hall? Or was there something more . . . sinister behind it? And why had Ray deferentially called him "Sir" in reply?

Before he'd joined the Dalhousie Law School faculty a decade ago, Montague had been one of the most successful criminal defence attorneys in Nova Scotia. His two most famous and discussed cases involved white men killing black men and getting away with it.

In the early sixties, he'd won an acquittal for a white policeman charged with murdering a young black man by shooting him five times in the back. The man's crime: looking too much like someone the police were seeking in connection with a shoplifting incident earlier in the day. Montague's defence was that the young man had turned away from the policeman to grab for a gun so the officer had no choice but to fire in self-defence. Montague did not produce the alleged gun, if there was one. But Montague did do his lawyerly best to put the victim on trial, slipping in hints about the deceased's lengthy criminal record without ever qualifying them with the fact that none of his petty crimes involved violence.

The Crown—out of laziness? stupidity? collusion?—never corrected the record. The judge let it pass. And the jury, all white men, of course, needed only enough time to finish their free lunch from the Department of Justice to acquit Montague's client and send him back out into the streets to serve and protect.

In 1964, just before he surprised the legal community by giving up his lucrative practice for what had turned out to be an almost monastic life as an academic, Montague helped another white man get away with murder. The man and his black neighbour lived next door to one another in backwoods Nova Scotia. One day, the two men argued over some trees the black man claimed the white man had cut from his property. So the white man got his rifle and shot his neighbour in the stomach. According to evidence at his trial, the gunshot didn't kill the black man immediately; he slowly bled to death while the white man finished splitting the wood in dispute and then stored it in his shed.

Montague's defence was that the black man had been drinking, though the autopsy report showed no evidence of alcohol in his system, and had threatened his client with physical harm, though there was no one other than his client alive to corroborate this. As for the four-hour delay in contacting the police to tell them what had happened, Montague explained that his client had just finished painting the floor in his kitchen and had to wait for it to dry before he could get to the phone. He too was acquitted.

There were those who suggested that Montague had become so disillusioned by his own success he decided to go into teaching to atone for it. But others believed there had to be something more than coincidence at work in Montague's choice of unsavoury clients and crimes.

Not that Ray found any evidence to support that belief in Montague's classroom. Indeed, Montague frequently admonished students that "defence lawyers do not have views, they have clients." Ray wanted to ask why he'd chosen to represent white clients who'd murdered black men, but he didn't. Montague intimidated him.

So did law school. Ray was the only indigenous black in the entire school. There had been days, especially during his first year, when Ray would have preferred to be white. Anything to disappear into the sea of white maleness around him. Though he'd never lived any place where he was a member of the majority race, there had always been other blacks around, and Ray had gravitated to them. Here, his difference made him an object of curiosity for faculty, students and staff, inspiring double takes and stares, or, worse, furtive glances. What were they thinking? That he didn't belong?

Ray thought that, too. Often. Not because he was a black man in a white institution, but because he was one of only a handful of students who'd been admitted to the law school without first having completed at least a few years of an undergraduate degree.

He had Mr. Eagleson to thank—or blame—for that. Jack Eagleson had written a glowing letter of recommendation to the Admissions Committee arguing that Ray should be admitted as a mature student based on his life experience. Not that Eagleson would have known very much about Ray's life experience. Or him, for that matter. Ray knew even less about his benefactor.

Ray hadn't even remembered, until Eagleson reminded him, the first time he invited Ray for "coffee and a little chat," that they'd met before, at Ray's high school graduation. "I was there to see Ward graduate and I was introduced to you and your father, and an older woman, I believe she was your aunt?"

"Oh, right. Aunt Annie. She's not my aunt really. Everyone just calls her that." Ray hadn't intended to make polite conversation with the man who'd tried to bribe his father with a suitcase full of cash. He wasn't sure why he'd agreed to meet him in the first place. Eagleson had called the day after the demonstration against the hiring of the police chief, four years ago now.

Ray almost hadn't shown up; what if someone from Black Pride happened to be at Calhoun's at the same time? What would they think? In the end, he'd arrived fifteen minutes early and taken up a strategic position in a booth at the far end of the narrow, train-car-like restaurant, partly so he could see everything and everyone coming in or leaving, and partly so Eagleson, when he sat opposite him, would be hidden from public view by the booth's high back.

"Nice woman, that Annie," Eagleson said after they'd ordered their coffees. "And she clearly thought the world of you."

Ray said nothing. The waitress came, put their coffees down on the green arborite tabletop in front of them. Ray drank his black, Eagleson emptied two creamers and two spoonfuls of sugar into his.

"So what're you hearing about the campaign?"

"What?"

"The election campaign. Sorry. I get so immersed in it I forget there's anything else going on in the world. Which is why I like to get out of the office now and again and talk to real people." Eagleson laughed. Other customers turned to see who was making the racket; Ray looked down at his coffee.

"But even when I'm supposed to be thinking about other things," Eagleson continued, "I can't help myself. I still have to ask how it's going. Especially here. We're convinced we'll form the next government but we're still not sure our leader's going to win his own riding. So . . . what're you hearing?"

"Haven't been paying much attention," Ray said. "Been kinda busy." It was true. He'd been busy organizing last night's demonstration, and the picketing at the landlord's the week before. And he was starting work on a new project to expose the electoral fraud and vote buying he knew went on in the black community every election. Ray didn't know at the time that Eagleson himself would turn out to be involved. But he did know that this election, like every election, was between two white men leading two white political parties whose only interest in the black community was in how many votes they could take from it.

Ray didn't say that to Eagleson. It sometimes annoyed him that he would think such things, even form the sentences in his head, but never speak them when he was talking one-to-one with a white person. Was that a hangover from slavery? Telling the "massa" only what it's safe to say? For some reason, Ray was much better in front of a TV camera, or performing for a crowd.

"That was quite a demonstration last night," Eagleson said. "Four thousand people, at least that's what they said on the news this morning. Pretty impressive." He paused, took a noisy slurp of his coffee. "I only wish Seamus could have been there. One of the problems with being party leader is that people expect you to be everywhere. So he was down in Digby talking at some old folks' home. They tell me he had twenty people, probably half of them senile and the other half Tory . . . maybe that's the same thing." Eagleson laughed again. Ray wanted to shrink into the seat. "Seriously, though," he continued, after a moment's silence, "I wish Seamus had been able to speak at your rally last night. He really *is* sympathetic to your point of view on the new police chief, you know." Ray didn't say anything, so Eagleson continued. "But it's more important right now for him to win the election so he can do—"

"I'm not sure I'm—"

"No, no, sorry. I'm sure you're not interested in my politicking. And that's not really why I wanted to talk to you anyway." He paused, collected his thoughts. "I've been keeping my eye on you, Raymond—do you prefer Ray or Raymond? Okay, Ray then—as I was saying, keeping my eye on you, partly because I remembered meeting you at the school that time but also because I've been very impressed by what you've been doing this past year."

Ray tried not to look puzzled, to keep his face impassive. Where was this guy coming from? Where was he going?

"I went down to City Hall myself last night. I thought you might be speaking. I was looking forward to hearing you speak to a crowd. I've watched you on TV a couple of times and thought you really had the gift, the speaker's gift."

For a coloured boy. Was that the subtext here? Was Eagleson complimenting him or insulting him? Ray tried to keep his face a mask.

"Do you know anything about the program for mature students at Dalhousie Law School? No. Well, it's for people like you, smart people who, for whatever reasons, don't meet the usual admission criteria but who've had the kind of life experiences you don't get from a B.A. and—"

"But I have a B.A."

"From Rochdale?" Eagleson laughed. How did he know that? "If you thought any university would accept that, you're not as smart as I thought."

"How did you—?"

"I make it my business to know things, Ray. That's what I do. The fact is you're smart, you know how to think on your feet, you speak well and you've got passion. The law could use more people like that."

"More *coloured* people, you mean?" Ray jabbed. He didn't, couldn't, shouldn't, wouldn't trust this white man, and he wanted to let him know.

"Coloured, white, black, green, who cares?" Eagleson parried his jab. "Smart people's what I mean. And smart isn't about race. You want to change the world? The law. That's the ticket."

"Tickets cost money," Ray replied.

"Money's easy. If you want something badly enough, you'll find the money. The question is, do you want it? Because if you do—and you should—I'd be happy to write a letter to the Admissions Committee on your behalf. I'm on the university's board of governors so a letter from me would carry weight."

"Why?"

"Because I like smart young men. And you're a smart young man."

That was the beginning. At first Ray had said no, not interested, too busy, too happy doing what I'm doing. But Eagleson kept calling every few months, even after the vote-buying incident. Ray knew from the reporter at the *Tribune* that Eagleson had somehow been involved in squelching that story. Eagleson must have known Ray was behind it. Still, he kept inviting Ray for coffee, bringing along brochures about the law school on one occasion, on another a book about how to prepare to take the LSATs, the law school admission tests.

The seed Eagleson had planted slowly took root in Ray's head. In the end, however, it wasn't Eagleson's blandishments so much as frustration with his fellow staff members that watered the seed, and anger at Black Pride's board that finally nurtured it into full flower.

Calvin had turned down Ray's plan to bring Tyrone Vincent from Black Hands to Halifax. "Board's against it," Calvin told him directly. "They say, 'What's any of that got to do with us?' Besides, they think it'd stir things up right when we're trying to convince the government to fund us for another year." The board, it seemed, was against anything that might generate media attention of any sort, assuming any publicity would be bad publicity in the white community, which was the only community they seemed to consider.

But attracting media attention was Ray's special talent at Black Pride. He'd learned that game watching Bartholomew Andrew Jackson III play to the cameras during "Halifax 2000." He'd learned well.

One week, Ray had organized three black men and three white men to go into a downtown barbershop, one after the other. The whites came out after a while with their hair neatly trimmed, the blacks immediately and unshorn. This was all faithfully recorded by the cameraman from CHAX-TV; Ray had chosen the barbershop in part because there was an alley across the street where the cameraman could film without being seen from inside. After interviewing the men who'd been refused service—"He said my hair's too kinky. I'd break his scissors," one old black man told the reporter—the reporter and his cameraman tried to interview the barber. He chased them out of the shop with a broom. The cameraman was still filming when the barber told them to "Get your nigger-loving asses out o' my place."

"Great TV," the reporter said, thanking Ray. "Keep us in mind next time."

But Ray had taken his next scheme to a reporter he knew at CBC, partly because he realized he'd get better play by spreading his exclusives around and partly because he was sure CHAX wouldn't be interested in a story about the hiring practices at Levant's, a women's clothing store that was one of its biggest advertisers. The story, this one filmed from down the block, featured a well-qualified black woman with a college degree and a resumé that included retail experience in Toronto. She was told the sales job advertised in the shop window had just been filled, but thanks for asking. After she left, a white woman—whose doctored qualifications showed her to be a high school dropout with no work experience—went in, applied and was hired.

"No more," Calvin said after that story appeared. "The board says enough, at least for now."

"But—"

"No *buts*, Ray, no *ifs*, no *ands* . . . Enough."

But Ray couldn't help but attract media attention, even when he was trying not to. Soon after he was told to stop staging events, he set up a drop-in centre for black teens from the projects. No publicity. But around the same time, the National Film Board decided to make a documentary about the racial situation in Halifax. Who better to centre the documentary around than those teens and the young black man whose media-savvy stunts had bubbled the smooth veneer on the city's self-image? That didn't sit well with some of Ray's fellow field workers, who toiled anonymously to convince local businesses to hire unemployed black kids or lobbied provincial politicians to raise the minimum wage. A few of them had taken to calling Ray "Hollywood," one to his face.

Perhaps the incident that marked the beginning of the end of Ray's career at Black Pride would have happened anyway, or perhaps, as some later suggested, it was the presence of the documentary crew that had precipitated the chain of events. Whatever the cause, the result was that, one afternoon while the cameras rolled, a half-dozen young people at the drop-in centre formulated a plan to stage a demonstration at the Department of Education. Initially, it was to protest descriptions of black people as savages in a world geography textbook. But it quickly became a demonstration against the entire racist education system.

They tried to enlist Ray to organize it; he demurred, but they persisted so, eventually, he agreed to help: "But you're going to have to do the work yourselves. I'll just be there to help when you need me."

Ray would marvel later to the interviewer from the NFB that "the kids did such a great job. They organized everything themselves."

In the end, more than one thousand blacks, many of them adults whose own humiliations in the school system were still raw, protested in front of the department's downtown offices. After about an hour, the Deputy Minister emerged to address the crowd. He defended the textbook. "Our experts have examined this textbook and they're satisfied it is an accurate representation of the places and events portrayed," he said, reading from a prepared statement. The reason there were not more "Negro" teachers in the classroom was that not enough black people chose to study education in college and university. "Perhaps," he told the young people, "you need to ask your parents why more of them didn't choose to become teachers." And he announced that any students who didn't return to their schools immediately would be suspended from classes for five days. He'd barely finished speaking when the first rock smashed through a second-floor window and into an empty department boardroom. Within seconds, the police riot squad emerged from nearby side streets dressed in their new, never-used riot gear, carrying full shields and heavy nightsticks. The next day's *Tribune* called it Halifax's first ever race riot and showed pictures of policemen clubbing demonstrators.

"Ironically, these rock-throwers and placard-wavers were supposedly protesting the portrayal in a school textbook of some African Negroes as savages," the paper's editorial declared. "We don't know about the Negroes in the textbook, but we can say for a certainty that those who took part in the demonstration this week acted like savages. We can only be thankful for the swift, decisive and restrained response of the forces of law and order, which prevented further property damage and hooliganism."

Black Pride held an emergency board meeting, after which it apologized for the "irresponsible actions of a few" and announced that the drop-in centre would close immediately. Some board members demanded that Calvin fire Ray, too, but he resisted, creating a split among board members, a few of whom hinted Calvin was protecting a "communist troublemaker" just because his sister was dating the young man.

The fallout from the demonstration itself had barely subsided when the local CBC broadcast the National Film Board documentary, which stirred things up all over again. In editing the film to fit its half-hour time slot, the filmmakers—intentionally or unintentionally—made it appear as though Ray had orchestrated the entire demonstration. Ray's praise for the young people for organizing the demonstration ended up on the cutting-room floor; his comments about the racist, capitalist education system became a damning voice-over for the dramatic film of the confrontation between the riot squad and the demonstrators.

Bowing to renewed pressure from the board, Calvin called in Ray to tell him he was being suspended for one week without pay for what the board described as "conduct detrimental to the future of Black Pride."

"I'm sorry, Ray, I truly am," Calvin said, "but what they really wanted was to fire your ass. So be thankful it didn't go that far."

"Thanks," Ray said. Then he got on the phone and called Jack Eagleson. "Mr. Eagleson," he said, "when's the next sitting for those admission tests?"

Jack Eagleson was as good as his word. And better. He not only wrote a compelling letter of reference for Ray, which, coupled with Ray's own high scores on his LSATs, got him accepted into the program, but he also arranged for Ray to receive a bursary to cover tuition, books and modest living expenses for all three years of law school. The cheques came from the Winners' Fund. "An organization I belong to has a fund that supports worthy causes," Eagleson explained with one his laughs. "You seemed worthy enough to me."

Ray had waited most of his first year for the other shoe to drop, for Eagleson to demand something in return, but he never did. In fact, the only communication Ray had from his benefactor was a note after his final exams that year, congratulating him on "doing far better than I did in my first year. Good luck with the rest of your studies."

Eagleson never once mentioned the suitcase full of money he'd tried to bribe Ray's father with, either to defend his actions or to apologize for them, although Ray figured that must have had something to do with Mr. Eagleson's support. But Ray, of course, never asked Eagleson about that either.

In that, he was not his father's son. Lawrence Carter frequently let his son know exactly what he thought—about Ray's decision to quit Black Pride "at the first sign of trouble"; about his decision to throw his lot in with "the white vultures preying on your own people"; about his decision to accept help and, worse, money from a man like

Jack Eagleson, "the very same fellow *I* told to go to hell"; and even about his decision to break up with Rosa, "the only one in that whole family who was worth a damn."

They'd split up just before Ray started law school. Ray's stupid idea. They had to stop seeing each other, he told her, so he could focus on his studies. He'd not only been out of school for seven years but he'd never even been inside an undergraduate university classroom, let alone a place like law school. So he wouldn't have time to be a proper boyfriend. Ray couldn't simply do well, he had to do better than his classmates. The dean, the profs, the students, probably even Mr. Eagleson himself, were all just waiting for him to live down to their expectations. He had to show them, he told her. Rosa could understand that; she could, couldn't she? Rosa couldn't. And didn't.

Ray couldn't blame her. He wasn't sure he understood either. Had he been honest, or was there something more to his inexplicable desire to walk away from a relationship that seemed to be everything he could have hoped for? Maybe he was just scared. Was he really ready to settle down with one woman? Shouldn't he see other girls, make sure Rosa was really the one for him? That would have been acceptable, but Ray wasn't even sure that was what was behind his decision. Could it be that he was embarrassed to introduce Rosa on campus as his girlfriend? Ray was twenty-four; Rosa was eighteen. And still in high school. Ray was going to be a law student. Could it be that Rosa was, well . . . that she was . . . too unsophisticated for the life he was about to lead? Unsophisticated? Was *unsophisticated* code for black? Jesus . . . could it be that he, a black man, was embarrassed to have a black girlfriend? Worried that the other students might think he wasn't smart enough, or ambitious enough, to have a girlfriend to fit his newly elevated social status?

Within days of breaking up with her, Ray had come to his senses, told Rosa he was sorry and asked, then begged her to forgive him his stupidity and take him back. Rosa refused. In the beginning, she'd been hurt, which morphed quickly into anger, and then finally obstinacy. She'd show him. And she did.

Within a week, she was dating a boy from her high school, a football player. Within the month, they were going steady.

Ray had been right about how hard first-year law school would be. But he was wrong that breaking off with Rosa would help him concentrate on his studies. In fact, it had the opposite effect. When he wasn't moping about how he'd screwed things up, he was hatching schemes to win her back, schemes he seemed incapable of following up. He passed his Christmas exams, but barely.

A few days after Christmas, he finally called Rosa to invite her over to his apartment for a drink, "because, well, it's Christmas and we should at least be friends."

She acquiesced, but there was a coldness in her tone. Perhaps that was why he'd felt the need to have a drink while he waited for her to arrive. And then another. And another. He was drunk by the time she got there. Drunk and maudlin and stupid. He careened from bragging about how well he'd done in law school to weeping about how much he missed her to complaining about how unfair she'd been to him.

"Unfair to *you!*" she fired back. "I wasn't the one who dumped you."

"But that was a mistake. I said I was sorry."

"Sorry? Sorry came way too late."

Afterward, he wouldn't remember how they'd ended up in bed together. Perhaps the answer was in the bottom of the empty quart of rye on his night table. At some point, they'd started passing it back and forth, drinking the alcohol straight from the bottle. And then suddenly—at least that's the way it seemed in Ray's memory of it—they were rolling around on the bed, frantically ripping at each other's clothes. There was nothing romantic about their lovemaking; it was aggressive, cathartic, as if they were taking out all their hurt, and anger, and love on each other's body. He was driving his hardness as deeply into her body as he could; she was clawing at the skin on his back, scratching, cutting. And then, in what seemed like a single, shuddering explosion, it was over. They fell asleep entangled in one another's arms and legs.

"This doesn't change anything, you know," she said the next morning, sitting on his bed, fastening her bra.

"But—"

"We shouldn't have. But we did. And now . . ." There was a hesitation, as if, he imagined when he replayed their conversation in his head later, her resolve was melting, but then she willed the ice back into her voice. "I have to go."

"Don't."

"Don't make it harder."

"But last night—"

"—was last night," she said, cutting him off. "You know, when you broke up with me, that hurt. A lot. But now I can see that it was the right thing to do. We're too different in too many ways. You were right to think I couldn't fit into your law school life."

"But that's not what I—"

"I know that's not what you said. You didn't have to say it. Your eyes said it for you." Ray looked away, tried not to let her see how right she'd been.

"I have to go," she said finally. And she was gone.

He found out she was pregnant during Reading Week that February. Aunt Annie told him. The story came out in fits and starts when he went to visit her to lie about how well he was doing at law school. And to ask, as casually as possible, if she'd heard how Rosa was doing.

"Gone," she said with a shake of her head. "Girl just done gone. Her and her daddy had a knock-down-drag-out. Heard 'em myself from down the hall. Shoutin' to beat the band. And then Rosa up and left. Just disappeared."

"You know what were they arguing about?"

"Not much I don't know," Aunt Annie said with a twinkle in her eye. "Seems our little Rosa is gonna be a mama."

"A what?"

"She's gonna have a baby."

Ray called Rosa's father's apartment; the Deacon said there was no one named Rosa living at that number. "It's Raymond, Raymond

Carter, Deacon Johnstone. Can you just tell me how I can get in touch with Rosa?"

"Young man," the Deacon said in his Reverend voice, "I don't know anyone named Rosa and I'd appreciate it if you wouldn't call here again."

He thought about calling Calvin, asking him about Rosa. He hadn't seen Calvin since he'd handed him his letter of resignation the day he was supposed to return to work after his suspension. They'd promised to keep in touch. But he hadn't. Now, it would be awkward. *Hi, Calvin. Sorry I knocked up your sister. You couldn't tell me where I could find her, could you?*

In the end, he'd waited for Rosa after school.

"Can I talk to you?"

"It's a free country," she said and started walking.

"Why didn't you tell me?" he demanded, more forcefully than he'd planned.

"Tell you what?"

"That you're having a baby."

"Is that any of your business?"

Ray was taken aback. But he pressed on. "It is if I'm the father. Look, Rosa, I'm sorry about everything that's happened but I do love you. And I'll make it right. I mean, we can get married . . . I'll quit law school, get a job, we can find a place, we can—"

She stopped, turned to face him. "What makes you think it's your baby?"

He hadn't even entertained the possibility, hadn't allowed the image of Rosa with someone else—her football player boyfriend?—to enter his mind. "Is it?" he asked weakly.

"Doesn't matter," she said. "I don't need your pity." And began walking again.

Ray remained rooted in place, considering. The baby was his. It had to be. But . . . what was he supposed to do if she wouldn't even acknowledge that? And maybe . . . maybe it really *wasn't* his baby. It had been just that one night. What made him think he *had* to be the father? Part of him wanted to run after her, make her tell him the truth. But part of him didn't want to know, didn't want to quit law school, give up on the future . . . he was too young to be a father . . .

And then she was gone. Turned the corner. Out of sight. He didn't follow. And he hadn't seen her since. He'd heard from Aunt Annie she'd had a son. "His name's Lawrence," she said. "And I hear he's a handsome one."

Ray had tried dating white girls again. There were only a few at the law school, but they were easier to talk to than the white guys. Maybe, like Becky back in high school, they were just looking for an adventure, a chance to rebel before they conformed, or perhaps they wanted to know if it was true what they said about black men and their big dicks. Ray wondered what they thought afterwards. He never asked. And they never offered.

Was that why once seemed enough for most of them? Curiosity satisfied, time to move on? Sometimes, after, they'd be friendly enough, even over-friendly, as if to make up for the fact that they didn't want to sleep with him again. Sometimes, like Sandy this morning, they'd pretend they didn't even see him.

He'd noticed her coming out of the library a few minutes before his hallway encounter with Montague. She'd seen him too, he was sure of that, but she'd looked away before "Good morning" could escape his lips. He'd swallowed the words as he felt another invisible curtain come crashing down. Was it something he'd said or done—or not—last night? Was it about the boyfriend back home she'd mentioned before and after? Or was it about the colour of his skin?

That was the problem, he thought. You never knew for sure whether someone was rejecting you, or your race. Or was race, at least some of the time, just the convenient receptacle into which you could put the blame you didn't want to take on yourself?

She doesn't like you because you were an asshole last night. You got drunk and stupid, came on to her. Pressured her to go to bed with you, wouldn't take no for an answer and then, after it was over, just walked away like you'd got what you wanted, and screw her. No wonder she didn't want to talk to you today.

But was that really it?

You saw her sitting at the bar in that miniskirt, legs winking open in invitation. She wanted your big black dick. She didn't say no to going back to her place. And she was the one who unbuckled your belt, who reached down and wrapped her hands around it. And now, now that she's got what she wanted, she knows what she doesn't want. A black man complicating her life.

Why did everything have to be so complicated? Like Montague's simple "Good morning, Mr. Carter."

Ray needed to get away from Sandy, and Cecil Montague, away from law school itself. Now. So he didn't go to his next class, just kept walking past other students and faculty, out the door, turned left on University Avenue and headed downtown.

He hadn't planned to end up at the Provincial Law Courts building, but once there, it seemed only logical to go inside, to see if he could find some reason not to quit.

"Arraignments are in Courtroom 1." The helpful deputy pointed down the hall. At first, Ray thought the sheriff's deputy must have realized he was a law student and was simply helping him find his way around. But then it struck him that the man couldn't know that and must have assumed Ray was here to be arraigned. That the deputy was black didn't ease the sting. Ray was tempted to go anywhere but Courtroom 1 just to prove there were other reasons for a black man to be in this courthouse, but he didn't. He slipped into the back of the courtroom, bowed to the still-empty judge's bench and looked for a seat. There was none. Just a sea of faces, many black, awaiting their turn to concede their guilt or assert their non-guilt.

Ray's eyes were drawn to the young woman standing alone at the front of the room. It took a moment for him to register that the woman was Rosa. In that same moment she recognized him, too. She looked at him, then away as if from a flame. She turned back to face the front of the empty room and sat down on the bench. She hunched over, trying, Ray thought, to make herself invisible. What was she doing there? he wondered. He should go up there, ask her about her son (his son?), apologize, tell her he loved her, beg her to take him back. He didn't. He turned on his heel and pushed the courtroom door open, ran down the hall past the startled deputy and out into the air. He needed to breathe.

"Hey." His come-on.

"Hey." Her response.

It was close to two in the morning; even the Derby Tavern—the usual excuse white south-enders offered for being on this part of Gottingen Street at night—had long since closed its doors.

"How much?"

"Depends . . ."

"On what?"

"Depends on what you want." She sounded bored, then forced. "But whatever you want, honey, I got."

Ward Justice could not see her face. He was staring at her midsection across the empty passenger seat and through the open window of his new Lincoln Town Car. She was standing on the curb, her face above the car's roof. It was dark, the electricity was out, and the only light came from the blowing, drifting snow. It was the first storm of the season, unexpected and unseasonably early, so the plows hadn't even been mobilized yet. Worse, it had rained just before the temperature dropped. The roads were slick with ice. What the hell was he doing out here in this weather at this hour?

Except for the girl, the streets were deserted. She wasn't dressed for the weather. Under an open jacket, he could see she was wearing a frilly white top that showcased her breasts and a micro-miniskirt that left little for him to have to imagine.

"You want anything or you just lookin'?" she said when he didn't answer. "Because it's frigging cold out here, you know. It's ten for the best blow job you ever had, twenty for the works."

Why was he doing this? Because he was drunk? He was definitely drunk, way too drunk to be driving. He'd told himself when he was elected he'd never do a Dauphinee but here he was, piss-drunk and at the wheel. He should have called the cops. Partying politicians regularly called the police for free cab rides. Ward had discovered that soon after he was elected. He'd been celebrating late into the night in Seamus O'Sullivan's hospitality suite at the Nova Scotian during the party's annual meeting when Jack suggested they head up to the Paradise, the all-night greasy spoon, for a burger and fries. "Just call the cops," Jack said. "They'll send a car for us." Ward thought he was joking. "They're just driving around anyway, so what the fuck?" Jack told him. "Consider it one of the perks of power. Just call the dispatcher." So Ward did. And sure enough, a few minutes later, a patrol car pulled up at the hotel entrance and drove them the three blocks to the Paradise.

Earlier tonight at Monique's, a couple of fellow Cabinet ministers had again encouraged him to call the dispatcher. "Just fucking tell them to send a car over to Monique's," Whitey suggested helpfully when Ward announced he was leaving. "They know the fucking way." The four men and one woman seated around the kitchen table playing cards guffawed loudly. Especially Monique.

"Tell them to send Sergeant Fralick," she said. "He's a real gentleman."

The weekly card game at Monique's had been an end-of-Cabinet-day ritual since the Liberals came to office in 1970. The Tories probably did it too. When Ward was first elected, the idea of being caught in the house of Halifax's most notorious madam would have frightened Ward, but he quickly came to realize there was almost no danger. Whenever the cops did raid her place, which was no more than once a year, one of Monique's good—and well-paid—friends on the vice squad would telephone a few hours in advance so she could shoo any clients out the door, relocate her girls to safer accommodations in one of the apartment buildings she owned and make sure all her carefully maintained business records were hidden in the secret storage room behind a living-room bookcase. The bookcase was filled with rare, first-edition books, many classics. Monique claimed to have read them all. Ward believed her.

Monique had arrived in Halifax from Montreal shortly after the war began. She'd found work in a waterfront brothel that catered to the roughest of the rough merchant navy trade. By the end of the war, she had her own place, a half-dozen girls working for her and a more genteel and better-heeled clientele. She paid bellhops at the finer hotels and baggage handlers at the railway station to direct inquiring visitors her way, offered a commission to any taxi driver who brought her customers and, of course, made sure the higher ranks in the city police department and all the top politicians knew they were welcome to sample her wares. Many did. Her girls were all good looking. And clean. Doc Wilson examined them before they were allowed to start working and he made weekly house calls to check for venereal diseases and any other medical complaints.

Why hadn't he asked Monique to get him a girl? Ward wondered. And why had he said no to calling for a cop-cabbie? Why was he here, drunk and picking up a street hooker? Why wasn't he home in bed with . . . well, he and Victoria were no longer sleeping in the same bed.

They had had one of their "conversations" this afternoon.

"Hello?" Hopeful. Her.

"Hi." Pretending she'd be happy to hear the sound of his voice.

"Oh, hi." Disappointed.

"Looks like I'm going to be late again," he said, trying to sound disappointed too. "Long day in Cabinet. Just got back to the office, and there's this mountain of messages and files to deal with."

"That's fine." She sounded relieved. "Should I save you dinner?"

"Don't worry about me," he said. "I'll get Sue Anne to send out for sandwiches, or I'll pick up something on the way home."

"Fine." She let that hang.

"Well, okay then." He tried to find a way out. "Guess I'd better get to it. Listen, kiss the girls for me. Tell them I'll see them in the morning."

"I will."

"Don't wait up."

"I won't."

"Okay. Bye."

"Bye."

They used to make a point of ending their conversations with exchanged *love-you/love-you-too*s. They didn't do that any more. Sometimes, he thought it was because she was no longer the free spirit he'd fallen in love with. But he wasn't much fun either. When Ward told her he had a lot of work left to do, he'd been telling the truth. There was always more to do than hours in a day.

Perhaps it was just Fisheries. If he wasn't meeting with this inshore fishermen's group or that offshore lobby, he was under siege from a fledging aquaculture association or an oil exploration consortium. And from Junior, of course. Junior called him two or three times a week. With this scheme or that problem. Everybody had a problem. The problem was they couldn't agree on what the problem was, let alone the solution. They did agree Canada needed to declare a two-hundred-mile coastal management zone around its perimeter, but that wasn't something Nova Scotia could do on its own. The fishery was one of the few areas where Ottawa and the provinces shared jurisdiction. Which meant even more meetings with his federal counterpart.

"You work too hard," Whitey would tell him. Whitey was Daniel James White, the Minister of Sport, who represented a Cape Breton riding. All the Cabinet ministers sported nicknames. "Makes you feel part of team," Whitey explained when they met for the first time after the election. "What'll we call you? Wardy? Justy? We could call you Ward Heeler, I guess . . . Great fucking nickname for a politician. But too long. Justy . . . that sounds just right. That's what we'll call you. Too bad our fucking Famous Seamus didn't appoint you Justice minister. Oh well, next time."

Whitey lived his job. He kept a running tab at Chez Henri for wining and dining. It was supposed to be just for Sports Department business, but Whitey believed his pleasure was Sports Department business. He travelled a lot, too. Wining and dining as he went. In the first six months of the new administration, he'd visited every Canadian Football League city except Regina—"Who the hell goes to Saskatchewan?"—to lobby for a Canadian Football League franchise for Halifax. And spent a week in Las Vegas trying to decide if

Nova Scotia should allow casinos. He'd covered his seven thousand dollars in gambling losses with a receipt for a lobster banquet he hadn't staged for the Vegas Chamber of Commerce. And he'd journeyed to the Turks and Caicos for two weeks of sun, sand and an occasional meeting with government officials to discuss the province annexing the Caribbean islands. Which justified the trip as a business expense. Whitey was all business. "The Yanks got fucking Hawaii, so why the fuck not?"

Fuck—in all its motherfucking permutations and combinations—was Whitey's favourite word. Ward marvelled at how he managed to make "fuck" every second word in private conversation and then, effortlessly, switched to his Sunday-school manners the moment he found himself in a public forum or with someone shoving a microphone in his face.

Whitey had been walking away from a post-Cabinet scrum with some reporters this afternoon when he'd spotted Ward walking back to his office. He caught up with him. "What say, Justy my lusty trusty, you handsome young fuck, you? Monique's at nine?"

Ward really did have too much work to do. He was meeting with the federal minister tomorrow to talk about next year's fish quotas. And Junior was coming in the afternoon to ask for his support in some scheme to lease a factory freezer trawler. Ward shouldn't spend tonight hanging out at Monique's. He looked at his watch. Nine o'clock? Four hours from now. Surely, by then, he'd have accomplished everything he was going to get done? He could go home after that, of course, but what was there at home?

"Sure, why not?"

Monique's was always fun. After a Cabinet meeting, half the government's front bench would end up in Monique's kitchen. Some came for the girls. One night a few months ago, Whitey had walked out of one of the girls' bedrooms and into the kitchen, wearing nothing but his socks and shoes, his ubiquitous fedora and a satisfied grin. He was chewing on an unlit cigar. "What the fuck you lookin' at?" he demanded, taking in the suddenly silent group sitting around the table. "This a fucking card game or what? Deal me in and stop your fucking gawking. What's the matter. You never seen a big dick before?"

"I never seen one yet," Monique replied, to hoots and hollers from the men. "Sit down, Whitey, and take a load off."

He grinned back at her. "Already shot my load, thanks."

Ward had never been with one of Monique's girls. Neither, he guessed, had most of the others in the room. Monique's was a place you went to say you'd been there, and let people imagine whatever they wanted. It added a certain macho mystique. The truth was that Ward hadn't been with any woman, including Victoria, since before the election. Until tonight.

"The works," Ward answered finally. "I'll have the works."

The girl opened the door, got in the car, glanced over at Ward, did a double take. So did Ward. She was coloured! He panicked? It seemed worse somehow. He'd never even imagined having sex with a—should he send her away, tell her he'd changed his mind?

"Why don't you just drive around that corner up there?" she instructed. "There's a parking lot. We can have some privacy." She wasn't looking at him now. She was staring straight ahead out the front windshield and into the snow void swirling in the car's headlights. She was younger than her world-weary voice seemed to suggest. Late teens or early twenties, he thought. And her face in profile was beautiful. He drank in the contours of her body as she shrugged off her jacket.

"Nice car." He didn't tell her it was one of the perks of his position. "At least it's warm in here," she said. She waited. He didn't move. "Are you okay?" she asked finally.

"Yeah, yeah. Sorry," he said. He put his foot on the gas, felt the tires spin, grab the pavement; the car lurched forward.

"In here," she said, pointing to what he assumed must be the entrance to the deserted parking lot. It wasn't. The car bumped up over the curb. "Sorry about that," she said. "It's hard to tell in all this snow."

"That's all right."

"You can stop anywhere. I don't think we're gonna be disturbed tonight."

He stopped the car, put it in park and left the engine running.

"Let's get the money out of the way first," she said. "That way we won't have to think about it later. It's like I said. Twenty dollars. For everything."

Ward reached into his back pants pocket, pulled out his wallet. It was fat with cash. He'd been to the bank before the Cabinet meeting this morning to withdraw the four hundred dollars cash he allowed himself for spending money each month. He should have taken the twenty out of his wallet before he drove down here. What if she decided to rob him? There was no turning back. He pulled two tens out of his wallet, handed them to her and quickly shoved the wallet back into his pants.

The girl took the money, slipped it into a pocket of her jacket. She turned around then and looked into the back seat. "If we move that briefcase, we'd probably be more comfortable in the back."

"Sure. Okay," he said.

The girl kneeled, then gracefully executed what looked to Ward like a swan dive over the top of the front seat and onto the plush back bench seat. As she did so, Ward got an tantalizing close-up glimpse of her white panties against chocolate skin. He could smell perfume. A hint of lavender.

"Come on in," she said, smiling, white teeth against dark skin, extending a slender hand his way. He noticed the lightness of the skin on her palms. "The water's fine."

He wasn't nearly as graceful, tumbling over the seat back, a tangle of arms and legs. He tried not to hit her as he landed. As soon as he'd adjusted himself on the seat, she reached over with her right hand and began to rub his stomach just above his belt. He put his arm around her shoulder, pulled her closer. Her hair was soft, shampoo-fresh. Perhaps that was the lavender. He ran his fingers through her hair, kissed her forehead. She unbuckled his belt, pulled down his pants' zipper. Her hand slipped inside his boxers. He sucked in his breath.

"Not yet." He exhaled. "I just want to hold you first." He was afraid that if she continued, he would explode and it would be over. He wanted to kiss her face and lips, explore the unfamiliar terrain of her darker nooks and crevices with his hands and tongue, feel the warmth of her skin against his, make it last.

What was the right way for a man to be with a girl who did it for money? He'd never been with a prostitute so he couldn't quite get his head around the etiquette. He had the sense he was supposed to let her lead, let her "do" him. But he didn't want to be done. He wanted to hold her, be held, get and give pleasure.

He kissed her face, her shoulder, the smooth bare skin above the top of her blouse. He reached around, unhooked her bra and watched as it fell away, exposing her breasts. His fingers lightly brushed across the dark nipples, felt them stiffen, took them, one by one, in his mouth and stroked them with his tongue. She moaned, a small, involuntary moan of pleasure. His eyes were closed. His right hand was down between her legs, inside her panties, his middle finger rubbing against the nub of her clitoris. Her legs opened and closed in a slow rhythm.

"I want you inside me," she said finally. Was that really what she meant, or was she just looking to get this over with quickly so she could . . . turn another trick? Go home? To her boyfriend? To her pimp?

She was straddling him now, lowering herself down, taking him inside her. Her muscles tightened, relaxed, tightened, relaxed around him. He opened his eyes. He wanted to tell her to slow down, make the feeling last, but he couldn't speak. The girl's eyes were closed now, her head was tilted back and the beginnings of a smile tickled her lips. Was she thinking about him? Or reliving some other, better moment in her head?

Suddenly, it was over in one stuttering concussive moment of ecstasy. His head fell back against the seat. He was utterly, completely, totally spent. It had been a long time.

She kept him inside her as his erection slowly subsided, her body leaning into his, wanting, he thought, to be held too.

"That felt good," he said as his breathing slowly returned to normal.

"Mmmm," she said, letting his penis slip out of her and dismounting. "Good. Yes . . . good." She reached behind her to reattach the clasps on her bra, found her panties on the floor and slipped them on over the high heels she was still wearing. With what seemed almost like modesty, she adjusted her skirt to cover herself.

Ward hadn't moved. He couldn't.

She looked at him. "I know who you are," she said.

Oh shit. Blackmail. He hadn't thought of that. Threaten to go to the papers. He could see the headline: "Negro Prostitute Claims Minister Paid to Have Sex With Her." Big type. Across the top of the front page—

Rewind.

What was that she'd said?

"You were friends with Ray. You used to visit him in Africville."

"Rose?" He tried to put the pieces together, shape a woman out of the little girl who wouldn't eat her corned beef and cabbage.

"Rosa," she corrected him. "It's Rosa."

"Sorry. I just didn't recognize you . . ."

"That's okay. Lots of times I don't recognize me either. You look different too. Better, I mean. But I knew it was you from TV. You're always on TV."

"How did . . . ?"

"How did a nice girl like me end up working the streets?" she finished his sentence, laughing. "It's a long story. Not worth telling. Not now." She paused. "You ever see Ray?"

"No, not for a long time." Strange, though, he'd been thinking about Ray today. This morning, Cabinet had voted to cut off funding for Black Pride immediately so the furor in the black community would have time to dissipate before the next election. Ward couldn't help but make the connection between Black Pride and Ray, Ray the Radical. It was hard to square the image of Ray on TV with the one that rolled through Ward's mind. Ray of the playground. Ray of Africville. Ray of . . . He missed *that* Ray, the Ray he'd known before Black Pride, before . . . before Ray had tried to expose him to the world as a vote buyer! Christ, how could he have been feeling nostalgia for the man who'd almost ruined his political career before it began? And yet, tonight, with Rosa in the car with him, his thoughts tumbled back to that time when he and Ray had been inseparable. When life was simpler.

Race hadn't mattered then. Was that what pushed them apart? Was that his fault? Or was it Ray who'd refused to open himself up to new friends, new experiences, white people? Whatever, they'd drifted apart. It was only now, ten years later, that Ward realized Ray had been his last best friend. There hadn't been anyone since. Jack and he were mentor and protegé. He and Junior had become friends, but there was a history there that would never be overcome. He liked the camaraderie of his Cabinet colleagues, but they were all older too. That was the problem with being too successful too soon. You were always out of sync.

What was Ray doing now? he wondered. Jack had said something one night about Ray enrolling in law school.

"Well," she said, hesitating, "I guess I'd better be going." She reached for the door handle.

"Let me drive you. This storm's too nasty to be out." *Stay.*

She looked out. Snow blanketed the car's windows. Beyond, she could hear the wind. There'd be no more customers tonight.

"You sure it's no trouble?"

"No trouble. Where do you live?"

"Uh, off Barrington. You can let me off by the bridge. That'd be great."

They drove in silence. There were so many questions he wanted to ask but his tongue couldn't seem to form the words. He pulled up beside the base of the bridge tower. The navy base was just up the street.

"You're sure this is okay? Is it safe to be walking around?"

She smiled. Her hand touched his sleeve. "You're sweet. But I'll be fine. I can take care of myself." She opened the door.

"Can I see you again?" He'd blurted it out. Now he looked away. What was he doing?

"You're sweet," she said again. "You really are." She closed the car door. And was gone.

9

Spring 2003

Ward slumped into the chair he now kept near the door to his office. He needed to catch his breath. There was nothing like being told you were dying to make you feel like death. These days, Ward rooted around inside every ache, pain, twinge, tickle and breath, examining it, turning it over, searching its insides for hidden meaning. Had the tumour grown? Had the cancer spread? Conversely, he rarely noticed when he had to pee. Perhaps this cancer, too, was only in his mind, not in his lungs and his bones.

"How long?" he'd asked. But they couldn't, or wouldn't tell him.

"I can tell you the course this disease usually takes," Dr. Hussein had said, "but there is no *usually* with lung cancer. Everyone is different and will experience the stages and the progression in different ways." She was professional, careful, cold. She had to be; she was, after all, sentencing patients to die. Like a judge. Ward admired her professionalism.

"But what do you think?" he insisted. For some reason—he knew the reason—the timeline seemed important.

He'd spent two days undergoing tests. At one point, they'd stuck a tube with a mini-camera up his nose, down his throat and into his chest, and snipped off a few pieces of tumour for testing. He'd been awake, but they'd given him a sedative to dull the pain, which had also dulled his memory.

The only thing he could remember from the procedure was somebody saying something about golf balls. It was only later, when Dr.

Hussein showed him the X-ray—"That tumour there," she said, pointing to something Ward's unschooled eyes saw only as a cloudy mass, "is the size of a golf ball"—that he understood. The golf ball was inoperable. And it was not the only tumour. In their poking and prodding and snipping and slicing, they'd discovered other enemy soldiers hunkered down inside his bones. The war was lost.

"What I think," the doctor answered, "is not important. I have seen patients presenting in much the same way as you who have survived six months, and others who've lived two years or more. So . . ." She let that hang in the air. "The fact is that medicine is continually developing new and better treatment options that can help to extend and enhance life—"

"No."

"I'm sorry?"

"No treatments. No chemotherapy, no radiation. If I have cancer and I know what the outcome is going to be, I'd rather just let nature take its course."

"But—"

"Pain management at the end. Okay. I'm no martyr, I don't want to die in pain. So fill with me drugs, whatever, but when I can't cope any more."

The doctor smiled. "Well," she said finally, "I see you've been thinking about this."

He had. He'd been thinking about it since he'd first convinced himself he had prostate cancer. It was different now, of course; he was more frightened *knowing* than he'd been merely *imagining*. Part of him wanted to rush off to Mexico or wherever miracle cures were on offer to swallow the seeds or bathe in the springs or rub mud all over or whatever he had to do to make himself whole again. But another part, the logical part, answered: *Why bother? What are you living for?* Not in some melodramatic, what-is-there-left-to-live-for way but in a clear-headed, what's-the-difference-if-it's-now-or-thirty-years-from-now way. He saw himself as a man in a canoe without a paddle, floating down a fast-moving river, being raked by a rock outcropping here, twisted around in an eddy there, flipped over a falls, shunted off to a quiet pool, sucked back into the current and now, the canoe leaking, hurtling toward a Niagara of a final falls. Over. Beyond his control.

Life, he now believed, had always been beyond his control. He would never have become a politician if Jack hadn't put that idea in his head. He would never have realized he liked being a politician if it hadn't suddenly been snatched away from him. He would never have chosen to be a judge. Does any little kid dream of growing up to become a judge? Whatever happened to being Bill Mazeroski? Ward had been a judge for twenty-five years now. He had been a good judge, judicious, conscientious, scrupulously fair, an upholder of all that is right and just . . . but he couldn't think of a single decision he'd made or opinion he'd written that would cast a shadow when he was gone.

So what difference would living longer make?

The doctors decided his resistance to treatment, his passivity in the face of death, indicated depression. They sent him to a shrink, who prescribed antidepressants. Ward didn't take them. Just as he didn't take the shrink's advice to confide in someone.

"Perhaps you'd like to have your wife join you when you talk with the doctor," the nurse had helpfully suggested when she'd set up his appointment with Dr. Hussein.

"We're separated."

"Oh, I'm sorry. Well, perhaps another family member, or a friend, then."

"No, I'll be fine."

Dr. Hussein made the same suggestions again after she told him he was dying. "Patients usually find it helpful to have someone to confide in," she said.

"Will it be obvious to anyone else that I have cancer?" Ward asked her.

She smiled again. He seemed to amuse her. "Well, there won't be a 'C' tattooed on your forehead. In the beginning, people may only notice that you're losing weight. You'll probably be coughing more, and your breathing may become more laboured."

"Can I keep working?"

"If you want. For a while. But you may not have the energy for a full day."

"So I don't have to tell anyone?"

"Again, not in the beginning. But there will come a time . . . Are you sure there isn't someone you can share this with?"

"I'm sure." He smiled back. "I'll be fine."

At first, he was. He spent his days juggling medical appointments around judicial obligations, and coming up with excuses for Kathleen in order to explain why he would be late returning from lunch this afternoon or why he would have to leave work early again today. His medical appointments provided all the opportunity he could want to discuss his condition. "Could you tell me again about . . . ?" Or, "Why do I feel this pain in my . . . ?" But when it became clear that Ward really had no interest in treatment, the doctors lost interest in him.

Which is when he began to rethink his decision not to tell Victoria. She had moved into a one-bedroom apartment in Clayton Park while she waited for her new three-bedroom Harbourland Estates condo to be completed. She needed the space, she'd explained, for when their daughters came to visit. That they would not choose to stay with him was a given, accepted if unacknowledged. Ward got along well enough with his daughters, but he had kept them at a distance while they were growing up, so their first loyalty was to Victoria.

He knew he should tell Victoria, if not to have someone to confide in, at least so there would be someone to discuss the practicalities with. Cremation? Burial? Halifax? Eisners Head? Should he write his own obituary? In writing that, how should he deal with his sudden departure from politics? And his will—could he still leave everything to Victoria and let her deal with it? How would their separation affect her survivor benefits? For a man whose career had been the law, there were remarkable gaps in his legal knowledge.

So yes, he should tell her. But if he did, would his resolve falter, would he change his mind about not raging at the closing of the day, or whatever saying it was that people trotted out whenever they talk about impending death?

His decision to go gently into that good night, he knew, was fragile. If he did tell Victoria, and if she decided to come back to him, even to nurse him through his final days—which she almost certainly would—his resolve would shatter. Strange. For twenty-five years, he'd imagined their separation as a Tom Rush song. In his imaginings, there were "no regrets, no tears goodbye." That's how much he knew.

With the time he had left, he would make things as right as they could be with Victoria, maybe reconnect with his children. And, oh yes, he would also do that other thing, the one he'd put off for too many years. What was that guy's name? He stood up finally, went to his desk and picked up the phone book.

"What'd I tell you?" Shondelle said triumphantly, her voice rising as it inevitably did whenever she scored a debating point. Sometimes she annoyed him. "I was right. Wasn't I right? I was, wasn't I?"

"You were," Uhuru said without enthusiasm. He knew this was going to be like his father's diary all over again. Shondelle had talked him into filing a federal Freedom of Information request for files the RCMP might have kept on him in the seventies.

He'd trapped himself; he had been trying to impress her, telling her stories of his days with Black Pride. And Shondelle had interrupted him in full flight. "It's a long shot, but you never know," she'd said. "We could find something to use in court. There could be stuff in those files that sheds light on the official view of Africville at that time."

There wasn't. So Shondelle wasn't quite as right as she was now claiming. In fact, there were only two reference to Africville in the 750 pages of reports and notes and transcripts. One was in a background memo on Raymond Carter early in the file: "Subject born and raised in Africville, black ghetto on edge of Halifax. Moved to Toronto 1967."

Reading the complete file on himself had disturbed Uhuru. While he'd known he was being watched, he was stunned that so many trees had been cut down to so little purpose. And he was intrigued that the Mounties, perhaps mindful of the cost of his surveillance, had done their best to make him seem like an important target—a dangerous radical preparing to lead a full-out insurrection against the established order. Chance encounters became clandestine meetings. The innocuous was made to seem ominous.

70/10/17. 12:45–14:30 hours. Downtowner Tavern. Subject met with [name blanked out for privacy reasons]. Topic of discussion unknown. Possible links to other strategy meetings of radical groups noted by officers in other Can. cities. Note to file: War Measures Act declared 70/10/16.

14:30: Subject left rendezvous, proceeded on foot to payphone corner Gottingen & Cogswell Sts. Made call. Approx. 2 min. 30 sec. No info available. Proceeded to 27 Cornwallis Street, Subject's domicile. Remained inside until 0930 70/10/18. Trace team reports no phone calls from apartment.

It had taken Uhuru a while to figure out whose name had been blacked out. It must have been that reporter—he couldn't remember his name—who'd written the vote-buying story the *Tribune* wouldn't publish. A few days after the election, he'd called Ray, asking to meet him at the Downtowner for lunch. Ray had assumed he was working on another story, but all the guy wanted to do was apologize that he hadn't been able to get the story into the newspaper.

"If you want, I'll quit. I'll call a press conference and tell everything that happened."

"No, man, don't be stupid," Ray replied. He'd never expected the paper to print the story; he'd just wanted Eagleson to know he was on to him, a none-too-subtle answer to Eagleson's suggestion that he abandon Black Pride for law school.

Ironic how that one had ultimately turned out, Uhuru thought now. The only thing he hadn't expected at the time was that Ward Justice would have been in the middle of it all. He wondered, just for an instant, if those photos of Ward handing out turkeys still existed somewhere. He'd better not mention that to Shondelle or she'd be off on yet another wild . . . turkey chase.

Uhuru couldn't help but marvel at the Mounties' thoroughness in documenting his life. There were even cryptic reports on his various meetings with Jack Eagleson. Eagleson's name wasn't blanked out in the files; the documents referred to him instead as CI#1376, which Uhuru eventually deduced must have stood for "confidential informant." Jack Eagleson a police informant? Was that why he'd contacted Ray? To fish for information for his Mountie masters? But why Eagleson, a white, well-connected downtown lawyer? And, if he was looking for material to pass on to the cops, what had he learned? Not much. CI#1376's reports of their meetings were bland. Interestingly, the reports never included references to Eagleson's attempts to convince Ray to apply for law school. That remained another mystery to Uhuru.

The identity of CI#2231 was no mystery. CI#2231 appeared only once in the files, but Uhuru knew immediately who he was. "CI#2231 first met Subject in 1963. Both teenagers. Became friends, spent time together, mostly at Subject's Africville domicile . . ." The second reference to Africville. And the first and only to . . . Ward Justice! If there was any doubt, it was dispelled by the detailed story of the initial "contact between Subject and CI#2231" when Ray saved Ward from a beating at the hands of Jeremiah Black. There was nothing in anything Ward had said to the Mounties that was incriminating. The closest he came to even a negative suggestion was that "he and Subject did not continue friendship in high school; Subject preferred company of his own kind." *His own kind?* Were those Ward's words, or some Mountie's interpretation of them?

He knew that as soon as Shondelle figured out CI#2231's identity—and she would—she would also see this as just more damning evidence to support her argument that he couldn't allow Ward Justice to preside at J. J.'s trial.

Uhuru would respectfully disagree.

There would be another fight.

He wasn't certain why he persisted in defending Ward Justice. No, that wasn't true. He just wasn't sure he wanted to explain his reasons to Shondelle. There were, of course, arguments he could, and did, make.

"Here's a guy who spent time in Africville when he was growing up, who saw it as a real community—"

"But look what he's done since those *good old days*," Shondelle countered. "Remember, this is the same guy who was directly involved in the plot to buy off your father, who treated you like shit that day in court, and who we now find out ratted you out to the cops."

"Don't be so dramatic. He didn't rat me out. All he did was tell them we'd been friends."

"But what was he doing talking about you to those guys?"

"I don't know." He was retreating now. "What's the difference?"

"The difference is that this guy holds the key to our whole fucking case. If he says we can't argue justification, we're fucked."

"Look, why don't we just forget it for now?" he said. "We have the documents. We can use them if we need to once we see what happens in court."

"Fine," she said, though he knew from the tone of her voice it was anything but fine. "But just answer me one question, will you, Mr. Magnanimous? Why—why *really*—are you protecting this guy?"

"No reason," he answered. But of course there was. Uhuru had known about Ward and Rosa. Aunt Annie had told him. She'd also told him Ward got Rosa off the streets and provided financial support for her and her child. At first he'd been jealous, but then, after the tragedy and Rosa's sudden disappearance, he'd begun to see Ward as the man who'd done his best in difficult circumstances to help Rosa and her son. Perhaps Ray's defence of Ward was just because he felt guilty about his own behaviour. What had *he* done for them? Whatever, he didn't/couldn't/wouldn't tell Shondelle about Rosa and Ward, Rosa and him.

When Shondelle had asked him about former girlfriends, he'd skipped over Rosa. Which meant that the sum total of the rest of his life confirmed Shondelle's view that he was "one of those self-hating black men with a thing for white women."

Uhuru wasn't certain she was wrong. Why had it always been so much easier with white women? Could it be because he understood those relationships weren't going anywhere—that he was in it to burnish his own self-image, to prove to himself that he could have a white girl and walk away?

Could that be true with Shondelle, too? Could he just fuck her and forget her? There'd been opportunities. He'd drive her home, she'd invite him in for a drink. He'd say yes but, once inside, could never make the next move. Was it because that next move might lead to another, and another, and soon there'd be no walking away? Did he suspect he was falling love with this woman? Damn right. Was he scared? Damn right.

R-i-n-g . . . r-i-n-g . . .

Moira was sitting at her desk in a corner of the newsroom, intently reading her horoscope and trying to stay out of Michelle's sightline, when she heard her phone. She tensed. There was a time when she would have grabbed it, knowing it had to be a callback on one of the half-dozen or so stories she was juggling at the time. Today, there were no calls out. So . . . it had to be the babysitter. Or, oh God, the police calling about the babysitter.

She'd come back from maternity leave much too soon. But what choice did she have? She and Todd had split up. The end had come early in the ninth month of her pregnancy over the issue of what to name their child if it was a boy. Moira had wanted to call him Patrick, after her father. Todd had insisted on naming their son Todd, Jr.: "You know, to carry on the family name."

"Todd is an insipid name," Moira had shot back, knowing exactly what she was saying, and saying it anyway. At least she hadn't said Todd was an insipid man, though she believed that was true, too. Todd had moved out the next morning.

The baby was a boy, and Moira named him Patrick. Her father

was thrilled, more so when his daughter told him that Todd was out of her life. Patrick Donovan considered it a bonus when the *Daily Journal* reported that Todd's condo project was in receivership.

Except that it meant his daughter, like his ex-wife before her, was now a single mother with an undependable ex-spouse. Patrick had volunteered to help out by babysitting his grandson, but Moira, whose memories of her father's parenting skills were not especially positive, demurred.

Instead, she hired a Thai woman recommended by a reporter at the paper who'd interviewed her for a story on new immigrants. The woman, who called herself May, had supposedly been an English professor in Bangkok but couldn't find work in Halifax, perhaps because her conversational English skills, while impressive at home, were modest at best. Still, she was a godsend. She not only took care of Patrick, even reading children's stories to him in her native language—he gurgled appreciatively and seemed, to Moira at least, to understand every word she was saying—she also cleaned the apartment and prepared delicious Thai dishes, which she left on the stove for Moira each night.

That made Moira suspicious. During the three months she'd stayed at home with Patrick, she'd never found time to clean and rarely to cook. Was this woman spending enough time with her son? What did Moira really know about her? And how much of that was true? What if . . . ?—She had to stop herself.

Being back at work was difficult enough. She'd lost her edge, that delicious thrill that comes with finding a person or a fact or a document no one else knows about. It had disappeared completely during the last months of her pregnancy, and it had not returned. Instead, she now filled her days at work trying not to work, doing any interviews she absolutely had to do by phone instead of in person and taking as long as possible on each assignment so Michelle wouldn't hand her another. It was working. She was, she'd told the City Editor that morning, "still waiting for a couple of callbacks," one on a story about plans by the local Voice of Women for a protest against the American invasion of Iraq, the other about local medical supply stores that were inundated with people wanting to buy respirator masks to ward off a possible SARS outbreak. Michelle left her alone after that.

The truth was it was unlikely Moira would get any callbacks since she hadn't yet placed any calls to anyone. She was glad she'd switched from courts to general assignment, where it was easier to pretend you were working.

She looked at her watch. Just after eleven. Seven more hours until she could go home to Patrick. Why was the damn phone still ringing?

"*Daily Journal*, Donovan here," she said, in the clipped voice she used to use when answering the shared phone in the press room at the Law Courts.

"Moira Donovan?" A woman's voice. Tentative.

"Yes."

"The one who's covering the Howe case?"

The Howe case? She couldn't remember . . . Oh, right. "I was. But I'm not covering courts any more. I can put you through to the City Editor, if you like."

There was a silence at the end of the line, as if the person was trying to figure out what to say. "I have some information, not about the case so much as about one of the participants. Would you be interested?"

"Depends," Moira replied. She wasn't sure what it depended on. "What's the information?"

"Well, I don't want to talk about it over the telephone, but it's got to do with the judge who's hearing the case."

Justice Justice! Moira felt guilt give her stomach a sudden wrench. She'd never done a thing with that tape of the judge telling racist jokes. At the time, she'd been too tired to pursue it. Since she'd returned from maternity leave, she'd avoided even mentioning it to Morton or Michelle because she knew they'd want her to tackle the story. And Moira wasn't keen; it would take too much time to corroborate. If it was even true. Still . . .

"Are you there?" It was the woman again.

"Yes, yes, I am," Moira said. "So what is this about the Judge? Can you tell me more?"

"Just that you won't be sorry. It's big. But I need to tell you in person."

"Okay." At the very least, Moira thought, this would get her out of the office for a while, convince Michelle she was working. "So how do we do this?"

"Why don't we meet for coffee this afternoon," the woman said. "Say, around three?"

"Where?"

"There's a little diner on Gottingen Street called Calhoun's."

"I know the one."

"So three o'clock?"

"See you then." Moira hung up the phone. She wasn't sure she was ready for a real story yet.

Shondelle Adams hung up the telephone and glanced quickly up and down Barrington Street before walking away from the phone booth. She could still back out, not show up. The woman would never know. And neither would Uhuru. She glanced down at the manila envelope that contained the papers she'd photocopied last night. She hoped Uhuru wouldn't be angry with her.

The air was heavy with the fresh-smoked smell of marijuana mingled with the apartment-hallway odour of cooking food and the locker room–stale stink of piss and sweat. He would need to take his suit to the dry cleaners to get rid of the smell. As he waited in one of the jail's glassed-in lawyers' cubicles for the guards to bring his client from the cells, Uhuru Melesse tried not to think about that, or about the fact that cash was so tight he couldn't really afford to have the suit dry cleaned.

J. J.'s case had transformed Uhuru back into the man-to-be-reckoned-with he hadn't been since the best of his Ray days at Black Pride. He'd been in demand during this year's Black History Month celebrations: keynote speaker at the Black Cultural Centre's fundraiser, presenter at a Chamber of Commerce breakfast on the changing face of Halifax, moderator of a panel discussion on the role of black professionals in social change, special guest at a Black Law Students' Association reception and a Nova Scotia Multicultural Association cocktail party, even a celebrity competitor on CBC Radio's black history trivia quiz.

"'Ru man." J. J. Howe offered him a grin and an aired high-five as a guard opened the door to allow him to enter the consultation room. Uhuru wasn't the only one who'd changed. J. J. swaggered now. Since he'd been in jail, J. J. had shaved all the hair from his head and grown a full beard that seemed designed to make him look menacing. It didn't. Despite putting on fifteen pounds from the jail's starchy diet—"Freshman Fifteen," the guards jokingly called it—J. J. had only gone from emaciated to skinny. With his still-bulging eyes and goofy grin, he looked more like another J. J.—Jimmy Walker's character on the old *Good Times* TV sitcom—than a scowling Mr. T.

But there were other, more significant changes, too. The first few times Uhuru had visited him in jail, J. J. had worn the haunted, frightened look of a man who'd been thrown into a cage with hungry lions. But then one day, at least as Uhuru heard the story, J. J. had openly challenged some arbitrary dictate—Uhuru still didn't know what—from a particularly nasty guard and taken his righteous complaint all the way to the superintendent. The guard was suspended, and J. J. became a jailhouse celebrity, the man other prisoners came to with their complaints about guards, about food, about overcrowding on the bus to the courthouse. J. J. began writing letters to the editor of the *Daily Journal* detailing their complaints and calling for a public inquiry.

Uhuru did his best to dissuade him—he was afraid potential jurors might be turned off by his client's combative prose—but J. J. wasn't listening to his lawyer any more.

In the year since he'd been charged, J. J. had gone from almost reverentially addressing Uhuru as "Mr. Melesse" or even "Sir" to greeting him with a gratingly familiar, almost dismissive, "'Ru man."

Perhaps that was because Uhuru himself sometimes felt like a messenger boy. He often brought interview requests—from a researcher at *the fifth estate* interested in doing a documentary on his case, a reporter from *The Toronto Star*, a couple of local TV reporters, a student at the journalism school who was working on a school project. A literary agent had written to J. J., care of Uhuru, asking if he would be interested in participating in an autobiography project the agent would broker. "I represent a prominent author who would like to tell your story," the letter explained. "We see this as a kind of Robin-Hood-meets-Russell-Crowe-in-*The-Insider* book." The agent had already held discussions with several major publishers. "Our movie rights division is very keen on the project. At the very least, they tell me, your story has great potential as a movie of the week."

Uhuru counselled against it. "Wait until after the trial," he said, though he could tell J. J. wasn't listening. "Reporters make you say things you shouldn't."

"Who was that I saw on the news last week?" J. J. demanded accusingly. "How come you can talk and I can't?"

"That was different," Uhuru replied. But was it really? It had been a routine hearing to set a date for pretrial legal arguments. Uhuru could have begged off requests from the TV reporters. He didn't. Instead, he'd played to the cameras, done his now-standard my-client-is-not-a-criminal-but-a-man-of-principle-as-will-become-clear-in-the-fullness-of-time routine, for no good reason other than to be on television. He didn't say that to J. J., of course.

"It's my job is to represent your best interests inside the courtroom and out. My job is to know what I can say—and what I can't."

"Tell the guy from *the fifth estate* I'll talk with him," J. J. instructed. "And give me the address of that agent. I'll write him back."

Today, Uhuru carried no messages from the outside world. Instead he reached into his briefcase, pulled out a business envelope, took out a letter, unfolded it and slid it across the table. "We need you to sign this," he said. "It's to your father, asking him to meet with us. We may want to call him as a witness for our pretrial motion and we need to interview him. So far, he's refused."

J. J. looked uncomfortable. "What do we need him for?" he asked.

"He's the missing piece of the puzzle, J. J.," Uhuru replied. "We've lined up other witnesses—elders—to tell the judge what life was like in Africville before the relocation. And we've got Calvin Johnstone all set to testify about the City's refusal to deal with the compensation issue for all those years. But we need someone to show the court how the relocation affected the children. Your father is the best evidence we have. Or your mother. But no one knows where she is."

"Why does it have to be them?" J. J. wanted to know. "I mean, I was there too. I could testify—"

"I'm not going to call you as a witness."

"Why not?"

"Because that would open you up to cross-examination. We don't need them muddying the waters, focusing on *what* you did instead of *why*."

"You mean I'm not going to testify at all?" J. J. sounded offended.

"I'm not planning on it."

"But don't I have the right to testify?"

"You do, but, as your lawyer, I'd advise against it,"

"But . . . if I want to?"

"Look, J. J., why don't we see what happens?" Uhuru was trying not to get impatient with his star client. It wasn't easy. "Right now, what I need you to do is sign this letter . . ."

J. J. picked up the letter, slumping back in his seat as he read the words on the page, boredom painted on his face. He finally took the pen Uhuru proffered, signed the letter and slid the piece of paper and pen back across the table.

"Hey!" J. J. brightened suddenly. "I just remembered. I got something for you, too, 'Ru man." He reached into the breast pocket of his Corrections Services jumpsuit. "My agent says I got to get you to sign this."

Uhuru took the paper, unfolded it. It was a release form, essentially allowing the still-unnamed writer to portray Uhuru in the book in any way he saw fit and the director to do the same in any film version that might be made of "*Black Robin: The J. J. Howe Story* (working title)."

"Your agent really thinks this will happen?" Uhuru was more interested than he let on.

"He says it's a sure thing . . . long as we win the case."

"Well, let's hope on that one," Uhuru said, and meant it.

"That's why you should put me on the stand," J. J. said. "What's it going to look like for the movie if I don't testify? . . . Hey, who do you want as you?"

"What?"

"In the movie. Who do you want to play you? I'm thinking Snoop Dogg as me . . . or maybe k-os . . . that rapper from Toronto. My agent says he'd be good . . . probably even write a song they could use for the soundtrack. For you? . . . I'm thinking that guy who played Malcolm X. What's his name?"

"Denzel Washington."

"Yeah, him. He'd be great as you."

"Listen, J. J., have you had anybody go over the contract with the agent?" Uhuru asked, changing the subject slightly. "To make sure you're getting the best deal?"

"You mean like a lawyer?" Uhuru nodded. "I figure I can read as good as any lawyer. I been doing a lot of reading about the law since I been in here. I'm thinking I might go to law school after. And then they could do the sequel about that." He laughed. "Seriously, 'Ru man, don't worry. I know how to look out for myself. It'll all be okay. You'll see."

Uhuru hoped so. If someone did make a movie about the case, J. J. would probably get enough money to pay for his own defence. Uhuru didn't say that, of course. "Let me take a closer look at this," Uhuru said, tapping the release form. "I'll bring it back next time I come see you."

If Aucoin was curious, he kept it to himself. He had that blandly unrevealing face and manner Ward associated with police officers. In fact, Aucoin was an ex-cop, a private investigator who specialized in finding people who didn't want to be found. He'd come to Ward's attention a few years before as a witness for the defence in a criminal case. Ward had been impressed by both the apparent thoroughness of his investigation and the matter-of-fact way in which he presented his findings. The jury had acquitted the defendant based largely on Aucoin's testimony.

So Ward had called him last week, arranged to meet this morning. He'd decided Aucoin should come to his house rather than meeting with him at either of their offices. Others might be more curious than Aucoin about why a judge wanted to hire a private investigator.

"More coffee?" Ward asked.

"Sure. But just half a cup this time, thanks, Judge. I drink too much coffee. Bad habit."

It was not his only bad habit. Ward could smell the stink of cigarettes on his clothing. Ward tried not to breathe in as he got up and slowly made his way across the kitchen to the coffee pot. He was, all of a sudden, an old man whose walk had become a foot-dragging shuffle. How long before people at work would begin to notice? Perhaps they had already.

"So Judge, what can you tell me about this person . . ." He flipped back to the first page of his notebook. "This Rosa Johnstone? Just to get me started."

Ward waited until he'd returned to the kitchen table with Aucoin's coffee before answering. He was having trouble walking and talking at the same time now. Besides, he needed time to decide how much to tell the private detective.

"I can't tell you a whole lot, Mr. Aucoin," Ward said finally. "I can tell you she was born in Africville"—Ward tried to read the detective's face; it was as unrevealing as ever—"sometime in the mid-fifties. Her father was a minister in the church . . . No. A Deacon, that's what they called it. She grew up in Halifax, went to Queen Elizabeth High but dropped out before she graduated . . ." He paused to catch his breath, to decide what to say next. "Sometime around 1976 she left town, and that's the last I know." He stopped again, choosing which story he would tell Aucoin from the variations he'd been auditioning in his head. "I knew her when I was a kid," he began. "We grew up in the north end and our paths crossed a few times. But then I lost touch with her. Last week, I was going through some stuff in the basement, trying to clear out old junk, when I came across something of hers I thought she might like to have. So I called you."

The story was lame, but Aucoin's face remained unreadable.

"Once I find her, do you want me to make contact, let her know you're looking for her?"

"No . . . I mean, that's not necessary, Mr. Aucoin. Once I know where she is, I'd like to be the one to contact her, surprise her." She would be surprised.

"Sure, no problem," Aucoin replied. "What's the timeline on this, Judge?"

"Well, it's not urgent"—*except for the fact that I'm dying*, he thought to himself—"but it would be nice to find her and, uh, get her stuff back to her sooner rather than later."

"Sure, no problem," Aucoin said again. "I got a couple of insurance frauds on the go, but I should be able to wrap them up next week and then . . . This doesn't sound too complicated. Shouldn't take me long to find her."

"Great."

"Should I bill Justice, or is this personal?"

"Personal," Ward answered. "And please bill me at my home, if you wouldn't mind."

"No problem, Judge. And I'm guessing this is confidential?"

"Yes, confidential, absolutely."

10

1976

The question was reporterly enough: "Mr. Minister, you've been 'Mr. Minister' for two years and, I was just wondering, what has surprised you the most about your job?"

Ward eyed the young man sitting opposite him this morning. He was not so young, in fact, probably a few years older than Ward, but being a Cabinet minister had a way of making a man seem older, even to himself. The man was a Legislature reporter from the *Tribune.* He'd called Ward a few days ago to ask for this interview. "A profile. For the Saturday paper. Our readers have been hearing a lot about you—youngest Cabinet minister, rising star, the two-hundred-mile limit and all—and my editor thinks our readers would like to know more."

"Sure." *Flattery will get you everywhere. Almost.* Ward knew the reporter wasn't really doing a benign personality profile. And the reporter probably knew Ward knew. But it was part of the game. Ward was learning. The reporter was looking down at his notebook now, his pen poised above it. Ready.

"What's surprised me the most about this job?" Repeat the question, make it seem as if that's what you've been pondering. "Well, Patrick . . ." Ward had learned to call reporters, even the older ones, by their first names. It seemed friendly enough, but it also established the power relationship; the reporters called him Mr. Minister or Mr. Justice. "I guess the thing that surprises me most about this job is that I have it." He smiled his best self-deprecating smile.

There were so many things Ward could tell him . . . that he couldn't. He could dazzle the reporter with details about the perks of office. Ward, for example, had "borrowed" ten thousand dollars from the Winners' Fund for the down payment on the Atlantic Street house, and then another fifteen thousand to renovate the kitchen. The mortgage had been arranged by Junior Eisner through a company he owned. "Prime minus prime," he'd said and winked. Zero percent interest! "And if you need to skip a payment, let me know. It can be arranged."

One of the other things that surprised Ward was just how many people wanted to help you out when you were a Cabinet minister. There was the Halifax real estate developer who needed Cabinet approval to buy a large block of government-owned land just outside the city to turn into a housing development. He took Ward out to dinner one night and, at the end, slipped him an envelope "for your re-election campaign." It contained ten fresh, crisp one-thousand-dollar bills. Ward was surprised at just how many campaign contributions came in the form of untraceable, unaccountable cash. It was almost as if the donor might be suggesting the recipient keep a little for himself. Ward, in fact, did just that, but never more than 10 percent. That seemed a reasonable amount for his troubles. And his needs.

Ah, yes, his needs. How could he tell Patrick about Rosa?

"You want to know about surprise? Well, let me tell you just how surprised I was when I fell in love with a black woman."

"How interesting, Mr. Minister. I'm sure my readers would like to know all about that. How did you two lovebirds meet?"

"Well, you see, I was cruising Gottingen Street one night and I picked up this hooker, and I didn't know she was black, and she fucked me and I fell in love with her."

"How romantic, Mr. Minister. And then what happened?"

Then? How could he put this? He'd become obsessed. Two nights after that first night, he'd been driving home to his wife and family and his life when he felt this magnetic pull on his heart, and his groin, tugging the car's steering wheel back to the stroll. He drove around the block three times, staring at the women in their short skirts and skimpy tops, watching them wave, listening to their come-ons. None was Rosa. Finally, he'd pulled up beside a young woman in hot pants who seemed slightly less pushy than the others. He rolled down his window, waited for her to approach.

". . . can I do you for tonight, mister?" she said. She was chewing gum.

"Nothing," Ward said. "Uh, I'm just looking for somebody, girl named Rosa, she works up here sometimes."

She leaned in through the window. He saw her reach into the top of her low-cut top, fish something out of her bra. It flashed. It was a badge. "Mr. Minister," she was whispering urgently now, "Tanya Smits. Vice. You just walked into the middle of a sting operation. So I suggest you get the hell out of here right now. This is no place for you." She slipped the badge back into her bra, stepped back and shouted at him, "You fuckin' perv! I don't do that shit for nobody so get the fuck out of here."

Ward didn't wait to roll up the passenger window, just gunned it down the street. After that, he didn't stop to ask questions. But he did continue to drive past the stroll several times a night every night, looking but not finding her. Finally he branched out, tried the two other downtown areas where prostitutes hung out, the one outside the lieutenant-governor's mansion on Barrington Street and the other in the park across from the Nova Scotian, the big railway hotel down near the docks, which is where he finally saw her. She was getting into someone else's car as he drove by. They drove away. He didn't follow, just drove around for fifteen long minutes until the car finally returned and she got out, waved, smiled at the person inside. Ward was jealous.

Standing under the streetlight, she looked so beautiful—more beautiful than any of the others—he was afraid someone else might try to pick her up, so he drove up beside her immediately. She recognized his car.

"Well, look who it isn't!" she said, opening the door, squatting down to see inside. Her smile said she was pleased to see him. "What can I do for you tonight?"

"Talk. Just talk." He hadn't planned that. "I'd just like to talk to you, that's all. I'll pay you. For your time, I mean. Don't worry about the money."

"I'm not worried," she said, slipping easily into the passenger seat.

He had paid her for the "full deal," and then offered her more at the end when she joked that she'd never had a trick who'd lasted as long as their conversation. She'd put the extra money back into his palm, closed her hand on his. "That's okay," she said. "It was nice. Maybe I should pay you."

Later, when he tried to remember what they'd talked about, he couldn't. Only that it had been good, wonderful, better than fucking. That night had been the beginning. Within a few months, he'd convinced her to give up prostitution. She was only doing it, she said, to support her son.

"I can support him. You too."

He wanted to set her up in an apartment downtown, but she said no. "No fancy apartment's going to rent to me. A black woman's bad enough, but me with a kid and no father . . . I'd rather stay where I'm comfortable. Besides, one of those apartments downtown would cost way too much and I'm taking enough of your money now."

Ward wanted to tell her the money didn't matter, that there was more where that came from. But he didn't. He also wanted to tell her how dangerous it was for him to visit her in the abandoned warehouse near the waterfront where she and little Larry lived. What if someone saw his car? What if the police decided to chase the squatters and he happened to be on the mattress on the floor in her place, making love to her when they came busting through the door? He didn't say that. He just wanted to be with her, and that was worth any risk.

He didn't think anyone knew. Except maybe Jack. Jack knew everything. One night at Monique's, Jack and Whitey and a few of the boys were sitting around the kitchen table playing cards when Jack asked, "Okay boys, a contest. What's the worst career move a politician can make?" Ward wasn't playing, just watching, and listening.

"That's easy," Whitey answered. "Calling a press conference and announcing you're a fucking homo. Bang. That's it. No more fucking career." Laughter, murmurs of agreement.

There were other suggestions too: having sex with animals or little girls, but not a word about the usual political scandals over money.

"What about getting caught in my house?" Monique asked.

"Nah," Whitey answered. "That'd probably get a man fucking votes. At least it fucking well would with men." He looked at Jack. "What about you, Jack? You asked the question. What's the worst fucking career move?"

"In Nova Scotia?" Jack glanced at Ward, back at Whitey, didn't look at Ward. "I'd say the worst thing a politician could do in this province is to shack up with a coloured girl. Voters will forgive a man a lot, but not that." More murmurs of assent. Ward said nothing. And Jack said nothing more.

Was that why Ward had told those stupid jokes at that dinner last month? Because he knew Jack was right? So he'd . . . he'd what? Played to the crowds? Tried to shock them out of their bigotry? Or maybe throw them off the scent?

He hadn't planned it. It had just been a bad day. Every day was bad, and getting worse. Junior and Jack were squeezing him. For a change, Ward was squeezing back. They didn't like that. And Victoria was complaining that he wasn't spending enough time with the girls. Not with her. Just with the girls. "Maybe you should start spending more time at home with your daughters instead of . . . doing whatever you do," she'd said. So she did know. Or at least she suspected.

And she was right. He did prefer the company of Rosa and her son to his own wife and daughters. His own daughters! Why? He wasn't sure. Was it because Meghan and Sarah seemed more like extensions of Victoria than his own flesh and blood? Was that because Victoria was always with them and he was never home? He loved his daughters, but he liked being with little Larry more. Perhaps because Larry was a boy, or because he needed him in ways his daughters did not. There were no kids his own age in the warehouse. And his mother had no other friends who'd visit, certainly none with children. No wonder Larry's eyes would light up whenever Ward would come over. Ward would sometimes bring presents—toy cars, plastic soldiers, a kid's bat and ball—and play with him on the floor. Those were the best moments. But they didn't last. He would look up from their game and see Rosa sitting on the sofa. Guilt. He'd go home to his wife and daughters. Guilt.

Was that why he'd slipped away to the Victory Lounge that day after work, before the dinner? He couldn't remember how many double Scotches he'd had. Five? Six? By the time he got to the press gallery dinner, he was hammered, and beyond knowing enough to know he'd had more than enough. By the time he stood up to speak, he was piss-eyed with alcohol. But he knew exactly what to say. He'd been planning it since his first drink at the Victory nearly four hours before.

At the podium, he took out the bland speech with its lame jokes that Norah Radcliffe, the Premier's speech writer, had prepared. "Save you the trouble," O'Sullivan had explained when he'd handed it to Ward the morning of the dinner. Ward had noted that the speech included a few pledges of loyalty to the Premier—Seamus O'Sullivan had heard the rumours, too. He smoothed out the folded pages on the podium, reached into his breast pocket, removed the Victory napkin with the notes he'd scrawled on it and placed the napkin beside the official text of the speech. It was amazing the number of nigger jokes bartenders knew. He'd intended to segue into the jokes earlier but put it off when he noticed there were black servers clearing the plates. He followed the prepared text while he waited for them to leave. Which meant he'd officially declared his loyalty to "my Premier and the man to lead Nova Scotia into the future" twice before he looked around the room and gave himself the all-clear.

By the time he'd dropped his second one-liner, they were throwing buns at him. He pressed on. What was he trying to prove? That he could be as racist as the next guy? Finally, Whitey tackled him, pushed him away from the mic and through the door to the kitchen. Over his shoulder, he could hear Jack doing his best to smooth things over, to pretend that what had happened hadn't.

A cone of silence quickly dropped over the whole affair. No one reported a word; it was, after all, off the record.

What about this guy he was talking to now? Was this reporter there? Probably . . . Oh, yes, Patrick. Here. Now. What was he on about? Surprised? Yes, surprised. Ward felt outside himself, looking down on another Ward Justice explaining to this reporter how surprised he'd been by the many complexities of the fishing industry, the starkly different views of the offshore and the inshore industry, the various bizarre jurisdictional tug-of-war battles.

"Even though I grew up in this industry," the other Ward was saying, echoing the line Jack had encouraged him to emphasize, "I have to admit I'm surprised at just how complex it is." He paused. How much longer before the reporter moved on to the question he really wanted answered?

"The good news, of course, is that Ottawa has finally agreed to declare the two-hundred-mile limit. On January first, we'll finally have control over our own fishing zones. We'll be able to manage the resource in the interests of our fishermen and the future of the stocks." Which was something else he couldn't talk to this journalist about.

"If we could move away from Fisheries for just a moment, Mr. Minister, to provincial politics." The segue had begun. "As you know, the government seems to be in political trouble right now. Power rates going through the roof. Offshore oil and gas exploration wells coming up dry. The cruise ship scandal. According to what I hear, internal polls are already saying this government can't win the next election . . . at least not under Premier O'Sullivan. But my sources say the party has done some secret polling to see how it would do under different leaders, and that those polls show that you're the only one who could beat the Tories. What's your comment on that?"

"Well . . ." Ward paused, as if to gather the thoughts for the lines he'd rehearsed in his head. "Well, Patrick, I'm not sure I have any comment on that. You have an awful lot of hypotheticals in your question and I don't think it's wise for a politician to speculate about things that haven't happened."

"But would you be *interested* in the job?" Patrick persisted.

Ward smiled. This was all going just as Jack had predicted. "I *have* a job, Patrick, and I'm very happy serving the people of Nova Scotia as their Minister of Fisheries in the government of Seamus O'Sullivan. I'm happy to do that as long as Premier O'Sullivan wants me to."

"So you're saying there's no truth to the rumour that you've set up a secret campaign team and are raising money to challenge the Premier at the next annual meeting?"

Ward knew how not to answer questions he didn't want to answer. "Patrick, Patrick," he tsk-tsked, smiling. "Where *do* you come up with this wild speculation? All I can tell you is Seamus O'Sullivan is my leader and I'm loyal to my leader."

"So is that a yes or a no to my question?"

"That's a definite no to responding to outlandish speculation." Ward smiled again, to make it clear this was part of the game, too. But also that the game was over. He looked at his watch. "I don't mean to cut this off, Patrick, but I'm running late already this morning and I have another appointment waiting."

"Can I call you? In case I have any other questions."

"Certainly, Patrick." He paused, then added quietly, "You might want to hold off on running this story for a few weeks. By then, I might have something more to say about this. And I'd be happy to talk to you first."

Jack would have been proud.

The officious little man in the blue blazer behind the reception desk was on his feet before Ray could manoeuvre the battered pine table through the entranceway and into the lobby. "Deliveries to the Hollis

Street entrance," the man declared, blocking Ray's path to the elevator. "Can't you read?"

Ray had been tired and sweating, now he was angry. He'd rescued this table from the trash outside a South Street house early this morning and dragged/carried it six long blocks through morning rush hour to his new office in the Bell Building on Barrington. And now this pompous prick was telling him to use the service entrance? Would he have done that if Ray had been white?

"I'm a tenant here," Ray told him, a little too fiercely. He took a breath. "New. Today. Just moving in. Suite 401. Raymond Carter and Associates." He reached into his pocket for one of his freshly printed business cards.

"Oh right, sorry about that, sir," the man replied without waiting for Ray to prove he was who he claimed to be. "I heard someone had taken that third-floor suite. Welcome to the Bell Building, Mr. . . . Carter?" Ray nodded. "Can I help you up with that table?"

"Uh, no, but, uh, thanks." Was the man sincere, or overcompensating, or even condescending? White people, Ray thought. He'd never figure them out.

"Well, you need anything, you just ask," the man said, pressing the elevator button for Ray. He seemed genuine.

"Right, thanks very much."

Upstairs, Ray stood outside the heavy wooden door with the frosted-glass window and admired. "SUITE 401" was stencilled in black block letters in the bottom right-hand corner of the glass panel. Above it, "R. Carter & Assoc." just as the landlord had promised.

In truth, there were no associates. Not yet anyway. And, except for his new-to-him used table, there was no office furniture either. He hadn't realized how expensive it would be to set up his own office. By the time he'd paid the first month's rent and the damage deposit and the deposit for the telephone, he'd used up his meagre savings from articling.

He'd made a mistake, he realized now, showing up in person to order his telephone. The woman at the counter had bustled off to talk to her supervisor, who took a long look at Ray and then went off to consult with his supervisor. Eventually the woman returned. "I'm afraid we'll require a deposit of two hundred dollars," she said. "If, after six months, there have been no problems with the account, we'll return it." She paused. "It's standard procedure for first-time business accounts."

"Is that why you had to talk to your supervisor and he had to talk with somebody else?" Ray asked.

She blushed. "I don't make the rules, sir. And those are the rules."

Ray considered asking to speak with her supervisor, but gave up. It probably was written in some rule book somewhere that new clients had to pay a deposit. But, as he'd discovered during his time at Black Pride, those kinds of rules generally applied only to blacks. If he'd been white, the deposit would have been waived.

The woman had told him his phone line would be installed sometime today. So for now he was stuck waiting for the installer in this echoing, empty space with his one table and no chair. Ray had originally planned to make the suite's inner room his private office. But that would have to wait until he found more furniture. He put the table in the middle of the room. Sat on it.

This wasn't the way he'd planned to begin his law career. And it wasn't his only choice. Ezekiel Abernathy had offered to take him on as an associate, but Ray had turned him down. Ray had articled with Abernathy, a black Barbadian who'd graduated from Dalhousie Law School in the late fifties, married a local girl from across the harbour in Preston and then set up private practice out of the basement of his house in the north end of Halifax. As one of the few black lawyers in the city, Abernathy handled the civil legal work for most of the city's black community. But few could afford his fees, so his was a hand-to-mouth existence at best, and it only got worse after Abernathy took Ray on as an article clerk after he graduated. Ray should have been grateful when Abernathy offered to make him an associate. But he wasn't. It wasn't fair, he knew, but Ray had developed a prejudice of his own—against black immigrants who came to Nova Scotia and thought they were smarter, better than the locals. Abernathy had never said anything derogatory about any of his local black clients, but Ray sensed that Abernathy looked down on them. And on him.

Ray didn't need that. And he didn't go to law school to spend the rest of his life a poor man. So, after he turned down Abernathy as politely as he could, Ray made an appointment to see Jack Eagleson. He asked Eagleson for a job.

Eagleson laughed. "You're not serious, are you?"

Ray was stunned, then indignant. "Yes, I'm serious. Of course I'm serious. Weren't you the one who said the legal profession needed more people like me?"

"I was. And it does. But it's not that simple, Ray," Eagleson said. "You have to understand, I have to think of my partners, our practice. I don't want you to think I'm prejudiced. I'm not. But I have clients who are . . . well, not so enlightened. They wouldn't like it if we had a black man working for the firm. They might decide to take their business elsewhere. And then my partners would be upset with me. And you couldn't blame them for that." He paused, waited for Ray to acknowledge the wisdom of his words. Ray didn't. "Listen, Ray, there are lots better ways to be a lawyer than being stuck in some big stuffy law firm like ours. Did you ever thinking of going out on your own, hanging out a shingle? You're smart. You'd do well."

Ray had been too angry to reply. But he'd taken Eagleson's advice. Perhaps because there seemed little choice. And now here he was sitting alone in his empty new office with no furniture and no clients.

Perhaps, after the installer finished hooking up his phone, Ray would call Rosa. All through law school, he'd imagined this day, the day he'd start his new career, the day he'd go back and make things right with Rosa and the son he'd become more and more convinced was really his. But now there was no going back. After little Larry was born, Ray had sent Rosa a cheque for one hundred dollars and a note promising to help out as much as he could. She'd sent the cheques and the note back with no other reply. He'd got the message. Still, he'd harboured the fantasy that, once he became a practising lawyer, she'd agree to start over. But that was before . . .

He'd heard about Rosa and Ward. Aunt Annie again. "She's taken up with that friend of yours," she said, "that white boy used to visit out home. Nice young man. Done all right for himself, too. But he's married. And not to Rosa. It's all supposed to be very hush-hush, but nothin's ever that quiet round here, you know what I'm sayin'. But I'll say one thing for him. He got Rosa to quit all that bad stuff she was doin'. And he's doin' right by little Larry, too. So he can't be all bad." Aunt Annie paused, looked Ray in the eye. "I just wish she'd taken up with one of her own kind. Someone like you."

There was a knock at his office door. The door opened slightly and a man leaned his head into the room. "Mr. Carter?"

"Yes." He was a young, Oriental-looking man. Ray looked at his watch. It was just after eleven in the morning. Maybe he'd have time to scrounge up a chair this afternoon. "Great," he said to the man. "The phone goes over here."

"Phone?" The man looked puzzled.

"You're not from the phone company?" Ray said.

"Phone company?"

Oh shit. "Look, I'm sorry," Ray said quickly. "My mistake. I just thought you were here to install the new phone . . . uh, what can I do for you?"

"I was looking for a lawyer." The man looked around the empty room. "Are you taking clients?"

Ray jumped down from the table, extended his hand to the man. "Absolutely," he said. "What would you like?"

It turned out his name was Lee and he had bought some land in Fairview where he wanted to build a small apartment building. He needed someone to handle the legal work. "I spoke to Mr. Eagleson and he suggested you. He recommended you very highly."

Eagleson? Recommended? Very highly? Fuck, Ray would never understand white men. "Well why don't you come in and we can talk . . ." There was no furniture. "Second thought, why don't we go get a coffee and you can tell me the details?"

Ray only hoped that Mr. Lee would spring for the coffee.

Ward knew it had to be serious when Junior called with instructions to meet for dinner that night at Claudie's. Usually Jack, Junior and Ward got together at the Halifax Club, or the Royal Nova Scotia Yacht Squadron, or the Chester Golf Club, places they would be sure to be seen. Claudie's was a fish-and-chips joint in the north end of the city, a place where they were unlikely to be seen by anyone who mattered. Which seemed to be the point.

Last month, Jack had chosen Claudie's when he wanted a quiet place to lay out the scenario he had concocted for Ward to replace Seamus O'Sullivan as party leader. Dan White, one of Jack's most trusted allies, had been primed to serve as Ward's stalking horse. Late in the summer, Jack had explained, Whitey would make a speech questioning whether O'Sullivan could lead the Liberals to electoral victory, and threaten to raise the issue during the party's annual meeting in October. As a result, Whitey—and not Ward—would become the lightning rod for angry O'Sullivan loyalists. But Whitey's speech would also pop the cork off what Jack was certain was the bottled-up discontent of many among the party's rank and file. Jack would then stir in a few well-timed leaks of secret poll results showing Ward—but not O'Sullivan—defeating the Tories. This would be followed by statements from members of the provincial executive loyal to Jack urging O'Sullivan to step down for the good of the party. And then by the establishment of a Draft Justice movement launched by another Jack surrogate. Junior, Jack said, was quietly raising money for Ward's war chest.

Although Whitey wasn't due to give his speech for another four months, Jack had begun to tantalize favoured reporters with rumours of internal discontent with O'Sullivan and growing support for Ward as his replacement.

"By October," he'd added, with one of his booming laughs, "Seamus will see the writing on the wall and be pleased as punch to answer a 'call' to the Senate. By the end of the year, you'll be Mr. Premier. At twenty-seven! Youngest ever! How's that sound?"

"Great." Ward's "great" had been more unenthusiastic than he'd intended. For his part, Jack had hardly seemed to notice Ward's discomfort.

Tonight's gathering at Claudie's seemed to be Junior's meeting. Somehow, Ward didn't find that comforting.

"So, gentlemen, what'll it be?" Shirley had been a waitress at Claudie's since Ward was a teenager picking up takeout orders of fish and chips for Friday night family suppers. Shirley hadn't been paying attention as she approached their booth, but now she recognized him, grinned a greeting. "Ward! How wonderful to see you!" Shirley was somehow related to the shop's owners, who originally came from Eisners Head and knew Ward's parents, so she considered him part of her extended family.

But her smile disappeared when she saw Junior. "Mr. Eisner," she acknowledged curtly. The mere sight of Junior brought back bitter memories for many fishing families from Cabot County, especially those who, like Shirley's relatives and Ward's parents, blamed Junior for forcing them to leave their hometowns forever.

Junior opted not to acknowledge Shirley's disdain. "Well, darlin'," he said, "what's fresh?" Claudie's had no printed menu, just a chalkboard on the wall where the day's catch was pencilled in, then erased as supplies were depleted.

"Everything," Shirley answered icily, gesturing over her shoulder. "It's on the wall. Like always."

"It is that," Junior said with a chuckle, as though Shirley had just been kidding. "So let's see what looks good." He eyed the list. "How about some of your best clams and chips, darlin', and don't spare the grease." Junior laughed. Shirley didn't. Ward, trying to please them both, offered a fleeting smile and silence. "Oh, yeah, and gimme a Keith's too, will ya, darlin'? A quart."

Shirley looked at Ward. Was it a look of anger or pity? Ward couldn't tell. "I'll have the same," he said quietly.

"Me too," added Jack. He also seemed more subdued than usual.

Shirley wrote it down, turned on her heel and left. "She's a cold old fish, that one," Junior said before Shirley was out of earshot. "Don't think she likes me."

Ward didn't say anything. He hoped Shirley would bring the beer soon.

"So, how was Florida?"

Ward had expected as much. Junior was predictable, always finding less than subtle ways to remind Ward of the favours he'd done for him. Usually these reminders were an appetizer to Junior's main course: a demand for yet another favour. Paving contracts for Junior's construction firm. An appointment to the Fisheries Loan Board for a friend. Ward knew what tonight's demand would be.

"Great," Ward answered. Ward, Victoria and the kids had spent the last week at Junior's condo outside Clearwater.

"Weather good?"

"Great."

"Only problem is you have to come back, eh?" Junior said with a laugh. "That's what I always find. Halifax gets the worst fucking springs . . . Makes you want to slit your throat."

"Yeah." Ward glanced out the window. It was snowing lightly. It was April.

"How's the wife? She like it down there?"

Junior rarely ever asked about Victoria. Was this a message that he knew about Ward and Rosa? Did he? Ward wouldn't be surprised. Jack might have told him. "Victoria loved it," Ward answered. "We all did. Thanks again."

"Yeah, well, you know, Florida's a great place for rejuvenating the old sex life. A little fun, a little sun, a couple of them fruity rum drinks and suddenly it's time for a little 'chitty chitty bang bang.'"

Ward didn't respond. There'd been no chitty chitty, and certainly no bang bang. One night, after Victoria and the kids were asleep,

Ward had slipped out of the condo and gone to a pay phone to call Rosa. But he hadn't brought enough change and they were cut off after only a few minutes.

"So," Junior said suddenly. "You get a chance to think about that thing we talked about?" Ward knew Junior had been circling the airport of what was on his mind. Now he was landing the plane.

"Yes, I did."

"So?"

"I don't think so," Ward said.

Ward had reached his decision a week ago, right here in Claudie's, his father sitting where Junior was sitting now.

Desmond Justice had been more than surprised when Ward called to invite him for supper at Claudie's; he'd been suspicious. Ward couldn't blame him. He never invited his father anywhere. The only times he saw his father these days were when he and Victoria and the kids stopped by for one of their occasional, perfunctory Saturday afternoon visits. While Victoria and his mother retired to the kitchen for tea—his mother fussing over her granddaughters while Victoria reported on their latest accomplishments—Ward and his father would sit silently in the living room, his father's attention riveted to whatever was on ABC-TV's *Wide World of Sports* that afternoon. Sometimes it was tolerable. A few months ago, they'd watched George Foreman stop some ex-con named Ron Lyle in the fourth, punch-filled round of what the announcer, Howard Cosell, called "one of the most exciting and titanic struggles in the entire history of boxing." The closest they came to a conversation that day was when his father asked Ward if he thought Cosell was wearing a wig. "It doesn't look real to me," he said, and Ward hadn't disagreed. They'd watched the rest of the show in silence.

So why had he called his father out of the blue last week and asked him to meet him that night at Claudie's?

Junior. Junior Eisner, and guilt. For more than a decade—almost, in fact, from the moment they'd moved to Halifax—Ward had managed to bury, and then throw dirt on, the memory of the man his father had once been. It wasn't entirely Ward's fault, of course. His father had chosen to inter those parts of his history, too, not to forget erecting a wall of disappointment between himself and his son's accomplishments. Nothing Ward did seemed to please his father.

It wasn't until after he'd become Fisheries minister that Ward finally began to put his father's life back into some perspective. It had begun with his first briefing as minister; Ward's deputy came to that meeting with stacks of reports and studies, even a few doctoral theses on current issues facing the province's fishery. There was also a thin paperback, which his deputy seemed almost embarrassed to give him.

"I'm sure you've already got your own copy of this," he said as he handed it over. "But Bernadette—she's the Department's librarian, you met her this morning—she said we should include it anyway. I think she just wanted to make sure you knew we had a copy."

Ward had never seen it before. The book was called *Troubled Waters: Nova Scotia Fishermen Fight For Their Union And Their Future, 1964*. The grainy cover photo, obviously photocopied from a newspaper page and blown up, showed his father standing in front of the *Sara Eisner*, his arms crossed over his chest, managing to look both defiant and awkward at the same time, as if he'd only reluctantly agreed to pose for the photo. That much was almost certainly true. His father hated to have his picture taken.

The book's author was one of the college professors from Halifax who'd supported the fishermen during the strike. Ward tried to place him from the author photo on the back cover, but couldn't. All the college professors—unnaturally thin with scruffy, wispy beards, dressed in almost identical corduroy sports jackets with thin, loosely knotted ties—looked the same to him. Although the professor's "first-hand account of this classic class struggle between oppressed workers and their capitalist oppressors" was as much about the professor's minuscule part in the strike—he was on the organizing committee for one of the Halifax protest marches—as it was about the strike itself, it was clear he regarded Ward's father as the hero of the piece. "Desmond Justice, a self-effacing, salt-of-the-earth worker whose rough, calloused hands belie his innate understanding of the Marxian dialectic for which Cod Capitalism is the thesis and Unionism and Revolution the antithesis, single-handedly united his fellow trawlermen in class struggle with their capitalist oppressors."

For all its Marxist bullshit rhetoric, reading/devouring the book that night had brought Ward's long-lost memories of protest and picket lines, his feelings of pride and paternal love, flooding back into his brain. And with them, a tidal wave of guilt. Guilt for everything, but especially for that lunch at the Halifax Club when Ward had allowed Junior, a capitalist oppressor if ever there was one, to transform the crushing of the fishermen and the permanent blackballing of his own father into "some problems" best filed and forgotten now. *Have another drink?* Ward had gone along. Why? Because going along meant Junior would underwrite his election campaign. So Ward could become the politician Jack wanted him to be. And Junior needed him to be.

Ward had become that politician, *their* politician. Occasionally, he would step outside himself for an instant and catch a sudden, sidelong glimpse of his new life, and realize it wasn't his. He wondered how his life might have turned out had he chosen it for himself. But he hadn't. As always, there was a price.

He was only surprised he hadn't seen it coming. Had this been their plan from the beginning? Find someone weak and malleable, buy him an election, connive to make him minister of the right department, flatter him, sweeten the pot with interest-free mortgages and forgivable loans, months in the country, weeks in the sunny south, and then, after he has well and truly taken the bait, jerk the hook in deep and haul him aboard. Ward couldn't be sure if it had been that Machiavellian or if there'd simply been a fortuitous collision of time and circumstance, but he did know he had been deeply hooked.

Now, Junior wanted payback—Ward's support for him to buy a fleet of factory freezer trawlers from Poland. Instead of allowing foreign-owned fleets to wipe out the fish stocks with their trawls and floating fish processing factories, Junior wanted Ward to help Eisner International do the dirty deed itself.

And do it with taxpayers' dollars. Junior wanted Ward to make the provincial Fisheries Loan Board lend Eisner 100 percent of the cost of buying the vessels, interest free. "I want the same deal I gave you, you know, prime minus prime," Junior told Ward, which also happened to be a convenient way of reminding him who held the mortgage on his house.

But there was more, and worse.

Junior wanted Ward to lobby the federal government to exempt Eisner International from the rule that Canadian fishing vessels must be Canadian registered and crewed. Junior planned to hire Thai workers to run the vessels and do all the fishing and processing, which would slash the company's operating expenses to about a quarter of the cost of a Canadian crew. And put Canadian fishermen and plant workers out of jobs.

"It's the only way we can compete with the big bastards," Junior had insisted when he'd outlined his plan to Ward last month. "Fishing's global now and we're playing with the big boys, so we have to find every advantage we can."

"I understand what you're saying," Ward replied, sounding far more understanding than he felt. "But you also have to understand that it will be difficult for us to show the benefits of all those interest-free loans and exemptions if there's no employment for our fishermen, our fish processors."

"There'd be taxes," Junior said helpfully. "We pay taxes."

"You haven't for the last five years," Ward pointed out. He'd checked.

"That's because we haven't been profitable." Junior looked miffed. "This will make us profitable and, when we're profitable, we'll pay taxes."

Ward knew better than to believe that. His department's officials were convinced Eisner International was already making money and using dodgy accounting tricks to obscure the fact.

Ward wondered what the fishermen of Eisners Head, the people who elected him, would have to say if they knew he was even considering such a proposal? What would his father think?

Ward knew exactly what his father would think, of course. Which was why he'd invited him to meet him at Claudie's last week. So that he could tell his father what Junior had in mind. And hear his father's response. His father had not let him down.

"Bastard!" Desmond Justice said through clenched teeth. "He's worse than his old man, that one." He looked at his son accusingly. "And you? You gonna let him get away with this?"

"No." Ward had not been sure precisely how he would answer that question until he spoke the word out loud to his father. "No," he said again, more strongly this time, "I'm not going to let him get away with it." The words felt good on his tongue. Saying them to his father felt even better.

But speaking them had served another, more important purpose; he knew he had to follow through this time. He couldn't disappoint his father. Not again.

Now Ward speared a breaded clam with his fork and looked directly into Junior's face. He could see his "I don't think so" had not been strong enough.

"No," he said. And then, again, "No, I won't support you."

Junior was incredulous. "What do you mean, no?" His voice was becoming louder again.

"Just what I said," Ward replied, his voice as cold and even as his thinking. "I'm not going to support your proposal for a factory freezer trawler fleet. So there'll be no need for an interest-free loan or crew exemptions or anything else. I said no and I mean no."

Junior's eyes hardened then. "That's not what I wanted to hear from you."

"I'm sorry," Ward said. He wasn't.

"Sorry? Sorry! You'll be more than fucking sorry!" Junior was shouting. Some of Claudie's other patrons looked over at them. Jack, who hadn't said anything to this point, put his hand on Junior's forearm as if to calm him. Junior lowered his voice then, but there was still an urgency to it. "Look, we have way too much tied up in this for you to fuck it up. We need you to eat shit and say it tastes like ice cream if that's what it takes to get this deal done. We need you to push this in Ottawa, and we need that loan. Do you understand me?"

Junior looked like he was about to reach across the table and throttle Ward. Ward was eerily calm.

Finally, Jack intervened. "Let's not be hasty," he said. "Why don't we just step back for a second before we talk ourselves into a corner we can't get out of, or do something we might regret?"

Ward had just walked out of the corner. He had no regrets. "Sure," he said. "Why don't we do that?"

11

Winter 2003

"So . . ." Aucoin flapped. The private detective's unflappable demeanour had become frightened, flitting, almost bird-like. Ward could sense his discomfort in every twitch. And his once inscrutable face had become, to Ward, suddenly very *scrutable.* Aucoin was nervous. He'd never had a judge for a client, and he didn't know what this judge knew, or wanted him to know, or—most important—wanted him to say. Gerald Aucoin knew only that he'd discovered far more than he should have.

"Wasn't that complicated, Your Honour. Routine, really." He was staring at the floor in Ward Justice's kitchen, not making eye contact. He coughed nervously. "I got lots of stuff in my notebook, but maybe you should tell me what you're looking for. Do you want me to go back to the beginning"—here he did finally look at Ward, then quickly resumed his examination of the grain in the hardwood floor—"or, you know, from when she left Halifax?"

"From when she left Halifax," Ward replied.

"Okay. Well. Let me see then." Aucoin seemed relieved. Ward knew he knew. Ward didn't care any more; he just wanted the information.

Aucoin consulted his notebook, more for show than to discover what he'd written. "Seems Miss Johnstone left Halifax in August 1976. She showed up almost immediately in Boston, where she found employment as a maid for the family of Charles O'Sullivan, a Boston lawyer and investor who is related to Seamus O'Sullivan." Aucoin glanced furtively at Ward as if seeking a sign, found none. "Became an American citizen September 1986. Never married. One child, out of wedlock, while still resident in Halifax. Father, according to the birth certificate . . ." The pause was profound. At least it felt that way to Ward. Aucoin kept his eyes fixed on the notebook, riffling through its pages without reading anything. The pause ended. ". . . Raymond Carter, a law student. He and Miss Johnstone never married. The boy—named Lawrence George, apparently after the paternal and maternal grandparents—died two years later . . . the result of an automobile . . . accident in 1976. Hit and run. Still unsolved. My sources at the police force say—"

"Where is she now?" Ward cut him off. Aucoin had told him something he'd only previously suspected, perhaps assumed, but certainly didn't want to know. He'd never asked Rosa about Larry's father, and she'd never volunteered. So Ward had, in fact . . . Don't go there. Not yet. Find Rosa first.

"That one's easy enough, Judge, though it may not be the answer you were hoping for," Aucoin replied, as relieved as the Judge to have been derailed from the issue of the police investigation. "Miss Johnstone is in Our Lady of Sorrows Cemetery in Cambridge, Massachusetts, in the O'Sullivan family section, the first non-O'Sullivan to be buried there, according to the obituary in the Boston *Globe.* She died of heart failure, September 19, 2002. Obituary's sort of interesting. Lots of stuff about her role as a nanny and maid, and her 'lifelong' love of the Red Sox, but it doesn't list a single surviving relative, even though I know for a fact some of her brothers and sisters still live here. And no mention of a son. Seems like she wanted to bury her past pretty deep . . ."

Rosa dead? Ward had not considered that. He had no Plan B.

"Christ, it's cold," she said. Because it was, and because there was nothing else she could think of to say. She stomped her feet on the sidewalk to try to shake off the damp November chill. "Bastards could at least let us wait inside."

"Now don't let the Father be hearing you talking that way, Moira, my dear," Mac upbraided her gently. "Or you'll find it'll be warmer than you want when you're in the eternal damnation of hell."

No wonder she had nothing to say. Mac was a moron. And not a very good photographer. How had she lucked into him for this assignment?

Michelle had called her that morning to tell her she didn't have to come into the office. She could just meet Mac at the Basilica at nine-thirty. Of course, Michelle hadn't told her the funeral didn't begin until ten-thirty, or that the family had requested no press inside the church. Michelle didn't even have the correct name of the deceased.

"He was big in politics in the sixties," Michelle had explained by way of background briefing. "Morton knew him. Anyway, he says it should be a big send-off. Lots of old pols and such. He wants a name-dropper for page three."

Lovely, Moira thought. Except she didn't know the names of any sixties politicians and wouldn't recognize their faces if she did.

"Let me see," Michelle had offered when Moira asked for details, "his name is, where's that note . . . Jeffrey Joseph Eagleson . . . Hmmm . . . Yes. And that's about all I have right now. You should be able to find something on the Net."

Thanks. Moira skipped breakfast and didn't even feed Patrick—"Why don't you watch *Sesame Street* until May gets here, honey? I'm sure May will make you something delicious for breakfast"—in a fruitless effort to find information about the late, and seemingly elusive, Jeffrey Joseph Eagleson. The closest she came was a reference to a legendary secretary-treasurer of the Nova Scotia Liberal Party in the forties. But he'd died in 1964. She'd only finally found the person she was looking for by accident.

She'd come across a listing for an Eagleson Charitable Trust, which turned out to be irrelevant—it was based in Savannah, Georgia, and gave money to "worthy Christian causes"—but its executive director's name was "Jeffrey Joseph Eagleson, 'Jack' to his many friends."

On a whim, Moira typed in "Jack Eagleson," *et voilà*, two web pages popped up that mentioned the Nova Scotia Liberal Party's chief strategist of the sixties and seventies. There were no useful details in either story, but at least she now knew the name he was known by, which might save her embarrassment when she began asking the mourners to talk about the late Mr. Eagleson.

As soon as May arrived, Moira grabbed a cab to St. Mary's Basilica, only to discover she was an hour early and consigned to watching from the sidewalk for people whose faces older readers might recognize but she would not.

Perhaps that was why Michelle had assigned Mac as her shooter. He'd been a news photographer since her father's time and knew most of the old politicians by first name. Or greeted them that way. Her father claimed to like him—"Mac's a great Cape Bretoner"—but he probably hadn't spent much time with Mac since that fateful night he'd got lost on his way to a bar and found the Lord.

"True as I'm standing here." Mac had told his tale—yet again—this morning. "God is my witness. There I was, on my way for another night of drinking and debauching when the Lord spoke to me. Just like me talking to you. 'Charles Macintosh,' God said, 'Repent ye of your sins, offer up your soul up to Mine hands and I will make room for thee in the Kingdom of Heaven.'" The Lord apparently spoke in Shakespearian English. "And I haven't had a drink since, Moira. Not one. Nor," and here he looked meaningfully at Moira, "blasphemed His name."

Oh fuck off, you Christly Jesus old fuck. Moira didn't say that, of course. But she did think it.

"Seamus, Seamus." Luckily, the arrival of the ex-premier distracted Mac before he launched into another proselytizing routine. Even Moira recognized Seamus O'Sullivan, a Liberal Party elder statesman whose successes were legend and whose failures were forgotten. His hair had turned the dull yellow-white of dirty, pissed-on snow. Moira wasn't sure if the former premier recognized Mac or if his vacant smile was merely a politician's Pavlovian response to the mention of his name. Mac did not wait for him to reply.

"Good to see you again, Seamus," he said as he brought the camera's viewfinder to his eye. "Only wish it were under happier circumstances. But at least we know Jack is now in a better place."

O'Sullivan looked fleetingly into the camera lens, and then moved on.

"Those two were quite a team," Mac said to her as the big wooden church doors swallowed the former premier.

Moira wished she knew more about the interconnectedness of the Nova Scotia Establishment. There were mourners she recognized, lawyers from the big downtown firms, a couple of real estate developers, even the Premier and the Mayor. Surely, they were too young to have worked with Eagleson. Perhaps she should call her father when she got back to the office. He'd know.

But then she'd have to listen to him berate her again for not following up on that Ward Justice racist-joke story. She'd made the mistake of telling him about the tape recording. But she'd learned her lesson; she hadn't mentioned what else the archivist had shown her, or the papers that woman who worked with Melesse had given her. She knew she should do something with it. But she didn't have the energy. Or perhaps she was afraid of asking the Judge for an interview.

My God, Uhuru Melesse! Moira hadn't expected to see him here. How did he know the dead guy? Melesse nodded solemnly in her direction as he walked past. He was accompanied by that woman from his office (Shauntay? Chenelle?) who saw Moira, flashed a face full of hostility—was she still angry Moira hadn't written about the Judge's decades-ago meeting with the Mounties?—and quickly looked away. Instead of going inside, the two of them huddled near the church entrance, talking as though trying to decide whether they really belonged among the parade of white politicians, lawyers and politicians streaming past them into the church.

There was a slight stir among the TV camera operators on the sidewalk when a limousine pulled up in front of the church. The

Nova Scotia Lieutenant-Governor and her husband got out and solemnly followed her uniformed aide-de-camp into the church. Whoever the dead guy was, Moira thought, he must have been important to merit the presence of the Queen's representative at his going-away party. She had to stop being cynical. She sounded like her father.

Speak of the devil . . . there he was, her father, slipping into the church behind the official party! He hadn't seen her. What was he doing here? She'd barely begun to try to sort that out when she saw Ward Justice himself approaching along Spring Garden Road.

"Ward, Ward . . ." Mac again. "You're looking hail-fellow-well-met this morning, my man." Moira thought he looked old and frail. "How about a little look at the camera for old times' sake?"

The Judge ignored him, his head down, shuffling slowly up the stairs.

"Stuck-up prick," Mac muttered. Moira only hoped she and Mac didn't end up in the eternal damnation of hell together. *That* would be true hell.

The Judge paused at the top of the stairs to catch his breath. Or was it because he saw Uhuru Melesse standing off to the side? The two men waved tentatively at each other. Melesse approached and shook the Judge's hand. They were too far away for Moira to know what they were saying. She stole a quick glance at Shondelle—that was her name—but she'd remained rooted in place. Moira would have to find the courage to call the Judge. She would. Someday.

The Judge's wife suddenly materialized beside him. Moira recognized her from a couple of Barristers' Society social functions Mrs. Justice had attended. What was her name? Victoria. As in Queen. Moira was surprised to see them together. Hadn't she just read a few weeks ago in *Frank* that the Judge and his wife were "splitsville," in *Frank*-speak? "Neither party returned our phone calls so we don't know the reasons for the marriage meltdown," the story said, "but friends insist there are no other parties involved. All anyone will say is that the Judge's wife recently stopped bedding down with the man who'd been her horizontal jogging partner for more than thirty years."

Moira was thankful the magazine's scandal radar, usually just as finely tuned to gossip involving younger members of the media and their liaisons, had missed her own marriage meltdown.

The Judge and his wife certainly didn't look splitsville. After the judge had introduced his wife to Melesse and they'd smiled and shaken hands politely, Victoria Justice fussed over her former horizontal jogging partner like a . . . well, a loving wife. Or perhaps a nurse. She turned up his collar to protect him from the wind and then inserted her arm in his and led him into the church.

Once the Judge and his wife were safely inside, Shondelle rejoined Melesse and, after another short discussion, they went in, too.

Maybe, Moira thought, she would approach the judge after the service.

He shouldn't have come here. And he certainly shouldn't have brought *her*. Uhuru and Shondelle sat down in the last row. Back of the bus. Heads turned. Curiosity? More? Their surprise—shock?—inevitably morphed into polite nods whenever someone accidentally made eye contact. Uhuru nodded back, felt Shondelle's silent disapproval. She'd been against this from the beginning. "You don't owe that man," she'd said. "That man owes *you* an apology from the grave."

They were at *that* stage of their relationship now.

They'd finally got over the hurdle of the first sex. It had been far less traumatic than Uhuru had anticipated in the knowing-it-must-happen-but-not-knowing-when-or-how lead-up. They'd gone for a Sunday drive in Shondelle's old Volvo. To see the leaves. "Everyone at the law school tells me I have to see the fall foliage in Nova Scotia," Shondelle had said. Uhuru could not remember the last time he'd even noticed this annual changing of the colours. When he was a kid in Africville? It was more spectacular than he'd imagined. And he said so. Which pleased Shondelle. As if she'd arranged the show herself.

But the leaves, of course, weren't the only item on Shondelle's agenda that day. She'd also arranged for them to visit Gloria Paris, a former resident of Africville who'd moved to a small black community in the Valley after her house was levelled. Shondelle had been told the City used a dump truck to move Mrs. Paris's belongings and then—once the truck got to its destination—the driver raised the front of the truck bed up and let all her furniture slide off the back, smashing most of it on the sidewalk. When Mrs. Paris complained, some City official—she'd have to find out who—told her she should be grateful they'd even put "that junk" on the truck at all. Her request for compensation was turned down. Shondelle hoped Mrs. Paris might make a compelling witness at trial.

She would not. She spoke to Uhuru as if he were his father and they were back in the 1940s. "Alzheimer's," explained her caregiver. When Shondelle tried to ask her about the relocation, Mrs. Paris acted as if Shondelle weren't even there. "Now, Lawrence Carter," she said coquettishly to Uhuru, "when are you gonna settle down with some nice young girl and start a family?"

On the drive back into the city, they began to see the humour in it. Shondelle stopped at a U-Pick farm, where they gathered more bags of apples and pears than they could possibly eat in a winter.

"Ever have my pear pie?" Shondelle asked.

"Can't say as I have."

"Well, you will. Tonight. I make a spectacular pear pie, so just consider yourself a lucky man."

Uhuru did. Even more so after Shondelle grilled steaks for them on the deck of her second-floor flat near the university. They ate on the floor of the living room in front of the fire while the pie baked in the oven. One thing led to another and soon they were naked.

"The pie," she said freeing her lips and tongue from inside his hungry mouth. "The pie's going to burn."

They ate it standing naked in the kitchen—the pie was as spectacular as advertised—and then moved on to the bedroom. Uhuru had been dreading this moment. It seemed like forever since he'd had sex with anyone he cared about, and almost that long since he'd been able to perform with any woman. The latter, though, was not completely true. He'd only failed to manufacture an erection on demand twice in his entire life—the last two times he'd picked up a woman in a bar. Both women, of course, had been white and blond, and both incidents had occurred just before he'd met Shondelle. Which made him even more nervous about going to bed with her. He'd waited for her to make the first move. And she had. Finally. After a year of working together, flirting, fighting, fighting the force of it. Still, it was almost as if she'd planned out the day in advance. Had she? Standing beside the bed that night, their bodies pressed together, feeling his own hardness pressing against her belly, Uhuru gave up trying to answer that question, or questioning whether he would be able to perform.

The only question then was: what did it mean? "I think I love you," he told her when his breathing finally began to slow down.

"Shhh," she said. She was right, of course. It was too soon. They were still telling each other the stories of their lives. And learning how to disagree without walking away.

He'd told her about his father and Africville and the fire, about living with his brother in Toronto and the process of becoming a radical, about coming back to Halifax and his growing disillusionment with the politics of Black Pride, about Jack Eagleson's role in his decision to go back to school and become a lawyer and his own continuing ambivalence about Eagleson's role in his life. He still hadn't told her about Rosa. She asked about his other girlfriends. "I can't remember any other girlfriends since I met you," he joked. She would not be that easily dissuaded, he knew. Sooner or later, he would have to tell her. Sooner or later, he would have to come to terms with what he had done.

Shondelle was the first to see Eagleson's obituary in the newspaper. "That lawyer guy you talked about," she said almost offhandedly. "He died. Story's in the paper this morning." And she passed him the obituaries.

She was surprised when he said he was going to attend the memorial service. "What for?" she demanded. He wasn't sure himself. He hadn't seen Eagleson since that day a thousand years ago when Eagleson had turned him down for an associate's position with his firm. Their only connection since had been through occasional new clients who'd mention that Eagleson had recommended him.

Telling Shondelle about Eagleson, in fact, had rekindled a long-forgotten impulse to go see the man again, to ask him to explain himself. But now, before he'd had a chance to act on that desire, Jack Eagleson was dead.

Uhuru sat in the church, listening to the orchestrated tributes and memorials being offered up by old men with fading voices: Eagleson's colleagues, friends from politics, the law, business. They were all white, of course. And none of them answered any of Uhuru's questions. Perhaps those questions were unanswerable. Perhaps Uhuru should stand up himself and testify. Tell all these white folks about the Jack Eagleson he'd known and they hadn't. Amen, brother. But this was not a black church. He reached out, put his hand over Shondelle's clasped hands, squeezed.

Ward Justice closed his eyes, tried to will his breathing back to something that might at least pass for normal. These days, even normal breathing felt like fighting against a fifty-pound weight pressing down on his chest; he had to struggle for every shallow breath. Walking was worse. A few steps. A pause. A few more steps. A longer pause. A few more steps. Sit down. Going out in public was worst of all. He couldn't have come here today if not for Victoria.

Thank God he'd finally told her. Over dinner at Valentino's, ostensibly to discuss the divorce settlement "like two civilized adults," as she'd put it. "Without lawyers."

He'd forgotten Valentino's was on the second floor.

"My God, you look awful," Victoria had said when he'd finally made it to their table. How late was he? How many times had he had to stop to catch his breath? "What's wrong with you?"

He hadn't had to say much. Just sketch in a few details. Doctor. Tests. Prostate of a much younger man, ha, ha. More tests. Lung. Cancer. Inoperable.

They hadn't discussed the divorce settlement that night. Or again.

Divorce was suddenly off the table. Instead, Victoria had moved back into the house—"Don't you ever vacuum?" was the extent of her criticism of his skills as a homemaker—and become his nurse.

Ward did not flatter himself that this changed anything. Victoria had been casting about for something to do post-divorce; Ward became her new project, her new high-fashion boutique for post-menopausal women, her new genealogical family tree. The difference was that this was a pre-death rather than post-divorce project. Ward was fine with that.

Perhaps, though, it was more than just that. For the first time in years, they could recall the times before the times had changed without rancour or regret: that first party at her parents' place where they'd smoked a joint on the widow's walk; those wild nights of drugs and sex in his first apartment; their wedding "on the rocks"; the first time he'd mangled the pronunciation of zabaglione; the day Meghan was born and Ward fainted ("One second you were standing beside the doctor at the end of the bed and the next you'd disappeared"); and the night Sarah was conceived ("Remember, we had lobster and two bottles of wine," she said, then laughed. "You *do* know I planned the whole thing").

But that was where the drive down memory lane still came to a gear-grinding halt. By the time Sarah was born, Ward had been appointed Cabinet minister. He'd been in meetings in Ottawa and missed the whole thing. His secretary sent flowers. And then, of course, there was Rosa, and all that that implied. Ward wanted to explain, if explanations were possible, his relationship with Rosa. He couldn't. He'd divided his life for so long into discrete compartments that he was incapable of opening doors between them. Perhaps that was for the best.

When he got the call from the young woman at McArtney, Eagleson—another compartment best left closed—to inform him, "as per Mr. Eagleson's last wishes," that his mentor was dead, and inviting him to the memorial service, Ward tried to beg off. *Very busy . . . May be out of town that day . . . Meetings . . .*

Victoria convinced him he should go. "He was a very important part of your life." Victoria had never liked Jack or his schemes; that she would encourage Ward to go to his memorial service seemed—well, perhaps he really should try to talk to her about Rosa. Or, perhaps not.

She let him off at the corner of Barrington and Spring Garden, half a block from the church, so he could maintain the illusion that he was still capable of walking. "I'll find a place to park and meet you inside," she said.

Luckily, he saw Ray—*Uhuru.* Would he screw up his name during the trial? Would he even be alive? Uhuru was standing at the entranceway to the church. It gave Ward a reason to stop at the top of the steps. To say hello. And catch his breath. And, oh yes, to plant the seed.

"Mr. Melesse," Ward mouthed in his direction.

"Your Honour," Melesse replied, approaching to shake his hand. Ward saw Ms. Adams was with him. He'd wondered about that. He'd met her during scheduling conferences. Ward had been impatient to get the trial underway. Uhuru had been okay with that, but Ms. Adams seemed suspicious of his motives. In the end, they'd agreed to begin the trial in late April, five months from now, which was the first open date for the prosecutors. The defence had already filed a pretrial motion, asking to be allowed to mount a defence of justification. That would be interesting.

"It's good to see you outside chambers for a change," Ward said lightly after Ray had shaken his hand. He wasn't sure why Ray was there. He remembered Jack had mentioned him a few times, but usually as "your friend, Ray." He'd called him a bright young man, but then he called everyone that.

"It's good to be outside, period," Melesse replied.

There was a silence then as both men tried to sort out what they might say to each other, given the court case hanging over them.

Ward finally began. "Maybe it's because I've been seeing so much of you lately, but I was thinking the other day about, you know, the old days. When we were kids. I know it isn't appropriate now, but, perhaps after, we can talk."

"I'd like that," Melesse replied.

"There some stuff I want to say . . ." Ward began again.

"Me too," Melesse said.

"Ward Justice. You shouldn't be standing out here in the cold like this." Victoria. She looked at the black man standing beside her husband. "He has a bad flu," she explained.

"Victoria," Ward said, "This is my friend . . . Uhuru Melesse."

"Pleased to meet you." Victoria extended her hand. Victoria knew who he was. Ward had long ago told her about his childhood friend Ray, so she had followed his career with a kind of vague curiosity.

"We'd better go inside and find a seat, Ward." Victoria turned to Melesse, smiled. "If you'll excuse us . . ."

"Certainly." He turned back to Ward. "Good to talk to you again, Ward. And, yes, let's get together after the trial. I'd like that."

Ward hoped he would still be alive then.

"The official citation reads: 'For gallantry, leadership and devotion to both mission and men during the landing at Normandy,'" the old man in the pulpit said as he held up Jack Eagleson's war medal. "But those official words don't begin to tell the half of what Jack Eagleson did that day. I know. I was there."

Apparently Jack Eagleson had lived his life in compartments too. He'd never talked—at least to Ward—about his heroism in World War II. And Ward had never thought to ask.

Ward had known Jack had a wife, but he could only remember meeting her two or three times, at the most formal of official government functions. She never had much to say. The priest had described her as "the love of his life." Ward couldn't picture it. Just as he couldn't imagine Jack's two now middle-aged sons. They'd been away at college when Ward met Jack; photos on the mantel. Now one was a university professor in British Columbia, the other a dentist in Toronto. Were they both Liberals? Ward wondered. Or had they run from their father's obsession? Was that why Jack was always on the lookout for "bright young men"? Ward would never know. He could only see the backs of their heads, sitting in the front pew with what must be their own families.

Compartments. Some had been opened today. Jack's war record, his success in helping elect Seamus O'Sullivan premier . . . There was no mention of his subsequent attempts to dethrone O'Sullivan. Or the envelopes of cash he kept in his desk drawer. Or the time he'd tried to buy off Ray's father with cash in a suitcase. Or how he'd arranged Ward's judicial appointment. Even in death, some things were best left behind closed compartment doors.

Ward wondered what people would say at *his* memorial service.

"Mr. O'Sullivan, what's your favourite memory of Jack Eagleson?" Fuck, Moira hated asking these insipid questions. But what choice did she have? Morton wanted a name-dropper. At least she had Eagleson's first name right.

"Jack was a wonderful man, a good friend and a loving father," Seamus O'Sullivan said. Moira had nabbed him, along with anyone else she even vaguely recognized, as they left the church. O'Sullivan's teeth, Moira noted now that she close to the man, were yellower than his hair.

"Any specific anecdotes?" she fished. She already had too much *wonderful, good, loving and blah, blah, blah.*

"Anecdotes? Ah, I don't think . . ." he answered, glancing back toward the church as if for inspiration. And found it. "Now there's the man you want to talk to," he said. "Ward Justice. He's a judge now, but he was a Cabinet minister in my second administration. One of Jack's protegés. He can tell you stories," He called out to Ward, obviously relieved to have found a graceful exit. "Over here. A young lady here from the paper. Wants to ask you about Jack."

Ward took his time walking over to where they stood. He was holding on to his wife's arm.

"Mr. Premier," Ward greeted him deferentially.

"Your Honour," O'Sullivan replied in kind.

The two men shook hands. "Now this young lady . . . I'm sorry, I didn't get your name . . ."

"Moira . . . Moira Donovan."

"Moira's writing a story about Jack and she was looking for some anecdotes. I said you'd be the one to talk to."

"Donovan?" Ward spoke directly to her. "I think I've seen your byline. You covered courts, right?" Moira nodded. "Used to be a reporter. Covered the Legislature. Patrick Donovan. You any relation to him?"

"My father," she said. He seemed to appraise her more carefully then.

"That so. A good reporter . . . Anyway, what can I tell you about Jack?"

Moira wasn't interested in hearing any more boring, pointless stories about Jack. But was this the place to ask about those other things?

"Well, sir," she began . . .

Ward's first reaction had been to say no, but the Chief Justice's directive last month practically ordered his judges to be more open and transparent with the press. "The media," David Fielding had written in the puffed-up memo-ese he favoured, "are surrogates for the broader public, so we have a responsibility, within the constraints of judicial probity and independence, to be accountable to the public through the media. I urge you, therefore, to take advantage of any and all opportunities to advance public understanding of our role, especially in these days when, as you know, the judicial role can sometimes be controversial."

So when Moira Donovan asked him for an interview outside the church last week, Ward Justice felt he had to say yes. That wasn't true; Ward had his own reasons to talk to this particular reporter, but he'd begun rehearsing his explanations for the Chief Justice, just in case it went wrong.

At first, the reporter reacted as if he'd said no. "I realize you aren't in a position to discuss specifics, sir," she continued. "But, as I'm sure you're aware, this case has generated a lot of public interest. Our readers would be interested in knowing more about the man at the centre of it all."

"Yes," Ward said again. "I'll do it."

"Essentially, I'm thinking of a profile that would talk about your background and—you'll do it?"

He couldn't help but smile. "Yes, Ms. Donovan, I'd be happy to. My schedule is clear for the next few days, so why don't you name the time?"

Now here they were, sitting opposite each other in an alcove off Ward's main office that had just enough room for two black leather chairs and a low round table between them. Donovan placed her tiny recorder on the table close to Ward. "I hope you don't mind," she said. "I just want to make sure the quotes are accurate."

"No problem."

But there was a problem. Ward had not thought this through. He'd fixated on the fact that she was Patrick Donovan's daughter. He'd planned to wait until she asked the question only Patrick Donovan's daughter would know to ask, and then make the pitch he'd been formulating in his head. He saw it as a dance, in which he would lead.

But she fooled him. She guided him through the predictable biographical questions, to which he gave the predictable answers. But then she circled back, came at him from an unexpected direction. She became the Grand Inquisitor, the Reporter.

It began innocuously. "I understand, sir, that you and Mr. Melesse were friends at one point. Can you tell me about your relationship with him?"

"Ah, that was a long time ago. We were both very young . . . We were friends, you know, like people are when they're kids, okay? But I haven't seen Ray—uh, Mr. Melesse—except in the courtroom now, of course, since . . . well, probably since high school." The more he tried, the more inarticulate he sounded, the more suspect his answer seemed.

"I have a copy of a transcript I'd like to show you," she said. She took some papers out of her purse, slid them across the table toward him. "This is from a 1970 report of an interview between you and two members of the RCMP's Security and Intelligence Division. About your knowledge of Mr. Melesse's political activities. Do you recognize these as your words?"

"Ah . . . let me see." He stared at the first page, uncomprehending, taking time to think about how to answer. He couldn't think. "I seem to recall something about being asked to meet with some members of the RCMP at that time," Ward said, clearing his throat, coughing nervously. "It was right after the October Crisis, I believe . . . and there were some concerns about Mr. Carter's— Mr. Melesse's activities. But I'm . . . not sure . . . I was much help to them."

Ward tried to remember what he might have said. Had he embellished his knowledge, tried to impress the cops? It was so long ago. He wanted to examine the document, consider the words and try to explain. But she'd already moved on. All she'd been looking for was a quickie quote she could use to show she'd offered him the chance to explain himself. And he'd failed.

What? Press gallery dinner? Speech? Joke? Oh, fuck!

"I do have a tape recording of your remarks from that night," she continued. She was in total control now. "I could play it for you if you'd like."

Ward shook his head. No.

"I guess what I'm looking for is a comment from you. I'm sure you know some people will read those jokes and see them as racist. Were they racist?"

"No . . . I mean, they were, but you'd need to understand the circumstances . . ." She was already asking another question. How long had he been babbling to himself, trying to explain the inexplicable, justify the unjustifiable?

He hadn't wanted to bring up his idea in this way; he'd wanted her to ask him the right question, the one he'd been waiting for, the question her father would have suggested, the one about the accident and his appointment, the one he'd been waiting to hear for twenty-seven years. And then, they could trade. She could tell him how close her father had been to publishing and he could tell her the whole story. And then they would agree—this was the essence of the pitch he'd intended to make—that he would tell her everything if she agreed to publish none of it until after he was dead.

But he'd lost his advantage. She seemed to know too much. What did he have to trade?

"—confess I was puzzled by what he'd showed me, and his interpretation of the documents and the photo." What now? "But Mr. Astor is a trained archivist, and he seems very convinced that he can trace your family tree . . ."

She passed him the photo.

Ward couldn't speak, couldn't move, couldn't understand, couldn't believe. What this woman was saying made no sense. He tried but he couldn't make his brain's tumblers fall into their proper places.

═══

"Oh, Judge Justice . . ." Gerry Donkin, the nursing home's administrator, fluttered about like a frightened bird as soon as he saw Ward limping into the lobby. "We weren't expecting you today." Realizing how that might sound now, he added quickly, "It's always a pleasure, of course . . . I—we—want you to know how sorry we are about what happened to your father."

Happened to my father!? Ward was stunned. *Dead? Before he could ask why!*

But Desmond Justice was very much alive.

"As soon as we realized what was going on," Donkin continued, in a for-the-record voice intended to indicate to the Judge—and to whatever lawyer he might hire down the road—that the nursing home had acted responsibly, "we called in the police and suspended the woman. According to what the police tell us now, Desmond may not have been the only one of our guests she's stolen from." He paused. "Not that that's any consolation, of course."

As Ward slowly untangled the story the administrator assumed was the reason for his visit that morning, he learned that one of the home's cleaners—the infamous "coloured girl" his father so often claimed was stealing his slippers—was indeed a thief! Ward and Victoria had both dismissed Desmond's ranting as paranoia, or senility, or yet another manifestation of his bigotry.

The coloured girl!

So the coloured girl really was a thief.

And Desmond Justice really was black.

Which made Ward Justice . . .

Desmond was neither embarrassed nor apologetic. "The races been mixing since before anybody knew there were races," he said, sounding like he'd been rehearsing it for years. "Who's to say who's white and who's black?"

"But why?" Ward demanded again. Ward wasn't angry to discover he was black; he wasn't even sure he'd managed to process that reality yet. It was that his own father had never told him the truth. "That's what I still don't understand. Why did you lie to me?"

Victoria had driven Ward to the nursing home, but she hadn't come inside. "I'll get a coffee at Tim's and come back for you in an hour," she'd said. "This is one conversation I think you and your father need to have alone."

Since Ward couldn't have driven the hour and a half to the nursing home by himself—one more sign of the shrinking borders of his life—he'd had to tell Victoria what Moira Donovan had told him. But Victoria had already known! She'd even known the reporter's source. "David Astor, that man I went to see at the Archives when I was researching your family tree," she said. "He found the photo."

Ward wanted to ask why Victoria had kept this little detail from him. But he didn't, perhaps because her deception now seemed trivial compared with the lifelong fraud his own father had perpetrated.

In the past fifteen hours, Ward had retraced, relearned, re-evaluated, reinterpreted his entire life history. And wondered why he'd never considered the question, or contemplated the possibility before now. Should he have?

His skin tone had always been slightly darker than that of the other—white—kids at school. Most of the time, that had seemed a plus, like having a year-round tan in high school. When anyone would comment on it, his pale-skinned mother would tell them, "He gets that from his father's side." But she said the same about Ward's predilection to pudginess and his tendency to keep his feelings bottled up inside. And, of course, his tightly curled black hair.

In the late sixties when he was in university, Ward had let his hair grow out into a then-fashionable Afro. Would he have called it that? Probably. Without even considering that he might be . . . Afro . . . himself. "You look like one of them coloured singers," his father had complained. "Get a haircut." But those were the days when fathers were always telling their sons to cut their hair. Ward thought nothing of it. And kept the Afro until it went out of style.

When he was little, Ward remembered asking about his "other" Grampy and Grandma, and his father telling him they had died in a fire. That much, at least, seemed to have been true.

Growing up, in fact, he'd known only a few of his relatives, all on his mother's side. But that seemed reasonable enough; his mother had grown up in Eisners Head, his father had not.

Had Ward ever asked his father where he was born? About his growing-up years? Probably. But when Ward was a child, his father most likely would have made a tall tale out of his answer. He did that a lot, especially before the strike. Once, when Ward asked his father what he'd done in World War II, his father had told him some fanciful story about floating on a torpedo in the North Atlantic for three days. Ward was young enough to believe him; he only discovered much later his father had never even served in the war.

By the time Ward was old enough to start asking serious questions and wanting serious answers, his father wasn't telling tall—or any—tales any more. After the strike and the exile to Halifax, his father had constructed a cocoon around himself Ward couldn't penetrate. Not that he'd tried very hard. As a teenager, Ward had become so absorbed in his own here and now that he had no interest in his father's then and there.

Besides, by then, he had secrets of his own. His friendship with

Ray, for starters. That little secret seemed more bizarre, even ridiculous, in light of . . . So many secrets . . . He really was his father's son. Ward hadn't told his father about his cancer; he didn't intend to now.

"Why?" Desmond Justice rolled the question around on his tongue. He was sitting up in his bed, a pile of pillows supporting his back, staring across the room at the big-screen TV. *Oprah* was on. He'd clicked the mute button on the remote when Ward came in. But he kept his thumb on the button, as if he might decide at any moment he'd rather watch Oprah than continue their conversation. "Why not?" he said.

"What kind of answer is that?" Ward demanded. Angry.

Desmond didn't answer directly. "My daddy told me the first Justice ever set foot in Nova Scotia was the son of a white plantation owner and his coloured slave girl," he offered instead. "Come up from Georgia after the American Revolution. British promised him his freedom and land. But the land they give him was the rockiest, most barren patch of dirt in the most out-of-the-way place in all of Nova Scotia. The good land all went to the whites. That's the way it always was. That's the way it's always going to be. He may have been half white but, to the British, he was still all black."

"But—"

"Still is. Forget your civil rights and your Martin Luther King, even your Malcolm X. You want to get ahead in this world, you got to be white. My daddy taught me that. He married white. So what did that make me? My daddy, he told me once I was probably three-quarters white man anyway. But the white men don't do the math that way.

"I was fourteen when my parents died in that fire. There was just me then. No brothers, no sisters. Just me. I didn't start out to make myself into a white man. I just wanted to get as far away from Kingville as I could get." He laughed. "Who knew I wouldn't get more than a couple hundred mile down the road? But that was a distance then. Nobody knew me in Eisners Head . . . When I showed up looking for work on the fishin' boats, people looked at me and just figured I must be a white man. I let 'em think what they wanted."

"Mum?"

"Your mother knew," Desmond Justice said. "I had to tell her. And she went along. She knew what people would say. That's why we decided not to have any kids. And then you came along. An accident. I tell you, we were both scared to death you were going to come out black as the ace of spades. It happens. But you didn't. You were even whiter than me."

"I don't get it," Ward tried again. "All my life, you've acted like a . . . like a racist. *Don't play with the black children. The coloureds* this and *the coloureds* that . . . and all the time you're black yourself. Why did you make me live your lie?"

"You have to understand, son," his father answered, as if the answer were obvious. "I did this for you. I figured if you spent too much time with coloured people, like that fellow down in Africville you were so fond of, I was afraid you'd end up coloured too and that would be the end of any chance you had . . . See, when I realized I could pass for white, I knew I could give you the chance I never had." Desmond Justice looked at Ward then. "And I was right. I was, wasn't I? You went to college. You been a lawyer, a Cabinet minister, a judge. You think you'd have been any of those things if they'd known you had the least trickle of black blood running through your veins?"

"But you never thought any of those were good things," Ward said. "You hated it when I told you I was going to go to law school."

"I did. But I didn't, too." Desmond Justice paused for a moment, tried to collect his thoughts. "Maybe I was white, but part of me was still coloured. The coloured part hated the lawyers and the politicians and the judges and the rest who kept us in our place. And, don't forget, I wasn't just white. I was poor white. Blacks, poor whites, we both resent the same rich white folks—the lawyers and fish plant owners—but we still want our kids to be them. It's not right. But that's just the way it is."

Desmond Justice stopped then, exhausted. He looked back at the

TV, his thumb still hovering over the mute button. "I may not have said it right, but I want you to know I was always proud of you and what you done," he said.

His father had never said that before.

But he'd said all he was going to say for now. He pressed down on the button and Oprah's voice filled the room.

12

July 1976

"John?" Ward Justice waved his empty glass in John's direction. "Another."

The bartender shrugged and reached behind him for the Glenfiddich bottle. Empty. How much of that bottle was already sloshing around in Ward Justice's stomach? he wondered. He opened another bottle, filled the jigger once, poured it into the glass, and then did the same again.

"Hope you're not planning to drive tonight, sir," John said as he put the glass down in front of Ward.

"No. Not driving. Not tonight," Ward said, his voice loose with slur.

John shrugged again. He knew the minister was lying and would get in his car as soon as he left the bar. "If you want, I can put in a call to the station for you, have them send somebody to drive you home," John offered.

"No, no . . . won't be necessary . . . But thanks, really, John. Thanks."

John nodded, picked up a cloth to wipe circular water stains off the bar countertop. Fuck it. What more could he do? He'd been a bartender here long enough to know just how hard he could push his customers, especially the politicians. The Victory Lounge, on Spring Garden Road beside the Lord Nelson Hotel, was a favourite hangout for provincial politicians. The out-of-towners, many of whom stayed in the hotel during legislative sessions, would drop in for a nightcap on the way to their rooms.

Justice had been only an occasional visitor to the bar. Usually with Mr. White and usually just for one, maybe two drinks. But lately, he'd been arriving alone, late in the afternoon, and staying until closing. Every night. John would see other MLAs stop at his stool and try to engage him in conversation, but it was as if there were an invisible, don't-come-too-close wall around him. They left.

Probably a woman, John thought. That was usually what pushed them over the edge. But Ward Justice always came alone, left alone. Maybe it wasn't a woman. Who knew? John looked at his watch. Quarter to one. Another Saturday night almost over. He began his final round along the bar stools.

"Just so you know, Mr. Minister," he said to Ward, "last call's in five minutes."

"One more for the road, then . . ."

It had not been a good day. Or a good week. A good month. A good year. How had it begun? With that stupid speech at the press gallery dinner? No one had mentioned a word about it since that night, of course, but Ward knew, just by the way the other MLAs and reporters spoke to him, approaching him gingerly, that it still hung over him. Or perhaps it had begun even before that, after Jack had floated the first rumours he was going to challenge the Premier. These days, O'Sullivan rarely called on him in Cabinet meetings or even spoke to him. And half of the Cabinet followed the Premier's lead. Then again, maybe it had started more recently, with that dinner at Claudie's with Jack and Junior.

Jack seemed to understand his position, even sympathized without saying it in so many words, but Junior was refusing to let it go. He'd demanded they meet this morning in Junior's office at the fish plant so he could make one final pitch for Ward's support.

Junior did the talking. Jack just stood by the window, watching a couple of deckhands loading supplies aboard a trawler.

Junior trotted out all the usual arguments. "Ottawa will go along, guaranteed, but only if you're in too," he said. Ward knew the feds just wanted to be able to deflect anger away from themselves and onto the province—onto him—for a controversial decision.

No. Ward said it again.

"You're as stubborn as your old man," Junior was shouting at him now, "and just as fucking stupid."

Jack tried to calm him but Junior was having none of it. "Don't think we don't know about you and your nigger whore," he said. "Oh, don't look so shocked. You think we wouldn't hear somethin' like that? And how do you think the voters in Cabot County will like that? Their MLA shaggin' a nigger?"

"Now why don't we all just step back and take a breath—" Jack began, but this time Junior cut him off.

"Give him the paper." Junior looked hard at Jack and pointed at Ward. "Give him the fucking letter. I'm sick of playing fucking games here."

Jack looked pained, but he reached into the inside breast pocket of his sports jacket, took out a business envelope and handed it to Ward. Ward couldn't help but think of all the envelopes, thick with cash, Jack had doled out to him in the last two years. This envelope was thin and flat.

"This meeting's fucking over," Junior shouted, louder now. "And so are you, you stubborn, stupid prick." With that, he stormed out of the office, leaving Jack and Ward alone in the silence of an empty building on a Saturday morning. They looked at each other.

"Sorry," Jack said simply. And then he left the room, too.

Ward was alone in Junior's office. He looked down at the envelope, at the familiar McArtney, Eagleson, Cullingham & O'Sullivan letterhead. He ripped it open, fished out the letter. Jack had signed it.

> Dear Mr. Justice:
>
> On behalf of our client, Eisner International Holdings Ltd., I am writing to inform you that, as per the terms of your agreement (Our File #6437A) with Eisner International Holdings, said company is demanding full and immediate repayment of

> the outstanding balance of all monies loaned to you for the purchase of the house and property known as 57 Atlantic Street in the City of Halifax, County of Halifax in the Province of Nova Scotia . . .

John set his final double Scotch on the bar in front of him. Ward felt inside his pocket now for the crumpled sheet of paper. Still there. So it was real and not just the alcohol. He swallowed the last of the Scotch, got to his feet.

"Yeah, okay, but what happens if they do find out?" Patrick Donovan said. "I'll be up shit's creek." Patrick didn't want to get into this discussion. He was too drunk to think clearly. Had Saunders planned it that way? Everyone knew Saunders was a malcontent, always blaming the publisher for everything that went wrong at the newspaper, everything that went wrong in his life.

Patrick hadn't been surprised that Saunders was the one organizing the union drive at the paper. It did surprise him that Keefe and Matthews were part of it too. They'd spent the day together at the oil company fishing derby/piss-up. No one had said a word about the union. Until now. This was supposed to be the last stop on their way home.

"One more victory round at the Victory for the victorious *Tribune* Trojans," Keefe had suggested during the drive back to the city. They'd found a corner table near the exit. And ordered a round. After the waiter had returned with their order, Saunders had hauled out a blank union card and handed it to Patrick.

Keefe and Matthews told Patrick they'd already signed.

"We've almost got the numbers to go for certification," Saunders told him. "And that's the best protection you can have."

Saunders was practically pushing the pen in his face now.

Patrick recoiled. And then saw his escape. "Mr. Minister, Mr. Minister, over here." Ward Justice was walking unsteadily toward the lounge's exit. Patrick caught his attention. Justice hesitated a second, then walked carefully, deliberately in their direction.

"Join us?"

"I'd love to, thanks, really," Ward replied. "But, you know, it's way past my bedtime." He exaggerated a yawn.

"So, Mr. Minister, when are you going to announce for leader?" It was Saunders. Saunders fancied himself a political reporter. He wanted Patrick's job.

Ward froze him with a look. Waited two beats. Then smiled and began to sing: "Seamus is my leader / I shall not be moved / Seamus is my leader / I shall not be moved . . ." He was still singing as he pushed open the door and stumbled on to the sidewalk.

Ward Justice awoke with an eyes-wide-open start, as if he'd suddenly remembered he was supposed to be paying attention. He looked around. There was no one to pay attention to. He wiped cold spittle from the corner of his mouth. Perhaps he'd woken himself up snoring. He was doing that more often these days. The alcohol? Or perhaps it was one of those myotonic jerks, the shocky, spastic sensation of falling out of bed he occasionally experienced in his last moments between wakefulness and sleep. Victoria had them all the time. Did she still have them? By the time Ward got home from "work," Victoria was inevitably deep into sleep, or some pretence of sleep. More often than not, he chose to bed down on the sofa in the den so as not to disturb her. In fact, he was sleeping on a sofa tonight, but not the same sofa. This was also not his den.

This was Rosa's everything-but-the-bedrooms room. There was a hot plate, a kettle and a toaster on the floor in one corner, which served as Rosa's kitchen (the bathroom down the hall, which she shared with two other families, provided what passed for a kitchen sink). In another corner, a card table, featuring an illustration of an English fox hunt on the top, and two mismatched folding lawn chairs worked as her dining-room set. The wall nearest the door was dominated by an oversized but stained red velour sofa that might have been popular in certain middle-class homes in the fifties but had outlived its style and its stuffing and been tossed out with someone else's trash. It was now Rosa's living-room suite. (Occasionally, when little Larry was sleeping and they were too eager to walk the few feet to Rosa's bedroom, the sofa did double duty as a narrow, lumpy bed for their lovemaking.)

To describe the place where Rosa slept as a bedroom overstated the reality. The entire apartment had started as one large, dark, open space on the third floor of an abandoned warehouse near the harbour. Rosa had created two bedrooms, one for her and one for her son, by hanging sheets from the low rafters and plunking mattresses on the floor behind them. She and Larry each had a battered suitcase instead of a dresser to hold their clothes.

Ward, awake now, looked around. Rosa and Larry must have gone to bed. How long had he been asleep on the sofa? He looked down at his watch. Quarter to four. Longer than he thought. Ward examined himself. He was still dressed in the dark-blue suit he'd worn to this morning's meeting with Jack and Junior; his paisley tie was still tight around the collar of his powder-blue dress shirt. So he and Rosa had not made love tonight. He wasn't surprised. They made love less and less these days, their once torrid, passionate affair now rutted into routine torpor. Like a marriage. Full of silences, or bickering, or both.

"You should have called," she'd said even before he'd sat down.

"I was in meetings."

"You smell like you were in meetings . . ."

"I'm here now."

"Why? Because you want to get laid?"

"No. Because I want to see you."

"Because you're too drunk to screw?"

"What happened to 'making love'?"

"Good question," she fired back. "It used to feel like making love. Now it feels like screwing."

"Maybe I should just go . . ." He let the sentence trail off.

"No. Stay," she said finally. "I'm sorry. I'm lonely, that's all." This was not a new complaint, and not entirely—though still partly—his fault. Rosa had been cut off (or cut herself off, Ward wasn't sure which) from her family. When he tried to ask her about her father or brothers, she changed the subject. Her family—in fact, just about every aspect of her life before that night in the back seat of his car in the parking lot off Gottingen Street—was off limits. Except for Africville. Or at least a narrow, nostalgic, vague band of memories of Africville—"out home," as Rosa called it—that did not include her father, her mother, her family or Ray. Ray especially. Except . . . except she would get this look—wistful? wishful?—whenever Ward mentioned his name. "I don't want to talk about him," she would say, while her eyes conveyed some other message. It wasn't that Ward wanted to talk about Ray either—he still felt vaguely guilty they'd drifted apart—but Ray was their only shared history. What else did they have to talk about? That was part of the problem. They had no life together outside this apartment. And Rosa had no life any more beyond the incomplete one she shared with Ward. She had no family, no friends. She'd stopped hanging out with her school friends when she dropped out of school to have Larry. She was no longer working the streets, so she didn't see her hooker friends any more. Given the clandestine nature of her relationship with Ward, of course, it was hard enough for them to be together, let alone socialize with other people.

She kissed him on the forehead and then stretched out on the sofa, her head resting in his lap. "It's just I'm so tired. And Larry won't sleep."

Larry had been awake and ready to play when Ward arrived at . . . that must have been one-thirty. After last call. "War'! War'!" he'd squealed with delight when Ward opened the door.

"P'ay t'uck?" Larry demanded now. "War' p'ay t'uck?" He wrapped his arms around Ward's leg.

"No, no truck tonight," Ward said as Larry raced to his room to get the Tonka truck Ward had given him for his birthday. "War' too tired to play. And you, young man," he added, "should be in bed. What are you doing still up?"

"Larry not tired," the boy replied, a grin on his face. "Larry wanna play."

"Maybe later, Larry, maybe later. Right now, I need to talk to your mama."

Ward did *need* to talk to Rosa, but he didn't want to. He didn't want to tell her about his meeting with Jack and Junior. (He didn't want to tell Victoria even more, of course, which may have been why he had ended up at Rosa's instead of at home confessing to his wife that Junior had called the mortgage on their house and Jack might or might not stop giving him envelopes of cash, so he almost certainly would not be able to keep her and the girls in the style to which they'd grown too accustomed.)

And Rosa and Larry? What would this mean for them? At first, Rosa had refused all Ward's offers to help her financially. But after he'd talked her into getting off the streets—she hadn't needed much persuasion—she'd reluctantly agreed to let him buy groceries "just until I find a job." But there were no jobs, so Ward began to give her cash to buy clothes for herself and Larry, then for taxis so she could take Larry to the doctor for his checkups and to the shopping centre for clothes and the supermarket for food. Most recently, he'd bought her a 1963 VW Beetle so she wouldn't have to spend all that money on taxis. The Bug was cheap enough—four hundred dollars—but then she needed money for insurance, and gas, and a new clutch, and who knew what next. The longer their relationship went on, the more Rosa depended on Ward's money, and the more Ward felt responsible for her financial well-being. And the more resentful he became because he felt responsible. Especially now. How could he support Victoria and Rosa, and the girls, and little Larry if he suddenly had to pay interest for a mortgage on a house he couldn't afford?

Ward wondered if he could call Junior, apologize, agree to write whatever letters, make whatever statements Junior wanted, perhaps even convince the Cabinet to approve his loan request. It was probably too late. They had crossed a line that morning as soon as Junior walked out of the office. Maybe Jack would intercede. Jack had seemed more disappointed than angry. Maybe Jack . . . ?

But did Ward really want to back down now? Saying no had felt good, clean, pure. Better than he'd felt in years. There had to be another way.

"Why so quiet?" Rosa asked. Little Larry was on the floor in the corner by the card table now, quietly stuffing his toy delivery van with plastic soldiers.

"Nothing. Just thinking."

"What about?"

"Nothing." Nothing, except the fact that Junior was threatening to expose their relationship, and put an end to his marriage and his political career.

She was silent then too. As if she were listening to him think out loud. "Do you think we should, you know . . . stop seeing each other?"

"No," he said, gently stroking her curls. "Is that what you want?"

"No," she said, turning to look up at him. "I want us to be together."

"Me too," he said. Then they were silent. Was that when he fell asleep?

He should go home now. Before Victoria and the kids got up. That way he could say he'd got home late from meeting Jack and Junior. Victoria slept heavily; she'd never know. Did she care?

He struggled to get up from the sofa, the springs of which had long since quit. Oh God. His head still oozed woozy. He felt like he might be sick. He reached for a wall to steady himself. He was still drunk. Christ, how many had he had? The fact that he couldn't remember was not a good sign.

Should he go in and kiss Rosa goodbye? No. She might wake up. And they might make love. Or screw. And then he might never go home. Larry? Just a kiss on the forehead? No, not that either. If the boy woke up, he'd want to play.

Ward carefully picked his way through the dark apartment. Luckily, the door was ajar so he could navigate by the hall light. He almost tripped going down the stairs. The rest of the way, he gripped the railing like an old man.

Outside, the night air was heavy with mist. It took Ward a minute to fish his keys out of his pocket, another to choose the right key and slip it into the door handle. But then he lucked out, finding the car's ignition on the first try. Perhaps he wasn't so drunk after all.

He turned the key and the ignition caught, but he held it too long and he heard a grinding sound. He let go. His foot was too heavy on the gas. The engine revved loudly. Finally, he slipped the car into gear and the car lurched . . . backward. Reverse! Shit. *Bang, crash.* He'd hit the garbage can. And smashed it into the wall of the building behind him. Christ. He was going to wake the neighbours. His wheels were still spinning on the damp pavement. Foot off the gas, take your foot of the gas. He hoped he hadn't woken anyone. Damn, he had to get out of here. He stared intently at the indicators on the automatic transmission. Find drive. Put it in drive. Go. His tires squealed as he pulled out of the lot. Christ, he was tired. Christ, he was drunk. He needed to get home. Which way now?

"Okay, okay, I'm sorry, but could you spell that last name again?" Patrick Donovan's stomach was still churning from his night before and his head was still aching from this morning's way-too-early wake-up call. The last thing he needed was a cop with attitude.

"I already did. Twice." The sergeant seemed determined to make this as difficult as possible. All for a three-paragraph brief with no byline.

The cop sighed. "Johnstone. J-O-H-N-S-T-O-N-E. Got it now?"

"Yeah."

"Okay, well let me give you the whole thing one more time just to be sure." The cop was mocking him, Patrick knew. He wanted to offer some witty riposte but he was afraid he really might have it all wrong. Damn this hangover.

"Kid's name: Lawrence Johnstone. Two years old, two-and-a-half if you want to be precise. Residence: 4 White Street . . . Black neighbourhood. Go figure. Next of kin, mother, Rosa Johnstone. Only kin listed. Hit-and-run case. Under investigation. And that's all she wrote. Anything else I can do for you?"

"No, nothing, thanks." Patrick Donovan wanted to go home to bed. Instead, he rolled another sheet of six-part carbon book into his typewriter and began to bang out the story.

He had to get out of here. Now. Before he threw up all over Barbie and Ken. But Ward was stuck, flat on his belly in the grass, his head and shoulders inside the flaps of My First House, a plastic pup tent shaped like a doll's house Victoria had bought for the girls. The smell of Sarah's wet diaper filled his nostrils. The heat from the sun, which had burned off the fog in the air but not in his head, magnified and intensified inside the airless, orange tent. He could feel the sweat trickling down his cheeks, taste the salt on his lips.

He'd been sitting on the deck, recovering, pretending to watch Meghan and Sarah while they played house with their dolls when Meghan came running over. "Daddy, can you come and play with us, please, please? We're going to have a tea party. Ken and Barbie will be there."

This then was his penance. For last night. For lying about where he was and when he got home. For everything. His lie hadn't worked.

"What time did you get in last night?" Victoria had asked when he'd walked into the kitchen this morning shortly after eleven. She'd asked sweetly. He should have known.

"Around two," he'd said. No need to be too precise. "My meeting lasted much longer than I expected." Mention the meeting with Junior and Jack. Maybe later, tell her about the mortgage. Or maybe he'd wait until Monday, see if he could make other arrangements with a bank first.

"That's interesting," she said, her voice congealing. "I thought I heard you come in around quarter to five."

"No," he said, shovelling dirt over the hole he'd dug for himself. "That must have been some teenagers making noise. It woke me, too."

"Strange," she said then. "I woke up around four-thirty and your car wasn't in the driveway. You weren't in bed. And when I went downstairs to look, you weren't in the den, either."

He couldn't think of an answer to that. He didn't have to. She turned on her heel and stormed out of the kitchen.

Ward made the girls a lunch of Honey Nut Cheerios and milk.

"'O's are for breakfast, not for lunch. Silly daddy," Meghan said. "Isn't he a silly daddy, Sarah?"

"Mmmph," Sarah offered in agreement, her grin exposing a mouthful of half-eaten cereal.

"Why don't you girls go play in the backyard," he told them as he put their dishes in the sink. "You can take your dollies out and play in the house Mummy got you." Ward could already smell Sarah's poopy diaper. He should change her. He couldn't face it. Later.

By the time later came, his head was trapped inside the tent.

"Sugar, missus?" Meghan asked her sister politely, and then dumped two imaginary spoonfuls of sugar into her tiny plastic cup. Sarah looked at her father and giggled. Ward tried to smile back. "And for you, Daddy—mister? Sugar?"

"Yes, please . . ." he said. Penance.

His head inside the tent, he didn't see or hear Victoria approaching from the house. "There's a call for you," she announced without preamble, without the saving grace of humanity.

"I'll be back in a few minutes," he told the girls, partly relieved at the possibility of escape and partly terrified of facing Victoria again. "Daddy just has to take a phone call." Ward felt Victoria looming over him as he manoeuvred his body backwards out of the tent. He got to his knees, then stood up.

"It's a woman," she said to his back as he walked toward the house. "It sounds like she's crying." She was following him, curious. He tried not to think.

"Hello?" he said as he pressed the receiver to his ear. Cautious, as if the phone would wrap itself around his neck and strangle him.

It was Rosa. He could tell by the sound of her sobbing. She continued to cry but she didn't say anything, at least nothing he could understand. He looked at Victoria, who was staring at him.

"Uh, okay, okay," he said then, in response to nothing. "I'll, ah, be right there." He hung up without waiting for a reply. He looked away from Victoria, tried to figure out what to say and do now.

"Is that your whore?" Victoria demanded. "Is it?"

Ward said nothing.

"Is she pregnant?" Pregnant! Ward hadn't even considered that. She could be. He'd thought about buying condoms but he was afraid someone might recognize him. What a stupid excuse. And now . . . Pregnant! Christ.

"I have to go," he said. "To see somebody. About work," he added, as if she hadn't been standing beside him during this conversation, as if she didn't know better.

"You lousy fucker," she shouted at him. She was crying now. "You lousy motherfucker."

"Mummy said a bad word," Meghan told her sister. They'd followed their parents into the house. "Bad mummy," she said, as if talking to one of her dolls.

But Mummy was gone from the room. Again.

Ward found his car keys on the floor in the den where he'd put them, or dropped them, or where they'd fallen out of his pocket last night. He went out the front door and down the walkway toward the driveway. The car was parked halfway up the lane as if he'd been unable to calculate the space remaining and erred on the side of caution by stopping in the middle of the driveway. Had he? He couldn't remember parking the car. Or the drive home. Walking around the back of the car to get to the driver's side, he noticed the dent in the left rear bumper, the chrome scraped off. Shit. What had he hit? And how? He tried to remember. Banging. The garbage can. He'd backed into the garbage can. Now he'd have to get the bumper fixed before—What? There was a dark, brownish-red colour splattered over the whitewalls. And what was that caught in the tire tread? A bluish-blackish-brownish piece of . . . He felt it with his fingers. Rubbery. Embedded with flecks of whitish-grey. Bone? Oh, Jesus! What had he done? He tried to conjure the details of the drive home, but none came to him. A dog? Someone? Oh, God . . . He got in the car, inhaled, exhaled, deep breaths, tried to stop himself from throwing up.

Think. Think. Car wash. Wash away whatever it is. Now. Before someone sees. He drove to the self-wash in the north end. A coin car wash. No operator to see his face, to see the . . . Was that really blood on the tire? He put his money in, took the hose, trained its spray on the rear tire, washed away the splatters and the pieces of whatever. He trained the hose on the pieces he'd washed out of the tread, followed them with the spray to the floor drain. Gone. He used five quarters' worth of water on the tire before realizing he had to wash the rest of the car too. So no one would know.

Rosa? Shit. He'd told her he'd be right there. Would she call the house again? What would Victoria say this time? He needed to get over to her place. East on Young to Barrington. South on Barrington to White. Left turn onto—Ward slammed on the brakes, jammed the car into reverse and backed onto Barrington again. There was a cop car outside Rosa's place. Were they looking for him? How had they connected him to Rosa?

He headed the car north on Barrington again, willed himself not to speed. Perhaps he should turn around, retrace his drive home after he left Rosa's last night. Maybe something along the route would bring back what really happened. He flipped on the radio. Driving rock music. And then the disc jockey. "Bachman-Turner Overdrive as you drive around on this beautiful Sunday afternoon. Don't worry. We won't stop the music. The Bay City Rollers are next, right after Steve tells us what's coming up on the news. Steve?"

"Thanks, Dan. Halifax Police are investigating a fatal hit-and-run accident last night on White Street in the city's north end. The victim: a two-and-a-half-year-old boy. I'll have all the details on Contemporary News at five to the—"

Ward snapped off the radio. Trying to pretend he hadn't heard what he'd heard. That he didn't know what it meant. But he had. And he did. He pulled the car over to the side of the road. Opened the door. Leaned over. Threw up.

The phone rang and rang. Ward was about to hang up when someone finally picked up. "Hello."

"Jack?"

"Ward! I'm glad you called. I didn't want to leave the things the way they were yesterday. We're all grown—"

"I need to talk to you," Ward interjected. "I think I did something . . . bad."

═══

Chickenshit bastards. Patrick was certain the missing paragraph hadn't been edited out for space. The local section was thin enough this morning the editors had even stuck some national wire stories in just to bulk it up. So it wasn't space. No, this smacked of the usual "*Tribune* Trepidation," a phrase of his own proud creation to describe the paper's aversion to controversy of any kind.

The missing paragraph read: "One eyewitness to the incident, a 12-year old Negro neighbour who wouldn't give his name"—not quite true; Patrick hadn't remembered to ask—"told this newspaper he saw a large white car driven by a white man leaving the scene of the hit-and-run Sunday morning. He said he'd seen the same car parked on the street on previous occasions."

Snipped from the printed version as if it had never even been there.

The phone rang. It was the desk calling. "How'd you like to do a follow-up on that hit-and-run story?" He was about to complain when Lucas, the City Editor, laughed out loud. "Just kidding, don't get yourself in a lather. Harkin left me a note about how happy you were to get that assignment. So, don't worry. I'll bounce that one back to the boys in the cop shop. But I do have a story you might be interested in. Nothing to do with car accidents. Got a note this morning. About some press conference in the Red Room at ten. The details are still sketchy but it's apparently going to be a kind of pep rally for some fish company pitch to convince Ottawa to give them a factory freezer trawler. I'm hearing Eisner but I can't say for sure. That more up your alley?"

"Yeah, thanks." The story didn't sound exciting but at least it didn't involve dead kids. That was a plus.

═══

Jack had been cryptic on the phone. "I have some information on that matter we discussed the other day," he said. "I'd like to come around and talk to you about it now if you have the time."

If he had the time! Ward had nothing but time. Time to think. And worry. About one thing. Certainly not Junior's press conference two days ago. Junior had announced Eisner's application to Ottawa to acquire a fleet of factory freezer trawlers. No mention where they would come from. Or who would crew them. Of course, the press wanted to know the provincial Fisheries Department's position on Junior's proposal.

"Tell them we're studying it," Ward had told Matheson, the department's press guy. "And no interviews. Tell them I'm too busy to talk to anyone right now."

Too busy? Ward had been busy cancelling appointments, postponing departmental meetings. So he could . . . sit alone in his office and think.

He had tried to call Rosa. And tried. No answer. He'd heard on one of the radio open-line shows—he listened to them all the time now—that the show had been trying to contact her too, "so we can ask *that woman* just what was she thinking, putting her child outside like that in the middle of the night." The host of *Open Mic with Mike in the Mornings* sounded angry with Rosa. "Listeners, I want you to know we called her number a dozen times yesterday and again this morning because we know you want to know the answer to that question too," Mike's Voice of Righteous Indignation boomed out from the radio on the credenza in Ward's office. He lowered his voice then, almost whispered. "She isn't answering her phone. What do you want to bet, dear listeners, that that woman is sitting there in her apartment and just doesn't want to talk to us, doesn't want to answer our questions, your questions? But who knows? Maybe she's got her radio on, is listening to us this morning. Is there something you want to say to that woman who left her little boy outside to die a horrible death? Our phone lines are open right now. Give us a call."

No wonder Rosa wasn't answering her phone. Not that Ward

would have known what to say if she did. What could he say? *I'm sorry I killed your son?* Did she know it was him?

"War' p'ay t'uck? War' p'ay t'uck?" Little Larry's voice played like a looped chorus, an endless accusation, in his head. It was playing now. Still. Ward's eyes filled with tears. Again.

He should have gone to the police. He'd wanted to, but Jack wouldn't hear of it. "It was an accident," Jack said after Ward blurted out the whole story and asked Jack to accompany him to the police station so he could turn himself in. "Don't make things any worse. There's nothing you can do now to change what happened. And you don't even know what the police know. They may not know anything. So just step back and take a deep breath . . . Look, I know you're upset and I know you want to do the right thing, but this is about more than just what happened. It's about your career and your future. It's about the government. I don't think we could survive a scandal like this. Not now." Ward was not convinced. Jack could see that. "And what about Victoria? And the kids? Are you really ready to put them through something like this?" Jack was beginning to make an impression now. He kept talking. "Give me a few days. Let me see what I can find out for you. I have some contacts. Meantime, don't do anything different. Just go about your business."

But Ward had done everything different. That night he'd told Victoria the whole story. The truth. Left nothing out. She'd screamed at him, beat at his chest with her fists. He took it. He deserved it. She'd cried then. He'd cried too, told her he was sorry for the mess he'd made for her and the kids, but he didn't say he was sorry he'd fallen in love with Rosa. And Victoria didn't say she forgave him. She didn't. The next day when he came home from the office, all his clothes were in the closet in the den. Their marriage, even the pretence their marriage had become, was finished. Nothing but the shell remained. For the sake of appearances. And the children. Which was why he had to wait for Jack, she told him. For the children.

But Jack didn't call. And didn't call. So last night, after the funeral,

Ward had driven to Rosa's apartment in Victoria's car. There were no cops. And no reporters. But no Rosa, either.

"Gone," her next-door neighbour yelled out from inside her apartment when she heard Ward knocking on Rosa's door. "Left this afternoon. In a cab. With her suitcase. Can't blame her. Why couldn't you guys just leave her to mourn in peace? Why you hafta be coming around here looking for your quotes and your pictures?" She thought he was a reporter! Ward turned and hurried back down the stairs before she came out and saw him. He'd probably passed her before in the hall. What if she recognized him? What if she put two and two together and . . . ? Coming here had been a terrible idea. He hadn't seen Rosa, hadn't been able to say he was sorry for her loss. Where had she gone, anyway?

He wished he'd gone to little Larry's funeral. He couldn't, of course, but he'd listened to the radio for all the details. There were only a few mourners inside the church, according to one newscast, but "dozens gathered outside to say goodbye to the little boy they didn't know but whose death touched their hearts."

Perhaps it was because of the circumstances in which he'd died. Perhaps it was simply a slow news week in the middle of summer. But Larry's death had become *the* news. There were stories in the newspaper. The *Tribune* stories inevitably made note of the fact that Rosa had been convicted for street prostitution two years before. As if that explained something.

The callers to *Open Mic with Mike in the Mornings* believed it did. They wondered where Child Welfare had been. "They shoulda taken that little boy away from that woman, Mike," one woman said, speaking for many. "I think Welfare's scared to do their jobs because they don't want the coloureds screaming discrimination, that's what I think."

"Leaving her little one run loose all night like that!" added another caller. "They should lock her up and throw away the key. Make sure she never gets the chance to do that to no baby again."

The open-line host agreed. And called the Police Chief to demand action.

"Well, Mike, I understand your callers' concerns," the Chief explained on the air. "We're concerned too. And we will be looking into what we can do to make sure this sort of thing doesn't happen again."

"So there you have it, callers." Mike spoke directly to his listeners. "The Chief's going to do what he can. By the way, Chief, what's the latest on the investigation? Have you found the bastard—sorry for my language but that's what he is—the bastard who did this terrible thing?"

"Not yet, Mike," the Chief replied. "But we are making progress. I hope your listeners saw the composite sketch of the suspect in the newspaper this morning, or on TV last night." He laughed lightly. "If you don't mind me mentioning TV on the radio."

Ward had seen the sketch. Of a black man! Dark. Nondescript. Could have been almost anyone. Anyone *black.*

"We're investigating the possibility this may have been connected to drugs," the Chief continued. "We have information the mother may have owed money to a drug pusher."

"A drug pusher! Well, well," Mike said, talking to his audience again. "What do you think of that, callers? We have lines open this morning and we're waiting for your call—"

The intercom buzzed, startled Ward. He turned down the volume, pressed the button. "Yes?"

"Mr. Eagleson is here to see you, sir," the disembodied voice announced. "Should I send him in?"

"Please do."

"I'm sorry it's taken so long," Jack said as he closed the door behind him. "But I had to call in some favours. The news isn't good, I'm afraid."

Ward nodded. He knew it.

"A kid apparently saw you driving away. He got a pretty good description of the car. The cops have talked to him."

"But the sketch?"

"Public consumption," Jack explained. "They're afraid of stirring up the black community, especially if they don't catch the guy."

"Do they suspect—?"

"No, not yet. At least from what my friend on the force tells me. Now that the boy has been buried and once the talk shows finish chewing over the bones, well, this isn't going to be at the top of anyone's to-do list." Jack paused then. "But the cops aren't our real problem."

"What is?" Ward asked.

"There's a reporter at the *Trib*, the one who covers the Legislature, you know, the prick who tried to nail us in '70 . . . Well, apparently, he's been sniffing around. Cops think he's on to something. Checked with a guy I know at the paper and it seems like they're right. My friend there tells me he's a day or two away from putting all the pieces together."

Ward found this news strangely comforting. Part of him just wanted the uncertainty over. He was guilty. He should be punished. Would he still feel that way when his name was on the front page?

". . . only way I can think of to head it off." Jack was still talking. "So I contacted some friends of mine in the Prime Minister's Office. They're willing, but they want to move quickly. They're afraid of winding up in the middle of a mess if it becomes public. So I have to phone them tonight, let them know if you want to go ahead . . ." He waited for Ward to say something.

"What?"

"Should they go ahead? They'd announce it tomorrow morning. Look, Ward, I know this isn't what you wanted. It isn't what I wanted either. But we need to be realistic. You could end up with nothing at all . . . or worse. This way, at least you'll be a judge."

A judge!

"The paper won't touch you then. My friend says he can make sure the *Trib* puts the leash on Donovan after you're appointed. The publisher has too much respect for the judiciary to allow one of his reporters to tarnish a judge."

Ward appeared doubtful.

"There's precedent," Jack added. "Everyone knew what happened with Williams and that hooker in Sydney." Al Williams had been the Municipal Affairs minister in O'Sullivan's first term. Ward didn't know anything about a hooker. Was he the only one? "He beat her pretty bad. Cops were still looking into it when O'Sullivan named him a Provincial Court judge. End of stories. All neat and clean. Same here . . . And Williams just got Provincial Court. You'll be a Justice of the Supreme Court of Nova Scotia. For life. So . . . ?"

So?

"I'm not sure there's really a choice . . ." Jack was waiting.

"Yes," Ward said finally. "Okay."

He had come so close to standing up to Jack and Junior. Now that all seemed a long time ago.

Holy shit! Patrick Donovan couldn't believe his eyes. But there it was in black and yellow. He hadn't expected much when he heard the *clack-clack-hiccup* of the government's information wire firing up in the back of his cubicle. They always seemed to be churning out fresh propaganda. Funding for this recreation group in Yarmouth, or that new rink in Canso. O'Sullivan must be planning an early election call, Patrick thought. Before things got worse. Before his own party turned against him. It was probably another nothing announcement, but Patrick was supposed to call the desk in fifteen minutes to tell them how he planned to spend the day. His notebook was still empty. So he got up from his desk and made his way to the teletype just as the roll of canary-yellow copy paper stopped turning and the machine went silent.

ATTENTION NEWS EDS

FOR IMMEDIATE RELEASE

HALIFAX—The Honourable Seamus J. O'Sullivan announced today he has accepted "with deep regret" the resignation of the Honourable Ward Justice as Nova Scotia's Minister of Fisheries and MLA for Cabot County.

Mr. Justice has accepted a federal appointment as a Justice of the Nova Scotia Supreme Court. That announcement will be made formally by the Prime Minister's Office later this morning.

> Premier O'Sullivan praised Mr. Justice for his "outstanding contributions" to public life and said his wise counsel will be missed at the Cabinet table, as well as by him personally.
>
> "All Nova Scotians are grateful to Mr. Justice, whose unstinting dedication to the people of his riding, to the future of the fishery, and to all the citizens of his native province has made this a better place to work and live. We wish him well as he continues to make a contribution as a Justice of the Supreme Court."
>
> A graduate of the Dalhousie University Law School, Mr. Justice was first elected as the Member for Cabot County in the General Election of 1974. He was appointed to the Cabinet as Minister of Fisheries, the youngest in provincial history, and has served in that portfolio since.
>
> Mr. Justice is married to the former Victoria Cullingham, daughter of a former Nova Scotia Premier, Gerald A. Cullingham. They have two daughters.

Patrick hurried to the telephone. He wanted to get to the desk before someone there checked the wires. That way, he could make it seem as if he'd picked up the story from one of his sources instead of off the wire like every other reporter in the province.

What a great story! You had to hand it to O'Sullivan. He was a wily old bastard. On the eve of what was shaping up to be a campaign to unseat him, the man managed to pull one out of the hat. How had he convinced his chief rival to quit? Even as he waited for someone to answer the phone back in the newsroom, Patrick began making notes. Jack Eagleson. He'd need to call him. Jack was his source on the party revolt. How would Justice's resignation affect his plans to get rid of O'Sullivan?

13

April 2004

At first, Michelle was nonplussed. "I thought you didn't want to cover courts any more," she said.

"I don't," Moira replied, "but this is different." She had no intention of telling her City Editor the real reason she was so keen to be assigned to J. J. Howe's fraud trial. "It's going to be a big deal. And I covered it when he was arraigned, so it would be nice to see a story all the way through for a change. Besides," she added, hoping it would clinch the argument, "I should be able to get at least a story a day."

"Works for me," Michelle said. Moira didn't know it at the time, but Michelle had been complaining to Morton about her just the day before. Since Moira had come back from maternity leave, Michelle told the Managing Editor, she seemed less interested in coming up with story ideas of her own, or even doing the stories Michelle assigned her. Maybe this would get her going again.

And so far, even before the pretrial hearing on Melesse's pitch to use justification as a defence at trial, Moira was generating plenty of copy: a backgrounder on the reparations movement, a feature on the history of the Africville relocation and even a profile of J. J., based mostly on a long interview with Calvin Johnstone, who was more than happy to fill her in on the young man's troubled family history and J. J.'s own heroic efforts to rise above it. (J. J. himself had turned down her request for an interview; Moira heard through the grapevine he'd sold the rights to his story to some Toronto publisher.)

There was another story about the case Moira could have written, but didn't, and had no intention of doing so. Luckily, neither Morton nor Michelle knew that. And Moira had no intention of telling them about it.

Moira's more immediate concern was that the Crown had just asked the Judge to ban publication of all evidence presented during the pretrial hearing. Although defence lawyers routinely apply for such bans, ostensibly to prevent potential jurors from hearing incriminating evidence in advance of their client's actual trials, Moira had assumed Melesse wouldn't ask for one. He *wanted* publicity. She was right. But Gettings fooled her.

"Your Honour, the Crown certainly believes the defence's motion concerning justification has no merit and that, after hearing it, Your Honour will so rule," Gettings began that morning, "but we fear that allowing the defence to make this argument in the court of public opinion as well as in this court of law may irreparably taint the jury pool with extraneous and prejudicial information, and make a fair trial impossible."

"Accepted," Justice Justice replied. Judges routinely approved such requests, but the speed and ease with which Ward Justice concurred prompted the reporters to look at one another. Was this going to be another arraignment story? The judge fixed his gaze on the journalists in the spectator section, zeroing in on Moira. "The media will not publish any evidence . . . presented during this hearing . . . until the trial is over."

Damn. How could she explain that to Michelle? *Sorry, I can't write a story today, but I want to stay here anyway.* Moira could argue that covering the hearing—even if she couldn't write about what happened until after the verdict—would give her useful context when she had to write about the trial itself. Michelle would counter that the paper needed copy, not context. The *Daily Journal* was all about volume now. The paper's new owners had installed a software program to allow editors—and their bosses—to measure how many stories and how many column inches each reporter generated. Quantity was always easier to measure than quality. What if Michelle reassigned her back to general reporting? What would become of her plan then? Moira decided not to call Michelle, at least not yet.

She focused on what was happening in the courtroom instead. Courtroom 5-1, a sterile, brick-walled barn of a room, was full to overflowing, even though this was only a pretrial hearing. There were lawyers, law professors, law students, the man Moira had interviewed from the Africville Descendants' Association, several dozen other black faces, mostly young, who'd apparently come to show their support for J. J., even a sprinkling of whites who seemed, for a change, uncomfortably out of place. Moira was pleased to see that the usual contingent of court watchers—retirees mostly, who handicapped each day's cases like horse players trying to pick a winner—had decided this was the case to watch today. They greeted Moira like a long-lost sister. "Where you been? We missed you down here."

There were reporters too, of course. Since there was no official press section, the sheriff's deputies had cordoned off the first two rows in the spectator gallery for them. The CBC took up most of the first row—there was a local radio reporter, a local TV reporter, one English network TV reporter, another from the French side, a courtroom artist with her sketch pad and a shifting group of self-important producers who would flit in, listen for a few minutes, get bored and leave to hang out in the corridor and talk on their cellphones before wandering back in to see if things had got more interesting while they were gone. The CBC contingent even included two Talking Heads that the network's all-news channel, Newsworld, had hired to serve as colour commentators for its coverage of the trial. Talking Head Number One was a black liberal former Crown prosecutor from Toronto, Talking Head Number Two a white conservative professor of criminal procedure at Dalhousie University. Moira had watched the two men on the news the night before previewing today's hearing. Despite their different backgrounds, they seemed to agree too often to be interesting.

For starters, they were like-minded on the question of whether Melesse's motion would succeed. It would not. "At this point in the proceedings, justification is simply not relevant," said Talking Head Two.

"Mr. Melesse will have plenty of opportunity to make that submission prior to sentencing if his client is found guilty," agreed Talking Head Number One. "The only question the jury should have to answer is, did he do the crime? If he did, then we can talk about whether he should have to do the time."

They also agreed that the defence had erred in not asking Justice Justice to step aside because of his apparent bias during arraignment. Talking Head Number Two speculated that the defence's decision might have been tactical. "Perhaps," he suggested, "Mr. Melesse hopes the judge will say something he shouldn't during the trial, and then the defence will use that in an appeal."

Then the two men chewed over the significance of last-minute changes to the makeup of the two legal teams. Elinor Evans, the prosecutor who'd handled the Crown's file since the arraignment, had been dumped. She'd been replaced by her boss, Henry Gettings, an ambitious young lawyer everyone knew was planning to quit soon to go into private practice.

"This will be an ideal showcase for his talents," said Talking Head Number Two.

"But only if he wins," added Talking Head Number One.

Talking Head Number Two: "Touché."

They were only slightly less in tune while discussing the significance of the news that Cecil Montague, who'd preceded Talking Head Number Two as the law school's resident expert on criminal procedure, would be sitting at the defence table as what Uhuru Melesse vaguely described as an "adviser and friend to the defence."

"Our younger viewers may not recognize his name but he was the foremost criminal defence lawyer in this town in his day," Talking Head Number Two said. "He won many cases others considered unwinnable."

"That's true," Talking Head Number One, the black former prosecutor, agreed, "but what's interesting is that it's my understanding some of his most high-profile victories were in cases involving white defendants accused of crimes against black people."

"Yes," said the law school professor equally affably, "you're absolutely right. But that may be the reason he's part of the defence team. Optics. The same reason you might want to have a woman lawyer if you're a man accused of sexual assault. It might help with a jury."

"It might, if the jury even knows who he is," responded Talking Head Number One, only slightly less agreeably. "Mr. Montague hasn't been a practising lawyer for more than thirty years and, with all due respect to my academic colleague here, most ordinary citizens won't have a clue who any law professor is, let alone a retired one."

Talking Head Number Two looked less agreeable, but said nothing.

The interviewer quickly got them back on the harmonic track when he asked about Shondelle Adams. "What is her role on the defence team?"

Neither seemed certain, but both thought it couldn't be significant. Her law school colleague was dismissive, noting that "Ms. Adams is a proponent of something called critical race theory, a marginal and obscure specialty that isn't accepted as legitimate by most legal scholars, so I'm not sure what she'll be able to contribute to Mr. Howe's defence in this criminal matter."

The black former Crown was only slightly more supportive, claiming Shondelle's background in academe probably didn't prepare her for "the rough and tumble of a courtroom."

Sitting alone in her living room, sipping on her second glass of white wine, Moira laughed out loud. "You're talking about the lady with the brown envelopes, buddy," she shouted back at the TV screen. "Deep Throat."

It wasn't quite so funny that morning when Moira ended up alone in an elevator with Shondelle. Shondelle didn't say a word as the elevator made its too-slow way from the parkade to the fifth-floor courtroom. Moira guiltily tried to fill up the silence by babbling that she hadn't given up on "that story you told me about.

I'm just waiting for some confirmations, that's all." It wasn't true. And Shondelle wasn't buying. She didn't even look at Moira, didn't reply, just strode purposefully away as soon as the elevator doors opened.

Now Moira watched Shondelle and Melesse conferring at the defence table. Montague was seated by himself at the end of the table, engrossed in notes he was writing on a yellow legal pad. Shondelle's role was as much a mystery to Moira as it had been to the Talking Heads. The only thing she knew for certain was that Uhuru Melesse was a very different lawyer now than he'd been at the arraignment. He hadn't a clue then, couldn't even answer the simplest question about reparations. Now he sounded like an expert. Was that Shondelle's doing? And there was something else, too. This morning, in the scrum outside the courtroom, Melesse had looked Moira in the eye—instead of staring at her chest—when he answered her questions. Shondelle?

The changes in Ward Justice since the arraignment were much more dramatic. There'd been a hush as he hesitantly shuffled in through the judges' entrance this morning. One of the sheriff's deputies held the door for him. Did Justice have the strength to push it open himself? Moira wondered. His progress up to the bench—a distance of no more than ten feet and three steps—was interrupted twice while he stopped to catch his breath. The courthouse was rife with rumours. The Judge had stomach cancer. The Judge had brain cancer. The Judge had lung cancer. The Judge was suffering from multiple sclerosis. Lou Gehrig's disease. Alzheimer's. The judge had a brain tumour and had weeks, maybe days left. The sheriff's deputies had organized a pool on how long he would last. "You can't win if you don't play," one of them said to Moira as they invited her to pick a date and plunk down her five dollars. She declined.

The Judge had finally collapsed into his seat. He appeared to study his notes while he caught his breath. During the discussion of the publication ban, he didn't ask any questions, simply let Gettings speak, and then issued his order with an economy of words. But even that seemed to exhaust him, and there was another long silence before he spoke again.

"Mr. Melesse . . . are you . . . ready to proceed?"

"Yes, Your Honour, we are." Uhuru looked at Ward Justice, nodding in acknowledgement or, perhaps, something more significant. Moira tried to interpret the gesture, couldn't, went back to making notes.

"Thank you, Your Honour," Uhuru said, then paused again before finally plunging in: "*Actus non facit reum nisi mens sit rea* . . . Every first-year law student is familiar with that Latin maxim. Literally, it means there is no guilty act without a guilty mind. It is one of the fundamental underpinnings of our system of criminal law. In order to find someone criminally responsible, the Crown must prove that the accused voluntarily committed a guilty act—an *actus reus*—and, of equal importance, that the accused knew that what he did was wrong, that is, he possessed a guilty mind—a *mens rea*. But there is a third element that must also be satisfied before we can determine criminal liability. The *actus reus* and *mens rea* requirements must be satisfied in circumstances where no legally accepted defence is available, where there is no justification for the conduct at issue."

It sounded like a law school lecture to Moira. Had Montague written it?

"Let us consider that maxim in the context of this case," Uhuru said. "Element number one. No one is disputing that my client committed what the law would call a guilty act. My friend here," Uhuru said with a nod to Gettings at the prosecution table, "will outline for you the facts of that act. I have told him that the defence is prepared to stipulate to those facts. As Your Honour is aware, we agreed to waive our right to a preliminary hearing and proceed directly to trial.

"Element number two. Did the defendant have a guilty mind? As Your Honour is also well aware, this question is usually raised in cases where the accused is not capable of determining right from wrong, or where an accused did not anticipate the consequences of his or her actions. Neither consideration applies here. My client is an intelligent young man who would have had no difficulty distinguishing between what is legal and what is illegal—as well as what is right and wrong, moral and immoral. It is also clear that Mr. Howe did not accidentally, or even recklessly, commit these acts. On the contrary, he did them with considered, deliberate forethought—and with pride."

Moira stole a glance at J. J. Howe. He was smiling to himself.

"So that brings us to the third element the court must consider in determining whether what happened is a crime. Justification. Over the course of history, there have been plenty of unjust laws. Many of those laws were changed or revoked only because individuals challenged them by violating them.

"So the question becomes: When does a person have the moral right, perhaps even obligation, to commit an act that would otherwise be a crime? And how should the criminal justice system, a system based on the notion that there is a right and wrong, a legal and an illegal, deal with ambiguous circumstance?

"If you walk just a few blocks from this courtroom you'll find a statue of Joseph Howe, the great Nova Scotia journalist, reformer and politician. Today, we venerate Howe, in part, for a crime he committed. In March of 1835, Howe published an attack on the local magistrates and police which accused them of stealing more than thirty thousand pounds from the public treasury. He was charged with criminal libel. At his trial, the presiding judge instructed the jury that the words in the article constituted a libel on the magistrates, the truth being no defence against libel. Howe admitted publishing the article, the judge told them, so the jury's duty was clear. Joseph Howe was guilty. Ten minutes later, the jury returned with a verdict of not guilty." Uhuru paused, looked around the courtroom. "What would that jury have said about the conduct of the Howe before you today . . . James Joseph Howe?"

Uhuru paused again, took a sip from a glass of water on the defence table, acknowledged Montague as if, Moira imagined, to say thanks for that.

"In the 1850s in the United States, there was a law, the Fugitive

Slave Law, that required federal officers to return runaway slaves to their 'rightful' owners. Although the law was on the books and people were charged under it, many juries in the northern states refused to convict anyone accused of that crime. The law was eventually repealed.

"In more recent times, in this country, Dr. Henry Morgentaler challenged Canada's abortion law by violating it. From 1969 to 1984, he was charged on four separate occasions with performing illegal abortions. In each case, a jury acquitted him. Finally, in 1988, the Supreme Court of Canada declared Canada's abortion law unconstitutional.

"In 1982, a Nova Scotia woman named Jane Stafford was charged with first-degree murder after she killed her husband with a shotgun while he slept. A clear case of murder? No, the jury decided. After listening to gruesome testimony about the physical and sexual abuse she and her children had suffered at the hands of her husband, the jury accepted the defence argument that Jane Stafford acted in self-defence, even though it was clear that the usual requirement for self-defence—an immediate threat—was not present.

"The common thread in those cases: the jury. When it comes to changing the law to meet the realities of changing times, juries—what we in the legal business like to call 'the conscience of the community'—have played a most critical role. Jurors are triers of fact; they pick and choose among the facts presented, give more weight to some facts and less to others. But juries can only exercise this very important role in society if they are given the opportunity to hear *all* of the evidence. We would submit, Your Honour, that in this particular case that means hearing about the history of Africville and the unjust treatment of its citizens by government officials during the past one hundred and fifty years. It also means hearing about the evolving legal concept of reparations and what role it may have played in my client's actions.

"During the 1960s, as Your Honour well knows"—Uhuru gave the judge a you-know-where-I'm-coming-from-here look; Moira was sure of it this time—"the City of Halifax connived to confiscate the homes and lands of the people of Africville. It destroyed their community. If the same thing were to happen today, it would almost certainly be challenged under Canada's Charter of Rights and Freedoms. There was no such Charter then.

"The City of Halifax *stole* their heritage and, for more than thirty years, it has refused to compensate the former residents for their loss, let alone acknowledge the wrong done to them.

"I'm not the only one to describe what happened to the citizens of Africville as state-sanctioned theft. The United Nations itself recently looked into this matter and last month issued a report calling on Canada to pay reparations for these crimes against the people of Africville, against humanity. So we are not reaching when we talk about theft, or about reparations.

"J. J. Howe is a child of Africville. His parents were both born in Africville. As teenagers in the sixties, they were among those whose families were forcibly uprooted from their homes and dumped in Maynard Square. J. J. Howe came of age in that soulless concrete jungle of public housing. He saw its deleterious effects on his mother and father, who both became drug addicts and petty criminals. He saw its impact on his relatives, friends and other former residents of Africville. And he couldn't help but see the City's indifference to the plight of the residents and to their legitimate claims for compensation.

"He saw all of that and . . . he acted." Uhuru looked back at his client, smiled. J. J. smiled back, his face smug with self-satisfaction. "James Joseph—J. J.—Howe acted in good conscience to right a terrible wrong," Uhuru said.

After a pause to allow his words to burrow into the heads of the spectators, Uhuru resumed. "Your Honour, we are prepared to call expert witnesses who will tell you all about the history of Africville and the sense of pride and community that existed there for more than one hundred years before the City of Halifax ripped apart the residents' homes and lives.

"If Your Honour permits, we will adduce evidence—deeds, documents, eyewitnesses, legal experts—to show how the City stole the land out from under the people who called it home, how the City paid the residents much less than their land was worth, and how it used blackmail and the threat of expropriation to achieve its nefarious ends.

"We will also tell you the very human story of what happened to the people whose community was destroyed. And to their children and grandchildren. You will hear from witnesses who will establish beyond doubt the human cost of this officially sanctioned theft of the soul of a community.

"And, finally, we will offer evidence demonstrating beyond any doubt the thirty years of official indifference, even hostility, that has greeted the efforts of the former residents to win compensation for their losses."

Uhuru paused, looked over at Gettings. "I can see my friend at the Crown table is getting impatient. What does any of this have to do with the case before us? he wants to know.

"My answer is: *everything*. We believe that understanding this history and background is critical to understanding the true nature of what my client did and, ultimately, enabling a jury to determine the guilt or innocence of my client.

"Can the courts really consider what Justice Hill in Ontario recently referred to as 'social factors' in criminal cases? In the case before Justice Hill, two women had been found guilty of acting as drug mules, bringing cocaine into this country from Jamaica. Both women were black single mothers of three children. In his decision, the judge reiterated an earlier court decision that, when sentencing offenders, judges are 'entitled to take judicial notice of the history of discrimination faced by disadvantaged groups in society.' Your Honour, the defence takes the position, and we shall argue, that those principles should be taken into account during trial, too.

"There is precedent for this right here in Nova Scotia. Your Honour will recall the case, I'm sure. In 1994, a Family Court judge named Corinne Sparks—the first African–Nova Scotian woman appointed to the bench in this province, I might add—acquitted a black teenager accused of assaulting a white police officer. In doing so, Her Honour brought her own experience as a black person to consideration of the evidence. As she explained it to the Crown: 'I'm not saying that the police officer overreacted, but certainly police officers do overreact, particularly when they're dealing with non-white groups.'

"Her decision was overturned by the Nova Scotia courts, which claimed her statement showed a bias against the police officer. The issue went to the Supreme Court of Canada. On September 26, 1997, the majority concluded that Judge Sparks was simply engaging in a process of 'contextualized judging,' which was entirely proper and conducive to a fair and just resolution of the case before her.

"What we are asking this court today is to allow us to provide the jurors in this case with the context to render a fair and just verdict. Thank you."

Uhuru sat down. The courtroom was quiet, as if everyone was trying to come to terms with the argument Uhuru had just made. Shondelle reached over and put her hand on his. Montague nodded approvingly.

"A fifteen-minute recess," Justice Justice announced into the void. "Then Mr. . . . Gettings . . . will have his say."

"All rise."

Moira looked at her watch. This morning's session had started thirty minutes later than scheduled and now, less than an hour into it, the judge was calling a break. Moira watched as Mr. Justice Justice hesitatingly made his way down the steps and out the door. Could he really last to the end of the trial? she wondered. She hoped so. For her sake as well as his.

By the time court resumed, more than half an hour after the announced fifteen-minute break, many of the private television reporters and their camera operators had left. Their bosses had decided there must be better things for them to do than listen to evidence they couldn't report. Moira had avoided a similar fate only because she hadn't called Michelle to tell her about the ban. Perhaps during the lunch break?

Now it was Henry Gettings's turn. While his prematurely white hair and horn-rimmed half-glasses gave him lawyerly *gravitas*, his boyish, unlined face and infectious smile offered a humanizing counterpoint.

"Your Honour," he began, with a bow in the direction of the Judge, "my friend here would like you to believe this case is something it's not. Despite everything that's been said inside this courtroom this morning and everything that's been in the press in the days leading up to this hearing, this is a routine, run-of-the-mill, open-and-shut criminal case. James Joseph Howe, who was in a position of public trust, took money that did not belong to him. He breached that trust. He stole money. There is no excuse for that. He is guilty. And he must pay a price for his criminal acts.

"A few moments ago, my friend offered this court an entertaining, if not completely illuminating—and certainly not complete—lecture on criminal liability in which he pointed out, correctly, that one of the elements the court must satisfy in determining criminal liability is that there is no legally accepted defence for the acts in question.

"Let me emphasize, as my friend did not: *legally accepted.* 'The Devil made me do it,' is not a legally accepted defence." There were titters in the audience. Score one for the prosecution. "In my respectful submission, Your Honour, that is exactly what the defence is asking you to accept here today. Mr. Melesse tells a good tale, and it is easy to get caught up in the morality of his little play.

"As an individual, I confess I found myself agreeing with Mr. Melesse that this city may very well have acted unfairly when it took that land back in the late sixties." Was Gettings rehearsing for his political future? "But that was . . . what? Thirty-five years ago? Almost forty? Certainly before this defendant was born. *That's* the problem—or should I say, one of the problems—with my friend's arguments. How can something that happened before the defendant was even born be used now to justify a criminal act? The answer is: it can't.

"There are legitimate legal forums where the issue of the Africville relocation, even reparations, can be debated. As I understand it," Gettings said, looking over at Shondelle, "there is already a civil suit dealing with this very matter working its way through the judicial system. *That* is the proper forum for this discussion.

"The defence says it will produce witnesses who can describe for this court the deleterious effects the relocation has had on various individuals and their children and their children's children. I'm sure they can. Should the Crown then counter those witnesses by calling its own witnesses—even my friend himself, perhaps—whose lives and careers can, equally, be taken out of context to demonstrate the *beneficial* effects of relocation? I am not being totally disingenuous here, Your Honour. My point is that, while it would be easy enough for Mr. Melesse and I to bring forward duelling witnesses to try to score debating points, that, in the end would prove nothing in terms of the case before you. In fact, such an exercise is irrelevant to the real matter at hand. And that matter is this. Is James Joseph Howe guilty of the charges against him? That . . . and only that . . . is the question we must answer at trial.

"I do take my friend's point—or at least part of his point—in reference to the drug courier case he referred to in his written submission and, again, here today. In that case the judge noted his right to take judicial notice of the history of discrimination against a particular group at the time of sentencing. Mr. Melesse talked about the case, but he glossed over that important qualification. *At the time of sentencing.* If there really are mitigating circumstances, they should be raised at the appropriate time . . . after a conviction and before sentencing.

"My friend was also less than fully forthcoming in his presentation of some of the other cases he mentioned this morning. It is worth noting, for example, that higher courts overturned the Morgentaler acquittals, once even substituting a guilty verdict for the jury's not guilty.

"The goal of the defence in those cases was different too. Dr. Morgentaler set out to change what he considered a bad law. He publicly flouted the Criminal Code of the day, practically inviting the police to charge him so he could challenge the law's legitimacy, so he could have his day in court. James Joseph Howe, on the other hand, got caught fudging the books. He got *caught.* Mr. Melesse's client doesn't want to change a bad law; he just wants the court to say that the law shouldn't apply to him.

"The final outcome of the Stafford case—not the interim ending my friend chose to focus on—may be more germane to the case before this court today. In that case, involving the woman who shot her husband, the Nova Scotia Court of Appeal threw out the jury's verdict and ordered a new trial. Before that new trial could take place, however, Ms. Stafford agreed to plead guilty to manslaughter. At *that* point, the judge took note of the acknowledged circumstances of her abuse and sentenced her to serve just six months in jail.

"So, Your Honour, it is my respectful submission that, if there is a time to deal with these issues, sentencing is the appropriate point in the legal process for the court to do so. I would ask Your Honour to reject the defence motion and instruct Mr. Melesse to save his documents and his witnesses for that more appropriate moment."

Justice Justice did not. Having already read their written submissions and listened to their oral arguments, the Judge didn't even retire to his chambers to consider his decision.

"Thank you, gentlemen," he said, his words coming in exhausting spurts. "You both make . . . excellent points. But I am more . . . persuaded . . . by Mr. Melesse. Defence may make arguments and call . . . witnesses . . . at trial based on the . . . claim of necessity. We will . . . begin jury . . . selection at . . . nine-thirty Monday . . . morning. We are . . . adjourned . . . till . . . then."

"All rise."

That was it? thought Moira. No learned citations of case law, no carefully weighed on-the-one-hand this, on-the-other-hand that balancing of legal principles? Just a gasped I-am-more-persuaded . . . ?

Moira looked over at the Talking Heads, who were already deep in conference with their producer. Probably trying to explain how they both could have been so wrong about the outcome of today's hearing. She made a mental note to tune in tonight to see how they would explain it away. Except, of course, they couldn't. By banning publication of the evidence, Justice Justice had effectively saved the Talking Heads from themselves. But not Moira from Michelle. She put her notebook in her purse, took out her cellphone and dialled her City Editor. She had some explaining to do too.

It was so much easier when he let the machine do all the hard work. Ward Justice slumped back in the high-backed leather chair he'd had his secretary position strategically just inside the door to his office, held the plastic mask to his face with his right hand and felt the life-giving oxygen fill what was left of his lungs.

He knew now he should have taken the tank with him into the courtroom. Why hadn't he? Vanity? Fear that people might realize just how sick he was? How could he have thought they wouldn't notice his condition, mask or no mask? he wondered now. He'd imagined it would be easier, that sitting up there on the bench looking down on the courtroom, the words would magically flow from his lips. The words! In his left hand, he still clutched the dozen sheets of foolscap he'd filled last night with so many fine but now unspoken words. He'd carefully weighed the lawyers' written arguments and counter-arguments, consulted cases, honed his phrases, crafted his decision, leaving room here and there to insert additional comments as needed, based on anything new the Crown or defence might add during oral arguments. He'd planned to read his decision aloud at the conclusion of this morning's hearing, but quickly realized after he made it to the bench this morning he would not have the strength or breath for such an exertion.

Why hadn't he just said thank you very much, he would consider the arguments and render a written decision in the fullness of time? Perhaps it was because he knew his days were limited, and he didn't want to waste any of them. Or perhaps, more likely, it was because he wasn't nearly as confident in his judicial reasoning as he wished he was. He knew what he wanted to conclude; he just couldn't find a solid legal basis for doing so. Now, it would be up to an appeal court—if it came to that—to interpret his cryptic decision. Perhaps they would find better reasons than he to uphold his judgment. Not that it would matter. Ward would be dead. He would have done his duty. Ray would have had the chance to make his case for J. J. Howe—and for Africville—in a public forum. Now it was up to Uhuru.

The trial itself had almost immediately settled into the predictable rhythms and routines that Moira—with more fondness now than in the days when she'd been the beat reporter—associated with courts. During a trial, the courtroom became a cocoon into which the larger world did not intrude. Moira could not have told you what was happening in the war in Iraq, for example, or which teams were playing for the Stanley Cup, or whether the provincial government was really going to rescind the 10 percent income tax cut it had announced last year. And she didn't care. With the exception of the hour or so she spent playing with or reading to little Patrick each night, her life centred around this courtroom and this case.

The trial itself played out as a series of dramatic set pieces with everyone—Crown, defence, judge, jury, court clerk, sheriff's deputies, reporters, spectators—performing their specific assigned roles within the larger play. But as soon as the Judge called a recess, it was if they really were actors on a rehearsal break who could slip out of their characters and joke and gossip with their fellow actors. And there were plenty of such recesses in this trial. Perhaps because of his health, Mr. Justice Justice had scheduled two fifteen-minute breaks during the mornings and two more in the afternoons (in truth, each recess usually dragged on for half an hour).

During these breaks, Moira loved to eavesdrop on the conversations around her. The court clerk flirted with a sheriff's deputy; this morning, Moira had overheard them making a dinner date. The deputy, Moira knew, was married. In another corner, J. J. and the Crown's forensic auditor, who'd testified against him on the second day of the trial, discussed the relative merits of two accounting software packages. In the spectator section, Shondelle held court with a group of a half-dozen black female law students who'd apparently decided to make the trial some sort of class project—and Shondelle their role model. Uhuru and Calvin Johnstone stood out in the hallway sipping coffee and swapping reminiscences of their childhoods in Africville.

No one talked about the trial, as if by unspoken agreement. Not that there'd been much worth talking about. Except, of course, for that brief, puzzling moment during jury selection when the defence had used one of its peremptory challenges to dismiss the only black person who had been selected from the jury pool. After a whispered discussion among the three defence lawyers, Uhuru stood up to ask the Judge to excuse the man. Even the Judge seemed surprised. But he did as he was asked. "The Court thanks . . . you for coming here . . . this morning. You are free . . . to go."

The Talking Heads could offer no logical explanation as to why the defence would not want to have a black man on the jury, but that didn't stop them from filling up that night's episode talking about it. Which turned out to be their best show all week.

The trial's first three days, in fact, had been boring. Gettings tediously laid out the Crown's case against J. J. Howe. Even though Uhuru had made it clear it was unnecessary—"the defence is prepared to stipulate to those facts," he'd said—Gettings insisted on establishing the details of the crime "for the sake of the record." Moira thought it more likely Gettings wanted to make sure he had his own moment in the media spotlight. He certainly did his best to prolong it. He used up most of a morning leading the City's internal auditor through an explanation of the procedures the City employed to monitor spending and flag possible cases of fraud or misappropriation before even arriving at the specifics of J.J.'s transgression. Later, he led the police detective in charge of the case through an equally interminable dissection of the techniques he'd used and how they'd led him, inevitably, inexorably, to the conclusion that J.J. had done the dirty deed.

Uhuru's cross-examinations were brief and to the point. He got the auditor to sheepishly admit that his laboriously explained auditing procedures had failed to detect $12,000 J. J. had—in Uhuru's delicate phrase—"redeployed," and that he had only discovered this additional missing money after J. J. had showed him where to find the records of each of the transactions.

His questioning of the detective was equally succinct.

"Detective, when you went to his rooming house to arrest Mr. Howe, did he resist?"

"No."

"How would you describe his demeanour at that time?"

"Well," the detective said, "he was co-operative. He said he'd been waiting for us to catch him and that he'd be happy to have his day in court. A lot of what he said—about Africville and reparations—didn't make much sense to me at the time and I don't remember the details very well." He paused, as if trying to conjure up those details. "Oh, yes, there was one other thing he said." The detective paused again, a smile playing at the corner of his lips.

"Yes, detective?" Uhuru encouraged him.

"He asked for you."

The spectators laughed.

Even though the Judge had already ruled that Uhuru could mount his justification defence, Gettings still popped up like a jack-in-the-box to challenge every single witness Uhuru tried to call.

"Professor Wilmot may be an expert on local history and may have written articles on Africville, Your Honour, but I fail to see what relevant testimony he has to offer the court in this case . . ."

"I'm sure I would find Dr. Robertson's dissertation on the history of reparations most enlightening and, if Mr. Melesse would like to rent a hall for him to speak, I'd be the first in the door. But I don't believe we should be spending taxpayers' dollars and taking up precious courtroom time with such extraneous matters when the real question before this court is whether Mr. Howe stole more than $300,000 from the taxpayers of this city."

The judge overruled every single one of Gettings's objections. "I think I'd . . . like to hear what . . . this witness has to say," was all he ever said, but it was more than enough to give the CBC's Talking Heads something to discuss. Which was also a good thing, since the expert testimony itself was as riveting as an academic essay. By the trial's sixth day, Moira's stories were being relegated to the inside of the paper and weren't even promoted in a box on the front page.

That's not to say some of the information wasn't interesting. Professor Wilmot quoted a 1954 report from the City Manager recommending the residents be relocated. "The area is not suited for residences," it said, "but, properly developed, is ideal for industrial purposes." So much, Moira thought, for the City's later claim that it had moved the residents "for humanitarian reasons."

But much of the testimony consisted of obscure legal arguments that might have been critical in law but were mind-numbing in print. "Maybe this wasn't such a good idea," Michelle fretted on the phone the morning after Wilmot's testimony. "Morton says we'll give it to the end of the week, but if there aren't any fireworks by then, he wants me to reassign you back into general and let Anne work it in around her other court stuff, maybe with a brief or something."

Moira did her best to be reassuring. "I think we're past the worst of it," she said. "Robertson should be finished today, and then I hear the defence is going to call former residents. J.J's parents. That should be a good show."

"I hope so," Michelle said.

"Me too," Moira added. She did not feel much more confident than her editor sounded.

"No further questions," Uhuru Melesse said. He turned away from Jeffrey Jack Howe—J.J. the Elder—and looked over at Henry Gettings. "Your witness," he said.

It had gone better than he'd hoped. Or had it? Uhuru Melesse was no longer sure whether he was winning or losing, or whether this—whatever "this" was—was the right strategy. He spent his days in the courtroom, his nights either reading transcripts of his days in the courtroom or prepping for the next day's witnesses. When he wasn't consumed by the case itself, he was trying to deal with its fallout. He worried about how he would pay this month's rent. He worried about whether to accept Shondelle's offer to pay last month's rent. What would saying yes mean? No? After they made love, Uhuru would fall asleep, wake up, worry, fall asleep, have a dream about winning, a nightmare about losing, wake up again. Sweating. Between times, he and Shondelle would argue about trial tactics and whether the toilet seat should be up or down.

Shondelle had urged him to begin J. J.'s defence case by calling one of the former residents to testify. "After Gettings finishes putting them to sleep," she argued, "you've got to wake the jury up, show them there's a human side." Uhuru had resisted. The key, he said, was to build their case carefully and conventionally, laying out the context with historians and experts, then bringing in the former residents to show what their lives had been like before and after the relocation. Once that was done, they could parade representatives from the various organizations to which J. J. had given money, all of whom would testify to the good—and vital—works the City's money had paid for. And then, finally, just before the jury began its deliberations, he would call J. J.'s parents to demonstrate, in the starkest terms possible, what ultimately drove J. J. to do what he did, what *justified* his otherwise illegal actions.

"I agree with everything you've said, Mr. Melesse, except for ending your case with Mr. Howe's parents," Cecil Montague had offered softly, almost apologetically, at their first meeting. "It's too risky."

Why hadn't he listened? Uhuru wondered now.

A month before the trial was scheduled to begin, Uhuru's old law school professor had called, seemingly out of the blue, to offer his services, *pro bono*, to the defence team. "I'd be pleased to do anything you feel would be helpful," he'd explained on the phone.

At first, Uhuru had been skeptical; it was Shondelle who had convinced him that Montague could be an asset. "Let's face it," she'd said, "neither of us has any experience with actual trials. Montague does."

"But—"

"And the fact is," she cut him off, "the man has won plenty of cases nobody thought he could—or should—win."

"But—"

"I know. A long time ago he got some racist white boys off who should still be in jail. But isn't that what we're trying to do here, too? Free a black man who, according to a strict interpretation of the law, should be going to jail?"

After he'd agreed to have Montague join the defence team, Uhuru discovered that Montague's surprising call to him had come as no surprise to Shondelle. Even though he'd been retired for close to a decade, Montague still maintained an office and some influence at the law school. In fact, he'd been a key champion of Shondelle's hiring, and was currently promoting her undeclared campaign to become the school's first African-Canadian dean when the current one retired in two years.

After he'd found out that Shondelle was involved in the Howe defence, Montague had begun sending her long, detailed memos full of legal theory—even suggesting at one point the possibility of a constitutional challenge—and courtroom strategies, many of which Shondelle had later presented to Uhuru as her own. At first, however, even she had dismissed outright Montague's contrarian ideas about jury selection. When he did finally convince her of their logic, Shondelle allowed that she wasn't sure she could get Uhuru to agree.

"Why not let me try?" Montague had suggested over lunch one day. "I've got time on my hands and, who knows, maybe there are some other ways I could be useful to your case." It was not lost on Shondelle that the presence of a distinguished-looking, white-haired white guy at the defence table might be reassuring to a jury, especially an all-white jury.

And that was the essence of Montague's counterintuitive argument on jury selection. "Pick yourself a jury that's white and middle class and new to Halifax," he urged Uhuru when they met. "This isn't the city it was when I was practising, or even when you graduated from law school, Mr. Melesse. It's more cosmopolitan. Lots of new people. They're better educated, more liberal, or at least want to be seen that way. They've probably never heard of Africville and they'll be appalled when they find out what the City did. They'll want to acquit Mr. Howe for that reason alone. You want folks like that on your jury.

"What you don't want are people who grew up here, ones like me. They'll remember Africville as a slum and believe the City was trying to do the right thing by moving the people out. Even if they don't remember much about Africville itself, they won't want to see their hometown's name dragged through the national press as some racist backwater. They've had enough of that over the years, and they'll blame your client for embarrassing them again.

"So what I'm suggesting, Mr. Melesse, is go for an all-white jury, but a middle-class white jury made up of folks who've lived in the city for no more than the last ten or fifteen years."

"Why all white?" Uhuru asked. Defensive now. Resentful, too. Was Montague really a racist? "Don't you think black people would be sympathetic to our case?" How could a white guy know how blacks think?

"Some would, of course," Montague answered without rancour. "But you can't assume all black people are going to think the way you want them to." He paused, smiled to himself. He knew it was ludicrous for a white man to be telling a black man how black people thought. He continued anyway. "They're just as different as white folks. So you have to be at least as careful about any blacks you select for your jury. Maybe more so. Your best prospects, it seems to me, will have characteristics opposite to your white jurors. You want poor, or at least working-class people who've lived in this community all their lives and who remember what it was like to be black in Halifax during the sixties and seventies. The problem is that, for whatever reason, those people aren't usually well represented in jury pools. So you may not have anyone like that to choose from.

"What you don't want—at least in my view—are black jurors from the business and professional classes, or blacks who've moved here from somewhere else. They're anxious to look forward, not backward. They're living in the white suburbs trying to fit in, and they aren't going to want to do anything that would make their colour an issue. The come-from-aways tend to look down on the locals anyway, and they'll figure this isn't their fight."

Montague stopped, allowed silence to weave its questions and doubts. Then he laughed. "What a crock!" he said. "Here I am sitting in a room with a black professional and a black come-from-away—both of whom I'd kill to get on my jury in a case like this!" Montague looked from one to the other; their expressions were puzzled now. "I apologize. It's the old professor in me," Montague explained. "I just wanted to make the point that you shouldn't get caught up thinking of your jury in simple black and white terms. In too many cases, the easiest stereotypes don't work. And even the more sophisticated stereotypes are stereotypes. Make no mistake: who you get on this jury is going to determine whether you win or lose. All I'm trying to do is get you to think outside the clichés, to know all you can about each potential juror before you say yea or nay."

All of which seemed intended as a backdrop and lead-up to Montague's offer to put together a dossier on each potential juror. Using his own money, Montague hired two law students to assist him in tracking down information.

That was how they'd discovered that jury pool member sixty-five—a black software engineer, originally from Uganda, who was married to a white woman and lived in an expensive south-end condo overlooking the Northwest Arm—was also a frequent contributor to an American online discussion group for black professionals opposed to affirmative action.

If it hadn't been for Montague, Uhuru knew, jury pool member sixty-five would almost certainly have been sitting in judgment of his client today. Still, Uhuru wasn't comfortable that they'd ended up with an all-white jury in a case that so clearly turned on race. Just as he wasn't sure any more that he should have insisted, against Montague's advice, on calling J. J.'s father as the final witness for the defence. When Uhuru had finally got the chance to interview him in jail, Howe had repeatedly answered his questions by asking him what he wanted him to say. "I'll say what you want," he'd said. "Just tell me what it is." (Uhuru had planned to put J. J.'s mother, Jaina, on the stand too, but no one had been able to find her to serve the subpoena.)

J. J. the Elder's sorry track record with the law, coupled with whatever all those drugs had done to his brain, would have made him a chancy witness under the best of circumstances. But Uhuru's bull-headedness in insisting on calling him as the final witness meant that his testimony—and worse, his cross-examination at the hands of Gettings—was what jurors would remember going into the jury room.

Gettings was smarter than Uhuru had given him credit for. And better prepared. In the beginning, Gettings had done little more than raise objections to Uhuru's witnesses. For the record. For the appeal, in case it ever came to that. He hadn't cross-examined any of Uhuru's expert witnesses, creating the impression for the jury that what they had to say wasn't all that significant.

Although he still bounced to his feet like a schoolboy to object every time Uhuru called a new witness, those interjections had now become perfunctory. Once Gettings had belatedly realized that Ward Justice, for whatever reason, was willing to give the defence latitude to present its case, he began to focus on subtly undermining each defence witness instead. His cross-examinations were delivered as little more than gentle pokings and proddings, but Uhuru could feel the bruises they were inflicting.

After Uhuru had led Calvin Johnstone through his examination-in-chief, for example—getting Calvin to paint a more idyllic than realistic picture of growing up in Africville, followed by an apocalyptic vision of the relocation ("When they came and bulldozed my Aunt Mame's house, they gave her just ten minutes to get out. She was crying. Everyone was upset . . ."), followed by a chronology of his own years of unsuccessful lobbying and negotiations to convince the City to compensate the former residents—Gettings got his chance on cross to do some damage.

"You told my friend that you are the president of the Africville Descendants' Association. Is that correct?"

"Yes."

"Now that association has filed a civil suit against the City in connection with these matters. Is that correct?"

"Yes."

"So you have a direct interest in the outcome of this case. Is that correct?"

"Uh—"

"Objection." Uhuru wasn't sure what he was objecting to, but it didn't matter.

"Withdrawn," Gettings said. He would let the question do its insidious work. "Is yours the only organization that purports to represent a cross-section of the former residents, Mr. Johnstone?"

"Yes. We're the only one."

"Now, as president of this organization, Mr. Johnstone, would you be aware of the names of most of your members?"

"Yes."

"Would you know whether the defendant was ever a member of your organization?"

"Not to my knowledge."

"Has Mr. Howe ever held an executive position with the organization?"

"No."

"So I take it then that Mr. Howe was never authorized to speak—or act—on behalf of the organization, or negotiate with the City in the name of former Africville residents, or . . . decide how much the former residents should get in compensation, or how it should be paid out and to whom. Correct?"

Calvin looked at Uhuru, his eyes pleading for rescue. But there was nothing Uhuru could do. "Y-y-yes," he said finally.

"Okay, let's leave that for now and let me ask you . . . have you ever been convicted of a criminal offence, Mr. Johnstone?"

Calvin looked suitably surprised, then indignant. "No."

"You're a teacher?"

"Retired."

"After forty years, I believe."

"Forty-one."

"Right, forty-one years. A long and, from what I have been told, distinguished career. For which you are to be congratulated. Now, Mr. Johnstone, you testified, in what I can only describe as pretty compelling terms, about the bad things that happened to young people from Africville after the relocation." He paused long enough for the spectators to connect the dots of his questions. "Luckily," he continued, "those bad things didn't seem to happen to you. Do you have any statistics to show that former residents of Africville are more likely to commit crimes or be dope addicts or end up involved in street prostitution than other members of the black community?"

"No, I don't." Gettings had phrased his question perfectly to elicit the instinctively huffy response he got from Calvin.

"Well, then, would you agree with me that, in this courtroom, we have at least two concrete examples—yourself and my friend, Mr. Melesse—of individuals who grew up in Africville, were part of this 'forced relocation' and became fine, upstanding, productive members of our community?"

"Your Honour, I—"

Gettings waved Uhuru off. "No need to answer, Mr. Johnstone. Perhaps it was an unfair question. But let me ask you one more thing. Was your father an intelligent man?" Calvin looked puzzled. "I ask that because, as you know, he was a part of the citizens' committee that negotiated the terms of the relocation with the City. Isn't that so?"

"Yes, but—" Calvin knew he was being set up. Again.

Gettings pulled out a photocopied page from a three-ring binder on the Crown table. "I have here a clipping from the Halifax *Tribune* dated August 12, 1970, that I'll give to the clerk in a moment. But first, Mr. Johnstone," he handed the paper to Calvin, "I wonder if you could read for the members of the jury the section highlighted in yellow marker."

Calvin pushed his glasses up on top of his head. "Ah, let me see . . ."

He used his finger to guide his eyes along the column of type. "Deacon Johnstone dismissed criticism of the settlements between the City and residents. 'This was a fair process and a fair outcome,' he told the *Tribune* Tuesday, the day after the last resident was relocated. 'Those who suggest otherwise are just making trouble. As God is my witness . . .'" Calvin stopped, wishing he didn't have to continue, then did. "'As God is my witness, this was an honourable outcome achieved by honourable men in an honourable process.'"

"Thank you, Mr. Johnstone." Gettings looked to the Judge. "That's all I have for this witness, Your Honour."

Uhuru did his best to mitigate the damage in redirect. "Now, Mr. Johnstone, my friend had you read from a newspaper clipping indicating that, in 1970, your father supported the relocation. Did he change his mind about that?"

Calvin looked relieved. "Yes, he did. In his later years, he became an outspoken critic of the settlement."

"Thank you, Mr. Johnstone."

There had been no salvaging Aunt Annie's testimony. Uhuru and Shondelle had prepped Aunt Annie carefully, but it all fell apart the moment she was called to the stand. "I think she's just a lonely old woman who realized she had an audience for the first time in a long time and decided to take advantage," Shondelle speculated later.

Annie referred to Uhuru as "Ray" and offered a familiar hello to the Judge that caused nervous laughter among the spectators. "You look like you're wasting away, young man," she said sternly to Ward. "You stop by my place and I'll fix you lunch."

When Uhuru asked her how she'd come into possession of Lawrence Carter's account of his encounter with Jack Eagleson, she called it "your daddy's diary," even though Uhuru and Shondelle had both cautioned her several times before she testified that she should refer to Uhuru's father as Lawrence Carter. "I'm sorry," she blurted out on the stand as soon as she realized her mistake. "I know you told me not to call him that, but I just keep forgetting." That, of course, only made matters worse.

Things went from worse to worst when Uhuru tried to get her to say that the relocation had led to greater poverty and more criminal behaviour among former residents and their children. Uhuru knew it was a tricky question. While there was truth to the argument, he also knew many former residents who'd done well for themselves resented that broad-brush characterization. That's why he'd spent so long with Aunt Annie, rehearsing the question and answer.

On the stand, it was as if Annie had suddenly decided the question itself offended her. "We're good people," she said, looking beyond Uhuru to the spectators, "no worse than nobody else." Uhuru tried a couple of other approaches but none had the desired effect so he finally gave up and sat down.

To crown his humiliation, Gettings got up, walked slowly toward Annie as if lost in thought, then turned back to the courtroom and smiled. "I have no questions," he said.

Gettings would, Uhuru knew, have questions for Jeffrey Jack Howe. They shouldn't have put him on the stand. What was he thinking? But J. J. the Elder was the only witness who could describe, in a way that might shock the jury into sympathy for his son, the family's personal history.

J. J. himself could have told that story, but Uhuru and Shondelle had agreed months ago not to let him testify. "Too dangerous," Uhuru said, and Shondelle agreed. So did Montague. It wasn't just that testifying would open him up to a potentially devastating cross-examination. The shy young man Uhuru had met in the holding cells two years ago had come to believe his own press clippings and was eager to make the courtroom his pulpit. "Loose cannon," Uhuru said, and Shondelle agreed. Luckily, J. J. had not insisted on his right to testify; he seemed to have lost interest in the case itself, spending most of his hours outside the courtroom meeting with the author who was ghost-writing his autobiography. But that meant J. J. the Elder had to carry the burden of the human side of the defence case.

"Mr. Howe, can you tell the court your present place of residence?" Uhuru had begun his examination-in-chief as gently as possible.

"Springhill." J. J. the Elder blinked every few seconds, as if he were unused to the light. His eyes darted nervously about the courtroom.

"When you say Springhill, are you referring to the medium-security institution in Springhill?"

"The jail, yeah."

"What are you in jail for?"

Howe thought for a moment, as if he couldn't remember what crime he'd been caught for this time. "Armed robbery . . . I had a gun."

"Have you been in jail before, Mr. Howe?"

"Uh-huh."

"How many times?"

Howe furrowed his brow, tried to calculate, gave up. "I can't remember," he said.

"More than . . . half a dozen?"

"Yeah, sure, more than that."

"Are you married, Mr. Howe?"

"Married?" He was having trouble keeping up with the change in topic.

"Do you have a wife?" Uhuru tried again.

"Oh, yeah, sure."

"Do you know where she is now?"

"Right now? No . . ."

"When was the last time you had contact with her?"

"The last time? Probably . . . you know . . . when I was sentenced."

"That would have been almost three years ago?"

"Yeah, I guess."

"Is your wife a drug addict, Mr. Howe?"

Howe looked at the Judge. "She gonna be in trouble?"

"Don't worry, Mr. Howe," Ward Justice offered gently. "I think Mr. Melesse . . . is simply trying to establish . . . a history here."

Howe thought about that for a moment. "Okay, yeah, Jaina uses."

"Crack cocaine?"

"That. Whatever's around."

"Have you ever been convicted of a drug offence, Mr. Howe?"

"Uh-huh." He squirmed uncomfortably in the witness chair.

"More than once?"

". . . Yeah."

"When did you first start to use drugs, Mr. Howe?"

"First time? When I was fifteen."

"Where were you living then?"

"Then? Maynard Square."

"Can you tell us the circumstances the first time you used drugs?"

"Well, it was just a bunch of us hanging around, you know, shootin' the—uh, and some guy comes up, like, and he asks if we wanna joint."

"Was he a dealer?"

"A dealer? He sold stuff if that's what you mean."

"Were drugs easily available in Maynard Square?"

Howe smiled for the first time. "Yeah, easy . . ."

"Where were you born, Mr. Howe?"

"Africville."

"How old were you when your family moved to Maynard Square?"

"Fourteen."

"Did you ever do drugs when you were living in Africville?"

Howe laughed. "Not and live to tell about it. No."

"Can you explain what you mean by that?"

"One of the Other Mothers see you doing somethin' like that, they'd probably clip you 'longside the head and drag you off to your own mama so she could whup you good."

"Other Mothers?"

"That's what we called 'em. Other Mothers. They was somebody else's mother, but they treated you like their own. It was bad when you done somethin' wrong. But if you fell and cut yourself, you could always go to wherever was the nearest house and one of the Other Mothers'd fix you up. It was good that way."

"Do you remember seeing drugs when you lived in Africville?"

"No, I wouldna even know what they were then . . ."

"Were you ever get convicted of a crime in Africville?"

"No. Not until later, after we moved to the Square."

By the time he sat down, Uhuru Melesse had convinced himself Jeffrey Jack was a better witness than he'd feared. Gettings proved him wrong.

"So, you were a perfect child back in Africville, and Maynard Square turned you into a criminal. Is that what you're saying, Mr. Howe?"

"I ain't saying I was ever perfect."

"That's good, Mr. Howe, because I think the record will agree with you on that. During what Mr. Melesse has painted as your idyllic childhood in Africville, I take it that you went to school? Is that correct?"

"School? Yeah. Richmond."

"What kind of student were you?"

"Okay, I guess."

"Okay? I happen to have the records in front of me—I'd like them marked as Crown Exhibit 41, Your Honour—and they indicate that you failed grades one, three, six and seven before you dropped out entirely. Is that so?"

Uhuru was on his feet. "Relevance, Your Honour? What has failing in school got to do with anything?"

"With respect, Your Honour, in the light of the broad scope Your Honour has allowed my friend in these proceedings, I believe I should be permitted to explore some avenues my friend prefers to ignore, avenues that raise doubts about the argument he's making. If you'll allow me to develop this line of questioning, I believe the relevance will be apparent."

"I'll allow it . . . for now, Mr. Gettings," Ward Justice said. "But we aren't here to discuss . . . Mr. Howe's academic achievements. I'll expect you to . . . get to your point . . . quickly. Proceed."

"Thank you, Your Honour. Now, Mr. Howe, did you attend school regularly?"

J. J. Howe was wary now. He didn't want to be caught again. "Most of the time, yeah, I went."

"Well, again, Mr. Howe, let's see what the record says." He glanced at the page, more for dramatic effect than to remind himself of what was written. "According to School Board records, you were absent without excuse 123 days—more than half the year—in grade six. And that doesn't count the fifteen days you missed because you were suspended for striking your teacher. Does that sound familiar?"

Howe looked down. "I guess," he mumbled.

"Now, my friend makes the point that you were never convicted of a crime while you lived in Africville. My question to you is this: Were you ever charged with a crime while you lived in Africville?"

"Uh, I don't remember."

"Well then, let me refresh your memory, Mr. Howe. According to the pre-sentence report on the first occasion when you were convicted of a crime—which was, indeed, when you were sixteen years old and had been living in Maynard Square *for less than a year*—it says you had also been charged as a juvenile on three previous occasions for a variety of offences. Let me see here . . . break and enter, vandalism, arson, public intoxication . . . all while you were living in Africville, but that those charges were dropped when you agreed to provide statements implicating other, older boys in these acts. Is that correct?"

Howe's voice was barely audible now. "Yeah."

Gettings paused again. Waited long enough to make Jeffrey Jack twitch nervously. "Mr. Howe, tell me . . . are you high right now?"

"Your Honour!" Uhuru was on his feet to object.

"Can I take the fifth?" J. J.'s father turned to the judge.

Ward Justice held up his hand before Uhuru had a chance to object. "No need, Mr. Melesse. You're out of line, Mr. Gettings. Move on." He turned to the witness, smiled an understanding smile. "And, no, Mr. Howe, unfortunately . . . for you, there is no . . . fifth amendment right against . . . self-incrimination in Canada. I think you've been watching . . . too many American TV shows." More sternly, he stared back at Gettings. Silently.

"My apologies, Your Honour," Gettings offered quickly, but he did not sound apologetic. "I have no further questions of this witness."

"Your duty now is to weigh all the evidence you've heard," Ward Justice wrote carefully on the legal pad in his lap. "It is up to you to decide which facts to believe, which facts to emphasize and which to ignore. It won't be easy. Perhaps the most difficult—" Ward scratched out the beginning of that sentence, tried again. "One of the important questions you must ask yourself is how much weight to give to the evidence the defence offered purporting to show that Mr. Howe was justified in doing what he is alleged to have done." Justice drew a stroke through "purporting"; he needed a better word, but what was it? He had barely begun and already he was exhausted.

He looked up from the pad of yellow foolscap on his lap. On the TV screen across the room, the Talking Heads—Moira had called them that—were still talking. He shouldn't be watching; he knew that. But how could he not?

Tonight they were trying not only to summarize and characterize two weeks' worth of testimony in just five minutes but also to predict what the jury would have to say about it all. And how long it would take them to say it.

"I think it's going to depend on what the Judge says in his instructions to the jury," Talking Head Two said. "If he explains the law and says the other evidence isn't relevant, I think this will be all over in a few hours. If he says they can take into account all the other evidence, it may take a little longer."

"But," interjected Talking Head Number One, "the outcome will be the same no matter what, right?"

"Right."

"Okay," the interviewer segued into the segment wrap-up, "so what are you predicting the verdict will be then?"

"Guilty," said Talking Head One.

"Guilty," said Talking Head Two.

Ward reached for the remote, pressed a button and the Talking Heads disappeared. He looked at the paper, took up his pen, began to write again.

"The Crown would like you to believe this is a simple whodunit," Uhuru Melesse said as he began his closing argument, addressing himself directly to the jurors now, ignoring the Judge, the Crown and everyone else in the courtroom. "Decide 'who done it,' the case is closed and we can all go home."

Moira looked at her watch. Henry Gettings had taken just half an hour this morning for his final pitch to the jury, rehashing the facts of the crime as he'd laid them out in the evidence, reading jurors the wording of each specific section of the Criminal Code J. J. was charged with breaking, and showing them the connection between the law and the facts. He dismissed the defence's justification argument as a smokescreen "to make you believe this case is about something it's not. Ladies and gentlemen of the jury," he finished with a flourish, "your duty is clear. I am confident you will do your duty." He did seem confident.

But then, so did Uhuru Melesse, Moira thought. He'd probably talk longer; he'd need to get the jury thinking about more than the facts. An hour, say. And then the Judge's charge to the jury. It would be brief, she guessed, because of his health, but then—also given his health—it would probably still take him close to an hour to deliver it. Two hours would take them to lunchtime. And then, who knew? The jury might even start deliberating this afternoon. How long it would take after that was anyone's guess.

"But if that was really true, none of us would have to be here today."

Moira checked her tape recorder. She hoped it was working. She was having trouble concentrating. That didn't surprise her. It had been an exhausting two weeks. But she'd been right; the trial had become much more interesting after the Crown had made its case and the defence had slogged its way through its initial parade of expert witnesses. Once the former Africville residents had begun to testify, her own daily stories had begun to write themselves. And to appear on the front page.

"I can't believe some of this stuff actually happened," Michelle marvelled one morning after complimenting Moira on her latest article. Moira knew her actual contribution that day had been modest; the story was mostly stitched-together snippets of Everett Dickson's testimony about the fire that had killed Uhuru Melesse's mother. "The fact the City wouldn't give them water, that's bad enough," Michelle continued. "But for the fire department not even to show up for an hour? That's criminal. I mean, they still might have saved that woman. It makes Halifax sound like the American South. Anyway . . ." She paused just long enough to change subjects. "What'll you have for us today?" Michelle was no longer fretting about whether Moira should continue to cover the trial. "Oh, and by the way," Michelle interjected before Moira had a chance to outline what would be happening in court, "I forgot to mention that Morton's excited. We're getting incredible reaction on this. Phone calls, letters, e-mails."

"For or against?" Moira was curious.

"Mostly for, at least if the question is whether people think the residents got a raw deal. But a lot still believe your accountant guy should go to jail. On the guilty-or-not question, I'd say it's about fifty-fifty. But it changes every day."

Moira wasn't surprised. Opinions inside the courtroom yo-yoed too. Over the years, she'd become used to the roller-coaster rides trials could become. Listening to a lawyer lead his witness gently through a field of marshmallow questions, you couldn't help but wonder why the person hadn't been inducted into sainthood. But once the other lawyer got the chance to grill the saint-in-waiting, the witness, even one as peripheral to the case before the court as the head of a school breakfast program, emerged as a deeply flawed, most likely criminal sinner.

Moira would not want to be on this jury. Up and down. Back and forth. Convict, acquit, convict, acquit . . .

The outcome would ultimately come down to whether the eight men and four women seated in the jury box were brave enough—or foolhardy enough—to substitute their own judgment for the Criminal Code.

Moira already knew, from sitting through the pretrial arguments, that jury nullification—when a jury returns a verdict of not guilty even though it believes the accused is guilty, either because it thinks the law is an ass, or that it's being wrongly applied to the defendant *du jour*—was a much tougher sell in the real world of Canada's judicial system than on the make-believe American TV shows she watched. For starters, the defence in Canada wasn't even supposed to tell the jury it had the right to judge the law as well as the facts. That had been part of the fallout from the Morgentaler cases. The jurors had to figure it out themselves.

Which made choosing the jury critical. Which made Moira wonder. She still had no clue why the defence had done what it had during jury selection. Moira had tried to broach the subject with Melesse during a scrum at the end of the day, but he, not surprisingly, wasn't saying anything more than a blandly predictable, "The defence is satisfied with the jury we have."

So Moira had added that to the growing list of questions she wanted to put to Melesse after the trial. If he would talk to her, of course. He would, wouldn't he? There were things she could tell him—truths she could trade—that he might not know. But what if he said no? Would that be the end of her plan . . . ? *Stay focused on what's happening now*, she told herself. How was the jury reacting to Melesse's closing argument?

"Members of the jury, the defence answered the whodunit question the day we began these proceedings," Uhuru's eyes swept back and forth across the jury like a searchlight. "We said, 'Our client did it.' James Joseph Howe personally appropriated every single penny of the $335,456.56 the Crown claims he took.

"So to see this as a simple whodunit is to ignore the important questions and the larger issues that flow from answering those questions. Question number one, of course, is: Why? Why did J. J. Howe do what the police and the Crown say he did, and what he himself has admitted he did? To answer that question, we must begin by doing what the Crown will not do. We need to follow the money. What happened to the money?"

Finally. Uhuru Melesse was coming to a point. But the point, which was that J. J. was justified in playing Robin Hood with taxpayers' money because the City had dragged its feet in negotiating with the former residents, and because the causes he supported were good, still seemed pretty thin to Moira. Not that it mattered what she thought. What would the jury think?

"You heard Mrs. Althea Thompson, the director of Square Deal, a breakfast and lunch program for poor children from Maynard Square. She told you how important that program is to her community, and how it was in danger of folding three years ago after City Council cut off its funding, and how it was saved by an anonymous donor who allowed Square Deal to continue its important work, an anonymous donor who asked for nothing in return, an anonymous donor we now know was . . ." he turned to look at the defendant, "James Joseph Howe." J. J. nodded at the jury. Acknowledgement.

Uhuru Melesse pointedly did not mention Gettings's attempt to put a very different spin on J. J.'s donation during his cross-examination of Thompson.

"You come before this court," Gettings had thundered at her, his tone incredulous, "and you swear an oath to tell the truth, the whole truth and nothing but the truth. And then you tell us this . . . story . . . this tale . . . about some mystery man who sends you a cheque for ten thousand dollars, and you aren't even curious to find out his name?"

"I didn't say I wasn't curious," Thompson corrected him. "I just said I never found out."

"Isn't it true, Mrs. Thompson," Gettings pushed on, riding a wave of faux righteous indignation over her caveat, "that you knew all along exactly where this money was coming from, and that you were, in fact, in collusion with the accused, with Mr. Howe, to obtain the funds *you* decided you were entitled to after City Council, the elected representatives of the people of Halifax, did what they are legally entitled to do and turned down your group's request for more funding? Isn't that so?"

"No, it's not."

Gettings's goal, Moira realized, had not been to get Mrs. Thompson to confess—Moira was convinced Gettings had invented the whole collusion scenario—but to plant the seed of doubt, any doubt would do, in the jurors' minds.

Uhuru Melesse's task this morning was to root out that seed before it could germinate and plant a few of his own. He had to get the jurors thinking about J. J. Howe's personal story, about the evils the City had wrought on the sons and daughters of the former citizens of Africville, about the good J. J. had done with the money he'd redeployed.

"Ladies and gentlemen of the jury, this is not a whodunit. It's a *why*-dunit. We have tried to show you why James Joseph Howe felt compelled . . ." Uhuru stopped then, eyed the jurors one by one, continued, "why he felt justified, why he felt he . . . *had* . . . *no* . . . *choice*," his voice rising with each word, then falling to a whisper, "but to do what he did. Now it is up to you to decide whether what he did was a crime or a cry from the heart for justice for the people of Africville. The defence is confident you will make the right decision."

Ward Justice struggled for breath. Again. He had tried to keep his rehash of the evidence and his explanations of the law as brief as possible, but even those had taxed his lungs beyond their capacity. He was exhausted, he needed to sleep. Less than a page to go now. Home stretch. He tried to take a deep breath, couldn't, coughed, felt the phlegm rise in his throat, swallowed, paused again.

"So," he said finally, looking down at the jurors, "it is now . . . up to you. How much . . . weight . . . should you give . . . to the evidence the defence . . . offered . . . to show that . . . Mr. Howe . . . was justified . . . in doing what . . . he is alleged . . . to have done." Had he cut "purporting" simply to shorten his charge to the jury, or was he trying to send them a message? The word indicated a lack of proof, a doubt; he didn't want to convey that. What did he want to convey, and how could he say what he wanted to say without going too far and risking an easy reversal by a higher court?

"If you look simply . . . at the statute . . . as the Crown . . . believes you should," he continued, "the evidence is . . . clear. Mr. Howe is

. . . guilty. But the defence wants . . . you to look at . . . the bigger picture. Should you? Can you? No one . . . will ask you . . . to explain . . . your decision. And I cannot . . . instruct you . . . how to weigh . . . and balance . . . the evidence before you. I can only . . . explain and interpret . . . the law as it . . . is written. *You* must decide . . . if the facts . . . support the contention . . . that what . . . Mr. Howe has done . . . constitutes . . . a crime. It is . . . up to you now. May wisdom . . . guide you . . . in your deliberations."

"Members of the jury," the clerk began, reading from the neatly typed card in front of her, "have you agreed on your verdict?"

"We have," replied the jury foreman.

It had taken them nearly four days. What did that mean? The Talking Heads, who'd initially predicted the jury would be back in an hour with a guilty verdict, had had to keep revising their estimates of how long it would take, and then, last night, Talking Head Number One had even broached the possibility of a hung jury. "Someone is holding out in there," he'd suggested petulantly.

Moira had watched the jurors file in; not one looked at J. J. That was supposed to be a sign too. If the jurors didn't make eye contact with the defendant, conventional wisdom was that the verdict would be guilty.

"What is your verdict on count number one," the clerk read, "theft over five thousand dollars?"

The silence seemed to stretch into next week.

"Not guilty," the jury foreman declared in a flat, unemotional voice.

So much for conventional wisdom. No one drew a breath as the clerk continued, asking for their verdict on the second count. Fraud.

"Not guilty."

Breach of trust.

"Not guilty."

It was if everyone exhaled at exactly the same moment. And then it was pandemonium. Everyone was on their feet. Shouting. Cheering.

Hugging. Shaking hands. Slapping backs. Reporters rushed past the railing to be the first to get to the lawyers. Moira grabbed her tape recorder and hurried after them. The sheriff's deputies didn't even try to stop them.

Henry Gettings was sitting at the Crown bench dwarfed by the reporters surrounding him.

". . . naturally disappointed . . ."

Moira, stuck behind a TV camera operator, her arm extending the tape recorder into the melee over his shoulder, could only make out snatches of what Gettings was saying.

". . . not supported by the evidence . . . not correct in law . . . seriously consider an appeal . . . yes, the decision on the pretrial motion was the turning point . . . not criticizing Mister Justice Justice . . . simply saying I believe his decision was wrong in law."

Moira pulled her tape recorder out of that scrum and hurried over to where Uhuru Melesse, Shondelle Adams and J. J. Howe were holding court. Cecil Montague had already disappeared. Moira had hoped for better from Melesse but, surrounded by a crush of well-wishers and reporters, he offered even more predictable responses to even more predictable questions.

". . . never surprised by what happens inside a courtroom . . . just grateful the jury understood the case we were making . . . not worried . . . confident this is a proper judgment . . . be upheld if the Crown does decide to appeal . . . going out with our client to celebrate . . ."

Moira felt the snap of the tape recorder, signalling it had reached the end of the tape. Not that it mattered. She pulled her arm back, stuffed the machine into her purse. She had more than enough material.

She glanced over toward the judges' exit. Ward Justice was standing beside the door, catching his breath, admiring the chaos he had helped create. He looked over at Moira, smiled and winked. She smiled back.

Uhuru Melesse averted his eyes from the couple in the SUV, focused on the old white man in the distance walking his black Lab alongside the chain-link fence. Were white man and black beast treading on the sacred ground of Seaview African United Baptist Church? Uhuru thought so, then didn't think so. The church was to the right, closer to the water. Or, was it still farther north . . . ?

In his mind's eye, Uhuru could recreate Africville whole: the church, Tibby's Pond, Up the Road, Aunt Annie's candy store, Aunt Lottie's bootlegging establishment, the Deacon's house, his father's place, even the Dump. But when he opened his eyes, Seaview Park's landfilled, landscaped green grass and gravel pathways overlaid his remembered Africville and disoriented him.

He was standing beside his battered '89 Volvo in the nearly deserted parking lot, waiting for the Judge to arrive. While he waited, he tried to find some landmark, some proof he really was where he was. To the north loomed the huge cranes of the new container terminal. New how long ago? Ten years? Fifteen? To the west, where the rocky scrubland rose up sharply, access roads now carved into the hillside looped up from Barrington Street onto ramps leading to the new bridge. The "new" bridge was even older than the container pier, but both were new since Africville was levelled. His eyes traced down the bridge's huge steel pylon to its concrete base at the water's edge. Though its supports were to the south of the boundary of Seaview Park, he knew they had been built on what was once also part of Africville.

Uhuru heard a low rumble from the bridge above. He looked up, watched an eighteen-wheeler cross the span above him, disappear briefly behind trees and into a turn at the end of the bridge, then re-emerge a moment later hurtling down the off-ramp toward Barrington and some downtown warehouse.

Almost involuntarily his eyes returned to the ground, to the parking lot, to the SUV facing him from across the gravel parking lot. Inside, a boy and a girl were fondling one another. Just two high school kids making a hormonal passion stop on their way home from afternoon classes? Except the boy was black, the girl white. Did their parents know? Would they care?

Halifax had changed. He had seen it himself. Though still unusual, it wasn't shocking now to see interracial couples strolling arm in arm downtown. Their mere presence didn't seem to provoke the hard stares he remembered. Or was that just wishful thinking? Had Halifax changed? Or did it just hide its hostilities better?

The boy's hand was on the girl's clothed breast. He was kissing her face, her ears, her neck, working his way south. Uhuru recognized the move. Then the girl, whose arms were around the boy's shoulders, opened her eyes and saw Uhuru. Staring? She pushed the boy away. He seemed startled, then turned in the direction she'd indicated with her eyes. Uhuru looked away, turned on his heel and began to walk purposefully toward the sundial memorial in the middle of the park. As if that had been his plan all along.

Damn the Judge, anyway. Uhuru could have been back at his office, basking in the warm afterglow of his own success. The party was probably still going on. The celebrating had begun immediately after the verdict. Without saying anything to Uhuru, Shondelle had bought a dozen bottles of champagne the day the jury began deliberating and kept them on ice in a cooler in her car. "I knew we'd win," she said as she hefted the heavy cooler onto her desk.

"Oh, you did, did you?" Uhuru replied with a smile. "So why did you wait until now to bring them out?"

"I didn't want to jinx us, that's all." She opened the cooler, handed a bottle to J. J., who was standing beside her. "Why don't you do the honours?" she said, then turned and kissed Uhuru. As everyone whooped and cheered, she whispered in his ear, "Congratulations, counsellor. You didn't screw it up!"

"And you," he whispered back, "don't weigh three hundred and fifty pounds." It had become their private joke. The night they'd made love for the first time, they'd played a post-coital game of True Confessions. "Okay," she'd started it, "so what did you really think that night in the Shoe Shop?"

After he'd told her, he asked her the same.

"I figured you were going to screw everything up. And . . ." She laughed. "I thought you were cute."

There had never been so many people in Uhuru's office at the same time. Court clerks, sheriff's deputies, reporters, a few courthouse regulars. Some tenants who shared the floor of the office building with Uhuru. Even the landlord dropped by to congratulate Uhuru—and remind him this month's rent was past due. By noon there was pizza, and someone—Calvin?—volunteered to make a run to the liquor store for beer.

Cecil Montague stopped by briefly, shook Uhuru's hand. Uhuru tried to thank him. Montague waved him off. "I thank you," he said, leaning in to be heard over the din in the office. "You slayed a few demons in there for me, too."

The phone kept ringing. Reporters. Uhuru had agreed to tape a phone interview with *As It Happens* later in the afternoon; he asked Shondelle to handle a live hit with *Canada Now* half an hour later. *Canada AM* had called several times to arrange for J. J. to fly to Toronto that night so he could appear live on the program tomorrow morning.

"Judge asked me to give this to you," the deputy said. When the sheriff's deputy handed him the note, Uhuru was huddled in a corner of the inner office, the phone receiver pressed to his ear, trying to hear questions from an interviewer for National Public Radio in Boston.

"Legally, of course, a decision in Canada doesn't have any impact on American law, or vice versa," Uhuru was explaining as he absent-mindedly opened the folded sheet of paper, "but I think the outcome of this case represents a moral victory for the cause everywhere . . ." Uhuru had been too busy answering questions to take in what the deputy said. Now he tried to pull the pieces together. At the top of the page, someone had written "Ray," then crossed it out and inserted "Uhuru." Below, the message was short and choppy, as if the writer had as much difficulty writing as breathing.

Can we meet? This afternoon, 4:00. Seaview Park.
Call my secretary if you can't.
—Ward

"Hello, hello? Mr. Melesse, are you still there?" the interviewer said, then asked his technician. "Did we lose him? Mr. Melesse?"

"I'm here. Sorry. It's very hectic here right now. What was the question?"

He hadn't told Shondelle where he was going. "When I was talking to the producer at *As It Happens*, I said I'd take his call at home because it's quieter there," he explained as he packed his briefcase with files he didn't need.

"But that's not for nearly two more hours," Shondelle said, looking at her watch. She was in party mode.

"I know, honey. I just need a little quiet time to clear my head. Why don't I pick you up at the studio after *Canada Now?* We can go out to dinner. Just the two of us. Valentino's maybe? We've never been there."

She smiled, kissed him on the cheek. "Sounds good to me."

He wasn't sure why he didn't want to tell her about the note. Perhaps because they'd never been able to agree on anything connected with Ward Justice. If he told her about Ward's note, she would discourage him from going and, if that failed, would want to know what happened. Uhuru couldn't be sure what that might be. Better to tell her later. If . . . As he drove north along Barrington to the park, Uhuru promised himself he would get better at this couple thing. Secrets were no way to build a relationship. And he wanted this one to last.

Now, standing behind the sundial in the middle of the park, he made a point of looking down at the list of the names of Africville's founding families, as if to show the young couple that really was why he was here. He cast a furtive glance back toward the parking lot. The SUV was leaving, passing a Lincoln Town Car on its way into the parking lot.

"You're sure about this?" Victoria asked again as she navigated Ward's oversized vehicle around the departing SUV and into the parking lot. She would have preferred her Toyota, he knew, but its front seat wasn't big enough for Ward and the portable oxygen tank that had become his travelling companion. He held the mask up to his mouth and nose. "That wind off the water is going to be cold," she continued as she turned off the engine, already resigned to his going ahead anyway. "The last thing you need is to get a chill."

"I'll be fine," he said, pulling the mask away from his face, feeling the invisible weight on his chest again. "I just need help getting out is all."

She was already out of the car and hurrying around to the passenger side. He could see Uhuru approaching from across the field. Victoria opened the door then, took Ward's hands, helped him swing his body around square to the door. He swung his legs out, let them dangle there while he reached out with his left hand and grabbed the door handle for support. Victoria put an arm on his shoulder to help him push forward. Until very recently, he'd insisted on getting in and out of the car himself; that he no longer did was a sign to both of them the end was coming.

"Uhuru," he rasped. "My wife, Vic—"

"We met. At the church," Victoria spoke over him, trying to save her husband the exertion. "Good to see you again, Mr. Melesse. And congratulations on the case. My husband says you were very impressive."

"Thank you," he said. He wasn't sure what else to say.

Victoria broke the silence. "I'll leave you two to talk but, please, Mr. Melesse, don't let Ward tire himself. He doesn't have much stamina these days." Ward waved her off with his hand. "I'll be in the car if you need me," she said.

Ward pointed to a bench near the edge of the park facing the harbour. "There," he said simply.

"You sure?" Uhuru asked. The bench was a hundred feet from where they were standing and they'd have to climb a short, steep hill to get there.

"Sure," he said, raising his right arm slightly from his side, indicating Uhuru should support him as they walked. "Not too fast."

They walked in silence, stopping every few yards so Ward could control his breathing. Uhuru wanted to ask him questions but worried Ward might try to answer. The questions could wait. When they finally reached the bench, Ward stood for a moment staring back into the park. "Not the same," he said.

"No, it isn't," Uhuru answered. "Not the same at all."

"Sit," Ward instructed. And then turned and eased his own body down onto the bench, leaned back, slowed his breathing. Uhuru sat down too. They were facing the harbour, away from the park.

"How are you?"

"Some days better than others . . . mornings better than afternoons." Ward smiled. "At least nobody's won the pool." When Uhuru looked shocked, Ward laughed, then coughed. "I know what goes on," he said, hauled out his handkerchief and spat phlegm into it.

They were silent again, neither seeming to know how to proceed. "Like Victoria said, I . . . was very . . . impressed by the . . . way you made your . . . case." Ward was speaking in complete sentences, but rushing, stopping and starting, gulping for air so often Uhuru had to listen carefully to patch the meaning together. "Are you going to . . . celebrate?"

"People have been in my office partying pretty much since the jury came back. Tonight, my—my associate and I are going to celebrate."

"Ms. Adams?"

"Yeah."

"She's very . . . bright. Attractive too. Are you two . . . ?"

"Yeah."

"Good." He was silent for a moment. "I sent a letter to the Chief Justice this afternoon . . . asked for immediate leave. I won't be back . . . Not sure whether that will help or hurt at appeal . . . But you'll do fine . . . You convinced me!" He laughed, coughed again, waited to catch his breath. "Remember Jeremiah Black? The . . . kid who tried to . . . beat me up?" Uhuru nodded. "I sentenced him . . . a couple of years back. For murder. I don't think he even recognized me . . ."

Ward was talking now to keep talking, searching for the route to where he needed to go. "When I used to come down here . . . with you . . . when I was a kid . . . this place felt like home. Your father . . . treated me well . . ." He stopped, considered. "I was there the day Eagleson . . . offered him the money, you know."

"I know."

"I'm sorry."

"It's okay."

"How is he?" Ward asked.

"My father? Dead. More than ten years . . ."

"I'm sorry. I didn't know."

"What about yours?" Uhuru asked.

"Eighty-seven. In a home in Antigonish. Crankier than ever."

Uhuru smiled. "I don't think he liked me very much."

"It wasn't . . . that simple." Ward told him the story.

"Fuck," Uhuru said when he finished. "That's fucking amazing."

"Have you ever wondered . . . what it would have been like . . . to be white?" Ward asked.

"Once in a while. But I'm too black to imagine I could ever be white. It was never an option. But I'm sure things would have been different." That high school guidance counsellor relegating him to the general stream. Jack Eagleson telling him he didn't want him to think he was prejudiced, his words seared in some recess of his mind: *I have clients who wouldn't like it if we had a black man working for the firm.* Yes, things would have been different.

"Being black is pretty much all I think about," Ward confided, inspecting a blade of grass on the ground in front of him. "I wouldn't have . . . done very well . . . as a black man. I'm not strong. I just let things happen to me . . . things that wouldn't have happened if I was black . . ." He stopped, corrected himself: "If people *knew* I was black."

They sat in silence again, Ward still looking for a way to say the rest of what he had come to say. Uhuru was the final person to whom he had decided he must make amends. Victoria already knew, of course. She'd known the facts since that night twenty-eight years ago when Ward had confessed everything—and she'd moved his clothes out of their bedroom. She knew the facts, but never the feelings. He finally told her those, too. A week after Jack's funeral. The night of the interview with Moira. The day before she drove him to the nursing home to see his father. Telling her had been far easier than he'd expected, perhaps because she'd already assumed most of it, or maybe because none of it mattered in the way it once had. Looming death could have that effect.

It had been Victoria's idea for him to tell the children. "If it's going to come out anyway," she explained, with her usual impeccable logic, "they should hear it from you first." Victoria had arranged for the girls to fly home from Toronto last Friday for a "family weekend."

The girls had been more understanding than he had any right to expect. Sarah's new boyfriend, it turned out, was from Grenada. "I can't wait to tell him, so he can tell his parents he's going out with a black girl," she joked. Even Meghan, the daughter who wanted nothing more than to fit in and who was now pregnant with her own first child, was far less upset than Victoria had feared. "Half our friends in Toronto are in mixed marriages," she said. "It's no big deal."

Rosa had been a bigger deal, of course, but Victoria had artfully orchestrated that conversation, leading Ward through his confession with gentle nudges and smoothing explanations, even a confession of her own.

"You remember Dr. Griffin?" she said to her daughters after Ward had stuttered through his own story. "I had an affair with him." Ward had known about it but he'd never heard her say it aloud before. "Those were unhappy times for both of us," Victoria explained, "but it was a long time ago, and it doesn't change my feelings for your father."

Ward admired how carefully she'd said that. She'd guided him even more carefully through the story of the "terrible accident," skating him around his drunkenness and his failure to report his involvement to the police. "That poor little boy was dead, it was awful, but there was nothing to be gained by ruining more lives."

Ward had tried to understand Victoria's motives. Was she still the politician's daughter, the judge's wife, smoothing out life's wrinkles for the sake of appearances? Or could this be . . . love? What was love, anyway?

And what of his daughters? Did they really understand in the way they claimed to understand, or . . . or what? He wished he knew them better. Too late for that now. But not too late for this.

"You know," he said, not looking at Uhuru, "I've been rethinking my whole life . . . trying to understand what . . . being black really means. Did I feel at home in Africville . . . because I was black? Or because . . . it reminded me of Eisners Head? Were we friends because . . . we shared something we didn't even know? Or just because? Was I in love with Rosa," he lifted his head then, looked into Uhuru's face, "because she was black—?"

"I always wanted to thank you for that," Uhuru cut him off. There were things he needed to say too. "For taking care of Rosa and . . . the baby. I know you didn't do it for me, and there were times I resented you and Rosa, but . . . I fucked up that whole situation. Badly. You gave her what I couldn't, what I wouldn't, for my own selfish reasons. So, thank you."

Ward knew this was the moment. Seize it. "There's something you need to know," he started, then stopped, trying once again to invent a reason not to say what he had to say. No! He had to. Now. Or it would never be said.

"I killed your son."

Ward had jumped off his cliff of guilt. Into the abyss. Now what? He stared into Uhuru's face. Uhuru stared back. Blank. Uncomprehending? Or unwilling to comprehend? Ward tried again. "Larry . . . I was driving the car . . . I didn't know . . . I'm sorry." He stopped. Now what?

"My son? Larry was my son?" Uhuru's voice was hollow. "Rosa would never tell me—"

"I saw the birth certificate."

Uhuru turned away, as if he'd been struck. He stared, unseeing, past the green expanse of park toward the container terminal where a massive, black-hulled ship sat at the dock. Spider-like cranes scurried back and forth loading containers onto its deck. Ward turned and watched them too, waiting wordlessly for the condemnation he knew would come. It did not.

"I knew," Uhuru said finally, talking to himself, convicting himself of the crime of self-deception. "I had to know. But Rosa would never admit it, so I never had to. Maybe I didn't want to . . . didn't want to have to—" He turned back, met Ward's gaze. "Why wouldn't she at least let me help her?" he demanded. "Help my son?"

Ward shrugged helplessly. What could he say? Had Uhuru even heard *his* confession?

He had. But it was too much to process. It stuttered into his brain now in staccato bursts of comprehension. *My son! Larry really was my son* . . . And then: *Ward?* . . . *Accident?* . . . *Ward driving the car?* . . . Ward!

Uhuru stood up. He didn't, couldn't, wouldn't look at Ward. He felt the red-hot poker of hate stab his heart. *Ward Justice murdered my son.* He stared out at the harbour, his eyes refusing to focus. His son's life that never would be flashed before his eyes. Saturday morning hockey games, shivering in the stands, watching, cheering, marvelling at the boy's flash and grace. Did he get that from his dad? Africville Reunion Weekends, hot summer sun, water slides. *Have you met my son, Larry? Doesn't he look just like his granddad?* Science fairs and graduations, girlfriends, college, career, marriage, kids, life . . . *death.* His son was dead. Before he could live. Ward Justice had killed little Larry. Uhuru Melesse/Ray Carter wanted to kill Ward Justice in return. Wanted justice. He could feel his fists clench, his muscles tighten, his shoulders knot, the rage bubble. He turned back toward the man who had murdered his son . . . and saw a broken old man sitting on a park bench, his shrunken face grey and sallow, his cloudy eyes pleading and rheumy—tears?—his body waiting for the blows to come. Uhuru exhaled, felt the hate mingling with his escaping breath, dissipating in the spring air. It was too late for hate. Too late for guilt, too. He sat down again.

"What happened?" Uhuru's tone held more curiosity than accusation. He just wanted to know.

"I was drunk . . . I didn't see . . ." The story spilled out, all of it, including how Eagleson had orchestrated his own appointment as a judge. "I should have said no . . . I should have gone to the police. Turned myself in. But . . . I was scared . . . I'm sorry . . ." He paused.

"Does Rosa know?" Uhuru asked finally.

"I don't know," Ward answered. "I hired a detective . . . to find her. I wanted to tell her . . . But she was already dead."

Uhuru let out a soft moan. Rosa too. In some recess of his mind, he had fantasized, without foundation or action on his part to make it reality, that he would find her again one day, or that she would find him, or that somehow, magically, mysteriously, mystically, they would find each other, and that he would have the chance to tell her he was sorry, she would forgive him, and they would live happily ever after. The fantasy had sustained him, restrained him and constrained him for more than thirty years. And now it was over. Rosa was dead. He was alive. Was it too late to live?

"I loved her," Ward said.

Uhuru looked over at Ward. "I know," he said finally. "We both did."

It had been said. And there was nothing more to say.

14

Spring 2005

"This is a true story, or as true as I can make it." Moira Donovan reread the words she had typed on the screen. "It began to take shape in my head the first day I interviewed Ward Justice. It's been changing shape ever since"—Moira stared at the blinking cursor and the expanse of emptiness beneath it. *What now?* she thought.

She hadn't set out to write a book. She'd initially envisioned a kind of "gotcha" front-page newspaper story in which Ward Justice, confronted with her assembled storehouse of documents, tapes and knowledge, would crumble and confess. Or—perhaps better—try to lie, fudge, obfuscate or wriggle his way out of all the traps she'd set. Either way: Snap! Crackle! Gotcha!

She hadn't been nearly as eager as that made her sound. When she'd asked him for the interview at the funeral, it was because she'd expected—hoped—he would say no. His willingness surprised her. She hadn't intended to ask the questions she'd ended up asking, either, but it was almost as if instinct took over. Perhaps her father had been right; she was a reporter and couldn't escape her fate even if she wanted to.

Ward Justice hadn't expected her to know about his previous relationship with Uhuru. In truth, of course, she knew much less then than he thought she did. She'd had to stifle the urge to shout "Yes!" as he stumbled through his non-answers. By the time he began to bumble his predictable those-were-different-times defence of his racist jokes at the press gallery dinner, she was writing the lead in her head:

"The judge in the controversial J. J. Howe reparations case not only told racist jokes at a private dinner for journalists in the seventies, he also met secretly with RCMP Security and Intelligence officers in late 1970 to tell them all he knew about a former friend named Raymond Carter. Carter, then a black radical, is better known today as Uhuru Melesse, J. J. Howe's defence lawyer."

She'd made a quick note on her steno pad to make a list of those she'd need to call for comment. Melesse, of course. The Mounties . . .

How should she handle the most explosive bit? A paragraph right after the lead? "Ironically . . ." No, scratch that, too fluffy, too cutesy. "Incredibly . . ." The desk would excise that—no editorializing. "Surprisingly . . ." Morton hated starting a sentence that way. Fuck it. Straight ahead: "Justice Ward Justice is himself black." Black? Afro-Canadian? Which one did the stylebook say to use? And was calling him either correct? How about: ". . . of mixed race. His grandfather was an African–Nova Scotian." That worked. Then: "Justice Justice confirmed his ancestry, which had been previously publicly unknown, in an exclusive interview with the *Daily Journal* Friday." Followed by a confirming quote from Justice.

New paragraph. First response from Melesse. Anger? Disappointment? Would he finally demand that the judge recuse himself? What about a mistrial? She'd have to check the finer legal points with the paper's lawyers—

Whoa . . . She was getting ahead of herself. And then, even further ahead. Imagining the night she would receive her first National Newspaper Award. Who would she thank? Her father? Absolutely. He could be her guest at the dinner. Point him out in the audience.

This feverishly imagined future had fallen apart moments after she showed Ward Justice a copy of the photograph David Astor had given to her. "The photo was taken by an itinerant photographer named Pyke who passed through Kingville in 1928 and must have done a family portrait for the Justices," Moira explained to Ward as Astor had explained to her. "See, there's Desmond, seated. He would have been about twelve. That's his mother and father behind him. His father's name was *Ward* Justice. When you compare the face in that photo with your own face, the resemblance is remarkable, don't you think?" She'd stolen a quick glance at Ward Justice's face looking at his own face staring back at him from the photo. His real face was a train wreck. He hadn't known!

"While the elder Mr. Justice is certainly a bit darker than you, he was also very light-skinned for a black man. It's difficult to be sure from the photo but his wife, Rebeckah—that's her there—may have been a white woman. Desmond himself could be mistaken—or *pass*—for a Caucasian. Which means . . . Well, Mr. Astor—he's the archivist—doesn't think there's any doubt." A pause to let him consider the import. Ward Justice still said nothing. "He seems convinced he can trace your family tree to the Justices of Kingville and then back all the way to the Black Loyalists. Now, I guess what I wanted to ask you—"

"Ms. Donovan," Ward Justice cut her off then. "This is all . . . especially this," he said pointing to the photo, "a surprise. I need some time to consider . . . I will answer any questions you want, but I'd like a little time."

She didn't know what to say. This wasn't in the scenario she'd written in her head. But he didn't wait for her answer.

"There's something else, something I think that ties in with this . . . this *information* . . . that could make your story even more . . . interesting." He paused, as if trying to figure out what and how much to say. "Can we—I know this is unusual . . . but then it's all very unusual—can we go off the record . . . for a minute or two . . . while I put a proposition to you?"

Moira's instinct was to say no. She already had an "interesting" story. And she didn't need Ward Justice begging her not to ruin his career with her revelations. She'd never developed the alligator hide she needed to be a reporter. She was afraid she might say yes. After all, Morton didn't know what she had . . .

"One minute," Ward Justice was pleading. "Just one minute . . . and then . . . if you still want to . . . we'll go back on the record and continue the interview." He pointed at the microcassette recorder. She reached over, turned it off. What the hell?

That's when he made his pitch. The whole story, beginning to end, no questions unanswered, no pathway unexplored, no stone unturned, do with it as you wish. The only stipulation was that she wasn't to publish a word of it until after he died. "Which"—and here he coughed a watery, wet cough, perhaps for effect—"will be sooner rather than later."

When he'd learned he was dying, he explained, he'd decided he needed to confess to some terrible things he'd done in his life, "starting with Rosa and the accident." Moira hadn't understood what he was talking about at the time. Ward was just assuming her father had already told her everything.

Her request for an interview had started him thinking about asking her to be his confessional Boswell. "I was sure you knew some things from your father, but I never expected you would know so much," he told Moira later—at a time when she was just beginning to realize how little she really knew.

In the five months between that initial interview and the Judge's death late last fall, she'd conducted more than forty hours of face-to-face interviews. Before he died, Ward had also prepared an all-purpose letter of introduction she could use in lining up her interviews. The letters explained that Moira was writing the story of his life, "warts and all," and encouraged the recipient to co-operate fully.

Some did. Moira interviewed Uhuru Melesse several times—before and after he legally changed his name back to Raymond Carter. During their last interview, he explained how he'd come to terms with Ward's confession. "It took me a long time to sort this out and, even now, I know this is going to sound wrong," he said, "but finding out what really happened was strangely liberating. Rosa was dead, Larry was dead. The guilt I'd been carrying around all those years, the regret . . . pointless now. Ward lived with the same kind of guilt, the same regret. And what good did it do him? He was dead now, too. But I was alive. I decided I had to go on living. That's when I decided to change my name back, and when I decided to ask Shondelle to marry me."

Moira had already written that anecdote in the first draft of the book's afterword. Unfortunately, so far, she'd only written that and the beginnings of the acknowledgements, which she kept on a file in her computer so she could update it after every interview—to make her feel as though she was actually accomplishing something. "I especially want to thank Raymond Carter, Shondelle Carter Adams, my father, Patrick Donovan, Victoria Justice, David Astor, INSERT ADDITIONAL NAMES HERE, all of whom gave generously of their time and then patiently responded to my many follow-up and often follow-follow-up questions . . ." She'd also already written another, all-purpose thank-you: "There were others, too, many of whom agreed to speak with me on condition that I not use their names in the text. They will know who they are, and I thank them for their assistance in preparing this manuscript . . ."

Moira only wished there really were a manuscript. There were still too many holes in her knowledge, too many gaps in her understanding.

Some people had refused to be interviewed. Desmond Justice wouldn't speak with her at all. Neither would J. J. Howe, who told her that everything he had to say would be in his own book, publication of which was on hold while the Crown's appeal—prosecutors claimed the judge had erred in law by allowing the justification defence—worked its way to the Supreme Court of Canada.

Kathleen O'Donohue, Ward Justice's secretary during his years as a judge, declined Moira's requests for an interview too, even after typing the Judge's letter of support for her book. "I'm sorry, but it doesn't seem right to me to undermine the reputation of a man I admired, even at his own request," she wrote in a letter to Moira shortly after the Judge's death.

Others, of course, couldn't be interviewed. Rosa Johnstone, whose perspective would have been invaluable, was dead before Moira even knew she was alive. Dale "Junior" Eisner had died of a heart attack in 1989, shortly after Global Fisheries of Chicago bought his company for the same kind of fire-sale price Junior had once used to expand his own business interests. Junior's company was among those caught by the collapse of the industry in the mid-eighties

Mr. Eisner's executors refused Moira permission to examine his personal files. Using federal and provincial access to information legislation, she did get copies of some of his official correspondence with various governments, but those letters—compared to what she had learned about the man from other interviews—were blandly unrevealing and corporate.

Perhaps most disappointing was the fact that she never had the chance to interview Jack Eagleson, Ward's mentor, Ray's benefactor and a dominating force in Nova Scotia business and politics for so many decades. As a result, there were many questions she could never resolve. Why, for example, had Eagleson chosen Ward Justice to be his protegé? Was he, as Ward himself told Moira, just one of many young men Eagleson had taken under his wing in hopes one would mature into a successful politician? Or had he seen something particular in Ward Justice? Moira would never know. Just as she'd never understand what was behind Eagleson's complicated and puzzling relationship with the young Raymond Carter. Carter told her he now believed Eagleson's actions were motivated both by genuine integrationist sentiments and also by white liberal guilt. "When he refused to publicly acknowledge me by taking me into his firm, even after he'd privately supported me all through law school, I think it represented an understanding—probably a correct understanding—of the limits of racial tolerance in Nova Scotia at that time. Although I didn't think so then, I think now that Mr. Eagleson wanted to do the right thing but couldn't bring himself to challenge a status quo he was very much part of."

There was one other question concerning Jack Eagleson's role in the events of the summer of 1976 that Moira had wanted, tried—and ultimately failed—to answer. Did Jack Eagleson (and/or Junior Eisner) arrange the accident that cost Ward Justice his political career and—not to be too melodramatic—the possibility of a future life with Rosa?

On the one hand, there was certainly evidence of Jack Eagleson's Machiavellian tendencies. The conspiracy-minded might see Ward Justice's decision not to support Eagleson's and Eisner's scheme for a licence to operate a factory freezer trawler fleet—with its potentially huge payoff for their company—as a motive, even for murder.

But there was one very practical conundrum. How could Eagleson (and/or Eisner) have orchestrated events so little Lawrence would be in the parking lot in the middle of that night?

"That is really far-fetched," Ward Justice himself told Moira when she put the theory to him. Although Ward insisted he had no memory of what happened that night, he never denied being solely responsible for the death of Rosa's son. "My own best guess now," he told Moira in one of their last interviews, "is that what happened was an accident . . . an accident that was entirely my fault . . . and Jack and Junior took advantage of that."

That much was true. The new Fisheries minister—not coincidentally—supported Eisner Fisheries International and helped grease the political wheels of Ottawa's approval of its application for a factory freezer trawler fleet.

And there was evidence Eagleson had orchestrated the events that unfolded after the accident, too. Moira knew, for example—from an interview she'd done with Charles O'Sullivan, Rosa's Boston employer—that Jack Eagleson personally made the arrangements for him to hire Rosa and bring her to Boston. "I'd had a call a few days before from my cousin Seamus, telling me Mr. Eagleson would be calling and urging me to do whatever I could to assist him with a 'delicate' matter. No one ever told me why the matter was delicate, although I guess I always assumed that Seamus himself had had a . . . relationship with Rosie and his wife found out, or some such. Whatever it was, I must say that I personally never had one day's regret over the decision to hire Rosie."

Moira had uncovered one more intriguing fact, which suggested that, at the very least, Jack Eagleson took advantage of Ward Justice's unfortunate accident. In 1976, Eagleson told Ward Justice—who eventually told Moira—that Ward had to decide immediately whether to accept the judicial appointment because a reporter named Patrick Donovan was about to break the story of Ward's liaison with Rosa Johnstone and his role in her son's death.

This came as a shock to Moira's father. He didn't even recall covering the original accident until Moira showed him a copy of the brief from the newspaper. "Oh Christ, that. I just remember I'd spent the day before drinking, got into trouble with your mother and then got called to go out before it was decent the next morning to cover it. It wasn't any big deal. I did it and forgot it."

And he remained adamant that he knew nothing about Ward Justice's role in the accident; he certainly wasn't about to publish an exposé, as Eagleson had suggested. "I wish I was. Who knows? Maybe things would have turned out differently for me if I'd ever broken a story like that. Maybe I'd still be a journalist instead of . . . doing what I'm doing now."

What Patrick Donovan was doing now—more happily, Moira knew, than that quote would suggest—was taking care of Moira's son, his grandson and namesake.

When Moira told him she was quitting the paper to write a book about the case, Patrick tried to talk her out of it. "Why don't you just write a magazine article?" he suggested. "It'll pay more, and it would take less time, and you wouldn't have to quit just when you're so close to becoming an editor." When he realized she was going to quit anyway, however, Patrick was quick to offer his support—and his willingness to take care of her little boy while she wrote. At first, Moira was reluctant—"Remember, I experienced your parenting skills once already"—but then she had to call on him temporarily a few months later after Moira's Thai babysitter abruptly quit and moved to Toronto to be closer to her ailing mother. Things turned out so well—"I guess I learned all the things *not* to do when you were a little girl," Moira's father told her—that she soon stopped looking for a replacement.

While Moira wrote each morning in her home office, actually a tidy corner of her apartment's master bedroom, Patrick the Old and Patrick the Young became inseparable. Moira, of course, was still available for mama emergencies and even the occasional cheerleading. Last week, her father had yelled for her to come quickly to witness Patrick's first ever whiz in his potty. They'd clapped so loudly they distracted him. He turned to see what the fuss was about and peed all over the bathroom floor.

Moira's father did not clean up the mess. But he was unstinting when it came to making sure Patrick the Young was educated in what he considered important matters. Each morning he read aloud to his grandson all of the stories on the front page of each of the local newspapers, and then engaged him in what turned out to be a largely one-sided discussion of their merits, or lack thereof.

Patrick himself saw few merits in either paper. "But that doesn't mean journalism has to be this way," he would insist to Moira's uncomprehending two-year-old. "Journalism, done right—the way you'll do it—is a sacred calling."

Moira knew her father was proud she was writing a book, but book writing was clearly a lesser calling than newspapering. "You could have been a great editor," he told her often, but he'd given up on rescuing Moira from her weaknesses and had moved on to preparing his grandson to take his rightful place in the world. Which was okay with Moira, too.

"The story has been changing shape ever since . . ." Moira reread the words on the screen one more time, and continued typing.

Acknowledgements

There was a real community called Africville, and much of the awful tale of its destruction happened as I have described it. Former residents—in fact as well as in fiction—have filed a civil suit seeking compensation for the loss of their community. And a recent United Nations' report really did urge the Canadian government to offer reparations to the displaced families.

There are other verifiable facts in this fiction, too. We now know the RCMP did follow and compile dossiers on local black activists during the 1960s and 1970s. We know large fishing companies did lobby governments in the lead-up to Canada's declaration of the two-hundred-mile limit to give them licences to operate factory freezer trawlers. And we know there really was a Liberal government in Nova Scotia during the 1970s, albeit not the one I have described.

This is a work of fiction.

Raymond Carter/Uhuru Melesse exists only in my imagination. So does Ward Justice. And Jack Eagleson. And Junior Eisner. And Moira Donovan. And virtually all the rest of my cast of characters. The details of the situations I put them in, of course, are invented as well.

During the course of researching, thinking and writing, however, many people helped me to understand what really happened—or could have happened—so I was better able to bend and shape that reality to fit my fictional purposes.

Lisa Taylor, a friend, lawyer and former host of the CBC-TV series *The Docket,* read early drafts of the manuscript and offered many helpful editorial as well as legal suggestions. So too did Molly

Kalkstein McGrath, another good friend and wise editor. Carol Aylward, who taught critical race theory at the Dalhousie Law School, suggested ways in which Uhuru Melesse might try to mount a reparations defence for J. J. Howe. So did Wayne MacKay, a friend and expert on criminal procedure. Andrea MacDonald, a reporter for the Halifax *Daily News,* walked me through a day in the life of a real court reporter. Brian Flemming, an expert on the law of the sea who served as a policy adviser to Prime Minister Pierre Elliott Trudeau from 1976 to 1979, helped me navigate the actual ins and outs of Canada's 1977 decision to declare a two-hundred-mile territorial limit.

Others helped too, often without knowing it. I drew heavily on writer Charles Saunders's vivid reconstruction of everyday life in Africville in the book *The Spirit of Africville* when I began to paint my own picture of community life. And, in my role as a journalist, I had interviewed Irvine Carvery, the president of the Africville Genealogy Society, many times. Irvine's loving descriptions of growing up in Africville and his continuing, passionate commitment to winning justice for the former residents helped inspire this book.

I thank them all for making the book better for their input, and absolve them all of any responsibility for its imperfections.

I also want to thank Anne McDermid, my agent; Iris Tupholme, my editor at HarperCollins, who took a chance on this book when it was little more than an idea and a few sample chapters; Catherine Marjoribanks, my copy editor; and, of course, as always, my wife, Jeanie.

STEPHEN KIMBER
Halifax
May 2005